THE PICTURE OF DORIAN GRAY

The Classic Gothic Novel By
OSCAR WILDE

Edited, Annotated, and Illustrated By
M. GRANT KELLERMEYER, M.A.

℘

Expand Your Supernatural Fiction Collection
By Acquiring These
— Annotated and Illustrated Editions —

www.OldstyleTales.com

<u>WEIRD FICTION & HORROR BY:</u>
Algernon Blackwood
Robert W. Chambers
F. Marion Crawford
William Hope Hodgson
Arthur Machen
Guy de Maupassant
Fitz-James O'Brien
Edgar Allan Poe
Ambrose Bierce
H. G. Wells

<u>CLASSIC GHOST STORIES BY:</u>
Charles Dickens
Sir Arthur Conan Doyle
W. W. Jacobs
Henry James
J. Sheridan Le Fanu
E. Nesbit
Robert Louis Stevenson
Bram Stoker
Washington Irving
E. T. A. Hoffmann

<u>CLASSIC GOTHIC NOVELS:</u>
Dracula
Frankenstein
The Phantom of the Opera
Dr. Jekyll and Mr. Hyde
The Turn of the Screw
The Invisible Man
The Picture of Dorian Gray

<u>FIRESIDE HORROR SERIES:</u>
Ghost Stories for Christmas Eve
Victorian Ghost Stories
Supernatural Cats
Demons and the Devil
Mummies and Curses
Pirates and Ghost Ships
Werewolves

OLDSTYLE TALES

This edition published 2019 by
OLDSTYLE TALES PRESS
2424 N. Anthony Blvd
Fort Wayne, Indiana
4 6 8 0 5 – 3 6 0 4

*For more information, or to request permission
to reprint selections or illustrations from
this book, write to the Editor at*
oldstyletales@gmail.com

NOTES, INTRODUCTIONS, AND ILLUSTRATIONS
COPYRIGHT © 2019 BY MICHAEL GRANT KELLERMEYER

Readers who are interested in further titles from
Oldstyle Tales Press are invited to visit our website at

— WWW.OLDSTYLETALES.COM —

— TABLE *of* CONTENTS —

Concerning What
You Are About to Read

EVER since its explosive publication in 1890, Oscar Wilde's Gothic treatise on decadence, sin, and corruption has been subject to scandal and intrigue. Revised and censored multiple times during Wilde's tragically short life, it is presented here in its original, un-muted form, complete with redacted phrases and sentences that would later be used against Wilde at his trials for homosexuality. Beyond its salacious subtext, however, is a rich and philosophical parable on morality -- one as powerful as a sermon but as sensually entrancing as an opium cigarette -- which slyly undermines its presumed thesis of hedonism with a heartbreaking appeal to human decency. Dorian Gray's transformation from innocent object of a shy painter's platonic lust to heartless, corrupting lady-killer with dozens of ruined lives, murders, and suicides on his conscience is etched into his soul without leaving a blemish on his lovely face. But as Wilde reveals throughout his hypnotic, Faustian novel, vanity, arrogance, and a lack of compassion may make for an indulgent life without regrets, but the devil will have his due.

Today Oscar Wilde is most remembered for his wit, flamboyance, and the tragic persecution of his homosexuality. *Dorian Gray* adds another fascinating and often underappreciated layer to his often cartoonish, caricature-like persona: a deeply vulnerable, astonishingly insecure idealist. This is best illustrated by a comment Wilde made following the book's publication: "Basil Hallward is what I think I am: Lord Henry is what the world thinks of me: Dorian is what I would like to be—in other ages, perhaps." Many casual fans of Wilde's are surprised that he sees himself in the shy, retiring, idealistic, conventionally moral, tragically flawed Basil – a man who dies bent over in desperate prayer – but a cursory understanding of the Decadence Movement and of Wilde's life before and after his trials, will help to bring this into perspective.

In some ways the Decadents were to the 1880s and 1890s what the Goths were to the 1980s and 1990s – though with significant more joie de vivre. Like the Goth subculture, Decadents reveled in the macabre, the morose, the gaudy, and the garish: they celebrated entropy and decay, but did so with gusto and indulgence rather than melancholy. Tracing their roots to Poe-inspired French naturalists and symbolists like Baudelaire, Huysmans, Redon, Rimbaud, and Moreau, British Decadents reveled in their French counterparts' elaborate materialism and powerful mysticism. The ethos of their philosophy sounds like something out of Ecclesiastes: eat, drink, and be merry, for tomorrow we die; there is nothing new under the sun; life can only be fully experienced at a mad-dash pace – which is destined to break the rider's neck. In *Dorian Gray*, the Decadents are represented by the insidious yellow book that Lord Henry leaves out where Dorian can find it. Just as the Goths of the 20th century came to be known by their telltale black, the Decadents were identified by a sulfurous, mustard yellow that epitomized indulgence in the black-and-white world of conservative Victoriana.

Colors were tremendously important symbols to the aesthetically-obsessed Decadents, and yellow was their personal badge: it stood for everything debauched and forbidden about life – everything that they wanted to sample and gorge. Deeply associated with the Decadence movement, the color yellow was first connected to themes of corruption and impropriety several decades earlier when the fops of Jane Austen's Regency period wore the garish color to suggest their appetites for the indulgent, grotesque, and shocking. Later in the century, French books banned in England for their lewd content were at first discreetly packaged in yellow jackets, but when the code was figured out, booksellers even went so far as to wrap relatively tame publications in the lurid amber color because it would increase sales amongst eager buyers. Yellow became a symbol for all that was diseased in the soul, all that was unconventional, contrarian, rebellious, and decadent. If something was "Yellow," it was gaudy, luscious, vulgar, decayed, infamous, scandalous, poisonous, sensual, leprous, golden, lurid, bawdy, ghastly, seductive, corruptive, grotesque, fantastic, alien, fabulous, alluring, shocking, fascinating, ribald, repulsive, and repellent.ing the late 19th century, scandalous French novels were traditionally jacketed in yellow paperbacks.

The novel Dorian reads is not given a name in many of the story's editions, but in its earliest forms it was called "The Secret of Raoul" and was written by the fictional aesthete Catulle Sarrazin. This fictional French decadent author's name is a portmanteau of two real-life ones: Catulle Mendes and Gabriel Sarrazin. The name Raoul – which was edited out of the various later editions (likely to avoid putting a name to a character who is so ignominious, and to avoid public concern that a "cult of Raoul" might spring up amongst rebellious young men) is a reference to a character in another decadent, French novel, "Monsieur Venus." This scandalous erotica by the mononymous female writer Rachilde follows a female crossdresser named Raoule, who enters into a sexual relationship with a girlish young man who becomes her "mistress." Another oft-cited modelled – alluded to by Wilde at his trial and found on his person during his arrest – is the yellow-jacketed "Against Nature," a decadent novel by Joris-Karl Huysmans, which tells of a bored, bourgeois youth who rebels against the dullness of the 19th century by acquiring a house in the country and filling it with lavish collections (compare to all of Chapter IX) of art, antiques, literature, perfumes, poisonous flowers, gems, and exotic animals.

While the Decadents were obsessed with hedonism and material indulgence, the very core of their philosophy was a distrusting of any fleshly appetite to satisfy the searcher of truth: as human beings we were required to sample as much of the world as possible, but as human beings we are hopeless to ever find satiation. Because of this, the Decadents had a surprisingly conservative foundation to their beliefs, and it was tremendously common for members of their community to turn to Catholicism later in life (Wilde, Rimbaud, Huysmans, Baudelaire, Moreau, and Redon would all tend this way, and John Gray – the widely-accepted model of Dorian – would even become a priest). When Huysmans had one of his friends read "Against Nature," they opined that anyone who wrote such a book would ultimately have to choose between the "muzzle of a pistol or the foot of the cross." Indeed, religiosity was very attractive to the Decadents – especially upon entering middle age – due to its mysticism, rejection of materialism, comfort with death, and psychological masochism.

In *Dorian Gray*, Basil Hallward dies while in the throes of a desperate prayer, Dorian mystically dies in a vain attempt to slay his conscience, and Lord Henry finds himself abandoned by his wife and terrified of death. For all of its controversy, the story is really quite a conservative one, and the message urges its readers to live an authentic life motivated by love (rather than the posed life motivated by attention that Lord Henry models). This wouldn't prevent the novel from being a centerpiece of Wilde's trials after suing the Marquess of Queensbury for libel after he publically accused him of being a "sodomite." Basil's devotion to Dorian, his embarrassment at a secret which Henry knows and which Dorian guesses, Dorian's role in the downfall of many young men, his sexually aggressive behavior, and his feminization as a scarlet-lipped, golden-haired Adonis lead to several passages being read verbatim in court. All three main characters appear to have homosexual leanings, and even Dorian's name – used like "Doric" to describe Greek culture – was a euphemism for gayness ("Greek love" and "Dorian love" were used to allude to Athens' tradition of pederasty). As a result of this evidence, Wilde was convicted of sodomy and sentenced to hard labor. His spirit broken and his body ruined by the harsh conditions, he left England for France and prepared himself for death, which came shortly after. Although many readers struggle to believe that the witty Oscar

Wilde could have much in common with the retiring, soul-crushed Basil Hallward, he spent his final months poured out in prayerful defeat.

Basil's character is the most likeable of the novel and second only to Sibyl in his tragedy. Like Wagner's Tannhauser – an opera which Dorian adores – Basil is torn between his worship of a vain idol and confronting his own moral complexity. We begin the novel almost immediately with the information that Basil had once disappeared inexplicably, leading to wild rumors. The implication is that he was jilted or otherwise embarrassed in a failed romance and that his flight from society was interpreted as a possible suicide before he returned in one piece. Basil's great habit is to empty his soul into his art, and his greatest muses are – like Dorian – people who represent some eternal ideal to him. In Dorian he finds innocence, beauty, and spiritual purity, but just as Dorian himself projects his spiritual emptiness onto Sibyl, who turns out to be another human with needs and problems, Dorian is a flawed idol who fails to live up to Basil's expectations. Basil isn't capable of admitting that Dorian is a selfish person until he sees the transformation of his portrait and is forced to see how the ideal in its ideal form has decayed. When Dorian easily moves past Sibyl's suicide, when rumors come to Basil of his corrupting influence, and when society turns its back on him in revulsion, Basil still holds out hope that these are somehow mistakes or misunderstandings. Only when faced with the tangible reflection of Dorian's leprous conscience can he fully understand the demon which he has erected as the god of his life. Like Wilde, Basil is at his heart driven to experience beauty for its own sake, and although Wilde was often mischaracterized as a hedonistic Lord Henry, at his core he shared Basil's vulnerability and insecurity, and Basil's miserable end uncannily predicted Wilde's own future desperation.

One of the greatest influences on the novel was Goethe's *Faust* and the Faust legend throughout its various adaptations (in many ways, Dorian Gray most resembles the wicked Faust of Marlowe more than the redeemed Faust of Goethe). This tells the story of the medieval alchemist who makes a pact with the demon Mephistopheles to sell his soul in exchange for knowledge – though he later asks for women, wealth, and many other less noble pursuits. Throughout the play Mephistopheles is an electric character: charmingly wicked, greasily persuasive, and unrelentingly corruptive. In his black and scarlet clothes, pointed beard, and curling moustache, he is always the most interesting character when he is on stage. The Mephistopheles of *Dorian Gray* is undoubtedly the urbane cynic Lord Henry, whom Wilde considered a representation of what the world thought of him. Lord Henry is nosy (potentially a blackmailer), sardonic, and cruel: he regularly laughs at Basil's homosexuality (more because he is in love with Dorian than because he is gay), encourages Dorian to become a self-involved ego-maniac, and greatly enjoys watching people fail. While Basil is painting Dorian, he essentially – though inadvertently – pimps Dorian out to Lord Henry (he is so distracted in his own worship of Dorian's physical idealism that he doesn't notice Lord Henry corrupting his soul), which causes a rift between the two friends (to Henry's delight). But even this Mephistophelean trickster has a vulnerable underbelly: by the end of the novel his wife (modelled closely after Wilde's own socially awkward spouse) has abandoned him for a pianist and despite his brave show, it is obvious that he is lonely and afraid. Basil foreshadows this from time to time when he chides Henry's devil-may-care pessimism – especially when concerning marriage and love – as a sham designed to attract others' shocked attention.

The only character to earn his respect – and the foil to his cynicism – is Sibyl Vane, who gleefully loses her ability to act after falling in love with Dorian and commits suicide when he rejects her. Henry is staggered in his response to the news – awed that someone could love so genuinely. To Henry, almost all human acts are forgeries designed to elicit a reaction, especially love, which he distrusts most of all. Sibyl (whose names – "Sibyl" being a Greek oracle and "Vane" being a weather instrument used to indicate the change in wind – suggest that Dorian's treatment of her will forecast the rest of his future development) stood in direct opposition to Lord Henry. Dorian himself comments on this, wondering aloud whom he will listen to: Henry's bitter philosophies of hedonism and stoicism or Sibyl's simple love and happiness. Deeply embarrassed by her failure to act in front of his friends (a change which symbolizes her rejection of "acting" – professionally or socially – in favor of authentic love), Dorian spurns her offer of quiet contentment for Lord Henry's ribald sensuality, and Sibyl commits suicide by swallowing chemicals found in paint (creating a physical link between the painting – viz. Dorian's conscience – and her death).

Dorian himself represents what Wilde "would like to be – in other ages, perhaps." His character has shades of Faust blended with elements from various Decadent novels (especially the world-weary protagonist of "Against Nature"), and his fate is at least partially inspired by two of the greatest Doppelganger stories in English literature: Edgar Allan Poe's "William Wilson," and Robert Louis Stevenson's "Dr Jekyll and Mr Hyde." Both stories involve a man who is hounded by an almost supernatural double who represents their guilty conscience, both attempt to evade the Doppelganger – of course in vain – and both are ultimately driven to suicide. Like Dorian, William Wilson's suicide, however, is accidental. Followed by a man who looks exactly like him and shares his name, Wilson always seems to encounter his "good twin" when he is in the middle of some scheme, fraud, or sin. By the end of the novel, he is about to have an affair with a married woman when he sees his twin at a masked ball. He lures the man into an empty hall where he runs him through with a rapier. At first smug at having slain his conscience, he is then shocked when the image points back to him and begs him to see how, by killing his conscience, he "utterly hast murdered" himself. To his horror, he realizes that he is standing before a full length mirror and bleeding from a self-inflicted wound.

Likewise, Dorian – who buys in on Lord Henry's philosophy of utter materialism and self-indulgence – hates his corrupting picture because it reminds him that as fair as he may look on the surface, he is diseased and dying within. In a moment of rage, he rushes to slit the painting from top to bottom, but in killing his conscience – by symbolically confronting his own sins – he metaphysically transposes the sin to his physical body, and then suffers the physical toll of his crimes: death. As previously mentioned, the novel has a surprisingly conservative message, and serves as a complex and powerful moral allegory for corruption. The true threat to Dorian's peace of mind isn't the portrait itself, but the soul that it corresponds to, and Dorian's attempt to divorce mind from matter and spirit from flesh results in a philosophical treatise on the indivisibility of soul and body. Jekyll also tried to peel good and evil apart in supposed bid to isolate his evil self, but only managed to make his ego enslaved to his id. Likewise, William Wilson's id tried to slay his super-ego, but only succeeded in "utterly ... murder[ing]" his ego. Dorian's bid at gutting his own super-ego, as embodied in Basil's corrupted painting, similarly results in the literal gutting of his ego – in physical form. By trying to pry conscience away from the flesh, he only manages to free the spirit from the body (and – especially considering the many, many allusions to sulfur and hellfire throughout the novel – strait off to hell). Dorian, Wilson, and Jekyll each attempt to avoid consequences, and each are driven to symbolic and literal suicide in the attempt to bifurcate the spiritual effects of their earthly behaviors.

The portrait is a convenient metaphor for the ego, and has been throughout modern literature as a motif of the self. Haunted portraits are a time-honored Gothic trope used for a variety of reasons: sometimes they suggest the continued existence of the sins of past generations; sometimes they symbolize the way that we cling to the deep-seated patterns and refuse to change; on other occasions, the portrait with moving eyes – or shifting positions, or changing expressions – is simply a very chilling thing to imagine. Washington Irving (*The Haunted Portrait, The Young Italian, My Aunt's Adventure*), Bram Stoker (*The Judge's House*), J. S. Le Fanu (*Schalken the Painter, Strange Disturbances in Aungier Street*), H. P. Lovecraft (*Pickman's Model, The Picture in the House, Charles Dexter Ward*), Edith Nesbit (*The Ebony Frame*), Edgar Allan Poe (*The Oval Portrait*), and many others have used the motif of a haunted or haunting portrait which is often tied to the history of the house it is hanged in, and sometimes reveals an uncanny similarity with a living relative of the centuries-dead sitter. *Dorian Gray* was written during a hey-day of portrait painters, with John Singer Sargent, J. A. M. Whistler, and Henri de Toulouse-Lautrec leading the wave of new, stylish portraitists who invested their art with energy and interest. Wilde himself had a full-length portrait done by one of Whistler's students, and counted it among his most prized possessions. For Dorian, the painting is a manifestation of Basil's worship and a reflection of how he is perceived and regarded by others. Following Henry's stoic philosophy, he doesn't mind if the painting turns diseased and leering so long as it doesn't conflict with his free will. Ultimately, it is his horror at his inability to change course when desired that drives him to destroy the work, and – as we've already discussed – this ultimately leads to his ego-suicide.

Since it was released to the public, the story of Dorian Gray – the narcissist who didn't age but was haunted by his portrait which did – has captivated the public imagination as only brilliant moral philosophy can. Like "Jekyll and Hyde" or "William Wilson" or "Faust," it comments on the human condition with metaphysical vigor and physical violence, leaving its readers to marvel at the protagonist's pathetic demise. Filmed nearly a dozen times – most notably in the brilliantly-shot, expressionistic 1944 masterpiece starring Hurd Hatfield, Donna Reid, and Angela Lansbury – and grafted into several miniseries, television shows, and Victorian pastiches, it remains a shocking monument to the power of vanity and corruption, the hope of love, and the relentless decay of the human soul.

M. Grant Kellermeyer
Fort Wayne, St. Patrick's Day 2019

NOTE ON THE TEXT

Dorian Gray was first published in thirteen chapters in 1890. This early version included several objectionable passages, phrases, and words which were edited out of the longer 1891 novel. This second publication – much like the 1832 edition of Frankenstein – toned down some of the more controversial material and tried to make it more of a polite novel of manners in the style of Edward Bulwer-Lytton and George Du Maurier. It expanded Lord Henry's role as a commentator on Dorian's background and social rank, included the new character, James Vane (Sibyl's vengeful brother who hunts Dorian down but is later killed in a hunting accident), and muddies Basil's romantic attraction to Dorian. While the 1891 version is more popular because of its length, we have made the editorial decision to print the 1890 version, along with material that was edited out of it before publication. As a result, it represents the uncensored story which Wilde delivered to Lippincott's before editors revised and obscured its more controversial material. You will be able to identify expunged words, phrases, or passages because they are printed in [*brackets and italics like this*] and sometimes have accompanying notes to explain what replaced them or why they may have been replaced.

— M. G. K.

CHAPTER I

THE studio was filled with the rich odor of roses, and when the light summer wind stirred amidst the trees of the garden there came through the open door the heavy scent of the lilac, or the more delicate perfume of the pink-flowering thorn.

From the corner of the divan of Persian saddle-bags[1] on which he was lying, smoking, as usual, innumerable cigarettes[2], Lord Henry Wotton[3] could just catch the gleam of the honey-sweet and honey-colored blossoms of the laburnum, whose tremulous branches seemed hardly able to bear the burden of a beauty so flame-like as theirs; and now and then the fantastic shadows of birds in flight flitted across the long tussore-silk curtains that were stretched in front of the huge window, producing a kind of momentary Japanese effect, and making him think of those pallid jade-faced painters who, in an art that is necessarily immobile, seek to convey the sense of swiftness and motion. The sullen murmur of the bees[4] shouldering their way through the long unmown grass, or circling with monotonous insistence round the black-crocketed spires of the early June hollyhocks, seemed to make the stillness more oppressive, and the dim roar of London was like the bourdon[5] note of a distant organ.

In the centre of the room, clamped to an upright easel, stood the full-length portrait of a young man of extraordinary personal beauty, and in front of it, some little distance away, was sitting the artist himself,

---

[1] That is, Persian carpet rugs

[2] A Late Victorian sign of intellectualism, decadence, and status

[3] About Lord Henry, Wilde said that he represented who the world considered him to be (whereas Basil represented who he believed himself to be and Dorian represented who he wished himself to be). Lord Henry is a Mephistophelean character (modelled after the devilish antagonist of Goethe's "Faust," who lures the eponymous protagonist away from the noble pursuits of wisdom and love with temptations of power and hedonism) whose delight in corruption leads to Dorian's ruin. Scholars concur that he was modelled off of Wilde's friend, Lord Ronald Sutherland, a socialite and art connoisseur known for his hedonism, homosexuality, and proximity to scandal

[4] Throughout the book, bees will be used to symbolize corruption, lust, and desire. In the Victorian era, bee cultivation was a popular hobby, and the nature of the drones (male bees whose only purpose in life is to impregnate the queen) made them a symbol of decadence and sensuality

[5] Drone note (a deep, pulsing bass chord played beneath a higher melody)

Basil Hallward[1], whose sudden disappearance some years ago caused, at the time, such public excitement, and gave rise to so many strange conjectures[2].

As he looked at the gracious and comely form he had so skilfully mirrored in his art, a smile of pleasure passed across his face, and seemed about to linger there. But he suddenly started up, and, closing his eyes, placed his fingers upon the lids, as though he sought to imprison within his brain some curious dream from which he feared he might awake.

"It is your best work, Basil, the best thing you have ever done," said Lord Henry, languidly. "You must certainly send it next year to the Grosvenor. The Academy is too large and too vulgar[3]. The Grosvenor is the only place."

"I don't think I will send it anywhere," he answered, tossing his head back in that odd way that used to make his friends laugh at him at Oxford[4]. "No: I won't send it anywhere."

Lord Henry elevated his eyebrows, and looked at him in amazement through the thin blue wreaths of smoke that curled up in such fanciful whorls from his heavy opium-tainted cigarette. "Not send it anywhere? My dear fellow, why? Have you any reason? What odd chaps you painters are! You do anything in the world to gain a reputation. As soon as you have one, you seem to want to throw it away. It is silly of you, for there is only one thing in the world worse than being

---

[1] Wilde considered himself most like Basil: devoted to art, platonic love, and Dorian, and tragically ruined by the power of his vices. While Lord Henry is Dorian's corrupter, Basil inadvertently serves as Dorian's pimp, allowing Henry to indoctrinate him while he poses for Basil's portrait

[2] This wild past will allow Basil's death to go unnoticed for months. The implication is that he has – in the past – been subject to such passionate fits of impulse that rumors arose that he killed himself following some romantic disaster (as we will later intuit, this was probably of a homosexual nature, and thereby all the more scandalous and mysterious to gossipy Victorians)

[3] The Royal Academy was the venue where more conventional, conservative art was exhibited, while the Grosvenor Gallery was known for its more daring, avant garde exhibitions – particularly of portraits with erotic flourishes

[4] Laughter is a recurring motif throughout the novel – the response that Basil fears to his homosexuality. Far more than anger, censure, or arrest, he worries that others (Dorian in particular) will "laugh at" him if they learn about the nature of his feelings for Dorian. This is the first of many implications that Basil's feelings for Dorian are romantic in nature (thus attracting the derision – the laughter – of others who might not understand or accept the breadth of homosexual feelings)

talked about, and that is not being talked about. A portrait like this would set you far above all the young men in England, and make the old men quite jealous, if old men are ever capable of any emotion."

"I know you will laugh at me," he replied, "but I really can't exhibit it. I have put too much of myself into it."

Lord Henry stretched his long legs out on the divan and shook with laughter.

"Yes, I knew you would laugh; but it is quite true, all the same."

"Too much of yourself in it! Upon my word, Basil, I didn't know you were so vain; and I really can't see any resemblance between you, with your rugged strong face and your coal-black hair, and this young Adonis[1], who looks as if he was made of ivory and rose-leaves. Why, my dear Basil, he is a Narcissus[2], and you–well, of course you have an intellectual expression, and all that. But beauty, real beauty, ends where an intellectual expression begins. Intellect is in itself an exaggeration, and destroys the harmony of any face. The moment one sits down to think, one becomes all nose, or all forehead, or something horrid. Look at the successful men in any of the learned professions. How perfectly hideous they are! Except, of course, in the Church. But then in the Church they don't think. A bishop keeps on saying at the age of eighty what he was told to say when he was a boy of eighteen, and consequently he always looks absolutely delightful. Your mysterious young friend, whose name you have never told me, but whose picture really fascinates me, never thinks. I feel quite sure of that. He is a brainless, beautiful thing, who should be always here in winter when we have no flowers to look at, and always here in summer when we want something to chill our intelligence. Don't flatter yourself, Basil: you are not in the least like him."

"You don't understand me, Harry. Of course I am not like him. I know that perfectly well. Indeed, I should be sorry to look like him. You shrug your shoulders? I am telling you the truth. There is a fatality about all physical and intellectual distinction, the sort of fatality that seems to dog through history the faltering steps of kings. It is better not to be different from one's fellows. The ugly and the stupid have the best of it in this world. They can sit quietly and gape at the play. If they know nothing of victory, they are at least spared the knowledge of defeat. They live as we all should live, undisturbed, indifferent, and without disquiet.

---

[1] Aphrodite's mortal lover, renowned for his youthful beauty, and often used as a homoerotic symbol in Victorian art and literature

[2] A vain and tragic figure in Greek mythology who starved to death while admiring his beauty in the reflection of a lake (hence our word "narcissist")

They neither bring ruin upon others nor ever receive it from alien hands. Your rank and wealth, Harry; my brains, such as they are,–my fame, whatever it may be worth; Dorian Gray's[1] good looks,–we will all suffer for what the gods have given us, suffer terribly."

"Dorian Gray? is that his name?" said Lord Henry, walking across the studio towards Basil Hallward.

"Yes; that is his name. I didn't intend to tell it to you."

"But why not?"

"Oh, I can't explain. When I like people immensely I never tell their names to any one. It seems like surrendering a part of them. You know how I love secrecy. It is the only thing that can make modern life wonderful or mysterious to us. The commonest thing is delightful if one only hides it. When I leave town I never tell my people where I am going. If I did, I would lose all my pleasure. It is a silly habit, I dare say, but somehow it seems to bring a great deal of romance into one's life. I suppose you think me awfully foolish about it?"

"Not at all," answered Lord Henry, [*laying his hand upon his shoulder*;] "not at all, my dear Basil. You seem to forget that I am married, and the one charm of marriage is that it makes a life of deception necessary for both parties. I never know where my wife is, and my wife never knows what I am doing. When we meet,–we do meet occasionally, when we dine out together, or go down to the duke's,– we tell each other the most absurd stories with the most serious faces[2]. My wife is very good at it,–much better, in fact, than I am. She never gets

---

[1] The name "Dorian" has been traditionally read as a reference to Ancient Greece (Doris was a part of the Turkish coast once inhabited by Dorians – ethnic Greeks). During the Victorian Age, homosexuality was referred to with dozens of various euphemisms, but some of the most common referenced the prevelance of homosexuality amongst the Ancient Athenians: "Greek love," "Athenian love," and "Dorian love" were common code words for homoeroticism. The surname "Gray" of course calls to mind a lack of color (in German it is synonymous with horror, hence "Nosferatu's" subtitle, "A Symphony in Gray"), but it may also be a reference to John Gray, a young friend of Wilde's who is largely considered the model for Dorian. Youthful, attractive, hedonistic, and gay, Gray once signed a letter to Wilde "Yours ever, Dorian," and was deeply proud of the association during his twenties. After the Oscar Wilde trials, however, he became resentful of the connection, denounced Wilde, joined the Catholic Church, and became a priest. Wilde claimed that Dorian represented a fantasy version of what he would have liked himself to be: "Basil Hallward is what I think I am: Lord Henry is what the world thinks of me: Dorian is what I would like to be—in other ages, perhaps"

[2] Wilde's wife Constance was not even aware of his bisexuality until he was outed by the Queensbury libel case

confused over her dates, and I always do. But when she does find me out, she makes no row at all. [*I sometimes wish she did*]; but she merely laughs at me."

"I hate the way you talk about your married life, Harry," said Basil Hallward, [*shaking his hand off*[1]], and strolling towards the door that led into the garden. "I believe that you are really a very good husband, but that you are thoroughly ashamed of your own virtues. You are an extraordinary fellow. You never say a moral thing, and you never do a wrong thing. Your cynicism is simply a pose[2]."

"Being natural is simply a pose, and the most irritating pose I know," cried Lord Henry, laughing; and the two young men went out into the garden together, and for a time they did not speak.

After a long pause Lord Henry pulled out his watch. "I am afraid I must be going, Basil," he murmured, "and before I go I insist on your answering a question I put to you some time ago."

"What is that?" asked Basil Hallward, keeping his eyes fixed on the ground.

"You know quite well."

"I do not, Harry."

"Well, I will tell you what it is."

"Please don't."

"I must. I want you to explain to me why you won't exhibit Dorian Gray's picture. I want the real reason[3]."

"I told you the real reason."

"No, you did not. You said it was because there was too much of yourself in it. Now, that is childish."

"Harry," said Basil Hallward, looking him straight in the face, "every portrait that is painted with feeling is a portrait of the artist, not of the sitter. The sitter is merely the accident, the occasion. It is not he who is revealed by the painter; it is rather the painter who, on the colored canvas, reveals himself. The reason I will not exhibit this picture is that I am afraid that I have shown with it the secret of my own soul."

---

[1] Likely deleted because of the erotic subtext of an unwelcome, lingering touch between two men

[2] Since Wilde considered himself more akin to Basil – sensitive, self-doubting, and noble – in contrast to his public image as a Henry-esque hedonist – there is probably something of autobiographical self-examination at work in this comment

[3] Since this is the first Henry has seen of the picture, but apparently not the first time that he has asked this question, the implication is that the two are related – in other words, Henry is prying into the nature of Basil's sexuality, which Henry has inferred to be the true reason that he is unwilling to exhibit the portrait

Lord Harry laughed. "And what is that?" he asked.

"I will tell you," said Hallward; and an expression of perplexity came over his face.

"I am all expectation, Basil," murmured his companion, looking at him.

"Oh, there is really very little to tell, Harry," answered the young painter; "and I am afraid you will hardly understand it. Perhaps you will hardly believe it."

Lord Henry smiled, and, leaning down, plucked a pink-petalled daisy from the grass, and examined it[1]. "I am quite sure I shall understand it," he replied, gazing intently at the little golden white-feathered disk, "and I can believe anything, provided that it is incredible."

The wind shook some blossoms from the trees, and the heavy lilac blooms, with their clustering stars, moved to and fro in the languid air. A grasshopper began to chirrup in the grass, and a long thin dragon-fly floated by on its brown gauze wings. Lord Henry felt as if he could hear Basil Hallward's heart beating, and he wondered what was coming.

"Well, this is incredible," repeated Hallward, rather bitterly,– "incredible to me at times. I don't know what it means. The story is simply this. Two months ago I went to a crush[2] at Lady Brandon's. You know we poor painters have to show ourselves in society from time to time, just to remind the public that we are not savages. With an evening coat and a white tie, as you told me once, anybody, even a stock-broker, can gain a reputation for being civilized. Well, after I had been in the room about ten minutes, talking to huge overdressed dowagers[3] and tedious Academicians, I suddenly became conscious that some one was looking at me. I turned half-way round, and saw Dorian Gray for the first time. When our eyes met, I felt that I was growing pale. A curious[4] instinct of terror came over me. I knew that I had come face to face with some one whose mere personality was so fascinating that, if I allowed it to do so, it would absorb my whole nature, my whole soul, my very art itself. I did not want any external influence in my life. You know yourself, Harry, how independent I am by nature. My father destined me for the army. I insisted on going to Oxford. Then he made me enter my

---

[1] Foreshadowing Henry's eventual "plucking" and examining of Dorian – a specimen of innocence which he tears from its natural environment of purity merely as a game

[2] Bustling party (so called because of the crowded, packed rooms)

[3] High-ranking widows

[4] Curious – a synonym for "queer" – was another homoerotic euphemism popular at the time

name at the Middle Temple[1]. Before I had eaten half a dozen dinners I gave up the Bar, and announced my intention of becoming a painter. I have always been my own master; had at least always been so, till I met Dorian Gray. Then–But I don't know how to explain it to you. Something seemed to tell me that I was on the verge of a terrible crisis in my life. I had a strange feeling that Fate had in store for me exquisite joys and exquisite sorrows. [*I knew that if I spoke to Dorian I would become absolutely devoted to him, and that I ought not to speak to him.*] I grew afraid, and turned to quit the room. It was not conscience that made me do so: it was cowardice. I take no credit to myself for trying to escape."

"Conscience and cowardice are really the same things, Basil. Conscience is the trade-name of the firm. That is all."

"I don't believe that, Harry. However, whatever was my motive,– and it may have been pride, for I used to be very proud,–I certainly struggled to the door. There, of course, I stumbled against Lady Brandon. 'You are not going to run away so soon, Mr. Hallward?' she screamed out. You know her shrill horrid voice?"

"Yes; she is a peacock in everything but beauty," said Lord Henry, pulling the daisy to bits with his long, nervous fingers[2].

"I could not get rid of her. She brought me up to Royalties, and people with Stars and Garters[3], and elderly ladies with gigantic tiaras and hooked noses. She spoke of me as her dearest friend. I had only met her once before, but she took it into her head to lionize me. I believe some picture of mine had made a great success at the time, at least had been chattered about in the penny newspapers, which is the nineteenth-century standard of immortality. Suddenly I found myself face to face with the young man whose personality had so strangely stirred me. We were quite close, almost touching. Our eyes met again. It was mad of me, but I asked Lady Brandon to introduce me to him. Perhaps it was not so mad, after all. It was simply inevitable. We would have spoken to each other without any introduction. I am sure of that. Dorian told me so afterwards. He, too, felt that we were destined to know each other."

"And how did Lady Brandon describe this wonderful young man? I know she goes in for giving a rapid *précis*[4] of all her guests. I remember her bringing me up to a most truculent and red-faced old gentleman

---

[1] One of Oxford's four intellectual clubs for fledgling lawyers

[2] Again, Lord Henry's studious, inquisitive dissection of the flower foreshadows his eventually study and dissection of Dorian's soul (which matters little more to him than the destruction of the daisy)

[3] That is, knighthoods (the Order of the Bath and the Order of the Garter)

[4] Summary; a brief outline

covered all over with orders and ribbons, and hissing into my ear, in a tragic whisper which must have been perfectly audible to everybody in the room, something like 'Sir Humpty Dumpty–you know–Afghan frontier–Russian intrigues: very successful man–wife killed by an elephant–quite inconsolable–wants to marry a beautiful American widow–everybody does nowadays–hates Mr. Gladstone[1]–but very much interested in beetles: ask him what he thinks of Schouvaloff[2].' I simply fled. I like to find out people for myself. But poor Lady Brandon treats her guests exactly as an auctioneer treats his goods. She either explains them entirely away, or tells one everything about them except what one wants to know. But what did she say about Mr. Dorian Gray?"

"Oh, she murmured, 'Charming boy–poor dear mother and I quite inseparable–engaged to be married to the same man–I mean married on the same day–how very silly of me! Quite forget what he does– afraid he–doesn't do anything–oh, yes, plays the piano–or is it the violin, dear Mr. Gray?' We could neither of us help laughing, and we became friends at once."

"Laughter is not a bad beginning for a friendship, and it is the best ending for one[3]," said Lord Henry, plucking another daisy.

Hallward buried his face in his hands. "You don't understand what friendship is, Harry," he murmured,–"or what enmity is, for that matter. You like every one; that is to say, you are indifferent to every one."

"How horribly unjust of you!" cried Lord Henry, tilting his hat back, and looking up at the little clouds that were drifting across the hollowed turquoise of the summer sky, like ravelled skeins of glossy white silk. "Yes; horribly unjust of you. I make a great difference between people. I choose my friends for their good looks, my acquaintances for their characters, and my enemies for their brains. A man can't be too careful in the choice of his enemies. I have not got one who is a fool. They are all men of some intellectual power, and consequently they all appreciate me. Is that very vain of me? I think it is rather vain."

"I should think it was, Harry. But according to your category I must be merely an acquaintance."

"My dear old Basil, you are much more than an acquaintance."

"And much less than a friend. A sort of brother, I suppose?"

---

[1] One of the 19th century's most prominent Liberal politicians, and a prime minister several times over

[2] A prominent Russian statesman and chief counselor to Tsar Alexander II

[3] Once again, "laughter" operates as a coded motif for homosexuality. Henry implies that a fine way to begin a male relationship is with nervous sexual attraction, and a fine way to end it is with resentful, head-shaking disgust

"Oh, brothers! I don't care for brothers. My elder brother won't die, and my younger brothers seem never to do anything else."

"Harry!"

"My dear fellow, I am not quite serious. But I can't help detesting my relations. I suppose it comes from the fact that we can't stand other people having the same faults as ourselves. I quite sympathize with the rage of the English democracy against what they call the vices of the upper classes. They feel that drunkenness, stupidity, and immorality should be their own special property, and that if any one of us makes an ass of himself [*we are poaching on their preserves.*[1]] When poor Southwark got into the Divorce Court, their indignation was quite magnificent. And yet I don't suppose that ten per cent of the lower orders [*live with their own wives*[2]]."

"I don't agree with a single word that you have said, and, what is more, Harry, I don't believe you do either."

Lord Henry stroked his pointed brown beard, and tapped the toe of his patent-leather boot with a tasselled malacca[3] cane. "How English you are, Basil! If one puts forward an idea to a real Englishman,– always a rash thing to do,–he never dreams of considering whether the idea is right or wrong. The only thing he considers of any importance is whether one believes it one's self. Now, the value of an idea has nothing whatsoever to do with the sincerity of the man who expresses it. Indeed, the probabilities are that the more insincere the man is, the more purely intellectual will the idea be, as in that case it will not be colored by either his wants, his desires, or his prejudices. However, I don't propose to discuss politics, sociology, or metaphysics with you. I like persons better than principles. Tell me more about Dorian Gray. How often do you see him?"

"Every day. I couldn't be happy if I didn't see him every day. [*Of course sometimes it is only for a few minutes. But a few minutes with somebody one worships mean a great deal.*

"*But you don't really worship him?*"

"*I do.*"]

"How extraordinary! I thought you would never care for anything but your painting,–your art, I should say. Art sounds better, doesn't it?"

"He is all my art to me now. I sometimes think, Harry, that there are only two eras of any importance in the history of the world. The first

---

[1] Changed to "he is poaching" by the editor to take away the insinuation that all of the upper classes are corrupt

[2] Changed to "live correctly" to remove the reference of polyamory

[3] A type of Malaysian cane wood

is the appearance of a new medium for art, and the second is the appearance of a new personality for art also. What the invention of oil-painting was to the Venetians, the face of Antinoüs[1] was to late Greek sculpture, and the face of Dorian Gray will some day be to me. It is not merely that I paint from him, draw from him, model from him. Of course I have done all that. He has stood as Paris in dainty armor[2], and as Adonis with huntsman's cloak and polished boar- spear. Crowned with heavy lotus-blossoms, he has sat on the prow of Adrian's barge, looking into the green, turbid Nile[3]. He has leaned over the still pool of some Greek woodland, and seen in the water's silent silver the wonder of his own beauty[4]. But he is much more to me than that. I won't tell you that I am dissatisfied with what I have done of him, or that his beauty is such that art cannot express it. There is nothing that art cannot express, and I know that the work I have done since I met Dorian Gray is good work, is the best work of my life. But in some curious way–I wonder will you understand me?–his personality has suggested to me an entirely new manner in art, an entirely new mode of style. I see things differently, I think of them differently. I can now re-create life in a way that was hidden from me before. 'A dream of form in days of thought[5],'– who is it who says that? I forget; but it is what Dorian Gray has been to me. The merely visible presence of this lad, –for he seems to me little more than a lad, though he is really over twenty,–his merely visible presence,–ah! I wonder can you realize all that that means? Unconsciously he defines for me the lines of a fresh school, a school that is to have in itself all the passion of the romantic spirit, all the perfection of the spirit that is Greek. The harmony of soul and body,–how much that is! We in our madness have separated the two, and have invented a realism that is bestial, an ideality that is void. Harry! Harry! if you only knew what Dorian Gray is to me! You remember that landscape of mine, for which Agnew[6] offered me such a huge price, but which I would not part with? It is one of the best things I have ever done. And why is it so? Because, while I was painting it, Dorian Gray sat beside me."

---

[1] Homosexual lover to the Roman emperor Hadrian, who was famed for his youthful beauty

[2] A character from the Trojan Wars who absconded with Helen of Troy. The imagery of "dainty" armor – presumably covering little of his body – is of course suggestively homoerotic

[3] Antinous is reported to have drowned after falling into the Nile while sailing on Hadrian's barge

[4] As Narcissus

[5] Austin Dobson said this in the poem "To a Greek Girl"

[6] One of London's leading art firms

"Basil, this is quite wonderful! I must see Dorian Gray." Hallward got up from the seat, and walked up and down the garden. After some time he came back. "You don't understand, Harry," he said. "Dorian Gray is merely to me a motive in art. He is never more present in my work than when no image of him is there. He is simply a suggestion, as I have said, of a new manner. I see him in the curves of certain lines, in the loveliness and the subtleties of certain colors. That is all."

"Then why won't you exhibit his portrait?"

"Because I have put into it all the [*extraordinary romance*[1]] of which, of course, I have never dared to speak to him. He knows nothing about it. He will never know anything about it. But the world might guess it; and I will not bare my soul to their shallow, prying eyes. My heart shall never be put under their microscope. There is too much of myself in the thing, Harry,–too much of myself!"

"Poets are not so scrupulous as you are. They know how useful passion is for publication. Nowadays a broken heart will run to many editions."

"I hate them for it. An artist should create beautiful things, but should put nothing of his own life into them. We live in an age when men treat art as if it were meant to be a form of autobiography. We have lost the abstract sense of beauty. If I live, I will show the world what it is; and for that reason the world shall never see my portrait of Dorian Gray."

"I think you are wrong, Basil, but I won't argue with you. It is only the intellectually lost who ever argue. Tell me, is Dorian Gray very fond of you?"

Hallward considered for a few moments. "He likes me," he answered, after a pause; "I know he likes me. Of course I flatter him dreadfully. I find a strange pleasure in saying things to him that I know I shall be sorry for having said. [*I give myself away*.] As a rule, he is charming to me, and we walk home together from the club arm in arm, or sit in the studio and talk of a thousand things. Now and then, however, he is horribly thoughtless, and seems to take a real delight in giving me pain. Then I feel, Harry, that I have given away my whole soul to some one who treats it as if it were a flower to put in his coat, a bit of decoration to charm his vanity, an ornament for a summer's day[2]."

---

[1] Changed to "curious artistic idolatry"

[2] Obvious parallels run between Dorian whom Basil feels treats him like a flower and Lord Henry, whose interest in Dorian is mimicked in his destruction of a flower

"Days in summer, Basil, are apt to linger. Perhaps you will tire sooner than he will. It is a sad thing to think of, but there is no doubt that Genius lasts longer than Beauty. That accounts for the fact that we all take such pains to over-educate ourselves. In the wild struggle for existence, we want to have something that endures, and so we fill our minds with rubbish and facts, in the silly hope of keeping our place. The thoroughly well informed man,–that is the modern ideal. And the mind of the thoroughly well informed man is a dreadful thing. It is like a bric-à-brac shop, all monsters and dust, and everything priced above its proper value. I think you will tire first, all the same. Some day you will look at [*him*[1]], and he will seem to you to be a little out of drawing, or you won't like his tone of color, or something. You will bitterly reproach him in your own heart, and seriously think that he has behaved very badly to you. The next time he calls, you will be perfectly cold and indifferent. It will be a great pity, for it will alter you. The worst of having a romance[2] is that it leaves one so unromantic."

"Harry, don't talk like that. As long as I live, the personality of Dorian Gray will dominate me. You can't feel what I feel. You change too often."

"Ah, my dear Basil, that is exactly why I can feel it. Those who are faithful know only the pleasures of love: it is the faithless who know love's tragedies." And Lord Henry struck a light on a dainty silver case, and began to smoke a cigarette with a self-conscious and self-satisfied air, as if he had summed up life in a phrase. There was a rustle of chirruping sparrows in the ivy, and the blue cloud- shadows chased themselves across the grass like swallows. How pleasant it was in the garden! And how delightful other people's emotions were!–much more delightful than their ideas, it seemed to him. One's own soul, and the passions of one's friends,–those were the fascinating things in life. He thought with pleasure of the tedious luncheon that he had missed by staying so long with Basil Hallward. Had he gone to his aunt's, he would have been sure to meet Lord Goodbody there, and the whole conversation would have been about the housing of the poor, and the necessity for model lodging-houses. It was charming to have escaped all that! As he thought of his aunt, an idea seemed to strike him. He turned to Hallward, and said, "My dear fellow, I have just remembered."

"Remembered what, Harry?"

"Where I heard the name of Dorian Gray."

"Where was it?" asked Hallward, with a slight frown.

---

[1] Replaced with the less intimate-sounding "Gray"
[2] Wilde replaced "a romance" with "any kind of romance"

"Don't look so angry, Basil. It was at my aunt's, Lady Agatha's. She told me she had discovered a wonderful young man, who was going to help her in the East End, and that his name was Dorian Gray. I am bound to state that she never told me he was good-looking. Women have no appreciation of good looks. At least, good women have not. She said that he was very earnest, and had a beautiful nature. I at once pictured to myself a creature with spectacles and lank hair, horridly freckled, and tramping about on huge feet. I wish I had known it was your friend."

"I am very glad you didn't, Harry."

"Why?"

"I don't want you to meet him."

"Mr. Dorian Gray is in the studio, sir," said the butler, coming into the garden.

"You must introduce me now," cried Lord Henry, laughing.

Basil Hallward turned to the servant, who stood blinking in the sunlight. "Ask Mr. Gray to wait, Parker: I will be in in a few moments." The man bowed, and went up the walk.

Then he looked at Lord Henry. "Dorian Gray is my dearest friend," he said. "He has a simple and a beautiful nature. Your aunt was quite right in what she said of him. Don't spoil him for me. Don't try to influence him. Your influence would be bad. The world is wide, and has many marvellous people in it. Don't take away from me the one person [*that makes life absolutely lovely to me, and*] that gives to my art whatever [*wonder or*] charm it possesses. Mind, Harry, I trust you." He spoke very slowly, and the words seemed wrung out of him almost against his will.

"What nonsense you talk!" said Lord Henry, smiling, and, taking Hallward by the arm, he almost led him into the house.

CHAPTER II

As they entered they saw Dorian Gray. He was seated at the piano, with his back to them, turning over the pages of a volume of Schumann's "Forest Scenes[1]." "You must lend me these, Basil," he cried. "I want to learn them. They are perfectly charming."

"That entirely depends on how you sit[2] to-day, Dorian."

"Oh, I am tired of sitting, and I don't want a life-sized portrait of myself[3]," answered the lad, swinging round on the music-stool in a wilful, petulant manner. When he caught sight of Lord Henry, a faint blush coloured his cheeks for a moment[4], and he started up. "I beg your pardon, Basil, but I didn't know you had any one with you."

"This is Lord Henry Wotton, Dorian, an old Oxford friend of mine. I have just been telling him what a capital sitter you were, and now you have spoiled everything."

"You have not spoiled my pleasure in meeting you, Mr. Gray," said Lord Henry, stepping forward and extending his hand. "My aunt has often spoken to me about you. You are one of her favourites, and, I am afraid, one of her victims also."

"I am in Lady Agatha's black books at present," answered Dorian with a funny look of penitence. "I promised to go to a club in Whitechapel[5] with her last Tuesday, and I really forgot all about it. We were to have played a duet together—three duets, I believe. I don't know what she will say to me. I am far too frightened to call."

"Oh, I will make your peace with my aunt. She is quite devoted to you. And I don't think it really matters about your not being there. The audience probably thought it was a duet. When Aunt Agatha sits down to the piano, she makes quite enough noise for two people."

---

[1] A series of nine piano pieces written by the German composer Robert Schumann in 1850. They are quiet, pastoral tunes that were heavily identified with sensitivity, purity, and introspection

[2] Pose for the portrait

[3] It is critical to note that Dorian begins the novel relatively untainted and unpolluted – disinterested in self-absorption

[4] An indication of self-awareness that suggests that Dorian is uncomfortable sharing this intimate moment with a stranger whom he cannot yet trust to be discreet

[5] A poor neighborhood in East London made notorious by the Jack the Ripper slayings. Aunt Agatha is probably hosting this concert as a fund raiser for the local poor

"That is very horrid to her, and not very nice to me," answered Dorian, laughing.

Lord Henry looked at him. Yes, he was certainly wonderfully handsome, with his finely curved scarlet lips, his frank blue eyes, his crisp gold hair. There was something in his face that made one trust him at once. All the candour of youth was there, as well as all youth's passionate purity. One felt that he had kept himself unspotted from the world. No wonder Basil Hallward worshipped him. [*He was made to be worshipped.*]

"You are too charming to go in for philanthropy, Mr. Gray—far too charming." And Lord Henry flung himself down on the divan and opened his cigarette-case.

The painter had been busy mixing his colours and getting his brushes ready. He was looking worried, and when he heard Lord Henry's last remark, he glanced at him, hesitated for a moment, and then said, "Harry, I want to finish this picture to-day. Would you think it awfully rude of me if I asked you to go away[1]?"

Lord Henry smiled and looked at Dorian Gray. "Am I to go, Mr. Gray?" he asked.

"Oh, please don't, Lord Henry. I see that Basil is in one of his sulky moods, and I can't bear him when he sulks. Besides, I want you to tell me why I should not go in for philanthropy."

"I don't know that I shall tell you that, Mr. Gray. It is so tedious a subject that one would have to talk seriously about it. But I certainly shall not run away, now that you have asked me to stop. You don't really mind, Basil, do you? You have often told me that you liked your sitters to have some one to chat to."

Hallward bit his lip. "If Dorian wishes it, of course you must stay. Dorian's whims are laws to everybody, except himself."

Lord Henry took up his hat and gloves. "You are very pressing, Basil, but I am afraid I must go. I have promised to meet a man at the Orleans[2]. Good-bye, Mr. Gray. Come and see me some afternoon in Curzon Street[3]. I am nearly always at home at five o'clock. Write to me when you are coming. I should be sorry to miss you."

"Basil," cried Dorian Gray, "if Lord Henry Wotton goes, I shall go, too. You never open your lips while you are painting, and it is horribly dull standing on a platform and trying to look pleasant. Ask him to stay. I insist upon it."

---

[1] Since his painting of Dorian is a spiritual act, he hopes to have the solitude that deep worship requires

[2] A sporting club in Mayfair

[3] A posh street in the Mayfair district

"Stay, Harry, to oblige Dorian, and to oblige me," said Hallward, gazing intently at his picture. "It is quite true, I never talk when I am working, and never listen either, and it must be dreadfully tedious for my unfortunate sitters. I beg you to stay."

"But what about my man at the Orleans?"

The painter laughed. "I don't think there will be any difficulty about that. Sit down again, Harry. And now, Dorian, get up on the platform, and don't move about too much, or pay any attention to what Lord Henry says. He has a very bad influence over all his friends, with the single exception of myself."

Dorian Gray stepped up on the dais with the air of a young Greek martyr[1], and made a little *moue*[2] of discontent to Lord Henry, to whom he had rather taken a fancy. He was so unlike Basil. They made a delightful contrast. And he had such a beautiful voice. After a few moments he said to him, "Have you really a very bad influence, Lord Henry? As bad as Basil says?"

"There is no such thing as a good influence, Mr. Gray. All influence is immoral—immoral from the scientific point of view."

"Why?"

"Because to influence a person is to give him one's own soul. He does not think his natural thoughts, or burn with his natural passions. His virtues are not real to him. His sins, if there are such things as sins, are borrowed. He becomes an echo of some one else's music, an actor of a part that has not been written for him. The aim of life is self-development. To realize one's nature perfectly—that is what each of us is here for. People are afraid of themselves, nowadays. They have forgotten the highest of all duties, the duty that one owes to one's self[3]. Of course, they are charitable. They feed the hungry and clothe the beggar. But their own souls starve, and are naked. Courage has gone out of our race. Perhaps we never really had it. The terror of society, which is the basis of morals, the terror of God, which is the secret of religion—these are the two things that govern us. And yet—"

---

[1] Wilde prefigures the way in which Dorian's innocence will be martyred on the altar of Basil's adoration at the hands of Henry's influence. Greek statues of male martyrs were notable for their youth, beauty, and masculine eroticism (another "Dorian" connection)

[2] Pout

[3] Lord Henry speaks as an oracle, foreshadowing Dorian's inevitable downfall – caused by his concern for others' perceptions. It also suggests the fate of Sybil Vane, who loses her ability to act after falling in love and becoming true to her self

"Just turn your head a little more to the right, Dorian, like a good boy," said the painter, deep in his work and conscious only that a look had come into the lad's face that he had never seen there before[1].

"And yet," continued Lord Henry, in his low, musical voice, and with that graceful wave of the hand that was always so characteristic of him, and that he had even in his Eton[2] days, "I believe that if one man were to live out his life fully and completely, were to give form to every feeling, expression to every thought, reality to every dream—I believe that the world would gain such a fresh impulse of joy that we would forget all the maladies of mediaevalism, and return to the Hellenic[3] ideal—to something finer, richer than the Hellenic ideal, it may be. But the bravest man amongst us is afraid of himself. The mutilation of the savage has its tragic survival in the self-denial that mars our lives. We are punished for our refusals. Every impulse that we strive to strangle broods in the mind and poisons us[4]. The body sins once, and has done with its sin, for action is a mode of purification. Nothing remains then but the recollection of a pleasure, or the luxury of a regret. The only way to get rid of a temptation is to yield to it. Resist it, and your soul grows sick with longing for the things it has forbidden to itself, with desire for what its monstrous laws have made monstrous and unlawful. It has been said that the great events of the world take place in the brain. It is in the brain, and the brain only, that the great sins of the world take place also. You, Mr. Gray, you yourself, with your rose-red youth and your rose-white boyhood, you have had passions that have made you afraid, thoughts that have filled you with terror, day-dreams and sleeping dreams whose mere memory might stain your cheek with shame—"

"Stop!" faltered Dorian Gray, "stop! you bewilder me. I don't know what to say. There is some answer to you, but I cannot find it. Don't speak. Let me think. Or, rather, let me try not to think."

For nearly ten minutes he stood there, motionless, with parted lips and eyes strangely bright. He was dimly conscious that entirely fresh influences were at work within him. Yet they seemed to him to have come really from himself. The few words that Basil's friend had said to him—

---

[1] Something has stirred in Dorian's spirit – the process of corruption has begun, and only Basil, the artist, is sensitive to the subtle spiritual change
[2] England's most prestigious prep school
[3] Greek – values steeped in Athenean philosophy rather than Christian theology
[4] Lord Henry's basic worldview is that you should never resist an impulse at the peril of suppressing your spirit. Dorian will learn that there are monsters to be found in this lifestyle, too, though

words spoken by chance, no doubt, and with wilful[1] paradox in them—had touched some secret chord that had never been touched before, but that he felt was now vibrating and throbbing to curious pulses[2].

Music had stirred him like that. Music had troubled him many times. But music was not articulate. It was not a new world, but rather another chaos, that it created in us. Words! Mere words! How terrible they were! How clear, and vivid, and cruel! One could not escape from them. And yet what a subtle magic there was in them! They seemed to be able to give a plastic form to formless things, and to have a music of their own as sweet as that of viol[3] or of lute. Mere words! Was there anything so real as words?

Yes; there had been things in his boyhood that he had not understood. He understood them now. Life suddenly became fiery-coloured[4] to him. It seemed to him that he had been walking in fire. Why had he not known it?

With his subtle smile, Lord Henry watched him. He knew the precise psychological moment when to say nothing. He felt intensely interested[5]. He was amazed at the sudden impression that his words had produced, and, remembering a book that he had read when he was sixteen, a book which had revealed to him much that he had not known before, he wondered whether Dorian Gray was passing through a similar experience. He had merely shot an arrow into the air. Had it hit the mark? How fascinating the lad was!

Hallward painted away with that marvellous bold touch of his, that had the true refinement and perfect delicacy that in art, at any rate comes only from strength. He was unconscious of the silence.

"Basil, I am tired of standing," cried Dorian Gray suddenly. "I must go out and sit in the garden. The air is stifling here."

"My dear fellow, I am so sorry. When I am painting, I can't think of anything else. But you never sat better. You were perfectly still. And I have caught the effect I wanted—the half-parted lips and the bright look in the eyes. I don't know what Harry has been saying to you, but he has certainly

---

[1] Lord Henry may not actually believe these statements, but finds pleasure in confusing and warping others – he is a bringer of chaos, discord, and moral confusion

[2] Although Lord Henry introduces the corruptive germs, Dorian is innately receptive to them: something natural within him has a kinship with Lord Henry's philosophy

[3] Small cello

[4] The allure of sin

[5] Reptilian and detached, Lord Henry is merely "interested" in others' moral conflicts. What happens to their lives afterwards makes no difference to him

made you have the most wonderful expression[1]. I suppose he has been paying you compliments. You mustn't believe a word that he says."

"He has certainly not been paying me compliments. Perhaps that is the reason that I don't believe anything he has told me."

"You know you believe it all," said Lord Henry, looking at him with his dreamy languorous eyes. "I will go out to the garden with you. It is horribly hot in the studio. Basil, let us have something iced to drink, something with strawberries in it."

"Certainly, Harry. Just touch the bell, and when Parker comes I will tell him what you want. I have got to work up this background, so I will join you later on. Don't keep Dorian too long. I have never been in better form for painting than I am to-day. This is going to be my masterpiece. It is my masterpiece as it stands."

Lord Henry went out to the garden and found Dorian Gray burying his face in the great cool lilac-blossoms, feverishly drinking in their perfume as if it had been wine[2]. He came close to him and put his hand upon his shoulder. "You are quite right to do that," he murmured. "Nothing can cure the soul but the senses, just as nothing can cure the senses but the soul."

The lad started and drew back. He was bareheaded, and the leaves had tossed his rebellious curls and tangled all their gilded threads. There was a look of fear in his eyes, such as people have when they are suddenly awakened. His finely chiselled nostrils quivered, and some hidden nerve shook the scarlet of his lips and left them trembling.

"Yes," continued Lord Henry, "that is one of the great secrets of life— to cure the soul by means of the senses, and the senses by means of the soul. You are a wonderful creation. You know more than you think you know, just as you know less than you want to know."

Dorian Gray frowned and turned his head away. He could not help liking the tall, graceful young man who was standing by him. His romantic, olive-coloured[3] face and worn expression interested him. There was something in his low languid voice that was absolutely fascinating. His cool, white, flowerlike hands, even, had a curious charm. They moved, as he spoke, like music, and seemed to have a language of their own. But he felt afraid of him, and ashamed of being afraid. Why had it been left

---

[1] Basil's worship has caused him to be an unknowing partner in Dorian's corruption. Playing the role of pimp, he has miscarried his duty to protect and mentor his protégée. This will later horrify him when he realizes how he has contributed to Dorian's fall

[2] Lilacs symbolize first love: Dorian has fallen in love with Lord Henry's philosophies of the Self, and thus, with himself

[3] Suggesting Greek-ness

for a stranger to reveal him to himself? He had known Basil Hallward for months, but the friendship between them had never altered him. Suddenly there had come some one across his life who seemed to have disclosed to him life's mystery. And, yet, what was there to be afraid of? He was not a schoolboy or a girl. It was absurd to be frightened.

"Let us go and sit in the shade," said Lord Henry. "Parker has brought out the drinks, and if you stay any longer in this glare, you will be quite spoiled, and Basil will never paint you again. You really must not allow yourself to become sunburnt. It would be unbecoming."

"What can it matter?" cried Dorian Gray, laughing, as he sat down on the seat at the end of the garden.

"It should matter everything to you, Mr. Gray."

"Why?"

"Because you have the most marvellous youth, and youth is the one thing worth having."

"I don't feel that, Lord Henry."

"No, you don't feel it now. Some day, when you are old and wrinkled and ugly, when thought has seared your forehead with its lines, and passion branded your lips with its hideous fires, you will feel it, you will feel it terribly. Now, wherever you go, you charm the world. Will it always be so? ... You have a wonderfully beautiful face, Mr. Gray. Don't frown. You have. And beauty is a form of genius—is higher, indeed, than genius, as it needs no explanation. It is of the great facts of the world, like sunlight, or spring-time, or the reflection in dark waters of that silver shell we call the moon. It cannot be questioned. It has its divine right of sovereignty. It makes princes of those who have it. You smile? Ah! when you have lost it you won't smile.... People say sometimes that beauty is only superficial. That may be so, but at least it is not so superficial as thought is. To me, beauty is the wonder of wonders. It is only shallow people who do not judge by appearances. The true mystery of the world is the visible, not the invisible.... Yes, Mr. Gray, the gods have been good to you. But what the gods give they quickly take away. You have only a few years in which to live really, perfectly, and fully. When your youth goes, your beauty will go with it, and then you will suddenly discover that there are no triumphs left for you, or have to content yourself with those mean triumphs that the memory of your past will make more bitter than defeats. Every month as it wanes brings you nearer to something dreadful. Time is jealous of you, and wars against your lilies and your roses. You will become sallow, and hollow-cheeked, and dull-eyed. You will suffer horribly....

"Ah! realize your youth while you have it. Don't squander the gold of your days, listening to the tedious, trying to improve the hopeless failure, or giving away your life to the ignorant, the common, and the vulgar. These are the sickly aims, the false ideals, of our age. Live! Live the wonderful life that is in you! Let nothing be lost upon you. Be always searching for new sensations. Be afraid of nothing.... A new Hedonism[1]— that is what our century wants. You might be its visible symbol. With your personality there is nothing you could not do. The world belongs to you for a season.... The moment I met you I saw that you were quite unconscious of what you really are, of what you really might be. There was so much in you that charmed me that I felt I must tell you something about yourself[2]. I thought how tragic it would be if you were wasted. For there is such a little time that your youth will last—such a little time. The common hill-flowers wither, but they blossom again. The laburnum will be as yellow next June as it is now. In a month there will be purple stars on the clematis, and year after year the green night of its leaves will hold its purple stars. But we never get back our youth. The pulse of joy that beats in us at twenty becomes sluggish. Our limbs fail, our senses rot. We degenerate into hideous puppets, haunted by the memory of the passions of which we were too much afraid, and the exquisite temptations that we had not the courage to yield to. Youth! Youth! There is absolutely nothing in the world but youth!"

Dorian Gray listened, open-eyed and wondering. The spray of lilac fell from his hand upon the gravel. A furry bee[3] came and buzzed round it for a moment. Then it began to scramble all over the oval stellated globe of the tiny blossoms. He watched it with that strange interest in trivial things that we try to develop when things of high import make us afraid, or when we are stirred by some new emotion for which we cannot find expression, or when some thought that terrifies us lays sudden siege to the brain and calls on us to yield. After a time the bee flew away. He saw

---

[1] Hedonism – the unfettered pursuit of desire – was a popular philosophy amongst Late Victorians who viewed a return to Greco-Roman ideals as a welcome response to the 19th century's tradition of moralism. Decadents like Wilde led the movement to make pleasure and aestheticism the crowning ideal of the Belle Epoque: instead of self-control and duty, indulgence and appetite would shape the new society

[2] There are clear parallels here between the Genesis narrative (and Milton's rendition of it in "Paradise Lost") of the serpent coaxing Eve into eating the forbidden fruit: the two men are in a garden, Dorian is innocent but awakening, and Lord Henry's appeals are to ambition and aspiration

[3] Bees are a recurring motif in the novel, symbolizing sensuality and desire

it creeping into the stained trumpet of a Tyrian convolvulus. The flower seemed to quiver, and then swayed gently to and fro[1].

Suddenly the painter appeared at the door of the studio and made staccato[2] signs for them to come in. They turned to each other and smiled.

"I am waiting," he cried. "Do come in. The light is quite perfect, and you can bring your drinks."

They rose up and sauntered down the walk together. Two green-and-white butterflies fluttered past them, and in the pear-tree at the corner of the garden a thrush[3] began to sing.

"You are glad you have met me, Mr. Gray," said Lord Henry, looking at him.

"Yes, I am glad now. I wonder shall I always be glad?"

"Always! That is a dreadful word. It makes me shudder when I hear it. Women are so fond of using it. They spoil every romance by trying to make it last for ever. It is a meaningless word, too. The only difference between a caprice and a lifelong passion is that the caprice lasts a little longer."

As they entered the studio, Dorian Gray put his hand upon Lord Henry's arm. "In that case, let our friendship be a caprice," he murmured, flushing at his own boldness, then stepped up on the platform and resumed his pose.

Lord Henry flung himself into a large wicker arm-chair and watched him. The sweep and dash of the brush on the canvas made the only sound that broke the stillness, except when, now and then, Hallward stepped back to look at his work from a distance. In the slanting beams that streamed through the open doorway the dust danced and was golden. The heavy scent of the roses seemed to brood over everything.

After about a quarter of an hour Hallward stopped painting, looked for a long time at Dorian Gray, and then for a long time at the picture, biting the end of one of his huge brushes and frowning. "It is quite finished," he cried at last, and stooping down he wrote his name in long vermilion letters on the left-hand corner of the canvas.

Lord Henry came over and examined the picture. It was certainly a wonderful work of art, and a wonderful likeness as well.

"My dear fellow, I congratulate you most warmly," he said. "It is the finest portrait of modern times. Mr. Gray, come over and look at yourself."

---

[1] The flower (Dorian) is yielding to the conquest of the lascivious bee (Lord Henry's Hedonistic philosophy)

[2] Short, plucky sounds

[3] Symbolic of freedom and steadfast relationships: Dorian has been won over eternally to Lord Henry's views of freedom

The lad started, as if awakened from some dream.

"Is it really finished?" he murmured, stepping down from the platform.

"Quite finished," said the painter. "And you have sat splendidly to-day. I am awfully obliged to you."

"That is entirely due to me," broke in Lord Henry. "Isn't it, Mr. Gray?"

Dorian made no answer, but passed listlessly in front of his picture and turned towards it. When he saw it he drew back, and his cheeks flushed for a moment with pleasure. A look of joy came into his eyes, as if he had recognized himself for the first time[1]. He stood there motionless and in wonder, dimly conscious that Hallward was speaking to him, but not catching the meaning of his words. The sense of his own beauty came on him like a revelation. He had never felt it before. Basil Hallward's compliments had seemed to him to be merely the charming exaggeration of friendship. He had listened to them, laughed at them, forgotten them. They had not influenced his nature. Then had come Lord Henry Wotton with his strange panegyric[2] on youth, his terrible warning of its brevity. That had stirred him at the time, and now, as he stood gazing at the shadow of his own loveliness, the full reality of the description flashed across him. Yes, there would be a day when his face would be wrinkled and wizen, his eyes dim and colourless, the grace of his figure broken and deformed. The scarlet would pass away from his lips and the gold steal from his hair. The life that was to make his soul would mar his body. He would become dreadful, hideous, and uncouth.

As he thought of it, a sharp pang of pain struck through him like a knife[3] and made each delicate fibre of his nature quiver. His eyes deepened into amethyst, and across them came a mist of tears. He felt as if a hand of ice had been laid upon his heart.

"Don't you like it?" cried Hallward at last, stung a little by the lad's silence, not understanding what it meant.

"Of course he likes it," said Lord Henry. "Who wouldn't like it? It is one of the greatest things in modern art. I will give you anything you like to ask for it. I must have it."

"It is not my property, Harry."

"Whose property is it?"

"Dorian's, of course," answered the painter.

---

[1] He sees how he is seen – how Basil and Lord Henry view him (as a god of youth) – and is enamored with their enamorment

[2] A passionate speech

[3] Foreshadowing several future events

"He is a very lucky fellow."

"How sad it is!" murmured Dorian Gray with his eyes still fixed upon his own portrait. "How sad it is! I shall grow old, and horrible, and dreadful. But this picture will remain always young. It will never be older than this particular day of June.... If it were only the other way! If it were I who was to be always young, and the picture that was to grow old! For that—for that—I would give everything! Yes, there is nothing in the whole world I would not give! I would give my soul for that!"

"You would hardly care for such an arrangement, Basil," cried Lord Henry, laughing. "It would be rather hard lines on your work."

"I should object very strongly, Harry," said Hallward.

Dorian Gray turned and looked at him. "I believe you would, Basil. You like your art better than your friends. I am no more to you than a green bronze figure. Hardly as much, I dare say."

The painter stared in amazement. It was so unlike Dorian to speak like that. What had happened? He seemed quite angry. His face was flushed and his cheeks burning.

"Yes," he continued, "I am less to you than your ivory Hermes or your silver Faun[1]. You will like them always. How long will you like me? Till I have my first wrinkle, I suppose. I know, now, that when one loses one's good looks, whatever they may be, one loses everything. Your picture has taught me that. Lord Henry Wotton is perfectly right. Youth is the only thing worth having. When I find that I am growing old, I shall kill myself."

Hallward turned pale and caught his hand. "Dorian! Dorian!" he cried, "don't talk like that. I have never had such a friend as you, and I shall never have such another. You are not jealous of material things, are you?—you who are finer than any of them!"

"I am jealous of everything whose beauty does not die. I am jealous of the portrait you have painted of me. Why should it keep what I must lose? Every moment that passes takes something from me and gives something to it. Oh, if it were only the other way! If the picture could change, and I could be always what I am now! Why did you paint it? It will mock me some day—mock me horribly!" The hot tears welled into his eyes; he tore his hand away and, flinging himself on the divan, he buried his face in the cushions, as though he was praying.

"This is your doing, Harry," said the painter bitterly.

---

[1] Hermes, or Mercury, is the messenger god of athletics (often used as a homoerotic motif), and fauns – half goats, half men – were rural gods symbolizing lust and desire

Lord Henry shrugged his shoulders. "It is the real Dorian Gray[1]—that is all."

"It is not."

"If it is not, what have I to do with it?"

"You should have gone away when I asked you," he muttered.

"I stayed when you asked me," was Lord Henry's answer.

"Harry, I can't quarrel with my two best friends at once, but between you both you have made me hate the finest piece of work I have ever done, and I will destroy it. What is it but canvas and colour? I will not let it come across our three lives and mar them."

Dorian Gray lifted his golden head from the pillow, and with pallid face and tear-stained eyes, looked at him as he walked over to the deal painting-table that was set beneath the high curtained window. What was he doing there? His fingers were straying about among the litter of tin tubes and dry brushes, seeking for something. Yes, it was for the long palette-knife, with its thin blade of lithe steel. He had found it at last. He was going to rip up the canvas.

With a stifled sob the lad leaped from the couch, and, rushing over to Hallward, tore the knife out of his hand, and flung it to the end of the studio. "Don't, Basil, don't!" he cried. "It would be murder[2]!"

"I am glad you appreciate my work at last, Dorian," said the painter coldly when he had recovered from his surprise. "I never thought you would."

"Appreciate it? I am in love with it, Basil. It is part of myself. I feel that."

"Well, as soon as you[3] are dry, you shall be varnished, and framed, and sent home. Then you can do what you like with yourself." And he walked across the room and rang the bell for tea. "You will have tea, of course, Dorian? And so will you, Harry? Or do you object to such simple pleasures?"

"I adore simple pleasures," said Lord Henry. "They are the last refuge of the complex. But I don't like scenes, except on the stage. What absurd

---

[1] Henry's pleasure is in rising up people's natural vices, not in introducing foreign ideas; he doesn't so much corrupt Dorian as he stirs up Dorian's innate weaknesses, giving Henry the satisfaction of truthfully claiming that he has only probed a latent, pre-existing vice, clearing him of responsibility

[2] Dorian now views his personified youth as more human than himself. Indeed, since his soul has become transposed into the oils (as demonstrated by its visual aging over the future years), the painting is now more human and more "Dorian" than Dorian the man

[3] Even Basil seems to innately recognize that the picture holds Dorian's soul – it is "him"

fellows you are, both of you! I wonder who it was defined man as a rational animal. It was the most premature definition ever given. Man is many things, but he is not rational. I am glad he is not, after all—though I wish you chaps would not squabble over the picture. You had much better let me have it, Basil. This silly boy doesn't really want it, and I really do."

"If you let any one have it but me, Basil, I shall never forgive you!" cried Dorian Gray; "and I don't allow people to call me a silly boy[1]."

"You know the picture is yours, Dorian. I gave it to you before it existed[2]."

"And you know you have been a little silly, Mr. Gray, and that you don't really object to being reminded that you are extremely young."

"I should have objected very strongly this morning, Lord Henry."

"Ah! this morning! You have lived since then."

There came a knock at the door, and the butler entered with a laden tea-tray and set it down upon a small Japanese table. There was a rattle of cups and saucers and the hissing of a fluted Georgian[3] urn. Two globe-shaped china dishes were brought in by a page. Dorian Gray went over and poured out the tea. The two men sauntered languidly to the table and examined what was under the covers.

"Let us go to the theatre to-night," said Lord Henry. "There is sure to be something on, somewhere. I have promised to dine at White's, but it is only with an old friend, so I can send him a wire to say that I am ill, or that I am prevented from coming in consequence of a subsequent engagement. I think that would be a rather nice excuse: it would have all the surprise of candour."

"It is such a bore putting on one's dress-clothes," muttered Hallward. "And, when one has them on, they are so horrid."

"Yes," answered Lord Henry dreamily, "the costume of the nineteenth century is detestable[4]. It is so sombre, so depressing. Sin is the only real colour-element left in modern life."

"You really must not say things like that before Dorian, Harry."

"Before which Dorian? The one who is pouring out tea for us, or the one in the picture?"

"Before either."

---

[1] The word "boy" applied to a young man was often a homosexual euphemism for "sub," implying the weaker, younger, more submissive partner in a sexual relationship, and suggesting a power dynamic which clearly offends Dorian

[2] The picture is the manifestation of Basil's worship

[3] Pertaining to the reigns of the four king Georges: 1714 – 1830

[4] Wilde and his wife were members of a movement to relax Victorian fashion and both dressed in looser, more flamboyant clothes evocative of earlier centuries

"I should like to come to the theatre with you, Lord Henry," said the lad.

"Then you shall come; and you will come, too, Basil, won't you?"

"I can't, really. I would sooner not. I have a lot of work to do."

"Well, then, you and I will go alone, Mr. Gray."

"I should like that awfully."

The painter bit his lip and walked over, cup in hand, to the picture. "I shall stay with the real Dorian," he said, sadly.

"Is it the real Dorian?" cried the original of the portrait, strolling across to him. "Am I really like that?"

"Yes; you are just like that."

"How wonderful, Basil!"

"At least you are like it in appearance. But it will never alter," sighed Hallward. "That is something."

"What a fuss people make about fidelity!" exclaimed Lord Henry. "Why, even in love it is purely a question for physiology. It has nothing to do with our own will. Young men want to be faithful, and are not; old men want to be faithless, and cannot: that is all one can say."

"Don't go to the theatre to-night, Dorian," said Hallward. "Stop and dine with me."

"I can't, Basil."

"Why?"

"Because I have promised Lord Henry Wotton to go with him."

"He won't like you the better for keeping your promises. He always breaks his own. I beg you not to go."

Dorian Gray laughed and shook his head.

"I entreat you."

The lad hesitated, and looked over at Lord Henry, who was watching them from the tea-table with an amused smile.

"I must go, Basil," he answered.

"Very well," said Hallward, and he went over and laid down his cup on the tray. "It is rather late, and, as you have to dress, you had better lose no time. Good-bye, Harry. Good-bye, Dorian. Come and see me soon. Come to-morrow."

"Certainly."

"You won't forget?"

"No, of course not," cried Dorian.

"And ... Harry!"

"Yes, Basil?"

"Remember what I asked you, when we were in the garden this morning."

"I have forgotten it."

"I trust you."

"I wish I could trust myself," said Lord Henry, laughing. "Come, Mr. Gray, my hansom[1] is outside, and I can drop you at your own place. Good-bye, Basil. It has been a most interesting afternoon."

As the door closed behind them, the painter flung himself down on a sofa, and a look of pain came into his face.

CHAPTER III

ONE afternoon, a month later, Dorian Gray was reclining in a luxurious arm-chair, in the little library of Lord Henry's house in Mayfair. It was, in its way, a very charming room, with its high panelled wainscoting of olive-stained oak, its cream-coloured frieze and ceiling of raised plasterwork, and its brickdust felt carpet strewn with silk, long-fringed Persian rugs. On a tiny satinwood table stood a statuette by Clodion[2], and beside it lay a copy of Les Cent Nouvelles, bound for Margaret of Valois by Clovis Eve[3] and powdered with the gilt daisies that Queen had selected for her device. Some large blue china jars and parrot-tulips were ranged on the mantelshelf, and through the small leaded panes of the window streamed the apricot-coloured light of a summer day in London.

Lord Henry had not yet come in. He was always late on principle, his principle being that punctuality is the thief of time. So the lad was looking rather sulky, as with listless fingers he turned over the pages of an elaborately illustrated edition of Manon Lescaut[4] that he had found in one of the book-cases. The formal monotonous ticking of the Louis Quatorze[5] clock annoyed him. Once or twice he thought of going away.

At last he heard a light step outside, and the door opened. "How late you are, Harry!" he murmured.

"I am afraid it is not Harry, Mr. Gray," said a woman's voice.

---

[1] Two-wheeled carriage with the driver sitting behind and above the occupants
[2] An 18th century French sculptor known for his rococo terra cotta sculptures
[3] A collection of 15th century fiction (the first short stories in French literature) of a comic and often lusty nature. Margaret of Valois was queen of France during the late 1500s, and Clovis Eve was a famous French bookbinder who created extravagant books for the aristocracy
[4] A controversial French novel about a prostitute who runs away with a nobleman in Louisiana
[5] Furniture made in the ornate style popularized by the French court of Louis XIV

He glanced quickly round, and rose to his feet. "I beg your pardon. I thought–"

"You thought it was my husband. It is only his wife. You must let me introduce myself. I know you quite well by your photographs. I think my husband has got twenty-seven of them."

"Not twenty-seven, Lady Henry?"

"Well, twenty-six, then. And I saw you with him the other night at the Opera." She laughed nervously, as she spoke, and watched him with her vague forget-me-not eyes. She was a curious woman, whose dresses always looked as if they had been designed in a rage and put on in a tempest[1]. She was always in love with somebody, and, as her passion was never returned, she had kept all her illusions. She tried to look picturesque, but only succeeded in being untidy. Her name was Victoria, and she had a perfect mania for going to church[2].

"That was at 'Lohengrin[3],' Lady Henry, I think?"

"Yes; it was at dear 'Lohengrin.' I like Wagner's music better than any other music. It is so loud that one can talk the whole time, without people hearing what one says. That is a great advantage: don't you think so, Mr. Gray?"

The same nervous staccato laugh broke from her thin lips, and her fingers began to play with a long paper-knife.

Dorian smiled, and shook his head: "I am afraid I don't think so, Lady Henry. I never talk during music,–at least during good music. If one hears bad music, it is one's duty to drown it by conversation."

"Ah! that is one of Harry's views, isn't it, Mr. Gray? But you must not think I don't like good music. I adore it, but I am afraid of it. It makes me too romantic. I have simply worshipped pianists,– two at a time, sometimes. I don't know what it is about them. Perhaps it is that they are foreigners. They all are, aren't they? Even those that are born in England become foreigners after a time, don't they? It is so clever of them, and such a compliment to art. Makes it quite cosmopolitan, doesn't it? You have never been to any of my parties, have you, Mr. Gray? You must come. I can't afford orchids, but I spare no expense in foreigners. They make one's rooms look so picturesque. But here is Harry!–Harry, I came in to look for you, to ask you something,–I forget what it was,–and I found Mr.

---

[1] Likely based on Wilde's wife Constance, who tried to emulate her husband's dandyish fashion sense but was widely considered more comical than picturesque in her attempts to look casual and foppish

[2] Constance Wilde was also known for her devotion to church attendance

[3] Wagner's famous opera about a German knight in search of a damsel in distress, remembered for its dramatic romance and particularly for its "Bridal Chorus" – the ultimate cliché of wedding processionals

Gray here. We have had such a pleasant chat about music. We have quite the same views. No; I think our views are quite different. But he has been most pleasant. I am so glad I've seen him."

"I am charmed, my love, quite charmed," said Lord Henry, elevating his dark crescent-shaped eyebrows and looking at them both with an amused smile.–"So sorry I am late, Dorian. I went to look after a piece of old brocade in Wardour Street[1], and had to bargain for hours for it. Nowadays people know the price of everything, and the value of nothing."

"I am afraid I must be going," exclaimed Lady Henry, after an awkward silence, with her silly sudden laugh. "I have promised to drive with the duchess.–Good-by, Mr. Gray.–Good-by, Harry. You are dining out, I suppose? So am I. Perhaps I shall see you at Lady Thornbury's."

"I dare say, my dear," said Lord Henry, shutting the door behind her, as she flitted out of the room, looking like a bird-of-paradise that had been out in the rain, and leaving a faint odor of patchouli behind her. Then he shook hands with Dorian Gray, lit a cigarette, and flung himself down on the sofa.

"Never marry a woman with straw-colored hair, Dorian," he said, after a few puffs.

"Why, Harry?"

"Because they are so sentimental."

"But I like sentimental people."

"Never marry at all, Dorian. Men marry because they are tired; women, because they are curious: both are disappointed[2]."

"I don't think I am likely to marry, Harry. I am too much in love. That is one of your aphorisms. I am putting it into practice, as I do everything you say."

"Whom are you in love with?" said Lord Henry, looking at him with a curious smile.

"With an actress," said Dorian Gray, blushing.

Lord Henry shrugged his shoulders. "That is a rather common-place début[3]," he murmured.

"You would not say so if you saw her, Harry."

"Who is she?"

---

[1] A street made famous for its antique stores. Brocade is a type of embroidered cloth made of colorful silk

[2] This is an allusion to sexual appetite: according to Henry, men marry when they tire of debauchery and women because they desire it, leaving both partners "disappointed" by their mismatched sex drives

[3] Ill-starred romances between aristocratic men and actresses were a cliché based in truth during the Victorian era, which usually ended in scandal, embarrassment, and divorce

"Her name is Sibyl Vane[1]."

"Never heard of her."

"No one has. People will some day, however. She is a genius[2]."

"My dear boy, no woman is a genius: women are a decorative sex. They never have anything to say, but they say it charmingly. They represent the triumph of matter over mind, just as we men represent the triumph of mind over morals[3]. There are only two kinds of women, the plain and the colored. The plain women are very useful. If you want to gain a reputation for respectability, you have merely to take them down to supper. The other women are very charming. They commit one mistake, however. They paint in order to try to look young. Our grandmothers painted in order to try to talk brilliantly. Rouge and *esprit*[4] used to go together. That has all gone out now. As long as a woman can look ten years younger than her own daughter, she is perfectly satisfied. As for conversation, there are only five women in London worth talking to, and two of these can't be admitted into decent society. However, tell me about your genius. How long have you known her?"

"About three weeks. Not so much. About two weeks and two days."

"How did you come across her?"

"I will tell you, Harry; but you mustn't be unsympathetic about it. After all, it never would have happened if I had not met you. You filled me with a wild desire to know everything about life. For days after I met you, something seemed to throb in my veins. As I lounged in the Park[5], or strolled down Piccadilly[6], I used to look at every one who passed me, and wonder with a mad curiosity what sort of lives they led. Some of them fascinated me. Others filled me with terror. There was an exquisite poison in the air. I had a passion for sensations.

"One evening about seven o'clock I determined to go out in search of some adventure. I felt that this gray, monstrous London of ours, with its myriads of people, its splendid sinners, and its sordid sins, as you once said, must have something in store for me. I fancied a thousand things.

---

[1] A "sibyl" is a fortune teller from Greek mythology and a "vane" – like a weathervane – is an instrument used to tell the direction of the wind. Both suggest that Sibyl is a character who will foretell or prefigure Dorian's fate: the way he treats her will determine his destiny

[2] The personification of an art (in this case, acting)

[3] According to the misogynistic Lord Henry, women succeed in life because their physical beauty ("matter") disguises their stupidity while men succeed because their intellect covers up their perversions

[4] Charm, wit, intelligence

[5] Hyde Park

[6] One of London's most urbane, posh streets

47

"The mere danger gave me a sense of delight. I remembered what you had said to me on that wonderful night when we first dined together, about the search for beauty being the poisonous secret of life. I don't know what I expected, but I went out, and wandered eastward[1], soon losing my way in a labyrinth of grimy streets and black, grassless squares. About half-past eight I passed by a little third- rate theatre[2], with great flaring gas-jets and gaudy play-bills. A hideous Jew, in the most amazing waistcoat I ever beheld in my life, was standing at the entrance, smoking a vile cigar. He had greasy ringlets, and an enormous diamond blazed in the centre of a soiled shirt. "Ave a box, my lord?' he said, when he saw me, and he took off his hat with an act of gorgeous servility. There was something about him, Harry, that amused me. He was such a monster. You will laugh at me, I know, but I really went in and paid a whole guinea[3] for the stage-box. To the present day I can't make out why I did so; and yet if I hadn't!–my dear Harry, if I hadn't, I would have missed the greatest romance of my life. I see you are laughing. It is horrid of you!"

"I am not laughing, Dorian; at least I am not laughing at you. But you should not say the greatest romance of your life. You should say the first romance of your life. You will always be loved, and you will always be in love with love. There are exquisite things in store for you. This is merely the beginning."

"Do you think my nature so shallow?" cried Dorian Gray, angrily.

"No; I think your nature so deep."

"How do you mean?"

"My dear boy, people who only love once in their lives are really shallow people. What they call their loyalty, and their fidelity, I call either the lethargy of custom or the lack of imagination. Faithlessness is to the emotional life what consistency is to the intellectual life,–simply a confession of failure. But I don't want to interrupt you. Go on with your story."

"Well, I found myself seated in a horrid little private box, with a vulgar drop-scene staring me in the face. I looked out behind the curtain, and surveyed the house. It was a tawdry affair, all Cupids and cornucopias,

---

[1] Towards the poor side of the city with its prostitutes, opium dens, and human trafficking

[2] Probably the Pavilion Theatre, a Whitechapel stage which was managed by Isaac Cohen (who was Jewish) during Wilde's career, and was decorated in the "tawdry" manner which Dorian later describes

[3] A coin worth one pound and one shilling, usually used to pay expert craftsmen (the extra shilling was usually considered a tip) such as tailors, cobblers, artists, and furniture makers. It is a surprisingly high price for such a low-class theater, which might imply that the shows involve nudity or burlesques

like a third-rate wedding-cake. The gallery and pit were fairly full, but the two rows of dingy stalls were quite empty, and there was hardly a person in what I suppose they called the dress-circle. Women went about with oranges and ginger-beer[1], and there was a terrible consumption of nuts going on."

"It must have been just like the palmy days of the British Drama[2]."

"Just like, I should fancy, and very horrid. I began to wonder what on earth I should do, when I caught sight of the play-bill. What do you think the play was, Harry?"

"I should think 'The Idiot Boy, or Dumb but Innocent[3].' Our fathers used to like that sort of piece, I believe. The longer I live, Dorian, the more keenly I feel that whatever was good enough for our fathers is not good enough for us. In art, as in politics, *les grand pères ont toujours tort[4].*"

"This play was good enough for us, Harry. It was 'Romeo and Juliet.' I must admit I was rather annoyed at the idea of seeing Shakespeare done in such a wretched hole of a place. Still, I felt interested, in a sort of way. At any rate, I determined to wait for the first act. There was a dreadful orchestra, presided over by a young Jew who sat at a cracked piano, that nearly drove me away, but at last the drop-scene was drawn up, and the play began. Romeo was a stout elderly gentleman, with corked eyebrows, a husky tragedy voice, and a figure like a beer-barrel. Mercutio was almost as bad. He was played by the low-comedian, who had introduced gags of his own and was on most familiar terms with the pit. They were as grotesque as the scenery, and that looked as if it had come out of a pantomime of fifty years ago. But Juliet! Harry, imagine a girl, hardly seventeen years of age, with a little flower-like face, a small Greek head with plaited coils of dark-brown hair, eyes that were violet wells of passion, lips that were like the petals of a rose[5]. She was the loveliest thing I had ever seen in my life. You said to me once that pathos left you

---

[1] Considered indulgences for the lower classes (as opposed to chocolate-dipped fruits and champagne, which would have been on hand in a high-brow opera house)

[2] Palmy means "successful" or "flourishing." Henry refers to the age of Shakespeare, Jonson, and Marlowe

[3] A fictitious adaptation of Wordsworth's poem which exults the spiritual purity of a mentally challenged child

[4] "Our grandparents are always wrong"

[5] Dorian's description of Sibyl is very similar to one of Wilde's letters describing his wife, Constance, shortly before their marriage. The juxtaposition between Lord Henry's wife (also modelled after Constance) and Sibyl may illustrate Wilde's own conflicting feelings about the girl he fell in love with and the woman she grew into

unmoved, but that beauty, mere beauty, could fill your eyes with tears. I tell you, Harry, I could hardly see this girl for the mist of tears that came across me. And her voice,- -I never heard such a voice. It was very low at first, with deep mellow notes, that seemed to fall singly upon one's ear. Then it became a little louder, and sounded like a flute or a distant hautbois[1]. In the garden-scene it had all the tremulous ecstasy that one hears just before dawn when nightingales are singing. There were moments, later on, when it had the wild passion of violins. You know how a voice can stir one. Your voice and the voice of Sibyl Vane are two things that I shall never forget. When I close my eyes, I hear them, and each of them says something different. I don't know which to follow. Why should I not love her? Harry, I do love her. She is everything to me in life. Night after night I go to see her play. One evening she is Rosalind, and the next evening she is Imogen[2]. I have seen her die in the gloom of an Italian tomb, sucking the poison from her lover's lips[3]. I have watched her wandering through the forest of Arden, disguised as a pretty boy in hose and doublet and dainty cap[4]. She has been mad, and has come into the presence of a guilty king, and given him rue to wear, and bitter herbs to taste of[5]. She has been innocent, and the black hands of jealousy have crushed her reed-like throat[6]. I have seen her in every age and in every costume. Ordinary women never appeal to one's imagination. They are limited to their century. No glamour ever transfigures them. One knows their minds as easily as one knows their bonnets. One can always find them. There is no mystery in one of them. They ride in the Park in the morning, and chatter at tea-parties in the afternoon. They have their stereotyped smile, and their fashionable manner. They are quite obvious. But an actress! How different an actress is! Why didn't you tell me that the only thing worth loving is an actress?"

"Because I have loved so many of them, Dorian."

"Oh, yes, horrid people with dyed hair and painted faces."

---

[1] An oboe. Oboes were (and continue to be) frequently used in classical music to represent pastoral scenes of nature, purity, and innocence. In works like Beethoven's Pastoral Symphony and Berlioz's Fantastical Symphony, oboes are used to represent birds in pastures and shepherds playing songs in the countryside, respectively. To Dorian, it is a call away from Lord Henry, towards innocence and love – a call he ultimately rejects
[2] Female characters (both of whom cross-dress to hide their identities) in the Shakespeare comedies "As You Like It" and "Cymbeline," respectively
[3] Romeo and Juliet
[4] As You Like It
[5] Hamlet (as Ophelia)
[6] Othello (as Desdemona)

"Don't run down dyed hair and painted faces. There is an extraordinary charm in them, sometimes."

"I wish now I had not told you about Sibyl Vane."

"You could not have helped telling me, Dorian. All through your life you will tell me everything you do[1]."

"Yes, Harry, I believe that is true. I cannot help telling you things. You have a curious influence over me. If I ever did a crime, I would come and confide it to you. You would understand me."

"People like you–the wilful sunbeams of life–don't commit crimes, Dorian. But I am much obliged for the compliment, all the same. And now tell me,–reach me the matches, like a good boy: thanks,–tell me, [*is Sibyl Vane your mistress*]?"

Dorian Gray leaped to his feet, with flushed cheeks and burning eyes. "[*How dare you suggest such a thing, Harry? It is horrible.*] Sibyl Vane is sacred!"

"It is only the sacred things that are worth touching, Dorian," said Lord Henry, with a strange touch of pathos in his voice[2]. "But why should you be annoyed? I suppose she will be [*your mistress*] some day. When one is in love, one always begins by deceiving one's self, and one always ends by deceiving others. That is what the world calls romance. You know her, at any rate, I suppose?"

"Of course I know her. On the first night I was at the theatre, the horrid old Jew came round to the box after the performance was over, and offered to bring me behind the scenes and introduce me to her. I was furious with him, and told him that Juliet had been dead for hundreds of years, and that her body was lying in a marble tomb in Verona. I think, from his blank look of amazement, that he thought I had taken too much champagne, or something."

"I am not surprised."

"I was not surprised either. Then he asked me if I wrote for any of the newspapers. I told him I never even read them. He seemed terribly disappointed at that, and confided to me that all the dramatic critics were in a conspiracy against him, and that they were all to be bought."

"I believe he was quite right there. But, on the other hand, most of them are not at all expensive."

"Well, he seemed to think they were beyond his means. By this time the lights were being put out in the theatre, and I had to go. He wanted

---

[1] Henry's demonic, Mephistophelean role in Dorian's life becomes increasingly sinister as he tightens his grip on the boy's soul

[2] Clearly even Lord Henry has been in love before, and even he is emotionally disturbed by his corruptive influence on his lovers

me to try some cigars which he strongly recommended. I declined. The next night, of course, I arrived at the theatre again. When he saw me he made me a low bow, and assured me that I was a patron of art. He was a most offensive brute, though he had an extraordinary passion for Shakespeare. He told me once, with an air of pride, that his three bankruptcies were entirely due to the poet, whom he insisted on calling 'The Bard.' He seemed to think it a distinction."

"It was a distinction, my dear Dorian,–a great distinction. But when did you first speak to Miss Sibyl Vane?"

"The third night. She had been playing Rosalind. I could not help going round. I had thrown her some flowers, and she had looked at me; at least I fancied that she had. The old Jew was persistent. He seemed determined to bring me behind, so I consented. It was curious my not wanting to know her, wasn't it?"

"No; I don't think so."

"My dear Harry, why?"

"I will tell you some other time[1]. Now I want to know about the girl."

"Sibyl? Oh, she was so shy, and so gentle. There is something of a child about her. Her eyes opened wide in exquisite wonder when I told her what I thought of her performance, and she seemed quite unconscious of her power. I think we were both rather nervous. The old Jew stood grinning at the door-way of the dusty greenroom, making elaborate speeches about us both, while we stood looking at each other like children. He would insist on calling me 'My Lord,' so I had to assure Sibyl that I was not anything of the kind. She said quite simply to me, 'You look more like a prince.'"

"Upon my word, Dorian, Miss Sibyl knows how to pay compliments."

"You don't understand her, Harry. She regarded me merely as a person in a play. She knows nothing of life. She lives with her mother, a faded tired woman who played Lady Capulet in a sort of magenta dressing-wrapper on the first night, and who looks as if she had seen better days."

"I know that look. It always depresses me."

"The Jew wanted to tell me her history, but I said it did not interest me."

---

[1] Henry understands that to meet an idol is to ruin an illusion – to experience a long desired consummation is to be disappointed and unfulfilled

"You were quite right. There is always something infinitely mean[1] about other people's tragedies."

"Sibyl is the only thing I care about. What is it to me where she came from? From her little head to her little feet, she is absolutely and entirely divine. I go to see her act every night of my life, and every night she is more marvellous."

"That is the reason, I suppose, that you will never dine with me now. I thought you must have some curious romance on hand. You have; but it is not quite what I expected."

"My dear Harry, we either lunch or sup together every day, and I have been to the Opera with you several times."

"You always come dreadfully late."

"Well, I can't help going to see Sibyl play, even if it is only for an act. I get hungry for her presence; and when I think of the wonderful soul that is hidden away in that little ivory body, I am filled with awe[2]."

"You can dine with me to-night, Dorian, can't you?"

He shook his head. "To night she is Imogen," he answered, "and tomorrow night she will be Juliet."

"When is she Sibyl Vane[3]?"

"Never."

"I congratulate you."

"How horrid you are! She is all the great heroines of the world in one. She is more than an individual. You laugh, but I tell you she has genius. I love her, and I must make her love me. You, who know all the secrets of life, tell me how to charm Sibyl Vane to love me! I want to make Romeo jealous. I want the dead lovers of the world to hear our laughter, and grow sad. I want a breath of our passion to stir their dust into consciousness, to wake their ashes into pain. My God, Harry, how I worship her!" He was walking up and down the room as he spoke. Hectic spots of red burned on his cheeks[4]. He was terribly excited.

Lord Henry watched him with a subtle sense of pleasure. How different he was now from the shy, frightened boy he had met in Basil Hallward's studio! His nature had developed like a flower, had borne blossoms of scarlet flame. Out of its secret hiding-place had crept his Soul, and Desire had come to meet it on the way.

---

[1] Basic, common, stark

[2] Very, VERY similar sentiments to Basil's worshipful praise of Dorian: the worshipped artform has now found another artform to worship himself

[3] Henry is probing at the obvious fact that Dorian is enamored with what Sibyl represents, not with the flawed, complex human being she truly is

[4] The cheeks were frequently used as a polite proxy for the genitals in Victorian fiction: Dorian is furiously aroused

"And what do you propose to do?" said Lord Henry, at last.

"I want you and Basil to come with me some night and see her act. I have not the slightest fear of the result. You won't be able to refuse to recognize her genius. Then we must get her out of the Jew's hands. She is bound to him for three years–at least for two years and eight months–from the present time. I will have to pay him something, of course. When all that is settled, I will take a West-End[1] theatre and bring her out properly. She will make the world as mad as she has made me."

"Impossible, my dear boy!"

"Yes, she will. She has not merely art, consummate art-instinct, in her, but she has personality also; and you have often told me that it is personalities, not principles, that move the age."

"Well, what night shall we go?"

"Let me see. To-day is Tuesday. Let us fix to-morrow. She plays Juliet to-morrow."

"All right. The Bristol[2] at eight o'clock; and I will get Basil."

"Not eight, Harry, please. Half-past six. We must be there before the curtain rises. You must see her in the first act, where she meets Romeo."

"Half-past six! What an hour! It will be like having a meat-tea[3]. However, just as you wish. Shall you see Basil between this and then? Or shall I write to him?"

"Dear Basil! I have not laid eyes on him for a week. It is rather horrid of me, as he has sent me my portrait in the most wonderful frame, designed by himself, and, though I am a little jealous of it for being a whole month younger than I am, I must admit that I delight in it. Perhaps you had better write to him. I don't want to see him alone. He says things that annoy me[4]."

Lord Henry smiled. "He gives you good advice, I suppose. People are very fond of giving away what they need most themselves."

["*You don't mean to say that Basil has got any passion or any romance in him?*"]

["*I don't know whether he has any passion, but he certainly has romance," said Lord Henry, with an amused look in his eyes. "Has he never let you know that[5]?*"]

---

[1] That is, a reputable theater in London's high society neighborhoods

[2] A fictitious social club

[3] A high tea at which dishes of meat were served

[4] Dorian seems to have graduated from object of adoration (the submissive partner) to the adorer of the subject (the dominant partner) and resents Basil's patronizing fawnings

[5] Henry is betraying Basil's secret and taunting him behind his back for being incapable of openly declaring his love

"Never. I must ask him about it. [*I am rather surprised to hear it.*] He is the best of fellows, but he seems to me to be just a bit of a Philistine[1]. Since I have known you, Harry, I have discovered that."

"Basil, my dear boy, puts everything that is charming in him into his work. The consequence is that he has nothing left for life but his prejudices, his principles, and his common sense. The only artists I have ever known who are personally delightful are bad artists. Good artists give everything to their art, and consequently are perfectly uninteresting in themselves. A great poet, a really great poet, is the most unpoetical of all creatures. But inferior poets are absolutely fascinating. The worse their rhymes are, the more picturesque they look. The mere fact of having published a book of second-rate sonnets makes a man quite irresistible. He lives the poetry that he cannot write. The others write the poetry that they dare not realize."

"I wonder is that really so, Harry?" said Dorian Gray, putting some perfume on his handkerchief out of a large gold-topped bottle that stood on the table. "It must be, if you say so. And now I must be off. Imogen is waiting for me. Don't forget about to-morrow. Good- by."

As he left the room, Lord Henry's heavy eyelids drooped, and he began to think. Certainly few people had ever interested him so much as Dorian Gray, and yet the lad's mad adoration of some one else caused him not the slightest pang of annoyance or jealousy. He was pleased by it. It made him a more interesting study. He had been always enthralled by the methods of science, but the ordinary subject-matter of science had seemed to him trivial and of no import. And so he had begun by vivisecting[2] himself, as he had ended by vivisecting others. Human life,– that appeared to him the one thing worth investigating. There was nothing else of any value, compared to it. It was true that as one watched life in its curious crucible of pain and pleasure, one could not wear over one's face a mask of glass, or keep the sulphurous fumes[3] from troubling the brain and making the imagination turbid with monstrous fancies and misshapen dreams. There were poisons so subtle that to know their properties one had to sicken of them. There were maladies so strange that one had to pass through them if one sought to understand their nature. And, yet, what a great reward one received! How wonderful the whole world became to one! To note the curious hard logic of passion, and the emotional colored life of the intellect,–to observe where they met, and

---

[1] A backwards, unsophisticated person lacking eloquence or taste
[2] Dissecting a living specimen
[3] Sulfur being associated with hell, these "sulphrous fumes" are a metaphor for guilt and conscience

where they separated, at what point they became one, and at what point they were at discord,–there was a delight in that! What matter what the cost was? One could never pay too high a price for any sensation.

He was conscious–and the thought brought a gleam of pleasure into his brown agate eyes–that it was through certain words of his, musical words said with musical utterance, that Dorian Gray's soul had turned to this white girl[1] and bowed in worship before her. To a large extent, the lad was his own creation. He had made him premature. That was something. Ordinary people waited till life disclosed to them its secrets, but to the few, to the elect, the mysteries of life were revealed before the veil was drawn away. Sometimes this was the effect of art, and chiefly of the art of literature, which dealt immediately with the passions and the intellect. But now and then a complex personality took the place and assumed the office of art, was indeed, in its way, a real work of art, Life having its elaborate masterpieces, just as poetry has, or sculpture, or painting.

Yes, the lad was premature. He was gathering his harvest while it was yet spring. The pulse and passion of youth were in him, but he was becoming self-conscious. It was delightful to watch him. With his beautiful face, and his beautiful soul, he was a thing to wonder at. It was no matter how it all ended, or was destined to end. He was like one of those gracious figures in a pageant or a play, whose joys seem to be remote from one, but whose sorrows stir one's sense of beauty, and whose wounds are like red roses.

Soul and body, body and soul–how mysterious they were! There was animalism in the soul, and the body had its moments of spirituality. The senses could refine, and the intellect could degrade. Who could say where the fleshly impulse ceased, or the psychical impulse began? How shallow were the arbitrary definitions of ordinary psychologists! And yet how difficult to decide between the claims of the various schools! Was the soul a shadow seated in the house of sin? Or was the body really in the soul, as Giordano Bruno thought[2]? The separation of spirit from matter was a mystery, and the union of spirit with matter was a mystery also.

He began to wonder whether we should ever make psychology so absolute a science that each little spring of life would be revealed to us. As it was, we always misunderstood ourselves, and rarely understood others. Experience was of no ethical value. It was merely the name we gave to our mistakes. Men had, as a rule, regarded it as a mode of warning,

---

[1] Both a reference to Sibyl's fair skin and to Dorian's treatment of her like a marble statue

[2] An Italian astronomer, philosopher, and mathematician who was executed for heresy in 1600. He argued a position called cosmic pluralism and believed that the soul was housed irretrievably in the physical body

had claimed for it a certain moral efficacy in the formation of character, had praised it as something that taught us what to follow and showed us what to avoid. But there was no motive power in experience. It was as little of an active cause as conscience itself. All that it really demonstrated was that our future would be the same as our past, and that the sin we had done once, and with loathing, we would do many times, and with joy.

It was clear to him that the experimental method was the only method by which one could arrive at any scientific analysis of the passions; and certainly Dorian Gray was a subject made to his hand, and seemed to promise rich and fruitful results. His sudden mad love for Sibyl Vane was a psychological phenomenon of no small interest. There was no doubt that curiosity had much to do with it, curiosity and the desire for new experiences; yet it was not a simple but rather a very complex passion. What there was in it of the purely sensuous instinct of boyhood had been transformed by the workings of the imagination, changed into something that seemed to the boy himself to be remote from sense, and was for that very reason all the more dangerous. It was the passions about whose origin we deceived ourselves that tyrannized most strongly over us. Our weakest motives were those of whose nature we were conscious. It often happened that when we thought we were experimenting on others we were really experimenting on ourselves.

While Lord Henry sat dreaming on these things, a knock came to the door, and his valet entered, and reminded him it was time to dress for dinner. He got up and looked out into the street. The sunset had smitten into scarlet gold the upper windows of the houses opposite. The panes glowed like plates of heated metal. The sky above was like a faded rose. He thought of Dorian Gray's young fiery-colored life, and wondered how it was all going to end.

When he arrived home, about half-past twelve o'clock, he saw a telegram lying on the hall-table. He opened it and found it was from Dorian. It was to tell him that he was engaged to be married to Sibyl Vane.

"I suppose you have heard the news, Basil?" said Lord Henry on the following evening, as Hallward was shown into a little private room at the Bristol where dinner had been laid for three.

"No, Harry," answered Hallward, giving his hat and coat to the bowing waiter. "What is it? Nothing about politics, I hope? They don't interest me. There is hardly a single person in the House of Commons worth painting; though many of them would be the better for a little whitewashing."

"Dorian Gray is engaged to be married," said Lord Henry, watching him as he spoke.

Hallward turned perfectly pale, and a curious look flashed for a moment into his eyes[1], and then passed away, leaving them dull." Dorian engaged to be married!" he cried. "Impossible!"

"It is perfectly true."

"To whom?"

"To some little actress or other."

"I can't believe it. Dorian is far too sensible."

"Dorian is far too wise not to do foolish things now and then, my dear Basil."

"Marriage is hardly a thing that one can do now and then, Harry," said Hallward, smiling.

"Except in America[2]. But I didn't say he was married. I said he was engaged to be married. There is a great difference. I have a distinct remembrance of being married, but I have no recollection at all of being engaged. I am inclined to think that I never was engaged."

"But think of Dorian's birth, and position, and wealth. It would be absurd for him to marry so much beneath him."

"If you want him to marry this girl, tell him that, Basil. He is sure to do it then. Whenever a man does a thoroughly stupid thing, it is always from the noblest motives."

"I hope the girl is good, Harry. I don't want to see Dorian tied to some vile creature, who might degrade his nature and ruin his intellect."

"Oh, she is more than good–she is beautiful," murmured Lord Henry, sipping a glass of vermouth and orange-bitters. "Dorian says she is beautiful; and he is not often wrong about things of that kind. Your

---

[1] The pang of jealousy is followed by the aging of Basil's own soul

[2] Divorce, though uncommon in the middle class, was fairly common for upper-class Americans during this time period, while it was still an infrequent and scandalous thing for their British counterparts

portrait of him has quickened his appreciation of the personal appearance of other people. It has had that excellent effect, among others. We are to see her to-night, if that boy doesn't forget his appointment."

"But do you approve of it, Harry?" asked Hallward, walking up and down the room, and biting his lip. "You can't approve of it, really. It is some silly infatuation."

"I never approve, or disapprove, of anything now. It is an absurd attitude to take towards life. We are not sent into the world to air our moral prejudices. I never take any notice of what common people say, and I never interfere with what charming people do. If a personality fascinates me, whatever the personality chooses to do is absolutely delightful to me. Dorian Gray falls in love with a beautiful girl who acts Shakespeare, and proposes to marry her. Why not? If he wedded Messalina[1] he would be none the less interesting. You know I am not a champion of marriage. The real drawback to marriage is that it makes one unselfish. And unselfish people are colorless. They lack individuality. Still, there are certain temperaments that marriage makes more complex. They retain their egotism, and add to it many other egos. They are forced to have more than one life. They become more highly organized. Besides, every experience is of value, and, whatever one may say against marriage, it is certainly an experience. I hope that Dorian Gray will make this girl his wife, passionately adore her for six months, and then suddenly become fascinated by some one else. He would be a wonderful study."

"You don't mean all that, Harry; you know you don't. If Dorian Gray's life were spoiled, no one would be sorrier than yourself. You are much better than you pretend to be."

Lord Henry laughed. "The reason we all like to think so well of others is that we are all afraid for ourselves. The basis of optimism is sheer terror. We think that we are generous because we credit our neighbor with those virtues that are likely to benefit ourselves. We praise the banker that we may overdraw our account, and find good qualities in the highwayman in the hope that he may spare our pockets. I mean everything that I have said. I have the greatest contempt for optimism. And as for a spoiled life, no life is spoiled but one whose growth is arrested. If you want to mar a nature, you have merely to reform it. But here is Dorian himself. He will tell you more than I can."

"My dear Harry, my dear Basil, you must both congratulate me!" said the boy, throwing off his evening cape with its satin-lined wings, and shaking each of his friends by the hand in turn. "I have never been so

---

[1] Third wife to the Roman emperor Claudius, who was infamous for her sexual appetite, cruelty to her political enemies, and utter moral debauchery

happy. Of course it is sudden: all really delightful things are. And yet it seems to me to be the one thing I have been looking for all my life." He was flushed with excitement and pleasure, and looked extraordinarily handsome.

"I hope you will always be very happy, Dorian," said Hallward, "but I don't quite forgive you for not having let me know of your engagement. You let Harry know."

"And I don't forgive you for being late for dinner," broke in Lord Henry, putting his hand on the lad's shoulder, and smiling as he spoke. "Come, let us sit down and try what the new chef here is like, and then you will tell us how it all came about."

"There is really not much to tell," cried Dorian, as they took their seats at the small round table. "What happened was simply this. After I left you yesterday evening, Harry, I had some dinner at that curious little Italian restaurant in Rupert Street[1], you introduced me to, and went down afterwards to the theatre. Sibyl was playing Rosalind. Of course the scenery was dreadful, and the Orlando[2] absurd. But Sibyl! You should have seen her! When she came on in her boy's dress she was perfectly wonderful. She wore a moss-colored velvet jerkin[3] with cinnamon sleeves, slim brown cross-gartered hose, a dainty little green cap with a hawk's feather caught in a jewel, and a hooded cloak lined with dull red. She had never seemed to me more exquisite. She had all the delicate grace of that Tanagra[4] figurine that you have in your studio, Basil. Her hair clustered round her face like dark leaves round a pale rose. As for her acting–well, you will see her to-night. She is simply a born artist. I sat in the dingy box absolutely enthralled. I forgot that I was in London and in the nineteenth century. I was away with my love in a forest that no man had ever seen. After the performance was over I went behind, and spoke to her. As we were sitting together, suddenly there came a look into her eyes that I had never seen there before. My lips moved towards hers. We kissed each other. I can't describe to you what I felt at that moment. It seemed to me that all my life had been narrowed to one perfect point of rose-colored joy. She trembled all over, and shook like a white narcissus. Then she flung herself on her knees and kissed my hands. I feel that I should not tell you all this, but I can't help it. Of course our engagement is a dead secret. She has not even told her own mother. I don't know what my

---

[1] In the Soho neighborhood – at the time a place of crime, intrigue, and bohemian living, popular among immigrants and artists, and known for its foreign restaurants
[2] The male counterpart to Rosalind in "As You Like It"
[3] A sleeveless jacket
[4] Greek terracotta statuettes dating back to the fourth century B.C.

guardians will say. Lord Radley is sure to be furious. I don't care. I shall be of age in less than a year, and then I can do what I like. I have been right, Basil, haven't I, to take my love out of poetry, and to find my wife in Shakespeare's plays[1]? Lips that Shakespeare taught to speak have whispered their secret in my ear. I have had the arms of Rosalind around me, and kissed Juliet on the mouth."

"Yes, Dorian, I suppose you were right," said Hallward, slowly[2].

"Have you seen her to-day?" asked Lord Henry.

Dorian Gray shook his head. "I left her in the forest of Arden, I shall find her in an orchard in Verona."

Lord Henry sipped his champagne in a meditative manner. "At what particular point did you mention the word marriage, Dorian? and what did she say in answer? Perhaps you forgot all about it."

"My dear Harry, I did not treat it as a business transaction, and I did not make any formal proposal. I told her that I loved her, and she said she was not worthy to be my wife. Not worthy! Why, the whole world is nothing to me compared to her."

"Women are wonderfully practical," murmured Lord Henry,- "much more practical than we are. In situations of that kind we often forget to say anything about marriage, and they always remind us."

Hallward laid his hand upon his arm. "Don't, Harry. You have annoyed Dorian. He is not like other men. He would never bring misery upon any one. His nature is too fine for that."

Lord Henry looked across the table. "Dorian is never annoyed with me," he answered. "I asked the question for the best reason possible, for the only reason, indeed, that excuses one for asking any question,- simple curiosity. I have a theory that it is always the women who propose to us, and not we who propose to the women, except, of course, in middle-class life. But then the middle classes are not modern."

Dorian Gray laughed, and tossed his head. "You are quite incorrigible, Harry; but I don't mind. It is impossible to be angry with you. When you see Sibyl Vane you will feel that the man who could wrong her would be a beast without a heart. I cannot understand how any one can wish to shame what he loves. I love Sibyl Vane. I wish to place her on a pedestal of gold, and to see the world worship the woman who is mine.

---

[1] Like Basil, who adores what Dorian represents but doesn't effectively grasp him as a complex human being, Dorian has fallen in love with Shakespeare's characters, not the actress performing them, and has failed to see her as a morally, emotionally, and spiritually multifaceted human being capable of disappointing him

[2] Basil recognizes his own idealistic passion in Dorian's misguided worship, and apparently feels incapable of discouraging a passion so alike to his own

What is marriage? An irrevocable vow. And it is an irrevocable vow that I want to take. Her trust makes me faithful, her belief makes me good. When I am with her, I regret all that you have taught me. I become different from what you have known me to be. I am changed, and the mere touch of Sibyl Vane's hand makes me forget you and all your wrong, fascinating, poisonous, delightful theories."

"You will always like me, Dorian," said Lord Henry. "Will you have some coffee, you fellows?–Waiter, bring coffee, and fine-champagne, and some cigarettes. No: don't mind the cigarettes; I have some.– Basil, I can't allow you to smoke cigars. You must have a cigarette. A cigarette is the perfect type of a perfect pleasure. It is exquisite, and it leaves one unsatisfied. What more can you want?– Yes, Dorian, you will always be fond of me. I represent to you all the sins you have never had the courage to commit."

"What nonsense you talk, Harry!" cried Dorian Gray, lighting his cigarette from a fire-breathing silver dragon that the waiter had placed on the table. "Let us go down to the theatre. When you see Sibyl you will have a new ideal of life. She will represent something to you that you have never known."

"I have known everything," said Lord Henry, with a sad look in his eyes, "but I am always ready for a new emotion. I am afraid that there is no such thing, for me at any rate. Still, your wonderful girl may thrill me. I love acting. It is so much more real than life. Let us go. Dorian, you will come with me.–I am so sorry, Basil, but there is only room for two in the brougham[1]. You must follow us in a hansom."

They got up and put on their coats, sipping their coffee standing. Hallward was silent and preoccupied. There was a gloom over him. He could not bear this marriage, and yet it seemed to him to be better than many other things that might have happened. After a few moments, they all passed down-stairs. He drove off by himself, as had been arranged, and watched the flashing lights of the little brougham in front of him. A strange sense of loss came over him. He felt that Dorian Gray would never again be to him all that he had been in the past. His eyes darkened, and the crowded flaring streets became blurred to him. When the cab drew up at the doors of the theatre, it seemed to him that he had grown years older.

---

[1] A light, four wheeled carriage

CHAPTER V

FOR some reason or other, the house was crowded that night, and the fat Jew manager who met them at the door was beaming from ear to ear with an oily, tremulous smile. He escorted them to their box with a sort of pompous humility, waving his fat jewelled hands, and talking at the top of his voice. Dorian Gray loathed him more than ever[1]. He felt as if he had come to look for Miranda and had been met by Caliban[2]. Lord Henry, upon the other hand, rather liked him. At least he declared he did, and insisted on shaking him by the hand, and assured him that he was proud to meet a man who had discovered a real genius and gone bankrupt over Shakespeare. Hallward amused himself with watching the faces in the pit. The heat was terribly oppressive, and the huge sunlight flamed like a monstrous dahlia with petals of fire. The youths in the gallery had taken off their coats and waistcoats[3] and hung them over the side. They talked to each other across the theatre, and shared their oranges with the tawdry painted girls[4] who sat by them. Some women were laughing in the pit; their voices were horribly shrill and discordant. The sound of the popping of corks came from the bar.

"What a place to find one's divinity in!" said Lord Henry.

"Yes!" answered Dorian Gray. "It was here I found her, and she is divine beyond all living things. When she acts you will forget everything. These common people here, with their coarse faces and brutal gestures, become quite different when she is on the stage. They sit silently and watch her. They weep and laugh as she wills them to do. She makes them as responsive as a violin. She spiritualizes them, and one feels that they are of the same flesh and blood as one's self."

"Oh, I hope not!" murmured Lord Henry, who was scanning the occupants of the gallery through his opera-glass.

"Don't pay any attention to him, Dorian," said Hallward. "I understand what you mean, and I believe in this girl. Any one you love must be marvellous, and any girl that has the effect you describe must be fine and noble. To spiritualize one's age,–that is something worth doing. If this girl can give a soul to those who have lived without one, if she can create the sense of beauty in people whose lives have been sordid and

---

[1] The Jew's character is regularly presented as a sort of pimp who hopes to profit from Dorian's attraction to Sibyl

[2] In "The Tempest," Miranda is the beautiful daughter of the magician Prospero, and Caliban is the loathsome, monstrous son of a witch

[3] Middle and upperclass men never allowed themselves to be seen in their shirtsleeves, even with close friends

[4] Prostitutes

ugly, if she can strip them of their selfishness and lend them tears for sorrows that are not their own, she is worthy of all your adoration, worthy of the adoration of the world. This marriage is quite right. I did not think so at first, but I admit it now. God made Sibyl Vane for you. Without her you would have been incomplete[1]."

"Thanks, Basil," answered Dorian Gray, pressing his hand. "I knew that you would understand me. Harry is so cynical, he terrifies me. But here is the orchestra. It is quite dreadful, but it only lasts for about five minutes. Then the curtain rises, and you will see the girl to whom I am going to give all my life, to whom I have given everything that is good in me."

A quarter of an hour afterwards, amidst an extraordinary turmoil of applause, Sibyl Vane stepped on to the stage. Yes, she was certainly lovely to look at,–one of the loveliest creatures, Lord Henry thought, that he had ever seen. There was something of the fawn in her shy grace and startled eyes. A faint blush, like the shadow of a rose in a mirror of silver, came to her cheeks as she glanced at the crowded, enthusiastic house. She stepped back a few paces, and her lips seemed to tremble. Basil Hallward leaped to his feet and began to applaud. Dorian Gray sat motionless, gazing on her, like a man in a dream. Lord Henry peered through his opera-glass, murmuring, "Charming! charming!"

The scene was the hall of Capulet's house, and Romeo in his pilgrim's dress had entered with Mercutio and his friends. The band, such as it was, struck up a few bars of music, and the dance began. Through the crowd of ungainly, shabbily-dressed actors, Sibyl Vane moved like a creature from a finer world. Her body swayed, as she danced, as a plant sways in the water. The curves of her throat were like the curves of a white lily. Her hands seemed to be made of cool ivory.

Yet she was curiously listless. She showed no sign of joy when her eyes rested on Romeo. The few lines she had to speak,–

> Good pilgrim, you do wrong your hand too much,
>   Which mannerly devotion shows in this;
> For saints have hands that pilgrims' hands do touch,
>   And palm to palm is holy palmers' kiss,–

with the brief dialogue that follows, were spoken in a thoroughly artificial manner. The voice was exquisite, but from the point of view of tone it was absolutely false. It was wrong in color. It took away all the life from the verse. It made the passion unreal.

---

[1] Basil might recognize that Henry's hardening influence on Dorian has been loosened by Sibyl's softening influence on him, and sees how love for her may mellow and mature his boyish heart

Dorian Gray grew pale as he watched her. Neither of his friends dared to say anything to him. She seemed to them to be absolutely incompetent. They were horribly disappointed.

Yet they felt that the true test of any Juliet is the balcony scene of the second act. They waited for that. If she failed there, there was nothing in her.

She looked charming as she came out in the moonlight. That could not be denied. But the staginess of her acting was unbearable, and grew worse as she went on. Her gestures became absurdly artificial. She over-emphasized everything that she had to say. The beautiful passage,–

Thou knowest the mask of night is on my face,
Else would a maiden blush bepaint my cheek
For that which thou hast heard me speak to-night,–

was declaimed with the painful precision of a school-girl who has been taught to recite by some second-rate professor of elocution. When she leaned over the balcony and came to those wonderful lines,–

Although I joy in thee,
I have no joy of this contract to-night:
It is too rash, too unadvised, too sudden;
Too like the lightning, which doth cease to be
Ere one can say, "It lightens." Sweet, good-night!
This bud of love by summer's ripening breath
May prove a beauteous flower when next we meet,–

she spoke the words as if they conveyed no meaning to her. It was not nervousness. Indeed, so far from being nervous, she seemed absolutely self-contained. It was simply bad art. She was a complete failure.

Even the common uneducated audience of the pit and gallery lost their interest in the play. They got restless, and began to talk loudly and to whistle. The Jew manager, who was standing at the back of the dress-circle, stamped and swore with rage. The only person unmoved was the girl herself.

When the second act was over there came a storm of hisses, and Lord Henry got up from his chair and put on his coat. "She is quite beautiful, Dorian," he said, "but she can't act. Let us go."

"I am going to see the play through," answered the lad, in a hard, bitter voice. "I am awfully sorry that I have made you waste an evening, Harry. I apologize to both of you."

"My dear Dorian, I should think Miss Vane was ill," interrupted Hallward. "We will come some other night."

"I wish she was ill," he rejoined. "But she seems to me to be simply callous and cold. She has entirely altered. Last night she was a great artist. To-night she is merely a commonplace, mediocre actress."

"Don't talk like that about any one you love, Dorian. Love is a more wonderful thing than art."

"They are both simply forms of imitation," murmured Lord Henry. "But do let us go. Dorian, you must not stay here any longer. It is not good for one's morals to see bad acting. Besides, I don't suppose you will want your wife to act[1]. So what does it matter if she plays Juliet like a wooden doll? She is very lovely, and if she knows as little about life as she does about acting, she will be a delightful experience. There are only two kinds of people who are really fascinating,—people who know absolutely everything, and people who know absolutely nothing. Good heavens, my dear boy, don't look so tragic! The secret of remaining young is never to have an emotion that is unbecoming. Come to the club with Basil and myself. We will smoke cigarettes and drink to the beauty of Sibyl Vane. She is beautiful. What more can you want?"

"Please go away, Harry," cried the lad. "I really want to be alone.--Basil, you don't mind my asking you to go? Ah! can't you see that my heart is breaking?" The hot tears came to his eyes. His lips trembled, and, rushing to the back of the box, he leaned up against the wall, hiding his face in his hands.

"Let us go, Basil," said Lord Henry, with a strange tenderness in his voice[2]; and the two young men passed out together.

A few moments afterwards the footlights flared up, and the curtain rose on the third act. Dorian Gray went back to his seat. He looked pale, and proud, and indifferent. The play dragged on, and seemed interminable. Half of the audience went out, tramping in heavy boots, and laughing. The whole thing was a fiasco. The last act was played to almost empty benches.

As soon as it was over, Dorian Gray rushed behind the scenes into the greenroom. The girl was standing alone there, with a look of triumph on her face. Her eyes were lit with an exquisite fire. There was a radiance about her. Her parted lips were smiling over some secret of their own.

When he entered, she looked at him, and an expression of infinite joy came over her. "How badly I acted to-night, Dorian!" she cried.

---

[1] When actresses married, especially into the upper classes, they traditionally retired from the stage

[2] Although Henry is fascinated by Dorian's corruption, he often slips and shows a buried sadness that seems to come from empathy with Dorian's declining innocence

"Horribly!" he answered, gazing at her in amazement,–"horribly! It was dreadful. Are you ill? You have no idea what it was. You have no idea what I suffered."

The girl smiled. "Dorian," she answered, lingering over his name with long-drawn music in her voice, as though it were sweeter than honey to the red petals of her lips,–"Dorian, you should have understood. But you understand now, don't you?"

"Understand what?" he asked, angrily.

"Why I was so bad to-night. Why I shall always be bad. Why I shall never act well again."

He shrugged his shoulders. "You are ill, I suppose. When you are ill you shouldn't act. You make yourself ridiculous. My friends were bored. I was bored."

She seemed not to listen to him. She was transfigured with joy. An ecstasy of happiness dominated her.

"Dorian, Dorian," she cried, "before I knew you, acting was the one reality of my life. It was only in the theatre that I lived. I thought that it was all true. I was Rosalind one night, and Portia the other. The joy of Beatrice was my joy, and the sorrows of Cordelia were mine also[1]. I believed in everything. The common people who acted with me seemed to me to be godlike. The painted scenes were my world. I knew nothing but shadows, and I thought them real. You came,–oh, my beautiful love!– and you freed my soul from prison. You taught me what reality really is. To-night, for the first time in my life, I saw through the hollowness, the sham, the silliness, of the empty pageant in which I had always played. To- night, for the first time, I became conscious that the Romeo was hideous, and old, and painted, that the moonlight in the orchard was false, that the scenery was vulgar, and that the words I had to speak were unreal, were not my words, not what I wanted to say. You had brought me something higher, something of which all art is but a reflection[2]. You have made me understand what love really is. My love! my love! I am sick of shadows. You are more to me than all art can ever be. What have I to do with the puppets of a play? When I came on to-night, I could not understand how it was that everything had gone from me. Suddenly it

---

[1] The heroines of "As You Like It," "Julius Caesar," "Much Ado About Nothing," and "King Lear," respectively

[2] This parallels Dorian and Basil's empty worship of the lifeless painting: life is not to be found in art, but in life itself – in fragile love and the weakness of mortal existence. Sibyl has found inspiration not in the false posturings of acting, but in the genuine emotion of human companionship. Dorian, however, is still to in love with the ideals of beauty, youth, and prestige to accept her for herself – a flawed, imperfect mortal

dawned on my soul what it all meant. The knowledge was exquisite to me. I heard them hissing, and I smiled. What should they know of love? Take me away, Dorian– take me away with you, where we can be quite alone. I hate the stage. I might mimic a passion that I do not feel, but I cannot mimic one that burns me like fire. Oh, Dorian, Dorian, you understand now what it all means? Even if I could do it, it would be profanation for me to play at being in love. You have made me see that."

He flung himself down on the sofa, and turned away his face. "You have killed my love," he muttered.

She looked at him in wonder, and laughed. He made no answer. She came across to him, and stroked his hair with her little fingers. She knelt down and pressed his hands to her lips. He drew them away, and a shudder ran through him.

Then he leaped up, and went to the door. "Yes," he cried, "you have killed my love. You used to stir my imagination. Now you don't even stir my curiosity[1]. You simply produce no effect. I loved you because you were wonderful, because you had genius and intellect, because you realized the dreams of great poets and gave shape and substance to the shadows of art. You have thrown it all away. You are shallow and stupid. My God! how mad I was to love you! What a fool I have been! You are nothing to me now. I will never see you again. I will never think of you. I will never mention your name. You don't know what you were to me, once. Why, once . . . . Oh, I can't bear to think of it! I wish I had never laid eyes upon you! You have spoiled the romance of my life. How little you can know of love, if you say it mars your art! What are you without your art? Nothing. I would have made you famous, splendid, magnificent[2]. The world would have worshipped you, and you would have belonged to me. What are you now? A third-rate actress with a pretty face."

The girl grew white, and trembled. She clinched her hands together, and her voice seemed to catch in her throat. "You are not serious, Dorian?" she murmured. "You are acting."

"Acting! I leave that to you. You do it so well," he answered, bitterly.

---

[1] Like Henry, he is now drawn to people by curiosity instead of compassion. Since Sibyl is authentic and sincere, she has lost her mystique, and although she offers a path to love and peace, Dorian would prefer one of drama and the social status afforded by insincere falsehoods

[2] Naturally, Dorian is more concerned with what he has lost in potential status and allure to society than Sibyl's feelings

70

She rose from her knees, and, with a piteous expression of pain in her face, came across the room to him. She put her hand upon his arm, and looked into his eyes[1]. He thrust her back. "Don't touch me!" he cried.

A low moan broke from her, and she flung herself at his feet, and lay there like a trampled flower. "Dorian, Dorian, don't leave me!" she whispered. "I am so sorry I didn't act well. I was thinking of you all the time. But I will try,–indeed, I will try. It came so suddenly across me, my love for you. I think I should never have known it if you had not kissed me,–if we had not kissed each other. Kiss me again, my love. Don't go away from me. I couldn't bear it. Can't you forgive me for to-night? I will work so hard, and try to improve. Don't be cruel to me because I love you better than anything in the world. After all, it is only once that I have not pleased you. But you are quite right, Dorian. I should have shown myself more of an artist. It was foolish of me; and yet I couldn't help it. Oh, don't leave me, don't leave me." A fit of passionate sobbing choked her. She crouched on the floor like a wounded thing, and Dorian Gray, with his beautiful eyes, looked down at her, and his chiselled lips curled in exquisite disdain. There is always something ridiculous about the passions of people whom one has ceased to love. Sibyl Vane seemed to him to be absurdly melodramatic. Her tears and sobs annoyed him.

"I am going," he said at last, in his calm, clear voice. "I don't wish to be unkind, but I can't see you again. You have disappointed me."

She wept silently, and made no answer, but crept nearer to him. Her little hands stretched blindly out, and appeared to be seeking for him. He turned on his heel, and left the room. In a few moments he was out of the theatre.

Where he went to, he hardly knew. He remembered wandering through dimly-lit streets with gaunt black-shadowed archways and evil-looking houses. Women with hoarse voices and harsh laughter had called after him. Drunkards had reeled by cursing, and chattering to themselves like monstrous apes. [*A man with curious eyes had suddenly peered into his face, and then dogged him with stealthy footsteps, passing and*

---

[1] She attempts a real connection – reaching out from the falsehood of oil paints and stagelights, trying to touch him in a genuine, human way, and he rebuffs this gesture

repassing him many times.[1]] He had seen grotesque children huddled upon door-steps, and had heard shrieks and oaths from gloomy courts[2].

When the dawn was just breaking he found himself at Covent Garden[3]. Huge carts filled with nodding lilies rumbled slowly down the polished empty street. The air was heavy with the perfume of the flowers, and their beauty seemed to bring him an anodyne for his pain. He followed into the market, and watched the men unloading their wagons. A white-smocked carter offered him some cherries. He thanked him, wondered why he refused to accept any money for them, and began to eat them listlessly. They had been plucked at midnight, and the coldness of the moon had entered into them. A long line of boys carrying crates of striped tulips, and of yellow and red roses, defiled in front of him, threading their way through the huge jade- green piles of vegetables. Under the portico, with its gray sun- bleached pillars, loitered a troop of draggled bareheaded girls, waiting for the auction to be over. After some time he hailed a hansom and drove home. The sky was pure opal now, and the roofs of the houses glistened like silver against it. As he was passing through the library towards the door of his bedroom, his eye fell upon the portrait Basil Hallward had painted of him. He started back in surprise, and then went over to it and examined it. In the dim arrested light that struggled through the cream-colored silk blinds, the face seemed to him to be a little changed. The expression looked different. One would have said that there was a touch of cruelty in the mouth. It was certainly curious.

He turned round, and, walking to the window, drew the blinds up. The bright dawn flooded the room, and swept the fantastic shadows into dusky corners, where they lay shuddering. But the strange expression that he had noticed in the face of the portrait seemed to linger there, to be more intensified even. The quivering, ardent sunlight showed him the lines of cruelty round the mouth as clearly as if he had been looking into a mirror after he had done some dreadful thing.

---

[1] This passage was deleted by Wilde himself, and has been widely interpreted as an encounter with a homosexual man eager to solicit Dorian for a one-night-stand

[2] He is surrounded by the worst vices and sufferings of humanity, and more than being surrounded by them, he has joined them – a symbol of cruelty and heartlessness

[3] A district in fashionable West London which was once the site of an open air market for flower vendors and grocers. This portrayal of the flower shops setting up is famously paralleled in one of the opening scenes in "My Fair Lady" as the background to the song "Wouldn't It be Loverley"

He winced, and, taking up from the table an oval glass[1] framed in ivory Cupids, that Lord Henry had given him, he glanced hurriedly into it. No line like that warped his red lips. What did it mean[2]?

He rubbed his eyes, and came close to the picture, and examined it again. There were no signs of any change when he looked into the actual painting, and yet there was no doubt that the whole expression had altered. It was not a mere fancy of his own. The thing was horribly apparent.

He threw himself into a chair, and began to think. Suddenly there flashed across his mind what he had said in Basil Hallward's studio the day the picture had been finished. Yes, he remembered it perfectly. He had uttered a mad wish that he himself might remain young, and the portrait grow old[3]; that his own beauty might be untarnished, and the face on the canvas bear the burden of his passions and his sins; that the painted image might be seared with the lines of suffering and thought, and that he might keep all the delicate bloom and loveliness of his then just conscious boyhood. Surely his prayer had not been answered? Such things were impossible. It seemed monstrous even to think of them. And, yet, there was the picture before him, with the touch of cruelty in the mouth.

Cruelty! Had he been cruel? It was the girl's fault, not his. He had dreamed of her as a great artist, had given his love to her because he had thought her great. Then she had disappointed him. She had been shallow and unworthy. And, yet, a feeling of infinite regret came over him, as he thought of her lying at his feet sobbing like a little child. He remembered with what callousness he had watched her. Why had he been made like that? Why had such a soul been given to him? But he had suffered also. During the three terrible hours that the play had lasted, he had lived centuries of pain, aeon upon aeon of torture. His life was well worth hers. She had marred him for a moment, if he had wounded her for an age.

---

[1] Magnifying glass

[2] Wilde himself referred to this as "the horrible sympathy ... between him and the picture," suggesting that the painting transforms in order to express Dorian's inner feelings without allowing them to mar his physical features

[3] Ghostly paintings were a common trope in Anglo-American literature, starting with "The Castle of Ontranto," and featuring in tales like Poe's "The Oval Portrait," Hawthorne's "Prophetic Pictures," Irving's "The Adventure of the Young Italian," and "The Adventure of My Aunt," Nesbit's "The Ebony Frame," Le Fanu's "Strange Disturbances in Aungier Street," Gogol's "The Portrait," Lovecraft's "Charles Dexter Ward," and Stoker's "The Judge's House" are among the most famous in this genre, which typically feature a painting that supernaturally impacts the world around it, sometimes changing in the process

Besides, women were better suited to bear sorrow than men. They lived on their emotions. They only thought of their emotions. When they took lovers, it was merely to have some one with whom they could have scenes. Lord Henry had told him that, and Lord Henry knew what women were. Why should he trouble about Sibyl Vane? She was nothing to him now.

But the picture? What was he to say of that? It held the secret of his life, and told his story. It had taught him to love his own beauty. Would it teach him to loathe his own soul? Would he ever look at it again?

No; it was merely an illusion wrought on the troubled senses. The horrible night that he had passed had left phantoms behind it. Suddenly there had fallen upon his brain that tiny scarlet speck that makes men mad. The picture had not changed. It was folly to think so.

Yet it was watching him, with its beautiful marred face and its cruel smile. Its bright hair gleamed in the early sunlight. Its blue eyes met his own. A sense of infinite pity, not for himself, but for the painted image of himself, came over him. It had altered already, and would alter more. Its gold would wither into gray. Its red and white roses would die. For every sin that he committed, a stain would fleck and wreck its fairness. But he would not sin. The picture, changed or unchanged, would be to him the visible emblem of conscience. He would resist temptation. He would not see Lord Henry any more,–would not, at any rate, listen to those subtle poisonous theories that in Basil Hallward's garden had first stirred within him the passion for impossible things. He would go back to Sibyl Vane, make her amends, marry her, try to love her again. Yes, it was his duty to do so. She must have suffered more than he had. Poor child! He had been selfish and cruel to her. The fascination that she had exercised over him would return. They would be happy together. His life with her would be beautiful and pure.

He got up from his chair, and drew a large screen right in front of the portrait, shuddering as he glanced at it. "How horrible!" he murmured to himself, and he walked across to the window and opened it. When he stepped out on the grass, he drew a deep breath. The fresh morning air seemed to drive away all his sombre passions. He thought only of Sibyl Vane. A faint echo of his love came back to him. He repeated her name over and over again. The birds that were singing in the dew-drenched garden seemed to be telling the flowers about her.

CHAPTER VI

IT was long past noon when he awoke. His valet had crept several times into the room on tiptoe to see if he was stirring, and had wondered what made his young master sleep so late. Finally his bell sounded, and Victor came in softly with a cup of tea, and a pile of letters, on a small tray of old Sèvres[1] china, and drew back the olive-satin curtains, with their shimmering blue lining, that hung in front of the three tall windows.

"Monsieur has well slept this morning," he said, smiling.

"What o'clock is it, Victor?" asked Dorian Gray, sleepily.

"One hour and a quarter, monsieur."

How late it was! He sat up, and, having sipped some tea, turned over his letters. One of them was from Lord Henry, and had been brought by hand that morning. He hesitated for a moment, and then put it aside. The others he opened listlessly. They contained the usual collection of cards, invitations to dinner, tickets for private views, programmes of charity concerts, and the like, that are showered on fashionable young men every morning during the season[2]. There was a rather heavy bill, for a chased silver Louis-Quinze toilet-set, that he had not yet had the courage to send on to his guardians, who were extremely old-fashioned people and did not realize that we live in an age when only unnecessary things are absolutely necessary to us; and there were several very courteously worded communications from Jermyn Street[3] money-lenders offering to advance any sum of money at a moment's notice and at the most reasonable rates of interest.

After about ten minutes he got up, and, throwing on an elaborate dressing-gown, passed into the onyx-paved bath-room. The cool water refreshed him after his long sleep. He seemed to have forgotten all that he had gone through. A dim sense of having taken part in some strange tragedy came to him once or twice, but there was the unreality of a dream about it.

As soon as he was dressed, he went into the library and sat down to a light French breakfast[4], that had been laid out for him on a small round table close to an open window. It was an exquisite day. The warm air seemed laden with spices. A bee[5] flew in, and buzzed round the blue-

---

[1] A French manufacturer of porcelain
[2] The London social season – a period during which the social elite throw annual balls, events, and galas – takes place from March to August
[3] A street known for its men's fashion businesses
[4] Coffee, bread and butter with jam
[5] Once again, the herald of sensuality and sex

dragon bowl, filled with sulphur-yellow[1] roses, that stood in front of him. He felt perfectly happy.

Suddenly his eye fell on the screen that he had placed in front of the portrait, and he started.

"Too cold for Monsieur?" asked his valet, putting an omelette on the table. "I shut the window?"

Dorian shook his head. "I am not cold," he murmured.

Was it all true? Had the portrait really changed? Or had it been simply his own imagination that had made him see a look of evil where there had been a look of joy? Surely a painted canvas could not alter? The thing was absurd. It would serve as a tale to tell Basil some day. It would make him smile.

And, yet, how vivid was his recollection of the whole thing! First in the dim twilight, and then in the bright dawn, he had seen the touch of cruelty in the warped lips. He almost dreaded his valet leaving the room. He knew that when he was alone he would have to examine the portrait. He was afraid of certainty. When the coffee and cigarettes had been brought and the man turned to go, he felt a mad desire to tell him to remain. As the door closed behind him he called him back. The man stood waiting for his orders. Dorian looked at him for a moment. "I am not at home to any one, Victor," he said, with a sigh. The man bowed and retired.

He rose from the table, lit a cigarette, and flung himself down on a luxuriously-cushioned couch that stood facing the screen. The screen was an old one of gilt Spanish leather, stamped and wrought with a rather florid Louis-Quatorze pattern. He scanned it curiously, wondering if it had ever before concealed the secret of a man's life.

Should he move it aside, after all? Why not let it stay there? What was the use of knowing? If the thing was true, it was terrible. If it was not true, why trouble about it? But what if, by some fate or deadlier chance, other eyes than his spied behind, and saw the horrible change? What should he do if Basil Hallward came and asked to look at his own picture? He would be sure to do that. No; the thing had to be examined, and at once. Anything would be better than this dreadful state of doubt.

He got up, and locked both doors. At least he would be alone when he looked upon the mask of his shame. Then he drew the screen aside, and saw himself face to face. It was perfectly true. The portrait had altered.

As he often remembered afterwards, and always with no small wonder, he found himself at first gazing at the portrait with a feeling of

---

[1] The color of hellfire and damnation

almost scientific interest. That such a change should have taken place was incredible to him. And yet it was a fact. Was there some subtle affinity between the chemical atoms, that shaped themselves into form and color on the canvas, and the soul that was within him? Could it be that what that soul thought, they realized?–that what it dreamed, they made true? Or was there some other, more terrible reason[1]? He shuddered, and felt afraid, and, going back to the couch, lay there, gazing at the picture in sickened horror.

One thing, however, he felt that it had done for him. It had made him conscious how unjust, how cruel, he had been to Sibyl Vane. It was not too late to make reparation for that. She could still be his wife. His unreal and selfish love would yield to some higher influence, would be transformed into some nobler passion, and the portrait that Basil Hallward had painted of him would be a guide to him through life, would be to him what holiness was to some, and conscience to others, and the fear of God to us all. There were opiates for remorse, drugs that could lull the moral sense to sleep. But here was a visible symbol of the degradation of sin. Here was an ever-present sign of the ruin men brought upon their souls.

Three o'clock struck, and four, and half-past four, but he did not stir. He was trying to gather up the scarlet threads of life, and to weave them into a pattern; to find his way through the sanguine labyrinth of passion through which he was wandering. He did not know what to do, or what to think. Finally, he went over to the table and wrote a passionate letter to the girl he had loved, imploring her forgiveness, and accusing himself of madness. He covered page after page with wild words of sorrow, and wilder words of pain. There is a luxury in self-reproach. When we blame ourselves we feel that no one else has a right to blame us. It is the confession, not the priest, that gives us absolution. When Dorian Gray had finished the letter, he felt that he had been forgiven.

Suddenly there came a knock to the door, and he heard Lord Henry's voice outside. "My dear Dorian, I must see you. Let me in at once. I can't bear your shutting yourself up like this."

He made no answer at first, but remained quite still. The knocking still continued, and grew louder. Yes, it was better to let Lord Henry in, and to explain to him the new life he was going to lead, to quarrel with him if it became necessary to quarrel, to part if parting was

---

[1] Dorian is pitching between a pseudo-scientific explanation and a supernatural one: either this is caused by some yet-unknown atomic phenomenon, or it is the work of Hell

inevitable. He jumped up, drew the screen hastily across the picture, and unlocked the door.

"I am so sorry for it all, my dear boy," said Lord Henry, coming in. "But you must not think about it too much."

"Do you mean about Sibyl Vane?" asked Dorian.

"Yes, of course," answered Lord Henry, sinking into a chair, and slowly pulling his gloves off. "It is dreadful, from one point of view, but it was not your fault. Tell me, did you go behind and see her after the play was over?"

"Yes."

"I felt sure you had. Did you make a scene with her?"

"I was brutal, Harry,–perfectly brutal. But it is all right now. I am not sorry for anything that has happened. It has taught me to know myself better."

"Ah, Dorian, I am so glad you take it in that way! I was afraid I would find you plunged in remorse, and tearing your nice hair."

"I have got through all that," said Dorian, shaking his head, and smiling. "I am perfectly happy now. I know what conscience is, to begin with. It is not what you told me it was. It is the divinest thing in us. Don't sneer at it, Harry, any more,–at least not before me. I want to be good. I can't bear the idea of my soul being hideous."

"A very charming artistic basis for ethics, Dorian! I congratulate you on it. But how are you going to begin?"

"By marrying Sibyl Vane."

"Marrying Sibyl Vane!" cried Lord Henry, standing up, and looking at him in perplexed amazement. "But, my dear Dorian–"

"Yes, Harry, I know what you are going to say. Something dreadful about marriage. Don't say it. Don't ever say things of that kind to me again. Two days ago I asked Sibyl to marry me. I am not going to break my word to her. She is to be my wife."

"Your wife! Dorian! . . . Didn't you get my letter? I wrote to you this morning, and sent the note down, by my own man."

"Your letter? Oh, yes, I remember. I have not read it yet, Harry. I was afraid there might be something in it that I wouldn't like."

Lord Henry walked across the room, and, sitting down by Dorian Gray, took both his hands in his, and held them tightly. "Dorian," he said, "my letter–don't be frightened–was to tell you that Sibyl Vane is dead."

A cry of pain rose from the lad's lips, and he leaped to his feet, tearing his hands away from Lord Henry's grasp. "Dead! Sibyl dead! It is not true! It is a horrible lie!"

"It is quite true, Dorian," said Lord Henry, gravely. "It is in all the morning papers. I wrote down to you to ask you not to see any one till I came. There will have to be an inquest, of course, and you must not be mixed up in it. Things like that make a man fashionable in Paris. But in London people are so prejudiced. Here, one should never make one's début with a scandal. One should reserve that to give an interest to one's old age. I don't suppose they know your name at the theatre. If they don't, it is all right. Did any one see you going round to her room? That is an important point."

Dorian did not answer for a few moments. He was dazed with horror. Finally he murmured, in a stifled voice, "Harry, did you say an inquest? What did you mean by that? Did Sibyl–? Oh, Harry, I can't bear it! But be quick. Tell me everything at once."

"I have no doubt it was not an accident, Dorian, though it must be put in that way to the public. As she was leaving the theatre with her mother, about half-past twelve or so, she said she had forgotten something up-stairs. They waited some time for her, but she did not come down again. They ultimately found her lying dead on the floor of her dressing-room. She had swallowed something by mistake, some dreadful thing they use at theatres. I don't know what it was, but it had either prussic acid[1] or white lead in it. I should fancy it was prussic acid, as she seems to have died instantaneously. It is very tragic, of course, but you must not get yourself mixed up in it. I see by the Standard that she was seventeen. I should have thought she was almost younger than that. She looked such a child, and seemed to know so little about acting. Dorian, you mustn't let this thing get on your nerves. You must come and dine with me, and afterwards we will look in at the Opera. It is a Patti[2] night, and everybody will be there. You can come to my sister's box. She has got some smart women with her."

"So I have murdered Sibyl Vane," said Dorian Gray, half to himself,– "murdered her as certainly as if I had cut her little throat with a knife. And the roses are not less lovely for all that. The birds sing just as happily in my garden. And to-night I am to dine with you, and then go on to the Opera, and sup somewhere, I suppose, afterwards. How extraordinarily dramatic life is! If I had read all this in a book, Harry, I think I would have wept over it. Somehow, now that it has happened

---

[1] Cyanide. Both this and white lead are ingredients in paints (such as might be used in scenes and backgrounds), which suggests that Sibyl drank paint to kill herself. While the papers may be trying to make her death seem ambiguous, it is obvious that no one would mistakenly drink enough paint to kill themselves. This also supplies an interesting, symbolic connection to Dorian's oil portrait: she has been stifled by the same material used to worship Dorian's youth and beauty

[2] Adelina Patti was one of the most famous opera singers of the Victorian Age

actually, and to me, it seems far too wonderful[1] for tears. Here is the first passionate love-letter I have ever written in my life. Strange, that my first passionate love- letter should have been addressed to a dead girl. Can they feel, I wonder, those white silent people we call the dead? Sibyl! Can she feel, or know, or listen? Oh, Harry, how I loved her once! It seems years ago to me now. She was everything to me. Then came that dreadful night–was it really only last night?–when she played so badly, and my heart almost broke. She explained it all to me. It was terribly pathetic. But I was not moved a bit. I thought her shallow. Then something happened that made me afraid. I can't tell you what it was, but it was awful. I said I would go back to her. I felt I had done wrong. And now she is dead. My God! my God! Harry, what shall I do? You don't know the danger I am in, and there is nothing to keep me straight. She would have done that for me. She had no right to kill herself. It was selfish of her."

"My dear Dorian, the only way a woman can ever reform a man is by boring him so completely that he loses all possible interest in life. If you had married this girl you would have been wretched. Of course you would have treated her kindly. One can always be kind to people about whom one cares nothing. But she would have soon found out that you were absolutely indifferent to her. And when a woman finds that out about her husband, she either becomes dreadfully dowdy, or wears very smart bonnets that some other woman's husband has to pay for[2]. I say nothing about the social mistake, but I assure you that in any case the whole thing would have been an absolute failure."

"I suppose it would," muttered the lad, walking up and down the room, and looking horribly pale. "But I thought it was my duty. It is not my fault that this terrible tragedy has prevented my doing what was right. I remember your saying once that there is a fatality about good resolutions,–that they are always made too late. Mine certainly were."

"Good resolutions are simply a useless attempt to interfere with scientific laws. Their origin is pure vanity. Their result is absolutely nil. They give us, now and then, some of those luxurious sterile emotions that have a certain charm for us. That is all that can be said for them."

"Harry," cried Dorian Gray, coming over and sitting down beside him, "why is it that I cannot feel this tragedy as much as I want to? I don't think I am heartless. Do you?"

"You have done too many foolish things in your life to be entitled to give yourself that name, Dorian," answered Lord Henry, with his sweet, melancholy smile.

---

[1] Curious, fantastical, bizarre

[2] That is, starts affairs with married men

The lad frowned. "I don't like that explanation, Harry," he rejoined, "but I am glad you don't think I am heartless. I am nothing of the kind. I know I am not. And yet I must admit that this thing that has happened does not affect me as it should. It seems to me to be simply like a wonderful ending to a wonderful play. It has all the terrible beauty of a great tragedy, a tragedy in which I took part, but by which I have not been wounded."

"It is an interesting question," said Lord Henry, who found an exquisite pleasure in playing on the lad's unconscious egotism,–"an extremely interesting question. I fancy that the explanation is this. It often happens that the real tragedies of life occur in such an inartistic manner that they hurt us by their crude violence, their absolute incoherence, their absurd want of meaning, their entire lack of style. They affect us just as vulgarity affects us. They give us an impression of sheer brute force, and we revolt against that. Sometimes, however, a tragedy that has artistic elements of beauty crosses our lives. If these elements of beauty are real, the whole thing simply appeals to our sense of dramatic effect. Suddenly we find that we are no longer the actors, but the spectators of the play. Or rather we are both. We watch ourselves, and the mere wonder of the spectacle enthralls us. In the present case, what is it that has really happened? Some one has killed herself for love of you. I wish I had ever had such an experience. It would have made me in love with love for the rest of my life. The people who have adored me–there have not been very many, but there have been some– have always insisted on living on, long after I had ceased to care for them, or they to care for me. They have become stout and tedious, and when I meet them they go in at once for reminiscences. That awful memory of woman! What a fearful thing it is! And what an utter intellectual stagnation it reveals! One should absorb the color of life, but one should never remember its details. Details are always vulgar.

"Of course, now and then things linger. I once wore nothing but violets[1] all through one season, as mourning for a romance that would not die. Ultimately, however, it did die. I forget what killed it. I think it was her proposing to sacrifice the whole world for me. That is always a dreadful moment. It fills one with the terror of eternity. Well,–would you believe it?–a week ago, at Lady Hampshire's, I found myself seated at dinner next the lady in question, and she insisted on going over the whole thing again, and digging up the past, and raking up the future. I had

---

[1] Violets (in this case worn in a man's coat lapel) symbolize a preoccupation with love – that the wearer (or the sender) is constantly smitten

buried my romance in a bed of poppies[1]. She dragged it out again, and assured me that I had spoiled her life. I am bound to state that she ate an enormous dinner, so I did not feel any anxiety. But what a lack of taste she showed! The one charm of the past is that it is the past. But women never know when the curtain has fallen. They always want a sixth act, and as soon as the interest of the play is entirely over they propose to continue it. If they were allowed to have their way, every comedy would have a tragic ending, and every tragedy would culminate in a farce. They are charmingly artificial, but they have no sense of art. You are more fortunate than I am. I assure you, Dorian, that not one of the women I have known would have done for me what Sibyl Vane did for you. Ordinary women always console themselves. Some of them do it by going in for sentimental colors. Never trust a woman who wears mauve, whatever her age may be, or a woman over thirty-five who is fond of pink ribbons. It always means that they have a history. Others find a great consolation in suddenly discovering the good qualities of their husbands. They flaunt their conjugal felicity in one's face, as if it was the most fascinating of sins. Religion consoles some. Its mysteries have all the charm of a flirtation, a woman once told me; and I can quite understand it. Besides, nothing makes one so vain as being told that one is a sinner. There is really no end to the consolations that women find in modern life. Indeed, I have not mentioned the most important one of all."

"What is that, Harry?" said Dorian Gray, listlessly.

"Oh, the obvious one. Taking some one else's admirer when one loses one's own. In good society that always whitewashes a woman. But really, Dorian, how different Sibyl Vane must have been from all the women one meets[2]! There is something to me quite beautiful about her death. I am glad I am living in a century when such wonders happen. They make one believe in the reality of the things that shallow, fashionable people play with, such as romance, passion, and love."

"I was terribly cruel to her. You forget that."

"I believe that women appreciate cruelty more than anything else. They have wonderfully primitive instincts. We have emancipated them, but they remain slaves looking for their masters, all the same. They love being dominated. I am sure you were splendid. I have never seen you

---

[1] Associated with opium and narcotics

[2] To Henry, who revels in people's falseness and two-faced-ness, Sibyl's suicide is a rare act of genuine sincerity, illustrating how true her love actually was. He is strangely touched by the depth of her feeling and respects this like he respects few other people

angry, but I can fancy how delightful you looked[1]. And, after all, you said something to me the day before yesterday that seemed to me at the time to be merely fanciful, but that I see now was absolutely true, and it explains everything."

"What was that, Harry?"

"You said to me that Sibyl Vane represented to you all the heroines of romance–that she was Desdemona one night, and Ophelia the other; that if she died as Juliet, she came to life as Imogen."

"She will never come to life again now," murmured the lad, burying his face in his hands.

"No, she will never come to life. She has played her last part. But you must think of that lonely death in the tawdry dressing-room simply as a strange lurid fragment from some Jacobean[2] tragedy, as a wonderful scene from Webster, or Ford, or Cyril Tourneur[3]. The girl never really lived, and so she has never really died. To you at least she was always a dream, a phantom that flitted through Shakespeare's plays and left them lovelier for its presence, a reed through which Shakespeare's music sounded richer and more full of joy. The moment she touched actual life, she marred it, and it marred her, and so she passed away. Mourn for Ophelia, if you like. Put ashes on your head because Cordelia was strangled. Cry out against Heaven because the daughter of Brabantio[4] died. But don't waste your tears over Sibyl Vane. She was less real than they are."

There was a silence. The evening darkened in the room. Noiselessly, and with silver feet, the shadows crept in from the garden. The colors faded wearily out of things.

After some time Dorian Gray looked up. "You have explained me to myself, Harry," he murmured, with something of a sigh of relief. "I felt all that you have said, but somehow I was afraid of it, and I could not express it to myself. How well you know me! But we will not talk again of

---

[1] In spite of his admiration for Sibyl's sincerity, Henry is still irresistibly delighted by the idea of Dorian's self-absorbed temper tantrum

[2] Dating back to the reign of James I (1603 – 1625). Jacobean drama was renowned for its dark, violent, and often melodramatic nature. Many of Shakespeare's darkest plays – Othello, Macbeth, King Lear – come from this period

[3] John Ford, John Webster, and Cyril Tourneur were Jacobean playwrights known for the emotional intensity of their dramas. The most famous is Ford's tragedy 'Tis Pity She's a Whore, a violent play about incest, lust, murder, and despair

[4] Desdemona's father in Othello

what has happened. It has been a marvellous[1] experience. That is all. I wonder if life has still in store for me anything as marvellous."

"Life has everything in store for you, Dorian. There is nothing that you, with your extraordinary good looks, will not be able to do."

"But suppose, Harry, I became haggard, and gray, and wrinkled? What then?"

"Ah, then," said Lord Henry, rising to go,–"then, my dear Dorian, you would have to fight for your victories. As it is, they are brought to you. No, you must keep your good looks. We live in an age that reads too much to be wise, and that thinks too much to be beautiful. We cannot spare you. And now you had better dress, and drive down to the club. We are rather late, as it is."

"I think I shall join you at the Opera, Harry. I feel too tired to eat anything. What is the number of your sister's box?"

"Twenty-seven, I believe. It is on the grand tier. You will see her name on the door. But I am sorry you won't come and dine."

"I don't feel up to it," said Dorian, wearily. "But I am awfully obliged to you for all that you have said to me. You are certainly my best friend. No one has ever understood me as you have."

"We are only at the beginning of our friendship, Dorian," answered Lord Henry, shaking him by the hand. "Good-by. I shall see you before nine-thirty, I hope. Remember, Patti is singing."

As he closed the door behind him, Dorian Gray touched the bell, and in a few minutes Victor appeared with the lamps and drew the blinds down. He waited impatiently for him to go. The man seemed to take an interminable time about everything.

As soon as he had left, he rushed to the screen, and drew it back. No; there was no further change in the picture. It had received the news of Sibyl Vane's death before he had known of it himself. It was conscious of the events of life as they occurred. The vicious cruelty that marred the fine lines of the mouth had, no doubt, appeared at the very moment that the girl had drunk the poison, whatever it was. Or was it indifferent to results? Did it merely take cognizance of what passed within the soul? he wondered, and hoped that some day he would see the change taking place before his very eyes, shuddering as he hoped it.

Poor Sibyl! what a romance it had all been! She had often mimicked death on the stage, and at last Death himself had touched her, and brought her with him. How had she played that dreadful scene? Had she cursed him, as she died? No; she had died for love of him, and love would always be a sacrament to him now. She had atoned for everything,

---

[1] Shocking, awe-inspiring

by the sacrifice she had made of her life. He would not think any more of what she had made him go through, that horrible night at the theatre. When he thought of her, it would be as a wonderful tragic figure [*to whom Love had been a great reality.*] A wonderful tragic figure? Tears came to his eyes as he remembered her child-like look and winsome fanciful ways and shy tremulous grace. He wiped them away hastily, and looked again at the picture.

He felt that the time had really come for making his choice. Or had his choice already been made? Yes, life had decided that for him,– life, and his own infinite curiosity about life. Eternal youth, infinite passion, pleasures subtle and secret, wild joys and wilder sins,–he was to have all these things. The portrait was to bear the burden of his shame: that was all.

A feeling of pain came over him as he thought of the desecration that was in store for the fair face on the canvas. Once, in boyish mockery of Narcissus[1], he had kissed, or feigned to kiss, those painted lips that now smiled so cruelly at him. Morning after morning he had sat before the portrait wondering at its beauty, almost enamoured of it, as it seemed to him at times. Was it to alter now with every mood to which he yielded? Was it to become a hideous and loathsome thing, to be hidden away in a locked room, to be shut out from the sunlight that had so often touched to brighter gold the waving wonder of the hair? The pity of it! the pity of it!

For a moment he thought of praying that the horrible sympathy that existed between him and the picture might cease. It had changed in answer to a prayer; perhaps in answer to a prayer it might remain unchanged. And, yet, who, that knew anything about Life, would surrender the chance of remaining always young, however fantastic that chance might be, or with what fateful consequences it might be fraught? Besides, was it really under his control? Had it indeed been prayer that had produced the substitution? Might there not be some curious scientific reason for it all? If thought could exercise its influence upon a living organism, might not thought exercise an influence upon dead and

---

[1] The figure in Greek mythology who was so entranced by his own beauty, that he starved to death while staring lovingly at his own reflection. Narcissus (whence we derive "narcissist") has been closely associated with "Dorian Gray" which is often seen as a blending of this myth with Faust. Narcissus' self-love caused him to become emblematic of homoeroticism during the Victorian Age, and he was a frequent icon of male beauty in the arts

inorganic things[1]? Nay, without thought or conscious desire, might not things external to ourselves vibrate in unison with our moods and passions, atom calling to atom, in secret love or strange affinity? But the reason was of no importance. He would never again tempt by a prayer any terrible power. If the picture was to alter, it was to alter. That was all. Why inquire too closely into it?

For there would be a real pleasure in watching it. He would be able to follow his mind into its secret places. This portrait would be to him the most magical of mirrors. As it had revealed to him his own body, so it would reveal to him his own soul. And when winter came upon it, he would still be standing where spring trembles on the verge of summer. When the blood crept from its face, and left behind a pallid mask of chalk with leaden eyes, he would keep the glamour of boyhood. Not one blossom of his loveliness would ever fade. Not one pulse of his life would ever weaken. Like the gods of the Greeks, he would be strong, and fleet, and joyous. What did it matter what happened to the colored image on the canvas? He would be safe. That was everything.

He drew the screen back into its former place in front of the picture, smiling as he did so, and passed into his bedroom, where his valet was already waiting for him. An hour later he was at the Opera, and Lord Henry was leaning over his chair.

CHAPTER VII

AS he was sitting at breakfast next morning, Basil Hallward was shown into the room.

"I am so glad I have found you, Dorian," he said, gravely. "I called last night, and they told me you were at the Opera. Of course I knew that was impossible[2]. But I wish you had left word where you had really gone to. I passed a dreadful evening, half afraid that one tragedy might be followed by another[3]. I think you might have telegraphed for me when

---

[1] Like his contemporaries Arthur Conan Doyle, Arthur Machen, and Algernon Blackwood, Wilde genuinely believed in the power of the supernatural and was a student of spiritualism
[2] Basil, unlike Henry, believes in the best in Dorian. He is unwilling to believe that Dorian would remorselessly attend the opera after hearing such crushing news
[3] Furthermore, he overestimates Dorian's conscience, fearing that he might commit suicide out of guilt

you heard of it first. I read of it quite by chance in a late edition of the Globe, that I picked up at the club. I came here at once, and was miserable at not finding you. I can't tell you how heart-broken I am about the whole thing. I know what you must suffer. But where were you? Did you go down and see the girl's mother[1]? For a moment I thought of following you there. They gave the address in the paper. Somewhere in the Euston Road[2], isn't it? But I was afraid of intruding upon a sorrow that I could not lighten[3]. Poor woman! What a state she must be in! And her only child, too! What did she say about it all?"

"My dear Basil, how do I know?" murmured Dorian, sipping some pale- yellow wine from a delicate gold-beaded bubble of Venetian glass, and looking dreadfully bored. "I was at the Opera. You should have come on there. I met Lady Gwendolen, Harry's sister, for the first time. We were in her box. She is perfectly charming; and Patti sang divinely. Don't talk about horrid subjects. If one doesn't talk about a thing, it has never happened. It is simply expression, as Harry says, that gives reality to things. Tell me about yourself and what you are painting."

"You went to the Opera?" said Hallward, speaking very slowly, and with a strained touch of pain in his voice. "You went to the Opera while Sibyl Vane was lying dead in some sordid lodging? You can talk to me of other women being charming, and of Patti singing divinely, before the girl you loved has even the quiet of a grave to sleep in? Why, man, there are horrors in store for that little white body of hers[4]!"

"Stop, Basil! [*I won't bear it!*]" cried Dorian, leaping to his feet. "You must not tell me about things. What is done is done. What is past is past."

"You call yesterday the past?"

"What has the actual lapse of time got to do with it? It is only shallow people who require years to get rid of an emotion. A man who is master of himself can end a sorrow as easily as he can invent a pleasure. I don't want to be at the mercy of my emotions. I want to use them, to enjoy them, and to dominate them."

"Dorian, this is horrible! Something has changed you completely. You look exactly the same wonderful boy who used to come down to my

---

[1] The decent thing to do (of course he hasn't and will not)

[2] A working class neighborhood that was known for its dilapidation and cheapness

[3] Even though he never met Sibyl, Basil feels compelled to visit her mother. Once again, his polar opposition to Lord Henry is staggeringly stark

[4] He wants Dorian to understand that Sibyl has not just gone away – her body is doomed to blacken, swell, and stink. Metaphorically speaking, he is begging Dorian to acknowledge that his actions have consequences

studio, day after day, to sit for his picture. But you were simple, natural, and affectionate then. You were the most unspoiled creature in the whole world. Now, I don't know what has come over you. You talk as if you had no heart, no pity in you. It is all Harry's influence. I see that."

The lad flushed up, and, going to the window, looked out on the green, flickering garden for a few moments. "I owe a great deal to Harry, Basil," he said, at last,–"more than I owe to you. You only taught me to be vain."

"Well, I am punished for that, Dorian,–or shall be some day."

"I don't know what you mean, Basil," he exclaimed, turning round. "I don't know what you want. What do you want?"

"I want the Dorian Gray I used to know."

"Basil," said the lad, going over to him, and putting his hand on his shoulder, "you have come too late. Yesterday when I heard that Sibyl Vane had killed herself–"

"Killed herself! Good heavens! is there no doubt about that[1]?" cried Hallward, looking up at him with an expression of horror.

"My dear Basil! Surely you don't think it was a vulgar accident? Of course she killed herself. It is one of the great romantic tragedies of the age. As a rule, people who act lead the most commonplace lives. They are good husbands, or faithful wives, or something tedious. You know what I mean,–middle-class virtue, and all that kind of thing. How different Sibyl was! She lived her finest tragedy. She was always a heroine. The last night she played–the night you saw her–she acted badly because she had known the reality of love. When she knew its unreality, she died, as Juliet might have died. She passed again into the sphere of art. There is something of the martyr about her. Her death has all the pathetic uselessness of martyrdom, all its wasted beauty. But, as I was saying, you must not think I have not suffered. If you had come in yesterday at a particular moment,– about half-past five, perhaps, or a quarter to six,–you would have found me in tears. Even Harry, who was here, who brought me the news, in fact, had no idea what I was going through. I suffered immensely, then it passed away. I cannot repeat an emotion. No one can, except sentimentalists. And you are awfully unjust, Basil. You come down here to console me. That is charming of you. You find me consoled, and you are furious. How like a sympathetic person! You remind me of a story Harry told me about a certain philanthropist who spent twenty years of

---

[1] Always willing to believe the best in people, Basil had hoped that the bowdlerized police reports of an "accident" were accurate. This is also probably due to his inability to believe that Dorian could be so cruel as to drive Sibyl to suicide. The fact that she kills herself is evidence of Dorian's hand in her death

his life in trying to get some grievance redressed, or some unjust law altered,–I forget exactly what it was. Finally he succeeded, and nothing could exceed his disappointment. He had absolutely nothing to do, almost died of ennui, and became a confirmed misanthrope. And besides, my dear old Basil, if you really want to console me, teach me rather to forget what has happened, or to see it from a proper artistic point of view. Was it not Gautier who used to write about *la consolation des arts*[1]? I remember picking up a little vellum-covered[2] book in your studio one day and chancing on that delightful phrase. Well, I am not like that young man you told me of when we were down at Marlowe[3] together, the young man who used to say that yellow satin could console one for all the miseries of life. I love beautiful things that one can touch and handle. Old brocades, green bronzes, lacquer-work, carved ivories, exquisite surroundings, luxury, pomp,–there is much to be got from all these. But the artistic temperament that they create, or at any rate reveal, is still more to me. To become the spectator of one's own life, as Harry says, is to escape the suffering of life. I know you are surprised at my talking to you like this. You have not realized how I have developed. I was a school-boy when you knew me. I am a man now. I have new passions, new thoughts, new ideas. I am different, but you must not like me less. I am changed, but you must always be my friend. Of course I am very fond of Harry. But I know that you are better than he is. You are not stronger,–you are too much afraid of life,–but you are better. And how happy we used to be together! Don't leave me, Basil, and don't quarrel with me. I am what I am. There is nothing more to be said."

Hallward felt strangely moved. [*Rugged and straightforward as he was, there was something in his nature that was purely feminine in its tenderness.*] The lad was infinitely dear to him, and his personality had been the great turning-point in his art. He could not bear the idea of reproaching him any more. After all, his indifference was probably merely a mood that would pass away. There was so much in him that was good, so much in him that was noble.

"Well, Dorian," he said, at length, with a sad smile, "I won't speak to you again about this horrible thing, after to-day. I only trust your name

---

[1] The 19th century French writer Theophile Gautier said that "Art is the best consolation for living"

[2] Pale yellow (as of parchment or leather). Foreign books were usually bound in yellow paper, especially those with scandalous contents. Of course, Lord Henry will eventually give Dorian the famous "yellow book" that clinches his corruption, and this too is implied to be a decadent French import

[3] A bucolic town some thirty miles west of London, popular amongst picnicking West-Enders

won't be mentioned in connection with it. The inquest is to take place this afternoon. Have they summoned you?"

Dorian shook his head, and a look of annoyance passed over his face at the mention of the word "inquest." There was something so crude and vulgar about everything of the kind. "They don't know my name," he answered.

"But surely she did?"

"Only my Christian name, and that I am quite sure she never mentioned to any one. She told me once that they were all rather curious to learn who I was, and that she invariably told them my name was Prince Charming. It was pretty of her. You must do me a drawing of her, Basil. I should like to have something more of her than the memory of a few kisses and some broken pathetic words."

"I will try and do something, Dorian, if it would please you. But you must come and sit to me yourself again. I can't get on without you."

"I will never sit to you again, Basil. It is impossible!" he exclaimed, starting back.

Hallward stared at him, "My dear boy, what nonsense!" he cried. "Do you mean to say you don't like what I did of you? Where is it? Why have you pulled the screen in front of it? Let me look at it. It is the best thing I have ever painted. Do take that screen away, Dorian. It is simply horrid of your servant hiding my work like that. I felt the room looked different as I came in."

"My servant has nothing to do with it, Basil. You don't imagine I let him arrange my room for me? He settles my flowers for me sometimes,–that is all. No; I did it myself. The light was too strong on the portrait."

"Too strong! Impossible, my dear fellow! It is an admirable place for it. Let me see it." And Hallward walked towards the corner of the room.

A cry of terror[1] broke from Dorian Gray's lips, and he rushed between Hallward and the screen. "Basil," he said, looking very pale, "you must not look at it. I don't wish you to."

"Not look at my own work! you are not serious. Why shouldn't I look at it?" exclaimed Hallward, laughing.

"If you try to look at it, Basil, on my word of honor I will never speak to you again as long as I live. I am quite serious. I don't offer any explanation, and you are not to ask for any. But, remember, if you touch this screen, everything is over between us."

---

[1] Dorian is fine with his corruption as long as no one else sees it, but the thought of Basil seeing how he has transformed spiritually is more than he can bear

Hallward was thunderstruck. He looked at Dorian Gray in absolute amazement. He had never seen him like this before. The lad was absolutely pallid with rage. His hands were clinched, and the pupils of his eyes were like disks of blue fire[1]. He was trembling all over.

"Dorian!"

"Don't speak!"

"But what is the matter? Of course I won't look at it if you don't want me to," he said, rather coldly, turning on his heel, and going over towards the window. "But, really, it seems rather absurd that I shouldn't see my own work, especially as I am going to exhibit it in Paris in the autumn. I shall probably have to give it another coat of varnish before that, so I must see it some day, and why not to- day?"

"To exhibit it! You want to exhibit it?" exclaimed Dorian Gray, a strange sense of terror creeping over him. Was the world going to be shown his secret? Were people to gape at the mystery of his life? That was impossible. Something–he did not know what–had to be done at once.

"Yes: I don't suppose you will object to that. Georges Petit is going to collect all my best pictures for a special exhibition in the Rue de Sèze[2], which will open the first week in October. The portrait will only be away a month. I should think you could easily spare it for that time. In fact, you are sure to be out of town. And if you hide it always behind a screen, you can't care much abut it."

Dorian Gray passed his hand over his forehead. There were beads of perspiration there. He felt that he was on the brink of a horrible danger. "You told me a month ago that you would never exhibit it," he said. "Why have you changed your mind? You people who go in for being consistent have just as many moods as others. The only difference is that your moods are rather meaningless. You can't have forgotten that you assured me most solemnly that nothing in the world would induce you to send it to any exhibition. You told Harry exactly the same thing." He stopped suddenly, and a gleam of light came into his eyes. He remembered that Lord Henry had said to him once, half seriously and half in jest, "If you want to have an interesting quarter of an hour, get Basil to tell you why he won't exhibit your picture. He told me why he wouldn't, and it was a revelation to me." Yes, perhaps Basil, too, had his secret[3]. He would ask him and try.

---

[1] Blue flames are associated with ghosts, hell, and supernatural evil

[2] A gallery known for exhibiting cutting edge paintings and sculpture during the height of French impressionism

[3] His implied secret, of course, is his homosexuality

"Basil," he said, coming over quite close, and looking him straight in the face, "we have each of us a secret. Let me know yours, and I will tell you mine. What was your reason for refusing to exhibit my picture?"

Hallward shuddered in spite of himself. "Dorian, if I told you, you might like me less than you do, and you would certainly laugh at me. I could not bear your doing either of those two things. If you wish me never to look at your picture again, I am content. I have always you to look at. If you wish the best work I have ever done to be hidden from the world, I am satisfied. Your friendship is dearer to me than any fame or reputation."

"No, Basil, you must tell me," murmured Dorian Gray. "I think I have a right to know." His feeling of terror had passed away, and curiosity had taken its place. He was determined to find out Basil Hallward's mystery.

"Let us sit down, Dorian," said Hallward, looking pale and pained. "Let us sit down. I will sit in the shadow, and you shall sit in the sunlight. Our lives are like that. Just answer me one question. Have you noticed in the picture something that you did not like?– something that probably at first did not strike you, but that revealed itself to you suddenly?"

"Basil!" cried the lad, clutching the arms of his chair with trembling hands, and gazing at him with wild, startled eyes.

"I see you did. Don't speak. Wait till you hear what I have to say. It is quite true that I have worshipped you with far more romance of feeling than a man [*should ever give*[1]] to a friend. Somehow, I had never loved a woman. I suppose I never had time. Perhaps, as Harry says, a really 'grande passion' is the privilege of those who have nothing to do, and that is the use of the idle classes in a country. Well, from the moment I met you, your personality had the most extraordinary influence over me. I quite admit that I adored you madly, extravagantly, absurdly. I was jealous of every one to whom you spoke. I wanted to have you all to myself. I was only happy when I was with you. When I was away from you, you were still present in my art. [*It was all wrong and foolish. It is all wrong and foolish still.*] Of course I never let you know anything about this. It would have been impossible. You would not have understood it; I did not understand it myself. One day I determined to paint a wonderful portrait of you. It was to have been my masterpiece. It is my masterpiece. But, as I worked at it, every flake and film of color seemed to me to reveal my secret. [*There was love in every line, and in every touch there was passion. There was love in every line, and in every touch there was passion*[2].] I grew

---

[1] Later changed to "usually gives" to change the homosexual overtones to something more plausibly platonic
[2] Deleted for obvious reasons

afraid that the world would know of my idolatry. I felt, Dorian, that I had told too much. Then it was that I resolved never to allow the picture to be exhibited. You were a little annoyed; but then you did not realize all that it meant to me. Harry, to whom I talked about it, laughed at me. But I did not mind that. When the picture was finished, and I sat alone with it, I felt that I was right. Well, after a few days the portrait left my studio, and as soon as I had got rid of the intolerable fascination of its presence it seemed to me that I had been foolish in imagining that I had said anything in it, more than that you were extremely good-looking and that I could paint. Even now I cannot help feeling that it is a mistake to think that the passion one feels in creation is ever really shown in the work one creates. Art is more abstract than we fancy. Form and color tell us of form and color,–that is all. It often seems to me that art conceals the artist far more completely than it ever reveals him. And so when I got this offer from Paris I determined to make your portrait the principal thing in my exhibition. It never occurred to me that you would refuse. I see now that you were right. The picture must not be shown. You must not be angry with me, Dorian, for what I have told you. As I said to Harry, once, you are made to be worshipped."

Dorian Gray drew a long breath. The color came back to his cheeks, and a smile played about his lips. The peril was over. He was safe for the time. Yet he could not help feeling infinite pity for the young man who had just made this strange confession to him. He wondered if he would ever be so dominated by the personality of a friend. Lord Harry had the charm of being very dangerous. But that was all. He was too clever and too cynical to be really fond of. Would there ever be some one who would fill him with a strange idolatry? Was that one of the things that life had in store?

"It is extraordinary to me, Dorian," said Hallward, "that you should have seen this in the picture. Did you really see it?"

"Of course I did."

"Well, you don't mind my looking at it now?"

Dorian shook his head. "You must not ask me that, Basil. I could not possibly let you stand in front of that picture."

"You will some day, surely?"

"Never."

"Well, perhaps you are right. And now good-by, Dorian. You have been the one person in my life of whom I have been really fond. I don't suppose I shall often see you again. You don't know what it cost me to tell you all that I have told you."

"My dear Basil," cried Dorian, "what have you told me? Simply that you felt that you liked me too much. That is not even a compliment."

"It was not intended as a compliment. It was a confession."

"A very disappointing one."

"Why, what did you expect, Dorian? You didn't see anything else in the picture, did you? There was nothing else to see?"

"No: there was nothing else to see. Why do you ask? But you mustn't talk about not meeting me again, or anything of that kind. You and I are friends, Basil, and we must always remain so."

"You have got Harry," said Hallward, sadly.

"Oh, Harry!" cried the lad, with a ripple of laughter. "Harry spends his days in saying what is incredible, and his evenings in doing what is improbable. Just the sort of life I would like to lead. But still I don't think I would go to Harry if I was in trouble. I would sooner go to you, Basil."

"But you won't sit to me again?"

"Impossible!"

"You spoil my life as an artist by refusing, Dorian. No man comes across two ideal things. Few come across one."

"I can't explain it to you, Basil, but I must never sit to you again. I will come and have tea with you. That will be just as pleasant."

"Pleasanter for you, I am afraid," murmured Hallward, regretfully. "And now good-by. I am sorry you won't let me look at the picture once again. But that can't be helped. I quite understand what you feel about it."

As he left the room, Dorian Gray smiled to himself. Poor Basil! how little he knew of the true reason! And how strange it was that, instead of having been forced to reveal his own secret, he had succeeded, almost by chance, in wresting a secret from his friend! How much that strange confession explained to him! Basil's absurd fits of jealousy, his wild devotion, his extravagant panegyrics, his curious reticences[1],–he understood them all now, and he felt sorry. There was something [*infinitely tragic in a romance that was at once so passionate and so sterile*[2]].

He sighed, and touched the bell. The portrait must be hidden away at all costs. He could not run such a risk of discovery again. It had been mad of him to have the thing remain, even for an hour, in a room to which any of his friends had access.

---

[1] Shyness

[2] The words "sterile" and "sterility" were Victorian euphemisms for homosexual and homosexuality, respectively. They were used to reflect the lack of "natural" sexual chemistry between a man and women

CHAPTER VIII

WHEN his servant entered, he looked at him steadfastly, and wondered if he had thought of peering behind the screen. The man was quite impassive, and waited for his orders. Dorian lit a cigarette, and walked over to the glass and glanced into it. He could see the reflection of Victor's face perfectly. It was like a placid mask of servility. There was nothing to be afraid of, there. Yet he thought it best to be on his guard.

Speaking very slowly, he told him to tell the housekeeper that he wanted to see her, and then to go to the frame-maker's and ask him to send two of his men round at once. It seemed to him that as the man left the room he peered in the direction of the screen. Or was that only his fancy?

After a few moments, Mrs. Leaf, a dear old lady in a black silk dress, with a photograph of the late Mr. Leaf framed in a large gold brooch at her neck, and old-fashioned thread mittens on her wrinkled hands, bustled into the room.

"Well, Master Dorian," she said, "what can I do for you? I beg your pardon, sir,"–here came a courtesy,–"I shouldn't call you Master[1] Dorian any more. But, Lord bless you, sir, I have known you since you were a baby, and many's the trick you've played on poor old Leaf. Not that you were not always a good boy, sir; but boys will be boys, Master Dorian, and jam is a temptation to the young, isn't it, sir?"

He laughed. "You must always call me Master Dorian, Leaf. I will be very angry with you if you don't. And I assure you I am quite as fond of jam now as I used to be. Only when I am asked out to tea I am never offered any. I want you to give me the key of the room at the top of the house."

"The old school-room[2], Master Dorian? Why, it's full of dust. I must get it arranged and put straight before you go into it. It's not fit for you to see, Master Dorian. It is not, indeed."

"I don't want it put straight, Leaf. I only want the key."

"Well, Master Dorian, you'll be covered with cobwebs if you goes into it. Why, it hasn't been opened for nearly five years,–not since his lordship died."

---

[1] The form of address given to a boy who is not yet of marrying age (e.g., roughly 18 – 20), after which they are addressed as "mister"

[2] The room where Dorian would have been taught by his governess or tutor

He winced at the mention of his dead uncle's name. He had hateful memories of him[1]. "That does not matter, Leaf," he replied. "All I want is the key."

"And here is the key, Master Dorian," said the old lady, after going over the contents of her bunch with tremulously uncertain hands. "Here is the key. I'll have it off the ring in a moment. But you don't think of living up there, Master Dorian, and you so comfortable here?"

"No, Leaf, I don't. I merely want to see the place, and perhaps store something in it,—that is all. Thank you, Leaf. I hope your rheumatism is better; and mind you send me up jam for breakfast."

Mrs. Leaf shook her head. "Them foreigners doesn't understand jam, Master Dorian. They calls it 'compot[2].' But I'll bring it to you myself some morning, if you lets me."

"That will be very kind of you, Leaf," he answered, looking at the key; and, having made him an elaborate courtesy, the old lady left the room, her face wreathed in smiles. She had a strong objection to the French valet. It was a poor thing, she felt, for any one to be born a foreigner.

As the door closed, Dorian put the key in his pocket, and looked round the room. His eye fell on a large purple satin coverlet heavily embroidered with gold, a splendid piece of late seventeenth- century Venetian work that his uncle had found in a convent near Bologna. Yes, that would serve to wrap the dreadful thing in. It had perhaps served often as a pall for the dead. Now it was to hide something that had a corruption of its own, worse than the corruption of death itself,—something that would breed horrors and yet would never die. What the worm was to the corpse, his sins would be to the painted image on the canvas. They would mar its beauty, and eat away its grace. They would defile it, and make it shameful. And yet the thing would still live on. It would be always alive.

He shuddered, and for a moment he regretted that he had not told Basil the true reason why he had wished to hide the picture away. Basil would have helped him to resist Lord Henry's influence, and the still more poisonous influences that came from his own temperament. The love that he bore him—for it was really love—had something noble and intellectual in it[3]. It was not that mere physical admiration of beauty that

---

[1] Several commentators have noted that it is not unreasonable to suspect that Dorian was molested or at least made very sexually uncomfortable by his uncle, which could explain several elements of his psychology

[2] "Compote" is a French dish consisting of slices of fruit cooked in a syrup

[3] Homosexual love had often been described – especially by Greek philosophers – as nobler and more intellectual than heterosexual attraction, which was considered vulgar and driven by animal lust. Well into the 20th century, so-called

is born of the senses, and that dies when the senses tire. It was such love as Michael Angelo had known, and Montaigne, and Winckelmann, and Shakespeare himself[1]. Yes, Basil could have saved him. But it was too late now. The past could always be annihilated. Regret, denial, or forgetfulness could do that. But the future was inevitable. There were passions in him that would find their terrible outlet, dreams that would make the shadow of their evil real.

He took up from the couch the great purple-and-gold texture that covered it, and, holding it in his hands, passed behind the screen. Was the face on the canvas viler than before? It seemed to him that it was unchanged; and yet his loathing of it was intensified. Gold hair, blue eyes, and rose-red lips,–they all were there. It was simply the expression that had altered. That was horrible in its cruelty. Compared to what he saw in it of censure or rebuke, how shallow Basil's reproaches about Sibyl Vane had been!–how shallow, and of what little account! His own soul was looking out at him from the canvas and calling him to judgment. A look of pain came across him, and he flung the rich pall over the picture. As he did so, a knock came to the door. He passed out as his servant entered.

"The persons are here, monsieur."

He felt that the man must be got rid of at once. He must not be allowed to know where the picture was being taken to. There was something sly about him, and he had thoughtful, treacherous eyes. Sitting down at the writing-table, he scribbled a note to Lord Henry, asking him to send him round something to read, and reminding him that they were to meet at eight-fifteen that evening.

"Wait for an answer," he said, handing it to him, "and show the men in here."

In two or three minutes there was another knock, and Mr. Ashton himself, the celebrated frame-maker of South Audley Street, came in with a somewhat rough-looking young assistant. Mr. Ashton was a florid, red-whiskered little man, whose admiration for art was considerably tempered by the inveterate impecuniosity[2] of most of the artists who dealt with him. As a rule, he never left his shop. He waited for people to come

---

"pederasts" used this belief to explain the benefits of same-sex-attraction (today we consider as just another example of complex human sexuality, but in previous generations it was alternatively considered either higher and nobler and heterosexual love or more bestial and debasing – but it was rarely considered equivalent)

[1] The Italian sculptor, French essayist, German historian, and English playwright were all widely known (or rumored to be known) for their homosexuality or bisexuality. There is no question that this is the "love" to which Wilde is referring

[2] Poverty

to him. But he always made an exception in favor of Dorian Gray. There was something about Dorian that charmed everybody. It was a pleasure even to see him.

"What can I do for you, Mr. Gray?" he said, rubbing his fat freckled hands. "I thought I would do myself the honor of coming round in person. I have just got a beauty of a frame, sir. Picked it up at a sale. Old Florentine. Came from Fonthill[1], I believe. Admirably suited for a religious picture, Mr. Gray."

"I am so sorry you have given yourself the trouble of coming round, Mr. Ashton. I will certainly drop in and look at the frame,–though I don't go in much for religious art,–but to-day I only want a picture carried to the top of the house for me. It is rather heavy, so I thought I would ask you to lend me a couple of your men."

"No trouble at all, Mr. Gray. I am delighted to be of any service to you. Which is the work of art, sir?"

"This," replied Dorian, moving the screen back. "Can you move it, covering and all, just as it is? I don't want it to get scratched going up-stairs."

"There will be no difficulty, sir," said the genial frame-maker, beginning, with the aid of his assistant, to unhook the picture from the long brass chains by which it was suspended. "And, now, where shall we carry it to, Mr. Gray?"

"I will show you the way, Mr. Ashton, if you will kindly follow me. Or perhaps you had better go in front. I am afraid it is right at the top of the house. We will go up by the front staircase, as it is wider."

He held the door open for them, and they passed out into the hall and began the ascent. The elaborate character of the frame had made the picture extremely bulky, and now and then, in spite of the obsequious protests of Mr. Ashton, who had a true tradesman's dislike of seeing a gentleman doing anything useful, Dorian put his hand to it so as to help them.

"Something of a load to carry, sir," gasped the little man, when they reached the top landing. And he wiped his shiny forehead.

"A terrible load to carry[2]," murmured Dorian, as he unlocked the door that opened into the room that was to keep for him the curious secret of his life and hide his soul from the eyes of men.

He had not entered the place for more than four years,–not, indeed, since he had used it first as a play-room when he was a child and then as a study when he grew somewhat older. It was a large, well-

---

[1] A famous manor house in Wiltshire renowned for its Gothic architecture
[2] Of course, he means this as a double meaning: the weight of his sins

proportioned room, which had been specially built by the last Lord Sherard for the use of the little nephew whom, being himself childless, and perhaps for other reasons, he had always hated and desired to keep at a distance. It did not appear to Dorian to have much changed. There was the huge Italian cassone[1], with its fantastically-painted panels and its tarnished gilt mouldings, in which he had so often hidden himself as a boy. There was the satinwood bookcase filled with his dog-eared school-books. On the wall behind it was hanging the same ragged Flemish tapestry where a faded king and queen were playing chess in a garden, while a company of hawkers rode by, carrying hooded birds on their gauntleted wrists. How well he recalled it all! Every moment of his lonely childhood came back to him, as he looked round. He remembered the stainless purity of his boyish life, and it seemed horrible to him that it was here that the fatal portrait was to be hidden away. How little he had thought, in those dead days, of all that was in store for him!

But there was no other place in the house so secure from prying eyes as this. He had the key, and no one else could enter it. Beneath its purple pall, the face painted on the canvas could grow bestial, sodden, and unclean. What did it matter? No one could see it. He himself would not see it. Why should he watch the hideous corruption of his soul? He kept his youth,–that was enough. And, besides, might not his nature grow finer, after all? There was no reason that the future should be so full of shame. Some love might come across his life, and purify him, and shield him from those sins that seemed to be already stirring in spirit and in flesh,–those curious unpictured sins whose very mystery lent them their subtlety and their charm. Perhaps, some day, the cruel look would have passed away from the scarlet sensitive mouth, and he might show to the world Basil Hallward's masterpiece.

No; that was impossible. The thing upon the canvas was growing old, hour by hour, and week by week. Even if it escaped the hideousness of sin, the hideousness of age was in store for it. The cheeks would become hollow or flaccid. Yellow crow's-feet would creep round the fading eyes and make them horrible. The hair would lose its brightness, the mouth would gape or droop, would be foolish or gross, as the mouths of old men are. There would be the wrinkled throat, the cold blue-veined hands, the twisted body, that he remembered in the uncle who had been so stern to him in his boyhood. The picture had to be concealed. There was no help for it.

"Bring it in, Mr. Ashton, please," he said, wearily, turning round. "I am sorry I kept you so long. I was thinking of something else."

---

[1] A large, ornate chest made for brides on their wedding days

"Always glad to have a rest, Mr. Gray," answered the frame-maker, who was still gasping for breath. "Where shall we put it, sir?"

"Oh, anywhere, Here, this will do. I don't want to have it hung up. Just lean it against the wall. Thanks."

"Might one look at the work of art, sir?"

Dorian started. "It would not interest you, Mr. Ashton," he said, keeping his eye on the man. He felt ready to leap upon him and fling him to the ground if he dared to lift the gorgeous hanging that concealed the secret of his life. "I won't trouble you any more now. I am much obliged for your kindness in coming round."

"Not at all, not at all, Mr. Gray. Ever ready to do anything for you, sir." And Mr. Ashton tramped down-stairs, followed by the assistant, who glanced back at Dorian with a look of shy wonder in his rough, uncomely face. He had never seen any one so marvellous.

When the sound of their footsteps had died away, Dorian locked the door, and put the key in his pocket. He felt safe now. No one would ever look on the horrible thing. No eye but his would ever see his shame.

On reaching the library he found that it was just after five o'clock, and that the tea had been already brought up. On a little table of dark perfumed wood thickly incrusted with nacre[1], a present from his guardian's wife, Lady Radley, who had spent the preceding winter in Cairo, was lying a note from Lord Henry, and beside it was a book bound in yellow paper, the cover slightly torn and the edges soiled[2]. A copy of

---

[1] Mother of pearl

[2] Colors were tremendously important symbols to the aesthetically-obsessed Decadents, and yellow was their personal badge: it stood for everything debauched and forbidden about life – everything that they wanted to sample and gorge. Deeply associated with the Decadence movement, the color yellow was first connected to themes of corruption and impropriety several decades earlier when the fops of Jane Austen's Regency period wore the garish color to suggest their appetites for the indulgent, grotesque, and shocking. Later in the century, French books banned in England for their lewd content were at first discreetly packaged in yellow jackets, but when the code was figured out, booksellers even went so far as to wrap relatively tame publications in the lurid amber color because it would increase sales amongst eager buyers. Yellow became a symbol for all that was diseased in the soul, all that was unconventional, contrarian, rebellious, and decadent. If something was "Yellow," it was gaudy, luscious, vulgar, decayed, infamous, scandalous, poisonous, sensual, leprous, golden, lurid, bawdy, ghastly, seductive, corruptive, grotesque, fantastic, alien, fabulous, alluring, shocking, fascinating, ribald, repulsive, and repellent.ing the late 19th century, scandalous French novels were traditionally jacketed in yellow paperbacks

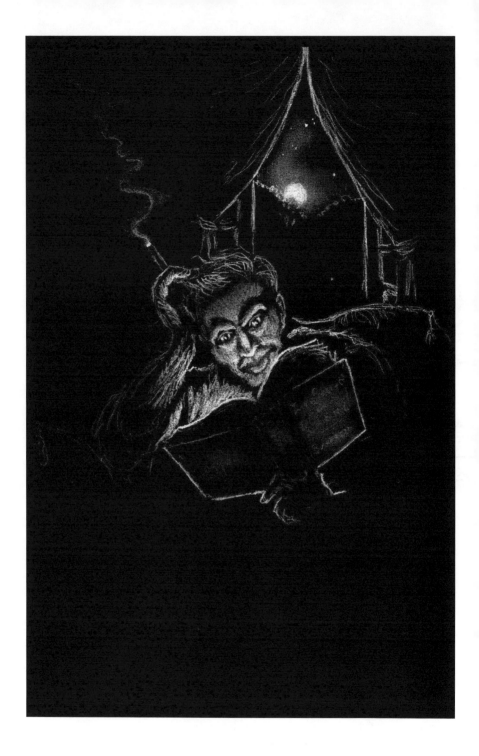

the third edition of the *St. James's Gazette*[1] had been placed on the tea-tray. It was evident that Victor had returned. He wondered if he had met the men in the hall as they were leaving the house and had wormed out of them what they had been doing. He would be sure to miss the picture,– had no doubt missed it already, while he had been laying the tea-things. The screen had not been replaced, and the blank space on the wall was visible. Perhaps some night he might find him creeping up-stairs and trying to force the door of the room. It was a horrible thing to have a spy in one's house. He had heard of rich men who had been blackmailed all their lives by some servant who had read a letter, or overheard a conversation, or picked up a card with an address, or found beneath a pillow a withered flower or a bit of crumpled lace.

He sighed, and, having poured himself out some tea, opened Lord Henry's note. It was simply to say that he sent him round the evening paper, and a book that might interest him, and that he would be at the club at eight-fifteen. He opened the St. James's languidly, and looked through it. A red pencil-mark on the fifth page caught his eye. He read the following paragraph:

INQUEST ON AN ACTRESS
An inquest was held this morning at the Bell Tavern, Hoxton Road, by Mr. Danby, the District Coroner, on the body of Sibyl Vane, a young actress recently engaged at the Royal Theatre, Holborn. A verdict of death by misadventure was returned. Considerable sympathy was expressed for the mother of the deceased, who was greatly affected during the giving of her own evidence, and that of Dr. Birrell, who had made the post-mortem examination of the deceased.

He frowned slightly, and, tearing the paper in two, went across the room and flung the pieces into a gilt basket. How ugly it all was! And how horribly real ugliness made things! He felt a little annoyed with Lord Henry for having sent him the account. And it was certainly stupid of him to have marked it with red pencil. Victor might have read it. The man knew more than enough English for that.

Perhaps he had read it, and had begun to suspect something. And, yet, what did it matter? What had Dorian Gray to do with Sibyl Vane's death? There was nothing to fear. Dorian Gray had not killed her.

His eye fell on the yellow book that Lord Henry had sent him. What was it, he wondered. He went towards the little pearl-colored octagonal stand, that had always looked to him like the work of some

---

[1] A conservative-learning intellectual and literary journal

strange Egyptian bees[1] who wrought in silver, and took the volume up. [*"Le Secret de Raoul, par Catulle Sarrazin." What a curious title![2]*] He flung himself into an arm-chair, and began to turn over the leaves. After a few minutes, he became absorbed. It was the strangest book he had ever read. It seemed to him that in exquisite raiment, and to the delicate sound of flutes, the sins of the world were passing in dumb show before him. Things that he had dimly dreamed of were suddenly made real to him. Things of which he had never dreamed were gradually revealed.

It was a novel without a plot, and with only one character, being, indeed, simply a psychological study of a certain young Parisian, who spent his life trying to realize in the nineteenth century all the passions and modes of thought that belonged to every century except his own, and to sum up, as it were, in himself the various moods through which the world-spirit had ever passed, loving for their mere artificiality those renunciations that men have unwisely called virtue, as much as those natural rebellions that wise men still call sin. The style in which it was written was that curious jewelled style, vivid and obscure at once, full of argot and of archaisms[3], of technical expressions and of elaborate paraphrases, that characterizes the work of some of the finest artists of the French school of Décadents[4]. There were in it metaphors as

---

[1] Bees again return as the symbol of temptation and eroticism

[2] This fictional French decadent author's name is a portmanteau of two real-life ones: Catulle Mendes and Gabriel Sarrazin. The name Raoul – which was edited out of the various later editions (likely to avoid putting a name to a character who is so ignominious, and to avoid public concern that a "cult of Raoul" might spring up amongst rebellious young men) is a reference to a character in another decadent, French novel, "Monsieur Venus." This scandalous erotica by the mononymous female writer Rachilde follows a female crossdresser named Raoule, who enters into a sexual relationship with a girlish young man who becomes her "mistress." Another oft-cited modelled – alluded to by Wilde at his trial and found on his person during his arrest – is the yellow-jacketed "Against Nature," a decadent novel by Joris-Karl Huysmans, which tells of a bored, bourgeois youth who rebels against the dullness of the 19th century by acquiring a house in the country and filling it with lavish collections (compare to all of Chapter IX) of art, antiques, literature, perfumes, poisonous flowers, gems, and exotic animals

[3] Argot: slang belonging to a particular class; archaisms: language with an obviously old-fashioned or antiquated flavor

[4] A school of French writers – Huysmans, Gautier, Baudelaire, Rimbaud, Mendes, de L'Isle Adam, and Verlaine being among the most famous – who were renowned for their eroticism, aesthetic indulgence, macabre themes, and anti-bourgeois elitism. Heavily influenced by writers like Poe, Hoffmann, and Gothic

monstrous as orchids, and as evil in color. The life of the senses was described in the terms of mystical philosophy. One hardly knew at times whether one was reading the spiritual ecstasies of some mediaeval saint or the morbid confessions of a modern sinner. It was a poisonous book. The heavy odor of incense seemed to cling about its pages and to trouble the brain. The mere cadence of the sentences, the subtle monotony of their music, so full as it was of complex refrains and movements elaborately repeated, produced in the mind of the lad, as he passed from chapter to chapter, a form of revery, a malady of dreaming, that made him unconscious of the falling day and the creeping shadows[1].

Cloudless, and pierced by one solitary star, a copper-green sky gleamed through the windows. He read on by its wan light till he could read no more. Then, after his valet had reminded him several times of the lateness of the hour, he got up, and, going into the next room, placed the book on the little Florentine table that always stood at his bedside, and began to dress for dinner.

It was almost nine o'clock before he reached the club, where he found Lord Henry sitting alone, in the morning-room, looking very bored.

"I am so sorry, Harry," he cried, "but really it is entirely your fault. That book you sent me so fascinated me that I forgot what the time was."

"I thought you would like it," replied his host, rising from his chair.

"I didn't say I liked it, Harry. I said it fascinated me. There is a great difference."

"Ah, if you have discovered that, you have discovered a great deal," murmured Lord Henry, with his curious smile. "Come, let us go in to dinner. It is dreadfully late, and I am afraid the champagne will be too much iced."

---

novelists, the Decadents celebrated sexual expression, drug-use, exoticism, moral and spiritual decay, fatalism, and hedonism. Their works were often luxurious but sinister, indulgent but gloomy, and manic but hopeless

[1] Wilde implies that the reason the book is so "poisonous" is because of its emphasis on materialism, moral relativism, and hedonism: it casts a doubt on reality, on the impact of choices, on the consequences of behaviors and on the passage of time. It further influences Dorian's self-obsession and darkens his ethical self-perspective

CHAPTER IX

FOR years, Dorian Gray could not free himself from the memory of this book. Or perhaps it would be more accurate to say that he never sought to free himself from it. He procured from Paris no less than five large-paper copies of the first edition, and had them bound in different colors[1], so that they might suit his various moods and the changing fancies of a nature over which he seemed, at times, to have almost entirely lost control. [Raoul], the wonderful young Parisian, in whom the romantic temperament and the scientific temperament were so strangely blended, became to him a kind of prefiguring type of himself. And, indeed, the whole book seemed to him to contain the story of his own life, written before he had lived it.

In one point he was more fortunate than [Catulle Sarrazin's] fantastic hero. He never knew–never, indeed, had any cause to know–that somewhat grotesque dread of mirrors, and polished metal surfaces, and still water, which came upon [Raoul] so early in his life[2], and was occasioned by the sudden decay of a beauty that had once, apparently, been so remarkable. It was with an almost cruel joy–and perhaps in nearly every joy, as certainly in every pleasure, cruelty has its place–that he used to read the latter part of the book, with its really tragic, if somewhat over-emphasized, account of the sorrow and despair of one who had himself lost what in others, and in the world, he had most valued.

He, at any rate, had no cause to fear that. The boyish beauty that had so fascinated Basil Hallward, and many others besides him, seemed never to leave him. Even those who had heard the most evil things against him (and from time to time strange rumors about his mode of life crept through London and became the chatter of the clubs) could not believe anything to his dishonor when they saw him. He had always the look of one who had kept himself unspotted from the world. Men who talked grossly became silent when Dorian Gray entered the room. There was something in the purity of his face that rebuked them. His mere presence seemed to recall to them the innocence that they had tarnished. They wondered how one so charming and graceful as he was could have escaped the stain of an age that was at once sordid and sensuous.

---

[1] This recalls the multi-colored rooms in Poe's "Masque of the Red Death," which was, in turn, heavily influential to French Decadents

[2] A perversion of the Narcissus myth: instead of being entranced by his own image, he is pathologically repulsed by it

He himself, on returning home from one of those mysterious and prolonged absences that gave rise to such strange conjecture among those who were his friends, or thought that they were so, would creep up-stairs to the locked room, open the door with the key that never left him, and stand, with a mirror, in front of the portrait that Basil Hallward had painted of him, looking now at the evil and aging face on the canvas, and now at the fair young face that laughed back at him from the polished glass. The very sharpness of the contrast used to quicken his sense of pleasure. He grew more and more enamoured of his own beauty, more and more interested in the corruption of his own soul. He would examine with minute care, and often with a monstrous and terrible delight, the hideous lines that seared the wrinkling forehead or crawled around the heavy sensual mouth, wondering sometimes which were the more horrible, the signs of sin or the signs of age. He would place his white hands beside the coarse bloated hands of the picture, and smile. He mocked the misshapen body and the failing limbs.

There were moments, indeed, at night, when, lying sleepless in his own delicately-scented chamber, or in the sordid room of the little ill-famed tavern near the Docks, which, under an assumed name, and in disguise, it was his habit to frequent, he would think of the ruin he had brought upon his soul, with a pity that was all the more poignant because it was purely selfish. But moments such as these were rare. That curiosity about life that, many years before, Lord Henry had first stirred in him, as they sat together in the garden of their friend, seemed to increase with gratification. The more he knew, the more he desired to know. He had mad hungers that grew more ravenous as he fed them.

Yet he was not really reckless, at any rate in his relations to society. Once or twice every month during the winter, and on each Wednesday evening while the season lasted, he would throw open to the world his beautiful house and have the most celebrated musicians of the day to charm his guests with the wonders of their art. His little dinners, in the settling of which Lord Henry always assisted him, were noted as much for the careful selection and placing of those invited, as for the exquisite taste shown in the decoration of the table, with its subtle symphonic arrangements of exotic flowers, and embroidered cloths, and antique plate of gold and silver. Indeed, there were many, especially among the very young men, who saw, or fancied that they saw, in Dorian Gray the true realization of a type of which they had often dreamed in Eton or Oxford days, a type that was to combine something of the real culture of the scholar with all the grace and distinction and perfect manner of a citizen of the world. To them he seemed to belong to those whom Dante describes as having sought to "make themselves perfect by the worship of beauty." Like Gautier, he was one for whom "the visible world existed."

And, certainly, to him life itself was the first, the greatest, of the arts, and for it all the other arts seemed to be but a preparation. Fashion, by which what is really fantastic becomes for a moment universal, and Dandyism[1], which, in its own way, is an attempt to assert the absolute modernity of beauty, had, of course, their fascination for him. His mode of dressing, and the particular styles that he affected from time to time, had their marked influence on the young exquisites of the Mayfair balls and Pall Mall club[2] windows, who copied him in everything that he did, and tried to reproduce the accidental charm of his graceful, though to him only half-serious, fopperies.

For, while he was but too ready to accept the position that was almost immediately offered to him on his coming of age, and found, indeed, a subtle pleasure in the thought that he might really become to the London of his own day what to imperial Neronian Rome the author of the "Satyricon" had once been[3], yet in his inmost heart he desired to be something more than a mere *arbiter elegantiarum*[4], to be consulted on the wearing of a jewel, or the knotting of a necktie, or the conduct of a cane. He sought to elaborate some new scheme of life that would have its reasoned philosophy and its ordered principles and find in the spiritualizing of the senses its highest realization.

The worship of the senses has often, and with much justice, been decried, men feeling a natural instinct of terror about passions and sensations that seem stronger than ourselves, and that we are conscious of sharing with the less highly organized forms of existence[5]. But it appeared to Dorian Gray that the true nature of the senses had never been understood, and that they had remained savage and animal merely because the world had sought to starve them into submission or to kill them by pain, instead of aiming at making them elements of a new spirituality, of which a fine instinct for beauty was to be the dominant

---

[1] Men obsessed with fashion and known for their flamboyant, colorful, and indulgent taste in clothes

[2] Two of the most elite neighborhoods in London

[3] Gaius Arbiter was a Roman novelist whose "Satyricon" was a fictionalized account of the wild debaucheries and moral indulgences of Nero's Rome

[4] "Judge of excellence" – a social influencer

[5] This is essentially the thesis of the Decadents: that indulgence of the senses is both exhilarating and terrifying – necessary to feel alive but ultimately doomed to disappoint those who survive the experience

characteristic[1]. As he looked back upon man moving through History, he was haunted by a feeling of loss. So much had been surrendered! and to such little purpose! There had been mad wilful rejections, monstrous forms of self-torture and self- denial, whose origin was fear, and whose result was a degradation infinitely more terrible than that fancied degradation from which, in their ignorance, they had sought to escape, Nature in her wonderful irony driving the anchorite[2] out to herd with the wild animals of the desert and giving to the hermit the beasts of the field as his companions.

Yes, there was to be, as Lord Henry had prophesied, a new hedonism that was to re-create life, and to save it from that harsh, uncomely puritanism that is having, in our own day, its curious revival. It was to have its service of the intellect, certainly; yet it was never to accept any theory or system that would involve the sacrifice of any mode of passionate experience. Its aim, indeed, was to be experience itself, and not the fruits of experience, sweet or bitter as they might be. Of the asceticism that deadens the senses, as of the vulgar profligacy that dulls them, it was to know nothing. But it was to teach man to concentrate himself upon the moments of a life that is itself but a moment.

There are few of us[3] who have not sometimes wakened before dawn, either after one of those dreamless nights that make one almost enamoured of death, or one of those nights of horror and misshapen joy, when through the chambers of the brain sweep phantoms more terrible than reality itself, and instinct[4] with that vivid life that lurks in all grotesques, and that lends to Gothic art its enduring vitality, this art being, one might fancy, especially the art of those whose minds have been troubled with the malady of revery. Gradually white fingers creep through the curtains, and they appear to tremble. Black fantastic shadows crawl into the corners of the room, and crouch there. Outside, there is the stirring of birds among the leaves, or the sound of men going forth to their work, or the sigh and sob of the wind coming down from the hills, and

---

[1] This is almost precisely the opposite of what Henry Jekyll strived for in Robert Louis Stevenson's own doppelganger masterpiece. Both men believe that evil can be tamed, but through different methods: Dorian seeks to integrate and tame it, whereas Jekyll seeks to isolate and cage it (although, admittedly, Jekyll's approach is self-deceptive: since he still prowls the streets at night as Hyde, he is trying to have it both ways)

[2] Hermit

[3] Wilde reaches out of the text with the plural pronoun to identify both himself and the reader with Dorian's corruption: this isn't the folly of one person, he reminds us – all of us have been a Dorian at some point

[4] Meaning endowed, infected, armed, imbued, or empowered with

wandering round the silent house, as though it feared to wake the sleepers. Veil after veil of thin dusky gauze is lifted, and by degrees the forms and colors of things are restored to them, and we watch the dawn remaking the world in its antique pattern. The wan mirrors get back their mimic life. The flameless tapers stand where we have left them, and beside them lies the half-read book that we had been studying, or the wired flower that we had worn at the ball, or the letter that we had been afraid to read, or that we had read too often. Nothing seems to us changed. Out of the unreal shadows of the night comes back the real life that we had known. We have to resume it where we had left off, and there steals over us a terrible sense of the necessity for the continuance of energy in the same wearisome round of stereotyped habits, or a wild longing, it may be, that our eyelids might open some morning upon a world that had been re-fashioned anew for our pleasure in the darkness, a world in which things would have fresh shapes and colors, and be changed, or have other secrets, a world in which the past would have little or no place, or survive, at any rate, in no conscious form of obligation or regret, the remembrance even of joy having its bitterness, and the memories of pleasure their pain.

It was the creation of such worlds as these that seemed to Dorian Gray to be the true object, or among the true objects, of life; and in his search for sensations that would be at once new and delightful, and possess that element of strangeness that is so essential to romance, he would often adopt certain modes of thought that he knew to be really alien to his nature, abandon himself to their subtle influences, and then, having, as it were, caught their color and satisfied his intellectual curiosity, leave them with that curious indifference that is not incompatible with a real ardor of temperament, and that indeed, according to certain modern psychologists, is often a condition of it[1].

It was rumored of him once that he was about to join the Roman Catholic communion[2]; and certainly the Roman ritual had always a great attraction for him. The daily sacrifice, more awful really than all the sacrifices of the antique world, stirred him as much by its superb rejection of the evidence of the senses as by the primitive simplicity of its elements

---

[1] Some Victorian psychologists argued that feelings were just jets of energy flaring-up from an apathetic state whenever the status quo was challenged: we only feel emotions when our central personality is disturbed

[2] John Gray, the rumored model for Dorian, was a hedonistic homosexual who originally loved his association with the novel (one time signing a letter to Wilde "Your Dorian"), but eventually grew to despise it. He became a devout Catholic and eventually became a priest. Wilde, too, became obsessed with Catholicism in his final days, and was given Last Rites on his deathbed

and the eternal pathos of the human tragedy that it sought to symbolize. He loved to kneel down on the cold marble pavement, and with the priest, in his stiff flowered cope[1], slowly and with white hands moving aside the veil of the tabernacle, and raising aloft the jewelled lantern-shaped monstrance[2] with that pallid wafer that at times, one would fain think, is indeed the "panis caelestis[3]," the bread of angels, or, robed in the garments of the Passion of Christ, breaking the Host into the chalice[4], and smiting his breast for his sins. The fuming censers[5], that the grave boys, in their lace and scarlet, tossed into the air like great gilt flowers, had their subtle fascination for him. As he passed out, he used to look with wonder at the black confessionals, and long to sit in the dim shadow of one of them and listen to men and women whispering through the tarnished grating[6] the true story of their lives.

But he never fell into the error of arresting his intellectual development by any formal acceptance of creed or system, or of mistaking, for a house in which to live, an inn that is but suitable for the sojourn of a night, or for a few hours of a night in which there are no stars and the moon is in travail. Mysticism, with its marvellous power of making common things strange to us, and the subtle antinomianism[7] that always seems to accompany it, moved him for a season; and for a season he inclined to the materialistic doctrines of the Darwinismus[8] movement in Germany, and found a curious pleasure in tracing the thoughts and passions of men to some pearly cell in the brain, or some white nerve in the body, delighting in the conception of the absolute dependence of the spirit on certain physical conditions, morbid or healthy, normal or diseased. Yet, as has been said of him before, no theory of life seemed to him to be of any importance compared with life itself. He felt keenly

---

[1] A religious garment

[2] A glass lens surrounded in gold and jewelry which is lifted up on a pole and used to symbolize the eye of God

[3] "Bread of heaven"

[4] During communion, Christians eat the bread and drink the wine in remembrance of the Last Supper. It is one of only a few holy rites which are universally recognized by nearly all mainstream Christian denominations, and is intended to be a moment of reflection, confession, and forgiveness

[5] Orbs held by chains and filled with slow-burning spices and resins, which are swung back and forth to fill the air with the aroma

[6] That is, in the confessional

[7] A theological perspective that rejects the need to pursue good behavior in order to find salvation, releasing Christians from the Ten Commandments

[8] A racist and eugenic movement that used Social Darwinism to argue for the superiority of the Nordic race

conscious of how barren all intellectual speculation is when separated from action and experiment. He knew that the senses, no less than the soul, have their mysteries to reveal.

And so he would now study perfumes, and the secrets of their manufacture, distilling heavily-scented oils, and burning odorous gums from the East. He saw that there was no mood of the mind that had not its counterpart in the sensuous life, and set himself to discover their true relations, wondering what there was in frankincense[1] that made one mystical, and in ambergris[2] that stirred one's passions, and in violets that woke the memory of dead romances, and in musk that troubled the brain, and in champak[3] that stained the imagination; and seeking often to elaborate a real psychology of perfumes, and to estimate the several influences of sweet-smelling roots, and scented pollen-laden flowers, of aromatic balms, and of dark and fragrant woods, of spikenard that sickens, of hovenia[4] that makes men mad, and of aloes that are said to be able to expel melancholy from the soul.

At another time he devoted himself entirely to music, and in a long latticed room, with a vermilion-and-gold ceiling and walls of olive-green lacquer, he used to give curious concerts in which mad gypsies tore wild music from little zithers[5], or grave yellow-shawled Tunisians plucked at the strained strings of monstrous lutes, while grinning negroes beat monotonously upon copper drums, or turbaned Indians, crouching upon scarlet mats, blew through long pipes of reed or brass, and charmed, or feigned to charm, great hooded snakes and horrible horned adders. The harsh intervals and shrill discords of barbaric music stirred him at times when Schubert's grace, and Chopin's beautiful sorrows, and the mighty harmonies of Beethoven himself, fell unheeded on his ear. He collected together from all parts of the world the strangest instruments that could be found, either in the tombs of dead nations or among the few savage tribes that have survived contact with Western civilizations, and loved to touch and try them. He had the mysterious *juruparis* of the Rio Negro

---

[1] A tree resin known for its sweet odor when burnt or distilled, often used in religious ceremonies, and remembered best for being one of the gifts given to the infant Jesus by the Magi
[2] A very valuable, waxy excretion from sperm whale intestines which has long been used in the production of musky perfumes and colognes
[3] An Asian evergreen considered holy by Buddhists
[4] A Japanese tree whose raisins are used to treat hangovers
[5] Plucked stringed instruments associated with Southern Europe and the Near East

Indians[1], that women are not allowed to look at, and that even youths may not see till they have been subjected to fasting and scourging, and the earthen jars of the Peruvians that have the shrill cries of birds, and flutes of human bones such as Alfonso de Ovalle[2] heard in Chili, and the sonorous green stones that are found near Cuzco[3] and give forth a note of singular sweetness. He had painted gourds filled with pebbles that rattled when they were shaken; the long clarin of the Mexicans, into which the performer does not blow, but through which he inhales the air; the harsh turé of the Amazon tribes, that is sounded by the sentinels who sit all day long in trees, and that can be heard, it is said, at a distance of three leagues; the teponaztli, that has two vibrating tongues of wood, and is beaten with sticks that are smeared with an elastic gum obtained from the milky juice of plants; the yotl-bells of the Aztecs, that are hung in clusters like grapes; and a huge cylindrical drum, covered with the skins of great serpents, like the one that Bernal Diaz saw when he went with Cortes into the Mexican temple[4], and of whose doleful sound he has left us so vivid a description. The fantastic character of these instruments fascinated him, and he felt a curious delight in the thought that Art, like Nature, has her monsters, things of bestial shape and with hideous voices. Yet, after some time, he wearied of them, and would sit in his box at the Opera, either alone or with Lord Henry, listening in rapt pleasure to "Tannhäuser[5]," and seeing in that great work of art a presentation of the tragedy of his own soul.

---

[1] The Rio Negro is a river in the Amazon Basin. The tribe there uses the juruparis, a sacred horn-like instrument, in its ceremonies, and hold it in such high regard that men are only allowed to see it after extensive repentance and self-flagellation, and any woman who sees it is put to death

[2] A 17th century Peruvian priest who recorded his encounters with the South American natives

[3] A city in southeastern Peru

[4] Diaz was a Spanish conquistador who traveled with Cortez to Mexico and recorded it in his history of the Conquest

[5] One of Wagner's greatest operas. Fittingly, the plot is about a man torn between sensuality (represented by the Goddess Venus, whom he had once been devoted to) and righteousness (represented by his fiancée Elisabeth, who prays for his soul). Tannhauser explores the lusts, desires, and indulgences of the world, but ultimately – out of love for Elisabeth – begs the pope to accept his repentance. Unimpressed, the pope sends him away claiming that his holy staff is likelier to bloom leaves than for God to forgive Tannhauser's debaucheries. Heartbroken, he returns home and finds that Elisabeth has died of grief and is being carried to her tomb. At this point Venus returns and calls to him, but he throws himself on Elisabeth's corpse, begs her to pray for his soul, and dies. At

On another occasion he took up the study of jewels, and appeared at a costume ball as Anne de Joyeuse[1], Admiral of France, in a dress covered with five hundred and sixty pearls. He would often spend a whole day settling and resetting in their cases the various stones that he had collected, such as the olive-green chrysoberyl that turns red by lamplight, the cymophane with its wire-like line of silver, the pistachio-colored peridot, rose-pink and wine-yellow topazes, carbuncles of fiery scarlet with tremulous four-rayed stars, flame- red cinnamon-stones, orange and violet spinels, and amethysts with their alternate layers of ruby and sapphire. He loved the red gold of the sunstone, and the moonstone's pearly whiteness, and the broken rainbow of the milky opal. He procured from Amsterdam three emeralds of extraordinary size and richness of color, and had a turquoise de la vieille roche that was the envy of all the connoisseurs.

He discovered wonderful stories, also, about jewels. In Alphonso's "Clericalis Disciplina[2]" a serpent was mentioned with eyes of real jacinth, and in the romantic history of Alexander he was said to have found snakes in the vale of Jordan "with collars of real emeralds growing on their backs." There was a gem in the brain of the dragon, Philostratus told us, and "by the exhibition of golden letters and a scarlet robe" the monster could be thrown into a magical sleep, and slain. According to the great alchemist Pierre de Boniface[3], the diamond rendered a man invisible, and the agate of India made him eloquent. The cornelian appeased anger, and the hyacinth provoked sleep, and the amethyst drove away the fumes of wine. The garnet cast out demons, and the hydropicus deprived the moon of her color. The selenite waxed and waned with the moon, and the meloceus, that discovers thieves, could be affected only by the blood of kids. Leonardus Camillus[4] had seen a white stone taken from the brain of a newly-killed toad, that was a certain antidote against poison. The bezoar, that was found in the heart of the Arabian deer, was a charm that could cure the plague. In the nests of Arabian birds was the aspilates, that, according to Democritus[5], kept the wearer from any danger by fire.

---

this point a group of pilgrims arrive bearing the pope's staff, which has blossomed with life

[1] A 16th century French nobleman best remembered for massacring French protestants during the Wars of Religion

[2] Dating to the early 12th century, this anthology compiled by the Spanish polymath Petrus Alphonso, is one the oldest collections of European fables and folktales

[3] A 14th century scientist known for his alchemical theories on precious stones

[4] A 16th century, Italian astronomer and mineralogist

[5] An Ancient Greek philosopher and proto-physicist

The King of Ceilan[1] rode through his city with a large ruby in his hand, as the ceremony of his coronation. The gates of the palace of John the Priest[2] were "made of sardius, with the horn of the horned snake inwrought, so that no man might bring poison within." Over the gable were "two golden apples, in which were two carbuncles," so that the gold might shine by day, and the carbuncles by night. In Lodge's strange romance "A Margarite of America[3]" it was stated that in the chamber of Margarite were seen "all the chaste ladies of the world, inchased out of silver, looking through fair mirrours of chrysolites, carbuncles, sapphires, and greene emeraults." Marco Polo had watched the inhabitants of Zipangu[4] place a rose-colored pearl in the mouth of the dead. A sea-monster had been enamoured of the pearl that the diver brought to King Perozes[5], and had slain the thief, and mourned for seven moons over his loss. When the Huns lured the king into the great pit, he flung it away,– Procopius[6] tells the story,–nor was it ever found again, though the Emperor Anastasius[7] offered five hundred-weight of gold pieces for it. The King of Malabar[8] had shown a Venetian a rosary of one hundred and four pearls, one for every god that he worshipped. [*It was a pearl that Julius Caesar had given to Servilia[9], when he loved her. Their young child had been Brutus.*]

[*The young priest of the Sun[10], who while yet a boy, had been slain for his sins liked to walk in jeweled shoes on dust of gold and silver.*] When the Duke de Valentinois, son of Alexander VI[11]., visited Louis XII. of France, his horse was loaded with gold leaves, according to Brantôme, and his cap had double rows of rubies that threw out a great light. Charles of

---

1 Ceylon

2 Prester John was a mythical Christian ruler in the Orient

3 A novel written by the English physician Thomas Lodge

4 Another name for Japan

5 Peroz I was a 5th century king of Iran

6 A 6th century Byzantine scholar

7 A 5th century Byzantine emperor

8 A region of India's southeast coast

9 Julius Caesar's mistress – a married woman – by whom he sired Marcus Junius Brutus, who would famously lead his assassination

10 Another reference to the emperor Elagabalus, who was assassinated at the age of 18 after a wildly indulgent reign whereby he developed a cult of personality

11 That is, Cesare Borgia, bastard son of Pope Alexander Vi, widely remembered for his violence, murders, vengefulness, and rumored incest with his sister Lucrezia

England[1] had ridden in stirrups hung with three hundred and twenty-one diamonds. Richard II. had a coat, valued at thirty thousand marks, which was covered with balas rubies. Hall described Henry VIII., on his way to the Tower previous to his coronation, as wearing "a jacket of raised gold, the placard embroidered with diamonds and other rich stones, and a great bauderike about his neck of large balasses." The favorites of James I. wore ear-rings of emeralds set in gold filigrane. Edward II. gave to Piers Gaveston a suit of red-gold armor studded with jacinths, and a collar of gold roses set with turquoise-stones, and a skull-cap parsemé[2] with pearls. Henry II. wore jewelled gloves reaching to the elbow, and had a hawk-glove set with twelve rubies and fifty-two great pearls. The ducal hat of Charles the Rash[3], the last Duke of Burgundy of his race, was studded with sapphires and hung with pear- shaped pearls.

How exquisite life had once been! How gorgeous in its pomp and decoration! Even to read of the luxury of the dead was wonderful.

Then he turned his attention to embroideries, and to the tapestries that performed the office of frescos in the chill rooms of the Northern nations of Europe. As he investigated the subject,–and he always had an extraordinary faculty of becoming absolutely absorbed for the moment in whatever he took up,–he was almost saddened by the reflection of the ruin that time brought on beautiful and wonderful things. He, at any rate, had escaped that. Summer followed summer, and the yellow jonquils bloomed and died many times, and nights of horror repeated the story of their shame, but he was unchanged. No winter marred his face or stained his flower-like bloom. How different it was with material things! Where had they gone to? Where was the great crocus-colored robe, on which the gods fought against the giants, that had been worked for Athena? Where the huge velarium[4] that Nero had stretched across the Colosseum at Rome, on which were represented the starry sky, and Apollo driving a chariot drawn by white gilt-reined steeds? He longed to see the curious table-napkins wrought for Elagabalus[5], on which were displayed all the dainties and viands that could be wanted for a feast; the

---

[1] Charles I, Richard II, James I, Edward II, Henry II, and Henry VIII were all infamous for their decadence, scandals, self-indulgent luxuries, and sexual intrigues
[2] Sprinkled, spangled
[3] A 15th century French noble
[4] An awning which was stretched over the stands of the coliseum to provide shade
[5] One of Rome's many famous decadent emperors

mortuary cloth of King Chilperic[1], with its three hundred golden bees[2]; the fantastic robes that excited the indignation of the Bishop of Pontus, and were figured with "lions, panthers, bears, dogs, forests, rocks, hunters,–all, in fact, that a painter can copy from nature;" and the coat that Charles of Orleans[3] once wore, on the sleeves of which were embroidered the verses of a song beginning "Madame, je suis tout joyeux[4]," the musical accompaniment of the words being wrought in gold thread, and each note, a square shape in those days, formed with four pearls. He read of the room that was prepared at the palace at Rheims for the use of Queen Joan of Burgundy[5], and was decorated with "thirteen hundred and twenty-one parrots, made in broidery, and blazoned with the king's arms, and five hundred and sixty-one butterflies, whose wings were similarly ornamented with the arms of the queen, the whole worked in gold." Catherine de Médicis[6] had a mourning-bed made for her of black velvet powdered with crescents and suns. Its curtains were of damask, with leafy wreaths and garlands, figured upon a gold and silver ground, and fringed along the edges with broideries[7] of pearls, and it stood in a room hung with rows of the queen's devices in cut black velvet upon cloth of silver. Louis XIV. had gold-embroidered caryatides[8] fifteen feet high in his apartment. The state bed of Sobieski, King of Poland[9], was made of Smyrna gold brocade embroidered in turquoises with verses from the Koran. Its supports were of silver gilt, beautifully chased, and profusely set with enamelled and jewelled medallions. It had been taken from the Turkish camp before Vienna, and the standard of Mohammed had stood under it[10].

---

[1] King of Western France during the 6th century

[2] Bees again appear as a sign of moral decadence

[3] A 15th century French nobleman and poet

[4] "Madame, I am all joy"

[5] Called "Joan the Lame," she served as regent while her husband, the King of Burgandy was fighting in the Hundred Years' War, and was considered evil and depraved by her contemporaries

[6] 16th century Italian-born queen of France remembered for her luxurious life, political power, and role in the massacre of French Portestants

[7] Embroideries

[8] A column shaped like a woman dressed in Ancient Greek robes

[9] John III Sobieski was a 17th century King of Poland and Duke of Lithuania known for his military prowess

[10] The 1683 Battle of Vienna was the last great repulsion of Islamic invaders from Europe, with the Polish-German forces defeating the Ottoman army in a decisive rout

And so, for a whole year, he sought to accumulate the most exquisite specimens that he could find of textile and embroidered work, getting the dainty Delhi muslins, finely wrought, with gold-threat palmates, and stitched over with iridescent beetles' wings; the Dacca gauzes, that from their transparency are known in the East as "woven air," and "running water," and "evening dew;" strange figured cloths from Java; elaborate yellow Chinese hangings; books bound in tawny satins or fair blue silks and wrought with fleurs de lys[1], birds, and images; veils of lacis worked in Hungary point; Sicilian brocades, and stiff Spanish velvets; Georgian work with its gilt coins, and Japanese Foukousas[2] with their green-toned golds and their marvellously- plumaged birds.

He had a special passion, also, for ecclesiastical vestments[3], as indeed he had for everything connected with the service of the Church. In the long cedar chests that lined the west gallery of his house he had stored away many rare and beautiful specimens of what is really the raiment of the Bride of Christ[4], who must wear purple and jewels and fine linen that she may hide the pallid macerated body that is worn by the suffering that she seeks for, and wounded by self-inflicted pain. He had a gorgeous cope of crimson silk and gold-thread damask, figured with a repeating pattern of golden pomegranates set in six-petalled formal blossoms, beyond which on either side was the pine-apple device wrought in seed-pearls. The orphreys[5] were divided into panels representing scenes from the life of the Virgin, and the coronation of the Virgin was figured in colored silks upon the hood. This was Italian work of the fifteenth century. Another cope[6] was of green velvet, embroidered with heart- shaped groups of acanthus-leaves, from which spread long-stemmed white blossoms, the details of which were picked out with silver thread and colored crystals. The morse[7] bore a seraph's head in gold-thread raised work. The orphreys were woven in a diaper[8] of red and gold silk, and were starred with medallions of many saints and martyrs, among

---

[1] National symbol of France in the shape of an unfolding lily
[2] A richly colored and embroidered cloth used as gift wrapping in Japan
[3] Robes and other clothing worn by priests during Mass
[4] A woman on her way to take vows to be a nun
[5] A richly and painstakingly embroidered strip of fabric hung around a priest's neck like a loose scarf
[6] A long, loose cloak worn during Mass
[7] The jeweled clasp on a cloak
[8] Pattern of crisscrossing threads in a diamond shape

whom was St. Sebastian[1]. He had chasubles[2], also, of amber-colored silk, and blue silk and gold brocade, and yellow silk damask and cloth of gold, figured with representations of the Passion and Crucifixion of Christ, and embroidered with lions and peacocks and other emblems; dalmatics[3] of white satin and pink silk damask, decorated with tulips and dolphins and fleurs de lys; altar frontals of crimson velvet and blue linen; and many corporals, chalice-veils, and sudaria[4]. In the mystic offices to which these things were put there was something that quickened his imagination.

For these things, and everything that he collected in his lovely house, were to be to him means of forgetfulness, modes by which he could escape, for a season, from the fear that seemed to him at times to be almost too great to be borne. Upon the walls of the lonely locked room where he had spent so much of his boyhood, he had hung with his own hands the terrible portrait whose changing features showed him the real degradation of his life, and had draped the purple-and-gold pall in front of it as a curtain. For weeks he would not go there, would forget the hideous painted thing, and get back his light heart, his wonderful joyousness, his passionate pleasure in mere existence. Then, suddenly, [*one night*[5]] he would creep out of the house, go down to dreadful places near Blue Gate Fields[6], and stay there, day after day, [*till the people almost drove him out in horror, and had to be appeased by monstrous bribes*[7]]. On his return he would sit in front of the picture, sometimes loathing it and himself, but filled, at other times, with that pride of rebellion that is half the fascination of sin, and smiling, with secret pleasure, at the misshapen shadow that had to bear the burden that should have been his own.

---

[1] Often depicted bound to a tree in a loincloth and pierced by arrows, St. Sebastian's physical beauty, vulnerability, and penetration by phallic arrows made him a queer icon as early as the Renaissance, and he is often seen as a symbol of homoeroticism or as the de facto patron saint of the gay community

[2] A sleeveless garment worn over the priest's clothes during Mass

[3] A wide-sleeved version of the chasuble

[4] Frontal: decorative cloth for the front of an altar; corporal: a cloth on which the chalice and wafers are placed during communion; chalice veil: a cloth used to cover the communion elements before and after communion; sudarium: a cloth used to wipe any wine dripping down the chalice

[5] Changed to "some night" in the 1891 version to make it seem more speculative/hypothetical and less like a plan

[6] A neighborhood infamous for its opium dens, foreign sailors, prostitution, and human trafficking

[7] Changed to "until he was driven away" to make it seem more casual (as if he were annoying) than scandalous (as if he has been doing something truly depraved)

After a few years he could not endure to be long out of England, and gave up the villa that he had shared at Trouville[1] with Lord Henry, as well as the little white walled-in house at Algiers[2] where he had more than once spent his winter. He hated to be separated from the picture that was such a part of his life, and he was also afraid that during his absence some one might gain access to the room, in spite of the elaborate bolts and bars that he had caused to be placed upon the door.

He was quite conscious that this would tell them nothing. It was true that the portrait still preserved, under all the foulness and ugliness of the face, its marked likeness to himself; but what could they learn from that? He would laugh at any one who tried to taunt him. He had not painted it. What was it to him how vile and full of shame it looked? Even if he told them, would they believe it?

Yet he was afraid. Sometimes when he was down at his great house in Nottinghamshire[3], entertaining the fashionable young men of his own rank who were his chief companions, and astounding the county by the wanton luxury and gorgeous splendor of his mode of life, he would suddenly leave his guests and rush back to town to see that the door had not been tampered with and that the picture was still there. What if it should be stolen? The mere thought made him cold with horror. Surely the world would know his secret then. Perhaps the world already suspected it.

For, while he fascinated many, there were not a few who distrusted him. He was blackballed at a West End club of which his birth and social position fully entitled him to become a member, and on one occasion, when he was brought by a friend into the smoking-room of the Carlton[4], the Duke of Berwick and another gentleman got up in a marked manner and went out. Curious stories became current about him after he had passed his twenty-fifth year. It was said that he had been seen brawling with foreign sailors in a low den in the distant parts of Whitechapel, and that he consorted with thieves and coiners[5] and knew the mysteries of their trade. His extraordinary absences became notorious, and, when he used to reappear again in society, men [*who were jealous of the strange love that he inspired in women*] would whisper to each other in corners, or pass him with a sneer, or look at him with cold searching eyes, as if they were determined to discover his secret.

---

[1] An English Channel beach resort in Brittany, Northern France
[2] Capital of Algeria, located on the Mediterranean coast
[3] A lush, wooded county in the Midlands in Central England
[4] A Conservative social club
[5] Counterfeiters

Of such insolences and attempted slights he, of course, took no notice, and in the opinion of most people his frank debonair manner, his charming boyish smile, and the infinite grace of that wonderful youth that seemed never to leave him, were in themselves a sufficient answer to the calumnies[1] (for so they called them) that were circulated about him. It was remarked, however, that those who had been most intimate with him appeared, after a time, to shun him. Of all his friends, or so-called friends, Lord Henry Wotton was the only one who remained loyal to him, [*and in the eyes of some it was a question of whether that was an honour or a disgrace*]. Women who had wildly adored him, and for his sake had braved all social censure and set convention at defiance, were seen to grow pallid with shame or horror if Dorian Gray entered the room. [*It was said that even the sinful creatures who prowl the streets at night*[2] *had cursed him as he passed by, seeing in him a corruption greater than their own, and knowing but too well the horror of his real life.*]

Yet these whispered scandals only lent him, in the eyes of many, his strange and dangerous charm. His great wealth was a certain element of security. Society, civilized society at least, is never very ready to believe anything to the detriment of those who are both rich and charming. It feels instinctively that manners are of more importance than morals, and the highest respectability is of less value in its opinion than the possession of a good chef. And, after all, it is a very poor consolation to be told that the man who has given one a bad dinner, or poor wine, is irreproachable in his private life. Even the cardinal virtues cannot atone for cold entrées, as Lord Henry remarked once, in a discussion on the subject; and there is possibly a good deal to be said for his view. For the canons of good society are, or should be, the same as the canons of art. Form is absolutely essential to it. It should have the dignity of a ceremony, as well as its unreality, and should combine the insincere character of a romantic play with the wit and beauty that make such plays charming. Is insincerity such a terrible thing? I think not. It is merely a method by which we can multiply our personalities.

Such, at any rate, was Dorian Gray's opinion. He used to wonder at the shallow psychology of those who conceive the Ego in man as a thing simple, permanent, reliable, and of one essence. To him, man was a being with myriad lives and myriad sensations, a complex multiform creature that bore within itself strange legacies of thought and passion, and whose very flesh was tainted with the monstrous maladies of the dead. He loved

---

[1] Slanders
[2] Johns, drug addicts, and rapists

to stroll through the gaunt cold picture-gallery of his country-house[1] and look at the various portraits of those whose blood flowed in his veins. Here was Philip Herbert, described by Francis Osborne, in his "Memoires on the Reigns of Queen Elizabeth and King James," as one who was "caressed by the court for his handsome face, which kept him not long company[2]." Was it young Herbert's life that he sometimes led? Had some strange poisonous germ crept from body to body till it had reached his own? Was it some dim sense of that ruined grace that had made him so suddenly, and almost without cause, give utterance, in Basil Hallward's studio, to that mad prayer that had so changed his life? Here, in gold-embroidered red doublet, jewelled surcoat[3], and gilt- edged ruff and wrist-bands, stood Sir Anthony Sherard, with his silver-and-black armor piled at his feet. What had this man's legacy been? Had the lover of Giovanna of Naples[4] bequeathed him some inheritance of sin and shame? Were his own actions merely the dreams that the dead man had not dared to realize? Here, from the fading canvas, smiled Lady Elizabeth Devereux, in her gauze hood, pearl stomacher[5], and pink slashed sleeves. A flower was in her right hand, and her left clasped an enamelled collar of white and damask roses. On a table by her side lay a mandolin and an apple. There were large green rosettes upon her little pointed shoes. He knew her life, and the strange stories that were told about [*the death of those to whom she granted her favors[6]*]. Had he something of her temperament in him? Those oval heavy-lidded eyes seemed to look curiously at him. What

---

[1] Aristocrats typically had a townhouse in London which they occupied during the winter (when the air was cleaner, disease less rampant, and activities in doors) and a country estate which they occupied during the summer (when outdoors occupations and London's dirtiness sent them towards country air). Picture galleries were a staple in these houses: a long, strait, tall hallway usually covered in dark wainscoting, and festooned with portraits of the family ancestors

[2] King James I was rumored to be bisexual (Osborne's original quotation – paraphrased from "Historical Memoires on Elizabeth and King James" – is a reference to one of James' supposed lovers)

[3] A loose robe worn over armor

[4] Ruler of Naples during the late 14th century, rumored to have murdered her husband in order to bed her own cousin

[5] A V-shaped piece of decorative cloth, worn over the chest and stomach on a dress from the 16th to 18th centuries

[6] The suggestion of suicide and sexual "favors" was toned down from this phrase to the word "lovers." The implication is that she was so depraved that her lovers – after being inducted into her orgies – tended to commit suicide after experiencing her debauched sexual appetites

of George Willoughby, with his powdered hair and fantastic patches[1]? How evil he looked! The face was saturnine[2] and swarthy, and the sensual lips seemed to be twisted with disdain. Delicate lace ruffles fell over the lean yellow hands that were so overladen with rings. He had been a macaroni[3] of the eighteenth century, and the friend, in his youth, of Lord Ferrars[4]. What of the second Lord Sherard, the companion of the Prince Regent[5] in his wildest days, and one of the witnesses at the secret marriage with Mrs. Fitzherbert? How proud and handsome he was, with his chestnut curls and insolent pose! What passions had he bequeathed? The world had looked upon him as infamous. He had led the orgies at Carlton House[6]. The star of the Garter[7] glittered upon his breast. Beside him hung the portrait of his wife, a pallid, thin-lipped woman in black. Her blood, also, stirred within him. How curious it all seemed!

Yet one had ancestors in literature, as well as in one's own race, nearer perhaps in type and temperament, many of them, and certainly with an influence of which one was more absolutely conscious. There were times when it seemed to Dorian Gray that the whole of history was merely the record of his own life, not as he had lived it in act and circumstance, but as his imagination had created it for him, as it had been in his brain and in his passions. He felt that he had known them all, those strange terrible figures that had passed across the stage of the world and made sin so marvellous and evil so full of wonder. It seemed to him that in some mysterious way their lives had been his own.

[*Raoul, t*]he hero of the dangerous novel that had so influenced his life had himself had this curious fancy. In [*the fourth*] chapter of the book he tells how, crowned with laurel, lest lightning might strike him, he had sat, as Tiberius, in a garden at Capri, reading the shameful books of Elephantis, while dwarfs and peacocks strutted round him and the

---

[1] Beauty marks made of black silk and pasted to the skin to cover blemishes. They were often in the shape of hearts, moons, stars, wands, diamonds, arrowheads, and even small men and ladies

[2] Gloomy

[3] Gold braid and elaborate lace used to line hat brims and coat lapels, cuffs, and collars

[4] A notoriously wild aristocrat who was hanged with a silk noose in 1760 for murdering a servant

[5] George IV was renowned – during his tenure as Prince Regent – for his foppish fashions, mindless social life, and depraved appetite for wine, women, and song. He secretly married Maria Fitzherbert in an illegal wedding

[6] The Prince of Wales' London residence

[7] One of England's oldest heraldries, it is reserved for only 24 members of the British aristocracy, not counting the Prince of Wales and the King

flute-player mocked the swinger of the censer[1]; and, as Caligula, [*had drank the love-philter of Caesonia[2], and worn the habit of Venus by night, and by day a false gilded beard[3], and*] had caroused with the green-shirted jockeys in their stables, and supped in an ivory manger with a jewel-frontleted horse[4]; and, as Domitian, had wandered through a corridor lined with marble mirrors, looking round with haggard eyes for the reflection of the dagger that was to end his days, and sick with that ennui, that taedium vitae, that comes on those to whom life denies nothing[5]; and had peered through a clear emerald at the red shambles of the Circus, and then, in a litter of pearl and purple drawn by silver-shod mules, been carried through the Street of Pomegranates to a House of Gold, and heard men cry on Nero Caesar as he passed by[6]; and, as Elagabalus, had painted his face with colors, and plied the distaff among the women, and brought the Moon from Carthage, and given her in mystic marriage to the Sun[7].

Over and over again Dorian used to read this fantastic chapter, and the chapter immediately following, in which [*Raoul*] describes the curious tapestries that he had had woven for him from Gustave Moreau's[8] designs, and on which were pictured the awful and beautiful forms of those whom [*Lust[9]*] and Blood and Weariness had made monstrous or mad[10]: [*Here was Manfred, King of Apulia, who dressed always in green,*

---

[1] Roman emperor from 14 AD – 37 AD, known for his impiety and corruption

[2] A mythic love potion

[3] These references to date rape drugs and crossdressing were removed for obvious reasons

[4] Son of Tiberius, Caligula reigned from 37 AD – 41 AD and is remembered for being one of the most debauched emperors, notorious for his sexual depravity and inhumanity

[5] Reigning from 81 AD – 96 AD, Domitian was a totalitarian egomaniac who developed a cult of personality about his supposed deity

[6] Nero, most famous for his cruelty, persecution of Christians, and rumored apathy at Rome's destruction in a fire, reigned from 54 AD to 68 AD before committing suicide

[7] Emperor from 218 AD to 222 AD, he is remembered for his sexual depravity, disregard for Roman morals, homosexuality, and self-worship. He was assassinated at the age of 18

[8] A French symbolist painter who specialized in decadent and imaginative portrayals of biblical and mythological characters

[9] Changed to "Vice"

[10] What follows throughout this paragraph are a series of Italian personalities famed for their debaucheries during the Renaissance; the majority of these references are borrowed from John Addington Symonds' "The Renaissance in Italy: The Age of Despots." The Italian Renaissance – particularly under the reign

and consorted only with courtezans and buffoons.] Filippo, Duke of Milan, who slew his wife, and painted her lips with a scarlet poison [*that her guilty lover might suck death from the dead thing he fondled*]; Pietro Barbi, the Venetian, known as Paul the Second, who sought in his vanity to assume the title of Formosus, and whose tiara, valued at two hundred thousand florins, was bought at the price of a terrible sin; Gian Maria Visconti, who used hounds to chase living men, and whose murdered body was covered with roses by a harlot who had loved him; the Borgia on his white horse, with [*Incest and*] Fratricide riding beside him, and his mantle stained with the blood of Perotto; Pietro Riario, the young Cardinal Archbishop of Florence, child and minion of Sixtus IV., whose beauty was equalled only by his debauchery, and who received Leonora of Aragon in a pavilion of white and crimson silk, filled with nymphs and centaurs, and gilded a boy that he might serve her at the feast as Ganymede or Hylas; Ezzelin, whose melancholy could be cured only by the spectacle of death, and who had a passion for red blood, as other men have for red wine,–the son of the Fiend, as was reported, and one who had cheated his father at dice when gambling with him for his own soul; Giambattista Cibo, who in mockery took the name of Innocent, and into whose torpid veins the blood of three lads was infused by a Jewish doctor; Sigismondo Malatesta, the lover of Isotta, and the lord of Rimini, whose effigy was burned at Rome as the enemy of God and man, who strangled Polyssena with a napkin, and gave poison to Ginevra d'Este in a cup of emerald, and in honor of a shameful passion built a pagan church for Christian worship; Charles VI., who had so wildly adored his brother's wife that a leper had warned him of the insanity that was coming on him, and who could only be soothed by Saracen cards painted with the images of Love and Death and Madness; and, in his trimmed jerkin and jewelled cap and acanthus-like curls, Grifonetto Baglioni, who slew Astorre with his bride, and Simonetto with his page, and whose comeliness was such that, as he lay dying in the yellow piazza of Perugia, those who had hated him could not choose but weep, and Atalanta, who had cursed him, blessed him.

There was a horrible fascination in them all. He saw them at night, and they troubled his imagination in the day. The Renaissance knew of strange manners of poisoning,–poisoning by a helmet and a lighted torch, by an embroidered glove and a jewelled fan, by a gilded pomander and by an amber chain. Dorian Gray had been poisoned by a

---

of the Borgia popes – was renowned for its intrigue, assassinations, and imaginative approach to poisoning (as described in the chapter's final paragraph) book. There were moments when he looked on evil simply as a mode through which he could realize his conception of the beautiful.

CHAPTER X

IT was on the 7th of November, the eve of his own thirty- second birthday[1], as he often remembered afterwards.

He was walking home about eleven o'clock from Lord Henry's, where he had been dining, and was wrapped in heavy furs, as the night was cold and foggy. At the corner of Grosvenor Square and South Audley Street[2] a man passed him in the mist, walking very fast, and with the collar of his gray ulster[3] turned up. He had a bag in his hand. He recognized him. It was Basil Hallward. A strange sense of fear, for which he could not account, came over him. He made no sign of recognition, and went on slowly, in the direction of his own house.

But Hallward had seen him. Dorian heard him first stopping, and then hurrying after him. In a few moments his hand was on his arm.

"Dorian! What an extraordinary piece of luck! I have been waiting for you ever since nine o'clock in your library. Finally I took pity on your tired servant, and told him to go to bed, as he let me out. I am off to Paris by the midnight train, and I wanted particularly to see you before I left. I thought it was you, or rather your fur coat, as you passed me. But I wasn't quite sure. Didn't you recognize me?"

"In this fog, my dear Basil? Why, I can't even recognize Grosvenor Square. I believe my house is somewhere about here, but I don't feel at all certain about it. I am sorry you are going away, as I have not seen you for ages. But I suppose you will be back soon?"

"No: I am going to be out of England for six months. I intend to take a studio in Paris, and shut myself up till I have finished a great picture[4] I have in my head. However, it wasn't about myself I wanted to

---

[1] In later editions, Wilde would change Dorian's age to 38. Some commentators have noted that while Wilde may have experimented with homosexuality in his youth, it wasn't until the age of 32 that he took a regular male lover

[2] Part of London's elite Mayfair district

[3] A wool overcoat with a short cape covering the shoulders

[4] Basil paints what inspires his soul, which suggests that he has moved beyond his worship of Dorian's beauty and found something else to aspire towards. He doesn't say "portrait," however, so we may wonder whether this new inspiration

talk. Here we are at your door. Let me come in for a moment. I have something to say to you."

"I shall be charmed. But won't you miss your train?" said Dorian Gray, languidly, as he passed up the steps and opened the door with his latch-key.

The lamp-light struggled out through the fog, and Hallward looked at his watch. "I have heaps of time," he answered. "The train doesn't go till twelve-fifteen, and it is only just eleven. In fact, I was on my way to the club to look for you, when I met you. You see, I shan't have any delay about luggage, as I have sent on my heavy things. All I have with me is in this bag, and I can easily get to Victoria in twenty minutes."

Dorian looked at him and smiled. "What a way for a fashionable painter to travel! A Gladstone bag[1], and an ulster! Come in, or the fog will get into the house. And mind you don't talk about anything serious. Nothing is serious nowadays. At least nothing should be."

Hallward shook his head, as he entered, and followed Dorian into the library. There was a bright wood fire blazing in the large open hearth. The lamps were lit, and an open Dutch silver spirit-case[2] stood, with some siphons of soda-water and large cut-glass tumblers, on a little table.

"You see your servant made me quite at home, Dorian. He gave me everything I wanted, including your best cigarettes. He is a most hospitable creature. I like him much better than the Frenchman you used to have. What has become of the Frenchman, by the bye?"

Dorian shrugged his shoulders. "I believe he married Lady Ashton's maid, and has established her in Paris as an English dressmaker. *Anglomanie*[3] is very fashionable over there now, I hear. It seems silly of the French, doesn't it? But--do you know?--he was not at all a bad servant. I never liked him, but I had nothing to complain about. One often imagines things that are quite absurd. He was really very devoted to me, and seemed quite sorry when he went away. Have another brandy-and-soda? Or would you like hock-and-seltzer[4]? I always take hock-and-seltzer myself. There is sure to be some in the next room."

---

is another human idol or whether it is something nobler and more spiritual. His final minutes suggests that this might be the case

[1] A shapeless leather bag often associated with doctors

[2] A small carrier that contains two or three decanters. Resembling a six pack carrier, it allows you to see the decanters from the sides, but to access them, a panel on the front must be unlocked, allowing spirits to be displayed to all visitors, but keeping servants or children from sampling them

[3] Or "Anglo-Mania" – an obsession with all things British

[4] Hock is a dry, white wine from Germany's Rhineland

"Thanks, I won't have anything more," said Hallward, taking his cap and coat off, and throwing them on the bag that he had placed in the corner. "And now, my dear fellow, I want to speak to you seriously. Don't frown like that. You make it so much more difficult for me."

"What is it all about?" cried Dorian, in his petulant way, flinging himself down on the sofa. "I hope it is not about myself. I am tired of myself to-night. I should like to be somebody else."

"It is about yourself," answered Hallward, in his grave, deep voice, "and I must say it to you. I shall only keep you half an hour."

Dorian sighed, and lit a cigarette. "Half an hour!" he murmured.

"It is not much to ask of you, Dorian, and it is entirely for your own sake that I am speaking. I think it right that you should know that the most dreadful things are being said about you in London[,--*things that I could hardly repeat to you*]."

"I don't wish to know anything about them. I love scandals about other people, but scandals about myself don't interest me. They have not got the charm of novelty."

"They must interest you, Dorian. Every gentleman is interested in his good name. You don't want people to talk of you as something vile and degraded. Of course you have your position, and your wealth, and all that kind of thing. But position and wealth are not everything. Mind you, I don't believe these rumors at all. At least, I can't believe them when I see you. Sin is a thing that writes itself across a man's face. It cannot be concealed. People talk of secret vices. There are no such things as secret vices. If a wretched man has a vice, it shows itself in the lines of his mouth, the droop of his eyelids, the moulding of his hands even. Somebody-- I won't mention his name, but you know him--came to me last year to have his portrait done. I had never seen him before, and had never heard anything about him at the time, though I have heard a good deal since. He offered an extravagant price. I refused him. There was something in the shape of his fingers that I hated[1]. I know now that I was quite right in what I fancied about him. His life is dreadful. But you, Dorian, with your pure, bright, innocent face, and your marvellous untroubled youth,--I can't believe anything against you. And yet I see you very seldom, and you never come down to the studio now, and when I am away from you, and I hear all these hideous things that people are whispering about you, I don't know what to say. Why is

---

[1] Wilde regularly draws attention to fingers as a symbol of vice (Lord Henry's are called long, white, and nervous, for instance). Something about this man's fingers (the digits with which he feels his way through life, connecting him to his vices whether they be stealing, drug use, prostitution, or murder) disturbs Basil

it, Dorian, that a man like the Duke of Berwick leaves the room of a club when you enter it? Why is it that so many gentlemen in London will neither go to your house nor invite you to theirs? You used to be a friend of Lord Cawdor. I met him at dinner last week. Your name happened to come up in conversation, in connection with the miniatures you have lent to the exhibition at the Dudley[1]. Cawdor curled his lip, and said that you might have the most artistic tastes, but that you were a man whom no pure-minded girl should be allowed to know, and whom no chaste woman should sit in the same room with. I reminded him that I was a friend of yours, and asked him what he meant. He told me. He told me right out before everybody. It was horrible! [*Why is it that every young man that you take up seems to come to grief or to go to the bad at once?*] There was that wretched boy in the Guards who committed suicide[2]. You were his great friend. There was Sir Henry Ashton, who had to leave England, with a tarnished name. You and he were inseparable. What about Adrian Singleton, and his dreadful end? What about Lord Kent's only son, and his career? I met his father yesterday in St. James Street. He seemed broken with shame and sorrow. What about the young Duke of Perth? What sort of life has he got now? What gentleman would associate with him? Dorian, Dorian, your reputation is infamous. I know you and Harry are great friends. I say nothing about that now, but surely you need not have made his sister's name a by-word. When you met Lady Gwendolen, not a breath of scandal had ever touched her. Is there a single decent woman in London now who would drive with her in the Park? Why, even her children are not allowed to live with her[3]. Then there are other stories,--stories that you have been seen creeping at dawn out of dreadful houses and slinking in disguise into the foulest dens in London. Are they true? Can they be true? When I first heard them, I laughed. I hear them now, and they make me shudder. What about your country-house, and the life that is led there? [*It is quite sufficient to say of a young man that he goes to stay at Selby Royal, for*

---

[1] A London art gallery known for its watercolors and minatures

[2] Officers committing suicide after being exposed or blackmailed for homosexuality were a recurring feature of British society, alluded to in the Sherlock Holmes case "Charles Augustus Milverton," and shown explicitly in the Granada Television adaptation of that story (starring Jeremy Brett as Holmes) wherein a young, engaged officer commits suicide after being blackmailed for having a transvestite lover

[3] You may recall that this is Lord Henry's sister. During a divorce or estrangement, it was far more common for the children to be put under the care of the father than the mother, but this is still a shocking restriction implying that the mother is not trusted to be a moral guardian

people to sneer and titter[1].] Dorian, you don't know what is said about you. I won't tell you that I don't want to preach to you. I remember Harry saying once that every man who turned himself into an amateur curate[2] for the moment always said that, and then broke his word. I do want to preach to you. I want you to lead such a life as will make the world respect you. I want you to have a clean name and a fair record. I want you to get rid of the dreadful people you associate with. Don't shrug your shoulders like that. Don't be so indifferent. You have a wonderful influence. Let it be for good, not for evil. They say that you corrupt every one whom you become intimate with, and that it is quite sufficient for you to enter a house, for shame of some kind to follow after you. I don't know whether it is so or not. How should I know? But it is said of you. I am told things that it seems impossible to doubt. Lord Gloucester was one of my greatest friends at Oxford. He showed me a letter that his wife had written to him when she was dying alone in her villa at Mentone[3]. [*It was the most terrible confession I ever read. He said that he suspected you.*] I told him that it was absurd,--that I knew you thoroughly, and that you were incapable of anything of the kind. Know you? I wonder do I know you? Before I could answer that, I should have to see your soul."

"To see my soul!" muttered Dorian Gray, starting up from the sofa and turning almost white from fear.

"Yes," answered Hallward, gravely, and with infinite sorrow in his voice,--"to see your soul. But only God can do that."

A bitter laugh of mockery broke from the lips of the younger man. "You shall see it yourself, to-night!" he cried, seizing a lamp from the table. "Come: it is your own handiwork[4]. Why shouldn't you look at it? You can tell the world all about it afterwards, if you choose. Nobody would believe you. If they did believe you, they'd like me all the better for it. I know the age better than you do, though you will prate about it so tediously. Come, I tell you. You have chattered enough about corruption. Now you shall look on it face to face."

There was the madness of pride in every word he uttered. He stamped his foot upon the ground in his boyish insolent manner. He felt

---

[1] Laughter once again returns as a motif of society's reaction to homosexuality
[2] Parson
[3] A district of the French Rivera. The implication is that the woman was socially banished due to some scandal, and her lingering death suggests – at least to my ear – a shameful, fatal venereal disease like syphilis
[4] Dorian doesn't just mean the portrait: his corruption can be partially blamed on Basil for allowing Henry to corrupt him with his ideas while Basil was engrossed in painting him

a terrible joy at the thought that some one else was to share his secret, and that the man who had painted the portrait that was the origin of all his shame was to be burdened for the rest of his life with the hideous memory of what he had done.

"Yes," he continued, coming closer to him, and looking steadfastly into his stern eyes, "I will show you my soul. You shall see the thing that you fancy only God can see."

Hallward started back. "This is blasphemy, Dorian!" he cried. "You must not say things like that. They are horrible, and they don't mean anything."

"You think so?" He laughed again.

"I know so. As for what I said to you to-night, I said it for your good. You know I have been always devoted to you."

"Don't touch me. Finish what you have to say[1]."

A twisted flash of pain shot across Hallward's face. He paused for a moment, and a wild feeling of pity came over him. After all, what right had he to pry into the life of Dorian Gray? If he had done a tithe of what was rumored about him, how much he must have suffered! Then he straightened himself up, and walked over to the fireplace, and stood there, looking at the burning logs with their frost-like ashes and their throbbing cores of flame.

"I am waiting, Basil," said the young man, in a hard, clear voice.

He turned round. "What I have to say is this," he cried. "You must give me some answer to these horrible charges that are made against you. If you tell me that they are absolutely untrue from beginning to end, I will believe you. Deny them, Dorian, deny them! Can't you see what I am going through? My God! don't tell me that you are infamous!"

Dorian Gray smiled. There was a curl of contempt in his lips. "Come up-stairs, Basil," he said, quietly. "I keep a diary of my life from day to day, and it never leaves the room in which it is written. I will show it to you if you come with me."

"I will come with you, Dorian, if you wish it. I see I have missed my train. That makes no matter. I can go to-morrow. But don't ask me to read anything to-night. All I want is a plain answer to my question."

"That will be given to you up-stairs. I could not give it here. You won't have to read long. Don't keep me waiting."

---

[1] Dorian is taunting Basil with his repressed homosexuality, demanding that if he wants to express his love, he should do so openly, not through innuendos or subtle touches

CHAPTER XI

HE passed out of the room, and began the ascent, Basil Hallward following close behind. They walked softly, as men instinctively do at night. The lamp cast fantastic shadows on the wall and staircase. A rising wind made some of the windows rattle.

When they reached the top landing, Dorian set the lamp down on the floor, and taking out the key turned it in the lock. "You insist on knowing, Basil?" he asked, in a low voice.

"Yes."

"I am delighted," he murmured, smiling. Then he added, somewhat bitterly, "You are the one man in the world who is entitled to know everything about me. You have had more to do with my life than you think." And, taking up the lamp, he opened the door and went in. A cold current of air passed them, and the light shot up for a moment in a flame of murky orange[1]. He shuddered. "Shut the door behind you," he said, as he placed the lamp on the table.

Hallward glanced round him, with a puzzled expression. The room looked as if it had not been lived in for years. A faded Flemish tapestry, a curtained picture, an old Italian cassone, and an almost empty bookcase,--that was all that it seemed to contain, besides a chair and a table. As Dorian Gray was lighting a half-burned candle[2] that was standing on the mantel-shelf, he saw that the whole place was covered with dust, and that the carpet was in holes. A mouse ran scuffling behind the wainscoting. There was a damp odor of mildew.

"So you think that it is only God who sees the soul, Basil? Draw that curtain back, and you will see mine."

The voice that spoke was cold and cruel. "You are mad, Dorian, or playing a part," muttered Hallward, frowning.

"You won't? Then I must do it myself," said the young man; and he tore the curtain from its rod, and flung it on the ground.

An exclamation of horror broke from Hallward's lips as he saw in the dim light the hideous thing on the canvas leering at him. There was something in its expression that filled him with disgust and loathing. Good heavens! it was Dorian Gray's own face that he was looking at! The horror, whatever it was, had not yet entirely marred that marvellous beauty. There was still some gold in the thinning hair and some scarlet

---

[1] Suggestive of hellfire
[2] Implying that Dorian visits the portrait at night

on the sensual lips. The sodden eyes had kept something of the loveliness of their blue, the noble curves had not yet passed entirely away from chiselled nostrils and from plastic throat. Yes, it was Dorian himself. But who had done it? He seemed to recognize his own brush-work, and the frame was his own design. The idea was monstrous, yet he felt afraid. He seized the lighted candle, and held it to the picture. In the left-hand corner was his own name, traced in long letters of bright vermilion[1].

It was some foul parody, some infamous, ignoble satire. He had never done that. Still, it was his own picture. He knew it, and he felt as if his blood had changed from fire to sluggish ice in a moment. His own picture! What did it mean? Why had it altered? He turned, and looked at Dorian Gray with the eyes of a sick man. His mouth twitched, and his parched tongue seemed unable to articulate. He passed his hand across his forehead. It was dank with clammy sweat.

The young man was leaning against the mantel-shelf, watching him with that strange expression that is on the faces of those who are absorbed in a play when a great artist is acting. There was neither real sorrow in it nor real joy. There was simply the passion of the spectator, with perhaps a flicker of triumph in the eyes. He had taken the flower out of his coat, and was smelling it, or pretending to do so.

"What does this mean?" cried Hallward, at last. His own voice sounded shrill and curious in his ears.

"Years ago, when I was a boy," said Dorian Gray, "you met me, devoted yourself to me, flattered me, and taught me to be vain of my good looks. One day you introduced me to a friend of yours, who explained to me the wonder of youth, and you finished a portrait of me that revealed to me the wonder of beauty. In a mad moment, that I don't know, even now, whether I regret or not, I made a wish. Perhaps you would call it a prayer . . . ."

"I remember it! Oh, how well I remember it! No! the thing is impossible. The room is damp. The mildew has got into the canvas. The paints I used had some wretched mineral poison in them. I tell you the thing is impossible."

"Ah, what is impossible?" murmured the young man, going over to the window, and leaning his forehead against the cold, mist-stained glass.

"You told me you had destroyed it."

"I was wrong. It has destroyed me."

"I don't believe it is my picture."

---

[1] Scarlet red

"Can't you see your romance[1] in it?" said Dorian, bitterly.

"My romance, as you call it . . ."

"As you called it."

"There was nothing evil in it, nothing shameful. This is the face of a satyr[2]."

"It is the face of my soul."

"[*Christ!*] what a thing I must have worshipped! This has the eyes of a devil."

"Each of us has Heaven and Hell in him[3], Basil," cried Dorian, with a wild gesture of despair.

Hallward turned again to the portrait, and gazed at it. "My God! if it is true," he exclaimed, "and this is what you have done with your life, why, you must be worse even than those who talk against you fancy you to be!" He held the light up again to the canvas, and examined it. The surface seemed to be quite undisturbed, and as he had left it. It was from within, apparently, that the foulness and horror had come. Through some strange quickening of inner life the leprosies of sin were slowly eating the thing away. The rotting of a corpse in a watery grave was not so fearful.

His hand shook, and the candle fell from its socket on the floor, and lay there sputtering. He placed his foot on it and put it out. Then he flung himself into the rickety chair that was standing by the table and buried his face in his hands.

"Good God, Dorian, what a lesson! what an awful lesson!" There was no answer, but he could hear the young man sobbing at the window[4].

"Pray, Dorian, pray[5]," he murmured. "What is it that one was taught to say in one's boyhood? 'Lead us not into temptation. Forgive us our sins. Wash away our iniquities[6].' Let us say that together. The prayer of your pride has been answered. The prayer of your repentance will be

---

[1] Another veiled allusion to Basil's homosexual passion for Dorian

[2] A Greek monster – half goat and half man – known for its sensuality and sexual perversions (usually depicted in Greco-Roman art with curling goat's horns and a massive erection)

[3] Paraphrasing from Milton's Satan, who famously claimed "The mind is its own place, and in itself can make a heaven of hell, a hell of heaven"

[4] Dorian, obviously, is not a caricatured monster: he too deeply regrets his corruption and weeps for his polluted soul

[5] Like Wilde himself, Basil (whom Wilde claimed to be most like him of the three main characters) found comfort and solace in religion in spite of his decadent lifestyle. By the end of his life, ruined and alone, Wilde was a devout Catholic and was given Last Rites on his deathbed

[6] This is a combination of the Lord's Prayer and Psalm 51

answered also. I worshipped you too much. I am punished for it. You worshipped yourself too much. We are both punished[1]."

Dorian Gray turned slowly around, and looked at him with tear-dimmed eyes. "It is too late, Basil," he murmured.

"It is never too late, Dorian. Let us kneel down and try if we can remember a prayer. Isn't there a verse somewhere, 'Though your sins be as scarlet, yet I will make them as white as snow[2]'?"

"Those words mean nothing to me now."

"Hush! don't say that. You have done enough evil in your life. My God! don't you see that accursed thing leering at us?"

Dorian Gray glanced at the picture, and suddenly an uncontrollable feeling of hatred for Basil Hallward came over him. The mad passions of a hunted animal stirred within him, and he loathed the man who was seated at the table, more than he had ever loathed anything in his whole life[3]. He glanced wildly around. Something glimmered on the top of the painted chest that faced him. His eye fell on it. He knew what it was. It was a knife that he had brought up, some days before, to cut a piece of cord, and had forgotten to take away with him. He moved slowly towards it, passing Hallward as he did so. As soon as he got behind him, he seized it, and turned round. Hallward moved in his chair as if he was going to rise[4]. He rushed at him, and dug the knife into the great vein[5] that is behind the ear, crushing the man's head down on the table, and stabbing again and again.

---

[1] Basil atones for his responsibility in Dorian's corruption: because he idealized him, he failed to perceive his complex humanity – capable of good and evil – and neglected to protect him from Henry while lost in his idolatrous reverie

[2] Isaiah 1:18

[3] Watching Basil turn to another deity and repenting of his worship of a false idol (mirroring the conclusion of "Tannhauser") appears to be the catalyst of Dorian's hatred. He doesn't mind being hated or loved as long as he is the objection of gossip and attention, but the sight of Basil bent over in prayer to another god summons a deep, psychological loathing because of its defiance to Dorian's sovereignty over the public's imagination: if Basil can reject him, then others may as well, and his response is to murder him before the infection of repentance spreads

[4] Basil's motion to stand is symbolic of his redemption: he is standing up for Dorian's salvation, making a move to correct what he had permitted Henry to soil, and Dorian stabs him before he can make that movement

[5] That would be the posterior auricular vein

There was a stifled groan, and the horrible sound of some one choking with blood[1]. The outstretched arms shot up convulsively three times, waving grotesque stiff-fingered hands in the air. He stabbed him once more, but the man did not move. Something began to trickle on the floor. He waited for a moment, still pressing the head down. Then he threw the knife on the table, and listened.

He could hear nothing, but the drip, drip on the threadbare carpet. He opened the door, and went out on the landing. The house was quite quiet. No one was stirring.

He took out the key, and returned to the room, locking himself in as he did so.

The thing was still seated in the chair, straining over the table with bowed head, and humped back, and long fantastic arms. Had it not been for the red jagged tear in the neck, and the clotted black pool that slowly widened on the table, one would have said that the man was simply asleep[2].

How quickly it had all been done! He felt strangely calm, and, walking over to the window, opened it, and stepped out on the balcony. The wind had blown the fog away, and the sky was like a monstrous peacock's tail, starred with myriads of golden eyes[3]. He looked down, and saw the policeman going his rounds and flashing a bull's-eye lantern on the doors of the silent houses. The crimson spot of a prowling hansom gleamed at the corner, and then vanished. A woman in a ragged shawl was creeping round by the railings, staggering as she went. Now and then she stopped, and peered back. Once, she began to sing in a hoarse voice. The policeman strolled over and said something to her. She stumbled away, laughing. A bitter blast swept across the Square. The gas-lamps flickered, and became blue[4], and the leafless trees shook their black iron branches as if in pain. He shivered, and went back, closing the window behind him.

He passed to the door, turned the key, and opened it. He did not even glance at the murdered man. He felt that the secret of the whole thing was not to realize the situation. The friend who had painted the

---

[1] With the knife having come in behind the ear and pinning itself into the table, Basil's throat has been gashed open on two sides

[2] Another biblical reference: "She is not dead, but sleeping" (Matthew 9:24), which implies that though murdered, Basil has been redeemed, while Dorian is still tangled up in his self-made hell

[3] Suggestive of the eyes of Heaven carefully watching his actions

[4] Blue flame, as earlier noted, is traditionally associated with the presence of ghosts and other supernatural powers of evil

fatal portrait, the portrait to which all his misery had been due, had gone out of his life. That was enough.

Then he remembered the lamp. It was a rather curious one of Moorish[1] workmanship, made of dull silver inlaid with arabesques of burnished steel. Perhaps it might be missed by his servant, and questions would be asked. He turned back, and took it from the table. How still the man was! How horribly white the long hands looked! He was like a dreadful wax image.

He locked the door behind him, and crept quietly down-stairs. The wood-work creaked, and seemed to cry out as if in pain. He stopped several times, and waited. No: everything was still. It was merely the sound of his own footsteps.

When he reached the library, he saw the bag and coat in the corner. They must be hidden away somewhere. He unlocked a secret press[2] that was in the wainscoting, and put them into it. He could easily burn them afterwards. Then he pulled out his watch. It was twenty minutes to two.

He sat down, and began to think. Every year--every month, almost-- men were strangled[3] in England for what he had done. There had been a madness of murder in the air. Some red star had come too close to the earth.

Evidence? What evidence was there against him? Basil Hallward had left the house at eleven. No one had seen him come in again. Most of the servants were at Selby Royal. His valet had gone to bed.

Paris! Yes. It was to Paris that Basil had gone, by the midnight train, as he had intended. With his curious reserved habits, it would be months before any suspicions would be aroused. Months? Everything could be destroyed long before then.

A sudden thought struck him. He put on his fur coat and hat, and went out into the hall. There he paused, hearing the slow heavy tread of the policeman outside on the pavement, and seeing the flash of the lantern reflected in the window. He waited, holding his breath.

After a few moments he opened the front door, and slipped out, shutting it very gently behind him. Then he began ringing the bell. In about ten minutes his valet appeared, half dressed, and looking very drowsy.

"I am sorry to have had to wake you up, Francis," he said, stepping in; "but I had forgotten my latch-key. What time is it?"

---

[1] North African
[2] Cabinet
[3] Specifically, hanged for murder

"Five minutes past two, sir," answered the man, looking at the clock and yawning.

"Five minutes past two? How horribly late! You must wake me at nine to-morrow. I have some work to do."

"All right, sir."

"Did any one call this evening?"

"Mr. Hallward, sir. He stayed here till eleven, and then he went away to catch his train."

"Oh! I am sorry I didn't see him. Did he leave any message?"

"No, sir, except that he would write to you."

"That will do, Francis. Don't forget to call me at nine tomorrow."

"No, sir."

The man shambled down the passage in his slippers.

Dorian Gray threw his hat and coat upon the yellow marble table, and passed into the library. He walked up and down the room for a quarter of an hour, biting his lip, and thinking. Then he took the Blue Book down from one of the shelves, and began to turn over the leaves. "Alan Campbell, 152, Hertford Street, Mayfair." Yes; that was the man he wanted.

CHAPTER XII

AT nine o'clock the next morning his servant came in with a cup of chocolate on a tray, and opened the shutters. Dorian was sleeping quite peacefully, lying on his right side, with one hand underneath his cheek. He looked like a boy who had been tired out with play, or study[1].

The man had to touch him twice on the shoulder before he woke, and as he opened his eyes a faint smile passed across his lips, as though he had been having some delightful dream. Yet he had not dreamed at all. His night had been untroubled by any images of pleasure or of pain. But youth smiles without any reason. It is one of its chiefest charms.

He turned round, and, leaning on his elbow, began to drink his chocolate. The mellow November sun was streaming into the room. The sky was bright blue, and there was a genial warmth in the air. It was almost like a morning in May.

Gradually the events of the preceding night crept with silent blood-stained feet into his brain, and reconstructed themselves there with terrible distinctness. He winced at the memory of all that he had suffered, and for a moment the same curious feeling of loathing for Basil

---

[1] Illustrating how little sin has come to mean to Dorian: he is no more perturbed by butchering one of his best friends than if he had spent the night roughhousing

Hallward, that had made him kill him as he sat in the chair, came back to him, and he grew cold with passion. The dead man was still sitting there, too, and in the sunlight now. How horrible that was! Such hideous things were for the darkness, not for the day.

He felt that if he brooded on what he had gone through he would sicken or grow mad. There were sins whose fascination was more in the memory than in the doing of them, strange triumphs that gratified the pride more than the passions, and gave to the intellect a quickened sense of joy, greater than any joy they brought, or could ever bring, to the senses. But this was not one of them. It was a thing to be driven out of the mind, to be drugged with poppies[1], to be strangled lest it might strangle one itself.

He passed his hand across his forehead, and then got up hastily, and dressed himself with even more than his usual attention, giving a good deal of care to the selection of his necktie and scarf-pin, and changing his rings more than once[2].

He spent a long time over breakfast, tasting the various dishes, talking to his valet about some new liveries[3] that he was thinking of getting made for the servants at Selby, and going through his correspondence. Over some of the letters he smiled. Three of them bored him. One he read several times over, and then tore up with a slight look of annoyance in his face. "That awful thing, a woman's memory[4]!" as Lord Henry had once said.

When he had drunk his coffee, he sat down at the table, and wrote two letters. One he put in his pocket, the other he handed to the valet.

"Take this round to 152, Hertford Street, Francis, and if Mr. Campbell is out of town, get his address."

As soon as he was alone, he lit a cigarette, and began sketching upon a piece of paper, drawing flowers, and bits of architecture, first, and then faces. Suddenly he remarked that every face that he drew seemed to have an extraordinary likeness to Basil Hallward. He frowned, and, getting up, went over to the bookcase and took out a volume at hazard. He was determined that he would not think about what had happened, till it became absolutely necessary to do so.

When he had stretched himself on the sofa, he looked at the title-page of the book. It was Gautier's "Emaux et Camées," Charpentier's

---

[1] Opium

[2] Once again emphasizing just how unbothered Dorian's conscience is: this murder means less to him than his choice in rings

[3] Uniforms for servants in the colors of their master's coat of arms

[4] Implying that the letter is from a one-night stand whose continued interest in Dorian is unrequited

Japanese-paper edition, with the Jacquemart etching[1]. The binding was of citron-green leather with a design of gilt trellis-work and dotted pomegranates. It had been given to him by Adrian Singleton. As he turned over the pages his eye fell on the poem about the hand of Lacenaire, the cold yellow hand "du supplice encore mal lavée[2]," with its downy red hairs and its "doigts de faune." He glanced at his own white taper fingers, and passed on, till he came to those lovely verses upon Venice:

> Sur une gamme chromatique,
>   Le sein de perles ruisselant,
> La Vénus de l'Adriatique
>   Sort de l'eau son corps rose et blanc.
>
> Les dômes, sur l'azur des ondes
>   Suivant la phrase au pur contour,
> S'enflent comme des gorges rondes
>   Que soulève un soupir d'amour.
>
> L'esquif aborde et me dépose,
>   Jetant son amarre au pilier,
> Devant une façade rose,
>   Sur le marbre d'un escalier.[3]

---

[1] Yet another book which was published with a decadent, yellow cover: Gautier's "Enamels and Cameos" was a collection of imaginative poems, and included an etching of the author by the artist Jacquemart and high quality Japanese paper by the Charpentier et Cie publishers

[2] A 19th century poet who was made infamous after he committed a double murder, and would later provide the inspiration for Dostoevsky's "Crime and Punishment." This line reads: "not yet washed clean of the fatal stain" and "faun-shaped fingers," respectively. The next time he looks at his portrait, it too will have a fatal stain of blood on its fingers

[3] The passage reads:

To see, her bosom covered o'er
With pearls, her body suave,
The Adriatic Venus soar
On sound's chromatic wave.

The domes that on the water dwell
Pursue the melody

How exquisite they were! As one read them, one seemed to be floating down the green water-ways of the pink and pearl city, lying in a black gondola with silver prow and trailing curtains. The mere lines looked to him like those straight lines of turquoise-blue that follow one as one pushes out to the Lido[1]. The sudden flashes of color reminded him of the gleam of the opal-and-iris-throated birds that flutter round the tall honey-combed Campanile[2], or stalk, with such stately grace, through the dim arcades. Leaning back with half- closed eyes, he kept saying over and over to himself,--

Devant une façade rose,
Sur le marbre d'un escalier.

The whole of Venice was in those two lines. He remembered the autumn that he had passed there, and a wonderful love that had stirred him to delightful fantastic follies. There was romance in every place. But Venice, like Oxford, had kept the background for romance, and background was everything, or almost everything. Basil had been with him part of the time, and had gone wild over Tintoret[3]. Poor Basil! what a horrible way for a man to die!

He sighed, and took up the book again, and tried to forget. He read of the swallows that fly in and out of the little café at Smyrna where the Hadjis[4] sit counting their amber beads and the turbaned merchants smoke their long tasselled pipes and talk gravely to each other; of the Obelisk in the Place de la Concorde[5] that weeps tears of granite in its lonely sunless exile, and longs to be back by the hot lotus-covered Nile, where there are Sphinxes, and rose-red ibises, and white vultures with gilded claws, and crocodiles, with small beryl eyes, that crawl over the

---

In clear-drawn cadences, and swell
Like breasts of love that sigh.

My chains around a pillar cast,
I land before a fair
And rosy-pale facade at last,
Upon a marble stair.

[1] A seven-mile long island in Venice, known for its sea bathing and brothels
[2] A free-standing bell tower
[3] Tintoretto was a 17th century Venetian painter noted for the boldness and energy of his art
[4] Smyrna is a city in Turkey and hadjis are Muslim pilgrims to Mecca
[5] The Luxor Obelisk, an Egyptian monument which was transported to Paris during the early years of Egyptology

green steaming mud; and of that curious statue that Gautier compares to a contralto voice, the "monstre charmant[1]" that couches in the porphyry-room of the Louvre. But after a time the book fell from his hand. He grew nervous, and a horrible fit of terror came over him. What if Alan Campbell should be out of England? Days would elapse before he could come back. Perhaps he might refuse to come. What could he do then? Every moment was of vital importance.

They had been great friends once, five years before,--almost inseparable, indeed. Then the intimacy had come suddenly to an end. When they met in society now, it was only Dorian Gray who smiled: Alan Campbell never did.

He was an extremely clever young man, though he had no real appreciation of the visible arts, and whatever little sense of the beauty of poetry he possessed he had gained entirely from Dorian. His dominant intellectual passion was for science. At Cambridge he had spent a great deal of his time working in the Laboratory, and had taken a good class in the Natural Science trips of his year. Indeed, he was still devoted to the study of chemistry, and had a laboratory of his own, in which he used to shut himself up all day long, greatly to the annoyance of his mother, who had set her heart on his standing for Parliament and had a vague idea that a chemist was a person who made up prescriptions. He was an excellent musician, however, as well, and played both the violin and the piano better than most amateurs. In fact, it was music that had first brought him and Dorian Gray together,--music and that indefinable attraction that Dorian seemed to be able to exercise whenever he wished, and indeed exercised often without being conscious of it. They had met at Lady Berkshire's the night that Rubinstein[2] played there, and after that used to be always seen together at the Opera, and wherever good music was going on. For eighteen months their intimacy lasted. Campbell was always either at Selby Royal or in Grosvenor Square. To him, as to many others, Dorian Gray was the type of everything that is wonderful and fascinating in life. Whether or not a quarrel had taken place between them no one ever knew. But suddenly people remarked that they scarcely spoke when they met, and that Campbell seemed always to go away early from any party at which Dorian Gray was present. He had changed, too,-- was strangely melancholy at times, appeared almost to dislike hearing music of any passionate character, and would never himself play, giving as his excuse, when he was called

---

[1] Charming monster (a reference to Gautier's poem about a replica statue of the intersex Greek deity, Hermaphroditus

[2] Anton Rubinstein was a tremendously famous 19th century pianist

upon, that he was so absorbed in science that he had no time left in which to practise. And this was certainly true. Every day he seemed to become more interested in biology, and his name appeared once or twice in some of the scientific reviews, in connection with certain curious experiments.

This was the man that Dorian Gray was waiting for, pacing up and down the room, glancing every moment at the clock, and becoming horribly agitated as the minutes went by. At last the door opened, and his servant entered.

"Mr. Alan Campbell, sir."

A sigh of relief broke from his parched lips, and the color came back to his cheeks.

"Ask him to come in at once, Francis."

The man bowed, and retired. In a few moments Alan Campbell walked in, looking very stern and rather pale, his pallor being intensified by his coal-black hair and dark eyebrows.

"Alan! this is kind of you. I thank you for coming."

"I had intended never to enter your house again, Gray. But you said it was a matter of life and death." His voice was hard and cold. He spoke with slow deliberation. There was a look of contempt in the steady searching gaze that he turned on Dorian. He kept his hands in the pockets of his Astrakhan[1] coat, and appeared not to have noticed the gesture with which he had been greeted.

"It is a matter of life and death, Alan, and to more than one person. Sit down."

Campbell took a chair by the table, and Dorian sat opposite to him. The two men's eyes met. In Dorian's there was infinite pity. He knew that what he was going to do was dreadful.

After a strained moment of silence, he leaned across and said, very quietly, but watching the effect of each word upon the face of the man he had sent for, "Alan, in a locked room at the top of this house, a room to which nobody but myself has access, a dead man is seated at a table. He has been dead ten hours now. Don't stir, and don't look at me like that. Who the man is, why he died, how he died, are matters that do not concern you. What you have to do is this--"

"Stop, Gray. I don't want to know anything further. Whether what you have told me is true or not true, doesn't concern me. I entirely decline to be mixed up in your life. Keep your horrible secrets to yourself. They don't interest me any more."

---

[1] Fluffy, dark fleece from lambs in Central Asia

"Alan, they will have to interest you. This one will have to interest you. I am awfully sorry for you, Alan. But I can't help myself. You are the one man who is able to save me. I am forced to bring you into the matter. I have no option. Alan, you are a scientist. You know about chemistry, and things of that kind. You have made experiments. What you have got to do is to destroy the thing that is up-stairs,--to destroy it so that not a vestige will be left of it. Nobody saw this person come into the house. Indeed, at the present moment he is supposed to be in Paris. He will not be missed for months. When he is missed, there must be no trace of him found here. You, Alan, you must change him, and everything that belongs to him, into a handful of ashes that I may scatter in the air."

"You are mad, Dorian."

"Ah! I was waiting for you to call me Dorian[1]."

"You are mad, I tell you,--mad to imagine that I would raise a finger to help you, mad to make this monstrous confession. I will have nothing to do with this matter, whatever it is. Do you think I am going to peril my reputation for you? What is it to me what devil's work you are up to?"

"It was a suicide, Alan."

"I am glad of that. But who drove him to it? You, I should fancy."

"Do you still refuse to do this, for me?"

"Of course I refuse. I will have absolutely nothing to do with it. I don't care what shame comes on you. You deserve it all. I should not be sorry to see you disgraced, publicly disgraced. How dare you ask me, of all men in the world, to mix myself up in this horror? I should have thought you knew more about people's characters. Your friend Lord Henry Wotton can't have taught you much about psychology, whatever else he has taught you. Nothing will induce me to stir a step to help you. You have come to the wrong man. Go to some of your friends. Don't come to me."

"Alan, it was murder. I killed him. You don't know what he had made me suffer. Whatever my life is, he had more to do with the making or the marring of it than poor Harry has had. He may not have intended it, the result was the same."

"Murder! Good God, Dorian, is that what you have come to? I shall not inform upon you. It is not my business. Besides, you are certain to

---

[1] Men almost universally referred to one another by last names (hence even best friends Holmes and Watson stick to each others' surnames) – to call him by his first name is to suggest a deep intimacy, and Dorian suggests that even hearing his name spoken summons up dangerous memories (presumably of a homosexual affair)

be arrested, without my stirring in the matter. Nobody ever commits a murder without doing something stupid. But I will have nothing to do with it."

"All I ask of you is to perform a certain scientific experiment. You go to hospitals and dead-houses, and the horrors that you do there don't affect you. If in some hideous dissecting-room or fetid laboratory you found this man lying on a leaden table with red gutters scooped out in it, you would simply look upon him as an admirable subject. You would not turn a hair. You would not believe that you were doing anything wrong. On the contrary, you would probably feel that you were benefiting the human race, or increasing the sum of knowledge in the world, or gratifying intellectual curiosity, or something of that kind. What I want you to do is simply what you have often done before. Indeed, to destroy a body must be less horrible than what you are accustomed to work at. And, remember, it is the only piece of evidence against me. If it is discovered, I am lost; and it is sure to be discovered unless you help me."

"I have no desire to help you. You forget that. I am simply indifferent to the whole thing. It has nothing to do with me."

"Alan, I entreat you. Think of the position I am in. Just before you came I almost fainted with terror. No! don't think of that. Look at the matter purely from the scientific point of view. You don't inquire where the dead things on which you experiment come from. Don't inquire now. I have told you too much as it is. But I beg of you to do this. We were friends once, Alan."

"Don't speak about those days, Dorian: they are dead."

"The dead linger sometimes. The man up-stairs will not go away. He is sitting at the table with bowed head and outstretched arms. Alan! Alan! if you don't come to my assistance I am ruined. Why, they will hang me, Alan! Don't you understand? They will hang me for what I have done."

"There is no good in prolonging this scene. I refuse absolutely to do anything in the matter. It is insane of you to ask me."

"You refuse absolutely?"

"Yes."

The same look of pity came into Dorian's eyes, then he stretched out his hand, took a piece of paper, and wrote something on it. He read it over twice, folded it carefully, and pushed it across the table. Having done this, he got up, and went over to the window.

Campbell looked at him in surprise, and then took up the paper, and opened it. As he read it, his face became ghastly pale, and he fell back in his chair. A horrible sense of sickness came over him. He felt as if his heart was beating itself to death in some empty hollow.

After two or three minutes of terrible silence, Dorian turned round, and came and stood behind him, putting his hand upon his shoulder.

"I am so sorry, Alan," he murmured, "but you leave me no alternative. I have a letter written already. Here it is. You see the address. If you don't help me, I must send it. You know what the result will be[1]. But you are going to help me. It is impossible for you to refuse now. I tried to spare you. You will do me the justice to admit that. You were stern, harsh, offensive. You treated me as no man has ever dared to treat me,--no living man, at any rate. I bore it all. Now it is for me to dictate terms."

Campbell buried his face in his hands, and a shudder passed through him.

"Yes, it is my turn to dictate terms, Alan. You know what they are. The thing is quite simple. Come, don't work yourself into this fever. The thing has to be done. Face it, and do it."

A groan broke from Campbell's lips, and he shivered all over. The ticking of the clock on the mantel-piece seemed to him to be dividing time into separate atoms of agony, each of which was too terrible to be borne. He felt as if an iron ring was being slowly tightened round his forehead, and as if the disgrace with which he was threatened had already come upon him. The hand upon his shoulder weighed like a hand of lead. It was intolerable. It seemed to crush him.

"Come, Alan, you must decide at once."

He hesitated a moment. "Is there a fire in the room up-stairs?" he murmured.

"Yes, there is a gas-fire with asbestos."

"I will have to go home and get some things from the laboratory."

"No, Alan, you need not leave the house. Write on a sheet of note-paper what you want, and my servant will take a cab and bring the things back to you."

Campbell wrote a few lines, blotted them, and addressed an envelope to his assistant. Dorian took the note up and read it carefully. Then he rang the bell, and gave it to his valet, with orders to return as soon as possible, and to bring the things with him.

When the hall door shut, Campbell started, and, having got up from the chair, went over to the chimney-piece. He was shivering with a

---

[1] Homosexuality was not only scandalous, but illegal well into the 20th century. If Dorian is in possession of a love letter from Alan, or is able to somehow prove that they had an affair, he can take Campbell down with him

sort of ague. For nearly twenty minutes, neither of the men spoke. A fly buzzed noisily about the room, and the ticking of the clock was like the beat of a hammer.

As the chime struck one, Campbell turned around, and, looking at Dorian Gray, saw that his eyes were filled with tears. There was something in the purity and refinement of that sad face that seemed to enrage him. "You are infamous, absolutely infamous!" he muttered.

"Hush, Alan: you have saved my life," said Dorian.

"Your life? Good heavens! what a life that is! You have gone from corruption to corruption, and now you have culminated in crime. In doing what I am going to do, what you force me to do, it is not of your life that I am thinking."

"Ah, Alan," murmured Dorian, with a sigh, "I wish you had a thousandth part of the pity for me that I have for you." He turned away, as he spoke, and stood looking out at the garden. Campbell made no answer.

After about ten minutes a knock came to the door, and the servant entered, carrying a mahogany chest of chemicals, with a small electric battery set[1] on top of it. He placed it on the table, and went out again, returning with a long coil of steel and platinum wire and two rather curiously-shaped iron clamps.

"Shall I leave the things here, sir?" he asked Campbell.

"Yes," said Dorian. "And I am afraid, Francis, that I have another errand for you. What is the name of the man at Richmond who supplies Selby with orchids?"

"Harden, sir."

"Yes,--Harden. You must go down to Richmond at once, see Harden personally, and tell him to send twice as many orchids as I ordered, and to have as few white ones as possible. In fact, I don't want any white ones. It is a lovely day, Francis, and Richmond is a very pretty place, otherwise I wouldn't bother you about it."

"No trouble, sir. At what time shall I be back?"

Dorian looked at Campbell. "How long will your experiment take, Alan?" he said, in a calm, indifferent voice. The presence of a third person in the room seemed to give him extraordinary courage.

Campbell frowned, and bit his lip. "It will take about five hours," he answered.

---

[1] First invented in 1886, electric batteries were cutting edge technology at the time. It's not clear exactly what it is that Wilde is implying Campbell's plan to be, but it seems that he is going to use an electric charge to slowly burn the body into powder, along with the help of some corrosive acids. This is of course a very far-fetched idea, but at the time was probably a plausible bit of science fiction

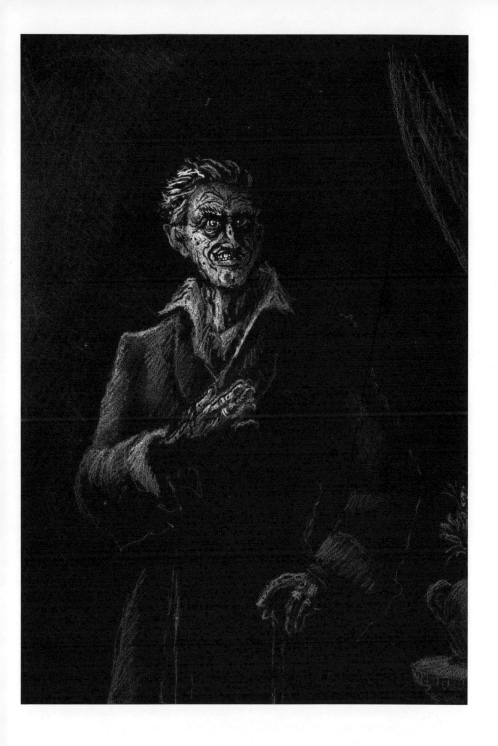

"It will be time enough, then, if you are back at half-past seven, Francis. Or stay: just leave my things out for dressing. You can have the evening to yourself. I am not dining at home, so I shall not want you."

"Thank you, sir," said the man, leaving the room.

"Now, Alan, there is not a moment to be lost. How heavy this chest is! I'll take it for you. You bring the other things." He spoke rapidly, and in an authoritative manner. Campbell felt dominated by him. They left the room together.

When they reached the top landing, Dorian took out the key and turned it in the lock. Then he stopped, and a troubled look came into his eyes. He shuddered. "I don't think I can go in, Alan," he murmured.

"It is nothing to me. I don't require you," said Campbell, coldly.

Dorian half opened the door. As he did so, he saw the face of the portrait grinning in the sunlight. On the floor in front of it the torn curtain was lying. He remembered that the night before, for the first time in his life, he had forgotten to hide it, when he crept out of the room.

But what was that loathsome red dew that gleamed, wet and glistening, on one of the hands, as though the canvas had sweated blood? How horrible it was!--more horrible, it seemed to him for the moment, than the silent thing that he knew was stretched across the table, the thing whose grotesque misshapen shadow on the spotted carpet showed him that it had not stirred, but was still there, as he had left it.

He opened the door a little wider, and walked quickly in, with half-closed eyes and averted head, determined that he would not look even once upon the dead man. Then, stooping down, and taking up the gold-and-purple hanging, he flung it over the picture.

He stopped, feeling afraid to turn round, and his eyes fixed themselves on the intricacies of the pattern before him. He heard Campbell bringing in the heavy chest, and the irons, and the other things that he had required for his dreadful work. He began to wonder if he and Basil Hallward had ever met, and, if so, what they had thought of each other.

"Leave me now," said Campbell.

He turned and hurried out, just conscious that the dead man had been thrust back into the chair and was sitting up in it, with Campbell gazing into the glistening yellow face. As he was going downstairs he heard the key being turned in the lock.

It was long after seven o'clock when Campbell came back into the library. He was pale, but absolutely calm. "I have done what you asked me to do," he muttered. "And now, good-by. Let us never see each other again."

"You have saved me from ruin, Alan. I cannot forget that," said Dorian, simply.

As soon as Campbell had left, he went up-stairs. There was a horrible smell of chemicals in the room. But the thing that had been sitting at the table was gone.

CHAPTER XIII

"THERE is no good telling me you are going to be good, Dorian," cried Lord Henry, dipping his white fingers into a red copper bowl filled with rose-water. "You are quite perfect. Pray don't change."

Dorian shook his head. "No, Harry, I have done too many dreadful things in my life. I am not going to do any more. I began my good actions yesterday."

"Where were you yesterday?"

"In the country, Harry. I was staying at a little inn by myself."

"My dear boy," said Lord Henry smiling, "anybody can be good in the country. There are no temptations there. That is the reason why people who live out of town are so uncivilized. There are only two ways, as you know, of becoming civilized. One is by being cultured, the other is by being corrupt. Country-people have no opportunity of being either, so they stagnate."

"Culture and corruption," murmured Dorian. "I have known something of both. It seems to me curious now that they should ever be found together. For I have a new ideal, Harry. I am going to alter. I think I have altered."

"You have not told me yet what your good action was. Or did you say you had done more than one?"

"I can tell you, Harry. It is not a story I could tell to any one else. I spared somebody. It sounds vain, but you understand what I mean. She was quite beautiful, and wonderfully like Sibyl Vane. I think it was that which first attracted me to her. You remember Sibyl, don't you? How long ago that seems! Well, Hetty was not one of our own class, of course. She was simply a girl in a village. But I really loved her. I am quite sure that I loved her. All during this wonderful May that we have been having, I used to run down and see her two or three times a week. [*Finally she promised to come with me to town. I had taken a house for her, and arranged everything[1].*] Yesterday she met me in a little orchard.

---

[1] This scandalous reference to premarital cohabitation didn't make the cut

The apple-blossoms kept tumbling down on her hair, and she was laughing. We were to have gone away together[1] this morning at dawn. [*Suddenly I said to myself 'I won't ruin this girl. I won't bring her to shame.' And*[2]] I determined to leave her as flower-like as I had found her."

"I should think the novelty of the emotion must have given you a thrill of real pleasure, Dorian," interrupted Lord Henry. "But I can finish your idyl[3] for you. You gave her good advice, and broke her heart. That was the beginning of your reformation."

"Harry, you are horrible! You mustn't say these dreadful things. Hetty's heart is not broken. Of course she cried, and all that. [*But her life is not spoiled. There is no disgrace on it.*] She can live, like Perdita[4], in her garden."

"And weep over a faithless Florizel[5]," said Lord Henry, laughing. "My dear Dorian, you have the most curious boyish moods. Do you think this girl will ever be really contented now with any one of her own rank? I suppose she will be married some day to a rough carter or a grinning ploughman. Well, having met you, and loved you, will teach her to despise her husband, and she will be wretched. [*Upon the other hand, had she become your mistress, she would have lived in the society of charming and cultured men. You would have educated her, taught her how to dress, how to talk, how to move. You would have made her perfect, and she would have been extremely grateful. After a time, no doubt, you would have grown tired of her. She would have made a scene. You would have made a settlement. Then a new career would have begun for her*[6].] From a moral point of view I really don't think much of your great renunciation. Even as a beginning, it is poor. Besides, how do you know

---

[1] That is, run off to commence an affair

[2] Likely removed due to the implication that this would not be the first girl that he deflowered and abandoned (presumably after a pregnancy)

[3] And idealized fantasy

[4] A heroine of "The Winter's Tale," whose life story consists of a series of abandonments (her name means "Lost One"). She is unaware that she is the long lost princess of Sicilia, and is raised as a simple peasant, unaware of her royal blood

[5] The Prince of Bohemia who falls in love with Perdita despite his parents' objections to her humble birth (unaware, of course, that she is a princess)

[6] This rhapsody on the pros of a scandalous affair seems to mirror Lord Henry's relationship with his own wife (whose fashion and intelligence he criticizes, but who has summoned the self-confidence to abandon him for a romantic pianist), suggesting that this may have been more of a personal reflection than a prognostication

that Hetty isn't floating at the present moment in some mill-pond, with water-lilies round her, like Ophelia[1]?"

"I can't bear this, Harry! You mock at everything, and then suggest the most serious tragedies. I am sorry I told you now. I don't care what you say to me, I know I was right in acting as I did. Poor Hetty! As I rode past the farm this morning, I saw her white face at the window, like a spray of jasmine. Don't let me talk about it any more, and don't try to persuade me that the first good action I have done for years, the first little bit of self-sacrifice I have ever known, is really a sort of sin. I want to be better. I am going to be better. Tell me something about yourself. What is going on in town? I have not been to the club for days."

"The people are still discussing poor Basil's disappearance."

"I should have thought they had got tired of that by this time," said Dorian, pouring himself out some wine, and frowning slightly.

"My dear boy, they have only been talking about it for six weeks, and the public are really not equal to the mental strain of having more than one topic every three months. They have been very fortunate lately, however. They have had my own divorce-case, and Alan Campbell's suicide. Now they have got the mysterious disappearance of an artist. Scotland Yard still insists that the man in the gray ulster who left Victoria by the midnight train on the 7th of November was poor Basil, and the French police declare that Basil never arrived in Paris at all. I suppose in about a fortnight we will be told that he has been seen in San Francisco. It is an odd thing, but every one who disappears is said to be seen at San Francisco[2]. It must be a delightful city, and possess all the attractions of the next world."

"What do you think has happened to Basil?" asked Dorian, holding up his Burgundy against the light, and wondering how it was that he could discuss the matter so calmly.

"I have not the slightest idea. If Basil chooses to hide himself, it is no business of mine. If he is dead, I don't want to think about him. Death is the only thing that ever terrifies me[3]. I hate it. One can survive everything nowadays except that. Death and vulgarity are the only two

---

[1] Who famously drowns herself (or by accident – Shakespeare is intentionally vague) after being driven mad by Hamlet's murder of her father and mistreatment of her

[2] Wilde adored San Francisco and was well-received there during his American tour. He called California a veritable "Italy, without its art"

[3] Decadent fiction was by its nature morbid, fatalistic, and death-obsessed. Everything, it argued, ends in decay. Interestingly enough, many of the leading decadents – including Wilde, Huysmans, Rimbaud, and Baudelaire – lived a life of indulgent, scandalous experiences only to end their days as penitent Catholics

facts in the nineteenth century that one cannot explain away. Let us have our coffee in the music-room, Dorian. You must play Chopin to me. The man with whom my wife ran away played Chopin exquisitely[1]. Poor Victoria! [*She was desperately in love with you at one time, Dorian. It used to amuse me to watch her paying you compliments. You were so charmingly indifferent. Do you know, I really miss her? She never bored me. She was so delightfully improbable in everything that she did.*] I was very fond of her. The house is rather lonely without her."

Dorian said nothing, but rose from the table, and, passing into the next room, sat down to the piano and let his fingers stray across the keys. After the coffee had been brought in, he stopped, and, looking over at Lord Henry, said, "Harry, did it ever occur to you that Basil was murdered?"

Lord Henry yawned. "Basil had no enemies, and always wore a Waterbury[2] watch. Why should he be murdered? He was not clever enough to have enemies. Of course he had a wonderful genius for painting. But a man can paint like Velasquez[3] and yet be as dull as possible. Basil was really rather dull. He only interested me once, and that was when he told me, years ago, that he had a wild adoration for you."

"I was very fond of Basil," said Dorian, with a sad look in his eyes. "But don't people say that he was murdered?"

"Oh, some of the papers do. It does not seem to be probable. I know there are dreadful places in Paris, but Basil was not the sort of man to have gone to them. He had no curiosity. It was his chief defect. Play me a nocturne[4], Dorian, and, as you play, tell me, in a low voice, how you have kept your youth. You must have some secret. I am only ten years older than you are, and I am wrinkled, and bald, and yellow. You are really wonderful, Dorian. You have never looked more charming than you do to-night. You remind me of the day I saw you first. You were rather cheeky, very shy, and absolutely extraordinary. You have changed, of course, but not in appearance. I wish you would tell me your secret. To get back my youth I would do anything in the world, except

---

[1] This brings the novel full circle: at the beginning it was Dorian who was the charming piano player by whom Lord Henry was fascinated, and in the end his wife leaves him for another young ingénue

[2] An inexpensive watch brand whose pieces were made of brass rather than precious metals – hardly likely to earn the attention of a murderous thief

[3] Diego Velazquez was a 17th century Spanish painter known for his rich colors, powerful realism, and striking mastery of the portrait

[4] A short piano piece with a dreamy, often melancholy mood, evocative of the night. Chopin, Beethoven, and Schumann were famous for theirs

take exercise, get up early, or be respectable. Youth! There is nothing like it. It's absurd to talk of the ignorance of youth. The only people whose opinions I listen to now with any respect are people much younger than myself. They seem in front of me. Life has revealed to them her last wonder. As for the aged, I always contradict the aged. I do it on principle. If you ask them their opinion on something that happened yesterday, they solemnly give you the opinions current in 1820, when people wore high stocks[1] and knew absolutely nothing. How lovely that thing you are playing is! I wonder did Chopin write it at Majorca[2], with the sea weeping round the villa, and the salt spray dashing against the panes? It is marvelously romantic. What a blessing it is that there is one art left to us that is not imitative! Don't stop. I want music to-night. It seems to me that you are the young Apollo, and that I am Marsyas[3] listening to you. I have sorrows, Dorian, of my own, that even you know nothing of. The tragedy of old age is not that one is old, but that one is young. I am amazed sometimes at my own sincerity. Ah, Dorian, how happy you are! What an exquisite life you have had! You have drunk deeply of everything. You have crushed the grapes against your palate. Nothing has been hidden from you. But it has all been to you no more than the sound of music. It has not marred you. You are still the same.

"I wonder what the rest of your life will be. Don't spoil it by renunciations. At present you are a perfect type. Don't make yourself incomplete. You are quite flawless now. You need not shake your head: you know you are. Besides, Dorian, don't deceive yourself. Life is not governed by will or intention. Life is a question of nerves, and fibres, and slowly-built-up cells in which thought hides itself and passion has its dreams. You may fancy yourself safe, and think yourself strong. But a chance tone of color in a room or a morning sky, a particular perfume that you had once loved and that brings strange memories with it, a line from a forgotten poem that you had come across again, a cadence from a piece of music that you had ceased to play,--I tell you, Dorian, that it is on things like these that our lives depend. Browning writes about that somewhere; but our own senses will imagine them for us. There are

---

[1] Neckcloths

[2] A Spanish island in the Mediterranean where Chopin was known to holiday

[3] While Apollo is the Greek god of music and beauty, Marsyas was an ugly, leering satyr who challenged the god to a music contest judged by the muses. Apollo played his lyre and Marsyas his hypnotic panpipes, but because he cheated, Marsyas was able to hold his own against the sun god, and the contest ended in a draw

moments when the odor of heliotrope[1] passes suddenly across me, and I have to live the strangest year of my life over again.

"I wish I could change places with you, Dorian. The world has cried out against us both, but it has always worshipped you. It always will worship you. You are the type of what the age is searching for, and what it is afraid it has found. I am so glad that you have never done anything, never carved a statue, or painted a picture, or produced anything outside of yourself! Life has been your art. You have set yourself to music. Your days have been your sonnets."

Dorian rose up from the piano, and passed his hand through his hair. "Yes, life has been exquisite," he murmured, "but I am not going to have the same life, Harry. And you must not say these extravagant things to me. You don't know everything about me. I think that if you did, even you would turn from me. You laugh. Don't laugh."

"Why have you stopped playing, Dorian? Go back and play the nocturne over again. Look at that great honey-colored moon that hangs in the dusky air. She is waiting for you to charm her, and if you play she will come closer to the earth. You won't? Let us go to the club, then. It has been a charming evening, and we must end it charmingly. There is some one at the club who wants immensely to know you,--young Lord Poole, Bournmouth's eldest son[2]. He has already copied your neckties, and has begged me to introduce him to you. He is quite delightful, and rather reminds me of you."

"I hope not," said Dorian, with a touch of pathos in his voice. "But I am tired to-night, Harry. I won't go to the club. It is nearly eleven, and I want to go to bed early."

"Do stay. You have never played so well as to-night. There was something in your touch that was wonderful. It had more expression than I had ever heard from it before."

"It is because I am going to be good," he answered, smiling. "I am a little changed already."

"Don't change, Dorian; at any rate, don't change to me. We must always be friends."

"Yet you poisoned me with a book once. I should not forgive that. Harry, promise me that you will never lend that book to any one. It does harm."

"My dear boy, you are really beginning to moralize. You will soon be going about warning people against all the sins of which you have

---

[1] A sweet, purple flower

[2] Always eager to contribute to a young person's ruination, Henry is acting as pimp to Dorian, bringing him Lord Poole as a potential lover

grown tired. You are much too delightful to do that. Besides, it is no use. You and I are what we are, and will be what we will be. Come round tomorrow. I am going to ride at eleven, and we might go together. The Park is quite lovely now. I don't think there have been such lilacs since the year I met you."

"Very well. I will be here at eleven," said Dorian. "Good-night, Harry." As he reached the door he hesitated for a moment, as if he had something more to say. Then he sighed and went out.

It was a lovely night, so warm that he threw his coat over his arm, and did not even put his silk scarf round his throat. As he strolled home, smoking his cigarette, two young men in evening dress[1] passed him. He heard one of them whisper to the other, "That is Dorian Gray." He remembered how pleased he used to be when he was pointed out, or stared at, or talked about. He was tired of hearing his own name now. Half the charm of the little village where he had been so often lately was that no one knew who he was. He had told the girl whom he had made love him that he was poor, and she had believed him. He had told her once that he was wicked, and she had laughed at him, and told him that wicked people were always very old and very ugly. What a laugh she had!--just like a thrush singing. And how pretty she had been in her cotton dresses and her large hats[2]! She knew nothing, but she had everything that he had lost.

When he reached home, he found his servant waiting up for him. He sent him to bed, and threw himself down on the sofa in the library, and began to think over some of the things that Lord Henry had said to him.

Was it really true that one could never change? He felt a wild longing for the unstained purity of his boyhood,--his rose-white boyhood, as Lord Henry had once called it. He knew that he had tarnished himself, filled his mind with corruption, and given horror to his fancy; that he had been an evil influence to others, and had experienced a terrible joy in being so; and that of the lives that had crossed his own it had been the fairest and the most full of promise that he had brought to shame. But was it all irretrievable? Was there no hope for him?

It was better not to think of the past. Nothing could alter that. It was of himself, and of his own future, that he had to think. Alan Campbell had shot himself one night in his laboratory, but had not

---

[1] What we would roughly term tuxedos or "white tie" attire
[2] Typical of country fashions (as opposed to the aristocracy's satin gowns and petite bonnets)

revealed the secret that he had been forced to know. The excitement, such as it was, over Basil Hallward's disappearance would soon pass away. It was already waning. He was perfectly safe there. Nor, indeed, was it the death of Basil Hallward that weighed most upon his mind. It was the living death[1] of his own soul that troubled him. Basil had painted the portrait that had marred his life. He could not forgive him that. It was the portrait that had done everything. Basil had said things to him that were unbearable, and that he had yet borne with patience. The murder had been simply the madness of a moment. As for Alan Campbell, his suicide had been his own act. He had chosen to do it. It was nothing to him.

A new life! That was what he wanted. That was what he was waiting for. Surely he had begun it already. He had spared one innocent thing, at any rate. He would never again tempt innocence. He would be good.

As he thought of Hetty Merton, he began to wonder if the portrait in the locked room had changed. Surely it was not still so horrible as it had been? Perhaps if his life became pure, he would be able to expel every sign of evil passion from the face. Perhaps the signs of evil had already gone away. He would go and look.

He took the lamp from the table and crept up-stairs. As he unlocked the door, a smile of joy flitted across his young face and lingered for a moment about his lips. Yes, he would be good, and the hideous thing that he had hidden away would no longer be a terror to him. He felt as if the load had been lifted from him already.

He went in quietly, locking the door behind him, as was his custom, and dragged the purple hanging from the portrait. A cry of pain and indignation broke from him. He could see no change, unless that in the eyes there was a look of cunning, and in the mouth the curved wrinkle of the hypocrite[2]. The thing was still loathsome,--more loathsome, if

---

[1] An allusion, perhaps, to Coleridge's "Rime of the Ancient Mariner," where Death and Living Death (personified as a skeleton and a diseased woman, respectively) gamble over the Mariner's soul. "Living Death" – viz. spiritual anguish and guilt – wins the game. Likewise, Basil's living death was his doglike devotion to the objects of his worship and the shame felt concerning his homosexuality – these inhibitions prevented him from living a full, actualized life (hence living death)

[2] This reflects the nature of his "sparing" of Hetty: nothing more than a half-hearted attempt to smooth over the past – if he really wanted to make amends, he would turn himself into the authorities and publicly confess his role in the multiple suicides and deaths referenced throughout the novel. No: his mercy on Hetty is a hypocrisy intended to fake his way to salvation

possible, than before,--and the scarlet dew that spotted the hand seemed brighter, and more like blood newly spilt.

Had it been merely vanity that had made him do his one good deed? Or the desire of a new sensation, as Lord Henry had hinted, with his mocking laugh? Or that passion to act a part that sometimes makes us do things finer than we are ourselves? Or, perhaps, all these?

Why was the red stain larger than it had been? It seemed to have crept like a horrible disease over the wrinkled fingers. There was blood on the painted feet, as though the thing had dripped,--blood even on the hand that had not held the knife.

Confess? Did it mean that he was to confess? To give himself up, and be put to death? He laughed. He felt that the idea was monstrous. Besides, who would believe him, even if he did confess? There was no trace of the murdered man anywhere. Everything belonging to him had been destroyed. He himself had burned what had been below-stairs. The world would simply say he was mad. They would shut him up if he persisted in his story.

Yet it was his duty to confess, to suffer public shame, and to make public atonement[1]. There was a God who called upon men to tell their sins to earth as well as to heaven. Nothing that he could do would cleanse him till he had told his own sin. His sin? He shrugged his shoulders. The death of Basil Hallward seemed very little to him. He was thinking of Hetty Merton.

It was an unjust mirror, this mirror of his soul that he was looking at. Vanity? Curiosity? Hypocrisy? Had there been nothing more in his renunciation than that? There had been something more. At least he thought so. But who could tell?

And this murder,--was it to dog him all his life? Was he never to get rid of the past? Was he really to confess? No. There was only one bit of evidence left against him. The picture itself,--that was evidence[2].

He would destroy it. Why had he kept it so long? It had given him pleasure once to watch it changing and growing old. Of late he had felt no such pleasure. It had kept him awake at night. When he had been away, he had been filled with terror lest other eyes should look upon it.

---

[1] Indeed, this is the solution: to be genuine and not obsessed with his public image. To be like Sibyl, who loved him authentically, not like Henry who is delighted only by humbuggery and hypocrites

[2] The picture corresponds to his soul, and while his youthful face doesn't illustrate the corruption of his soul, he feels that the budget of his sins has been artfully recorded in the painting (which, by the way, can be seen as a symbol of the ego or conscience: Dorian's decision to slay his ego has the unintended result of a physical as well as spiritual suicide)

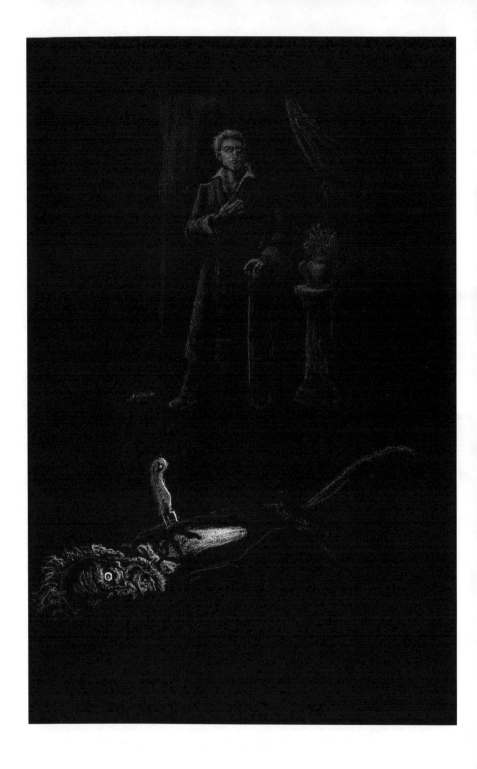

It had brought melancholy across his passions. Its mere memory had marred many moments of joy. It had been like conscience to him. Yes, it had been conscience. He would destroy it.

He looked round, and saw the knife that had stabbed Basil Hallward. He had cleaned it many times, till there was no stain left upon it. It was bright, and glistened. As it had killed the painter, so it would kill the painter's work, and all that that meant. It would kill the past, and when that was dead he would be free. He seized it, and stabbed the canvas with it, ripping the thing right up from top to bottom[1].

There was a cry heard, and a crash. The cry was so horrible in its agony that the frightened servants woke, and crept out of their rooms. Two gentlemen, who were passing in the Square below, stopped, and looked up at the great house. They walked on till they met a policeman, and brought him back. The man rang the bell several times, but there was no answer. The house was all dark, except for a light in one of the top windows. After a time, he went away, and stood in the portico of the next house and watched.

"Whose house is that, constable?" asked the elder of the two gentlemen.

"Mr. Dorian Gray's, sir," answered the policeman.

They looked at each other, as they walked away, and sneered. One of them was Sir Henry Ashton's[2] uncle.

Inside, in the servants' part of the house, the half-clad domestics were talking in low whispers to each other. Old Mrs. Leaf was crying, and wringing her hands. Francis was as pale as death.

After about a quarter of an hour, he got the coachman and one of the footmen and crept up-stairs. They knocked, but there was no reply. They called out. Everything was still. Finally, after vainly trying to force the door, they got on the roof, and dropped down on to the balcony. The windows yielded easily: the bolts were old.

When they entered, they found hanging upon the wall a splendid portrait of their master as they had last seen him, in all the wonder of

---

[1] Although we are led to believe that this is a supernatural novel and that it would be possible for Dorian to stab the portrait and for it to cause the injury to supernaturally reflect itself in his body, it is also arguable that Dorian – dizzied by his fear and self-loathing – literally stabs the object of his hate – himself – without realizing it

[2] This is the ruined friend of Dorian's of whom Basil says: "There was Sir Henry Ashton, who had to leave England with a tarnished name. You and he were inseparable"

his exquisite youth and beauty[1]. Lying on the floor was a dead man, in evening dress, with a knife in his heart[2]. He was withered, wrinkled, and loathsome of visage. It was not till they had examined the rings that they recognized who it was.

The End.

---

[1] In the act of confronting and assaulting his wickedness, Dorian transfers his soul back into his body, transforming the painting back to its original form, and absorbing the sin into his physical body

[2] Since the heart symbolizes the essence of a thing, Dorian – having tried to stab the painting (symbolic of his sin) – finds the knife transmuted into his own heart. Wilde's final message is clear: Dorian's essence – and all of ours – is the summation of his wickedness, and cannot be successfully redeemed without dire consequences: confrontation, atonement, arrest, shame, censure, prison, suicide, or death. This ending resembles Poe's "William Wilson," wherein a man is dogged by his doppelganger whenever he is about to do something vile. Just before he is about to seduce a married woman at a party, he sees the double lurking in the crowd and is seized with rage. Following the doppelganger into an empty room, he stabs it in the chest. The bleeding image tells him that by slaying his conscience, he has killed himself in the process, whereupon Wilson realizes that he is looking into a mirror, and that he has indeed stabbed his own self

WILDE was fascinated by the concept of duty – not by its merits, but by its ludicrousness. When Dorian realizes that it is his "duty" to marry Sibyl Vane (unaware of her suicide), there is a youthful silliness about his resolution (one at which Lord Henry would undoubtedly have laughed). Even as much as we may want him to make amends with her, we realize that marrying a woman because it is one's duty is a great way to begin a terrible marriage. "Lord Arthur Saville's Crime" was given the subtitle "A Study in Duty" to underscore its basic message: that a society dominated by the burdens of obligation will eventually find itself at the mercy of mindless lunatics driven to wage wars of honor in the name of "duty" with little concern for collateral damage.

Lord Arthur Saville's Crime: A Study of Duty
{1887}

CHAPTER I

IT was Lady Windermere's last reception before Easter, and Bentinck House was even more crowded than usual. Six Cabinet Ministers had come on from the Speaker's Levée in their stars and ribands, all the pretty women wore their smartest dresses, and at the end of the picture-gallery stood the Princess Sophia of Carlsrühe, a heavy Tartar-looking lady, with tiny black eyes and wonderful emeralds, talking bad French at the top of her voice, and laughing immoderately at everything that was said to her. It was certainly a wonderful medley of people. Gorgeous peeresses chatted affably to violent Radicals, popular preachers brushed coat-tails with eminent sceptics, a perfect bevy of bishops kept following a stout prima-donna from room to room, on the staircase stood several Royal Academicians, disguised as artists, and it was said that at one time the supper-room was absolutely crammed with geniuses. In fact, it was one of Lady Windermere's best nights, and the Princess stayed till nearly half-past eleven.

As soon as she had gone, Lady Windermere returned to the picture-gallery, where a celebrated political economist was solemnly explaining the scientific theory of music to an indignant virtuoso from Hungary, and began to talk to the Duchess of Paisley. She looked wonderfully beautiful with her grand ivory throat, her large blue forget-me-not eyes, and her heavy coils of golden hair. *Or pur* they were—not that pale straw colour that nowadays usurps the gracious name of gold, but such gold as is woven into sunbeams or hidden in strange amber; and they gave to her face something of the frame of a saint, with not a little of the fascination of a sinner. She was a curious psychological study. Early in life she had discovered the important truth that nothing looks so like innocence as an indiscretion; and by a series of reckless escapades, half of them quite harmless, she had acquired all the privileges of a personality. She had more than once changed her husband; indeed, Debrett credits her with three marriages; but as she had never changed her lover, the world had long ago ceased to talk scandal about her. She was now forty years of age, childless, and with that inordinate passion for pleasure which is the secret of remaining young.

Suddenly she looked eagerly round the room, and said, in her clear contralto voice, 'Where is my cheiromantist?'

'Your what, Gladys?' exclaimed the Duchess, giving an involuntary start.

'My cheiromantist, Duchess; I can't live without him at present.'

'Dear Gladys! you are always so original,' murmured the Duchess, trying to remember what a cheiromantist really was, and hoping it was not the same as a cheiropodist.

'He comes to see my hand twice a week regularly,' continued Lady Windermere, 'and is most interesting about it.'

'Good heavens!' said the Duchess to herself, 'he is a sort of cheiropodist after all. How very dreadful. I hope he is a foreigner at any rate. It wouldn't be quite so bad then.'

'I must certainly introduce him to you.'

'Introduce him!' cried the Duchess; 'you don't mean to say he is here?' and she began looking about for a small tortoise-shell fan and a very tattered lace shawl, so as to be ready to go at a moment's notice.

'Of course he is here; I would not dream of giving a party without him. He tells me I have a pure psychic hand, and that if my thumb had been the least little bit shorter, I should have been a confirmed pessimist, and gone into a convent.'

'Oh, I see!' said the Duchess, feeling very much relieved; 'he tells fortunes, I suppose?'

'And misfortunes, too,' answered Lady Windermere, 'any amount of them. Next year, for instance, I am in great danger, both by land and sea, so I am going to live in a balloon, and draw up my dinner in a basket every evening. It is all written down on my little finger, or on the palm of my hand, I forget which.'

'But surely that is tempting Providence, Gladys.'

'My dear Duchess, surely Providence can resist temptation by this time. I think every one should have their hands told once a month, so as to know what not to do. Of course, one does it all the same, but it is so pleasant to be warned. Now if some one doesn't go and fetch Mr. Podgers at once, I shall have to go myself.'

'Let me go, Lady Windermere,' said a tall handsome young man, who was standing by, listening to the conversation with an amused smile.

'Thanks so much, Lord Arthur; but I am afraid you wouldn't recognise him.'

'If he is as wonderful as you say, Lady Windermere, I couldn't well miss him. Tell me what he is like, and I'll bring him to you at once.'

'Well, he is not a bit like a cheiromantist. I mean he is not mysterious, or esoteric, or romantic-looking. He is a little, stout man, with a funny, bald head, and great gold-rimmed spectacles; something between a family doctor and a country attorney. I'm really very sorry, but it is not my fault. People are so annoying. All my pianists look exactly like poets, and all my poets look exactly like pianists; and I remember last season asking a most dreadful conspirator to dinner, a man who had blown up ever so many people, and always wore a coat of mail, and carried a dagger up his shirt-sleeve; and do you know that when he came he looked just like a nice old clergyman, and cracked jokes all the evening? Of course, he was very amusing, and all that, but I was awfully disappointed; and when I asked him about the coat of mail, he only laughed, and said it was far too cold to wear in England. Ah, here is Mr. Podgers! Now, Mr. Podgers, I want you to tell the Duchess of Paisley's hand. Duchess, you must take your glove off. No, not the left hand, the other.'

'Dear Gladys, I really don't think it is quite right,' said the Duchess, feebly unbuttoning a rather soiled kid glove.

'Nothing interesting ever is,' said Lady Windermere: '*on a fait le monde ainsi.* But I must introduce you. Duchess, this is Mr. Podgers, my pet cheiromantist. Mr. Podgers, this is the Duchess of Paisley, and if you say that she has a larger mountain of the moon than I have, I will never believe in you again.'

'I am sure, Gladys, there is nothing of the kind in my hand,' said the Duchess gravely.

'Your Grace is quite right,' said Mr. Podgers, glancing at the little fat hand with its short square fingers, 'the mountain of the moon is not developed. The line of life, however, is excellent. Kindly bend the wrist. Thank you. Three distinct lines on the *rascette*! You will live to a great age, Duchess, and be extremely happy. Ambition—very moderate, line of intellect not exaggerated, line of heart—'

'Now, do be indiscreet, Mr. Podgers,' cried Lady Windermere.

'Nothing would give me greater pleasure,' said Mr. Podgers, bowing, 'if the Duchess ever had been, but I am sorry to say that I see great permanence of affection, combined with a strong sense of duty.'

'Pray go on, Mr. Podgers,' said the Duchess, looking quite pleased.

'Economy is not the least of your Grace's virtues,' continued Mr. Podgers, and Lady Windermere went off into fits of laughter.

'Economy is a very good thing,' remarked the Duchess complacently; 'when I married Paisley he had eleven castles, and not a single house fit to live in.'

'And now he has twelve houses, and not a single castle,' cried Lady Windermere.

'Well, my dear,' said the Duchess, 'I like—'

'Comfort,' said Mr. Podgers, 'and modern improvements, and hot water laid on in every bedroom. Your Grace is quite right. Comfort is the only thing our civilisation can give us.

'You have told the Duchess's character admirably, Mr. Podgers, and now you must tell Lady Flora's'; and in answer to a nod from the smiling hostess, a tall girl, with sandy Scotch hair, and high shoulder-blades, stepped awkwardly from behind the sofa, and held out a long, bony hand with spatulate fingers.

'Ah, a pianist! I see,' said Mr. Podgers, 'an excellent pianist, but perhaps hardly a musician. Very reserved, very honest, and with a great love of animals.'

'Quite true!' exclaimed the Duchess, turning to Lady Windermere, 'absolutely true! Flora keeps two dozen collie dogs at Macloskie, and would turn our town house into a menagerie if her father would let her.'

'Well, that is just what I do with my house every Thursday evening,' cried Lady Windermere, laughing, 'only I like lions better than collie dogs.'

'Your one mistake, Lady Windermere,' said Mr. Podgers, with a pompous bow.

'If a woman can't make her mistakes charming, she is only a female,' was the answer. 'But you must read some more hands for us. Come, Sir Thomas, show Mr. Podgers yours'; and a genial-looking old gentleman, in a white waistcoat, came forward, and held out a thick rugged hand, with a very long third finger.

'An adventurous nature; four long voyages in the past, and one to come. Been ship-wrecked three times. No, only twice, but in danger of a shipwreck your next journey. A strong Conservative, very punctual, and with a passion for collecting curiosities. Had a severe illness between the ages sixteen and eighteen. Was left a fortune when about thirty. Great aversion to cats and Radicals.'

'Extraordinary!' exclaimed Sir Thomas; 'you must really tell my wife's hand, too.'

'Your second wife's,' said Mr. Podgers quietly, still keeping Sir Thomas's hand in his. 'Your second wife's. I shall be charmed'; but Lady Marvel, a melancholy-looking woman, with brown hair and sentimental eyelashes, entirely declined to have her past or her future exposed; and nothing that Lady Windermere could do would induce Monsieur de Koloff, the Russian Ambassador, even to take his gloves off. In fact, many people seemed afraid to face the odd little man with his stereotyped smile, his gold spectacles, and his bright, beady eyes; and when he told poor Lady Fermor, right out before every one, that she did not care a bit for music, but was extremely fond of musicians, it was generally felt that cheiromancy was a most dangerous science, and one that ought not to be encouraged, except in a *tête-à-tête*.

Lord Arthur Savile, however, who did not know anything about Lady Fermor's unfortunate story, and who had been watching Mr. Podgers with a great deal of interest, was filled with an immense curiosity to have his own hand read, and feeling somewhat shy about putting himself forward, crossed over the room to where Lady Windermere was sitting, and, with a charming blush, asked her if she thought Mr. Podgers would mind.

'Of course, he won't mind,' said Lady Windermere, 'that is what he is here for. All my lions, Lord Arthur, are performing lions, and jump through hoops whenever I ask them. But I must warn you beforehand that I shall tell Sybil everything. She is coming to lunch with me to-morrow, to talk about bonnets, and if Mr. Podgers finds out that you have a bad temper, or a tendency to gout, or a wife living in Bayswater, I shall certainly let her know all about it.'

Lord Arthur smiled, and shook his head. 'I am not afraid,' he answered. 'Sybil knows me as well as I know her.'

'Ah! I am a little sorry to hear you say that. The proper basis for marriage is a mutual misunderstanding. No, I am not at all cynical, I have merely got experience, which, however, is very much the same thing. Mr. Podgers, Lord Arthur Savile is dying to have his hand read. Don't tell him that he is engaged to one of the most beautiful girls in London, because that appeared in the *Morning Post* a month ago.'

'Dear Lady Windermere,' cried the Marchioness of Jedburgh, 'do let Mr. Podgers stay here a little longer. He has just told me I should go on the stage, and I am so interested.'

'If he has told you that, Lady Jedburgh, I shall certainly take him away. Come over at once, Mr. Podgers, and read Lord Arthur's hand.'

'Well,' said Lady Jedburgh, making a little *moue* as she rose from the sofa, 'if I am not to be allowed to go on the stage, I must be allowed to be part of the audience at any rate.'

'Of course; we are all going to be part of the audience,' said Lady Windermere; 'and now, Mr. Podgers, be sure and tell us something nice. Lord Arthur is one of my special favourites.'

But when Mr. Podgers saw Lord Arthur's hand he grew curiously pale, and said nothing. A shudder seemed to pass through him, and his great bushy eyebrows twitched convulsively, in an odd, irritating way they had when he was puzzled. Then some huge beads of perspiration broke out on his yellow forehead, like a poisonous dew, and his fat fingers grew cold and clammy.

Lord Arthur did not fail to notice these strange signs of agitation, and, for the first time in his life, he himself felt fear. His impulse was to rush from the room, but he restrained himself. It was better to know the worst, whatever it was, than to be left in this hideous uncertainty.

'I am waiting, Mr. Podgers,' he said.

'We are all waiting,' cried Lady Windermere, in her quick, impatient manner, but the cheiromantist made no reply.

'I believe Arthur is going on the stage,' said Lady Jedburgh, 'and that, after your scolding, Mr. Podgers is afraid to tell him so.'

Suddenly Mr. Podgers dropped Lord Arthur's right hand, and seized hold of his left, bending down so low to examine it that the gold rims of his spectacles seemed almost to touch the palm. For a moment his face became a white mask of horror, but he soon recovered his *sang-froid*, and looking up at Lady Windermere, said with a forced smile, 'It is the hand of a charming young man.

'Of course it is!' answered Lady Windermere, 'but will he be a charming husband? That is what I want to know.'

'All charming young men are,' said Mr. Podgers.

'I don't think a husband should be too fascinating,' murmured Lady Jedburgh pensively, 'it is so dangerous.'

'My dear child, they never are too fascinating,' cried Lady Windermere. 'But what I want are details. Details are the only things that interest. What is going to happen to Lord Arthur?'

'Well, within the next few months Lord Arthur will go a voyage—'

'Oh yes, his honeymoon, of course!'

'And lose a relative.'

'Not his sister, I hope?' said Lady Jedburgh, in a piteous tone of voice.

'Certainly not his sister,' answered Mr. Podgers, with a deprecating wave of the hand, 'a distant relative merely.'

'Well, I am dreadfully disappointed,' said Lady Windermere. 'I have absolutely nothing to tell Sybil to-morrow. No one cares about distant relatives nowadays. They went out of fashion years ago. However, I suppose she had better have a black silk by her; it always does for church, you know. And now let us go to supper. They are sure to have eaten everything up, but we may find some hot soup. François used to make excellent soup once, but he is so agitated about politics at present, that I never feel quite certain about him. I do wish General Boulanger would keep quiet. Duchess, I am sure you are tired?'

'Not at all, dear Gladys,' answered the Duchess, waddling towards the door. 'I have enjoyed myself immensely, and the cheiropodist, I mean the cheiromantist, is most interesting. Flora, where can my tortoise-shell fan be? Oh, thank you, Sir Thomas, so much. And my lace shawl, Flora? Oh, thank you, Sir Thomas, very kind, I'm sure'; and the worthy creature finally managed to get downstairs without dropping her scent-bottle more than twice.

All this time Lord Arthur Savile had remained standing by the fireplace, with the same feeling of dread over him, the same sickening sense of coming evil. He smiled sadly at his sister, as she swept past him on Lord Plymdale's arm, looking lovely in her pink brocade and pearls, and he hardly heard Lady Windermere when she called to him to follow her. He thought of Sybil Merton, and the idea that anything could come between them made his eyes dim with tears.

Looking at him, one would have said that Nemesis had stolen the shield of Pallas, and shown him the Gorgon's head. He seemed turned to stone, and his face was like marble in its melancholy. He had lived the delicate and luxurious life of a young man of birth and fortune, a life exquisite in its freedom from sordid care, its beautiful boyish insouciance; and now for the first time he became conscious of the terrible mystery of Destiny, of the awful meaning of Doom.

How mad and monstrous it all seemed! Could it be that written on his hand, in characters that he could not read himself, but that another could decipher, was some fearful secret of sin, some blood-red sign of crime? Was there no escape possible? Were we no better than chessmen, moved by an unseen power, vessels the potter fashions at his fancy, for honour or for shame? His reason revolted against it, and yet he felt that some tragedy was hanging over him, and that he had been suddenly called upon to bear an intolerable burden. Actors are so fortunate. They can choose whether they will appear in tragedy or in comedy, whether they will suffer or make merry, laugh or shed tears. But in real life it is different. Most men and women are forced to perform parts for which they have no qualifications. Our Guildensterns play Hamlet for us, and our Hamlets have to jest like Prince Hal. The world is a stage, but the play is badly cast.

Suddenly Mr. Podgers entered the room. When he saw Lord Arthur he started, and his coarse, fat face became a sort of greenish-yellow colour. The two men's eyes met, and for a moment there was silence.

'The Duchess has left one of her gloves here, Lord Arthur, and has asked me to bring it to her,' said Mr. Podgers finally. 'Ah, I see it on the sofa! Good evening.'

'Mr. Podgers, I must insist on your giving me a straightforward answer to a question I am going to put to you.'

'Another time, Lord Arthur, but the Duchess is anxious. I am afraid I must go.'

'You shall not go. The Duchess is in no hurry.'

'Ladies should not be kept waiting, Lord Arthur,' said Mr. Podgers, with his sickly smile. 'The fair sex is apt to be impatient.'

Lord Arthur's finely-chiselled lips curled in petulant disdain. The poor Duchess seemed to him of very little importance at that moment. He walked across the room to where Mr. Podgers was standing, and held his hand out.

'Tell me what you saw there,' he said. 'Tell me the truth. I must know it. I am not a child.'

Mr. Podgers's eyes blinked behind his gold-rimmed spectacles, and he moved uneasily from one foot to the other, while his fingers played nervously with a flash watch-chain.

'What makes you think that I saw anything in your hand, Lord Arthur, more than I told you?'

'I know you did, and I insist on your telling me what it was. I will pay you. I will give you a cheque for a hundred pounds.'

The green eyes flashed for a moment, and then became dull again.

'Guineas?' said Mr. Podgers at last, in a low voice.

'Certainly. I will send you a cheque to-morrow. What is your club?'

'I have no club. That is to say, not just at present. My address is—, but allow me to give you my card'; and producing a bit of gilt-edge pasteboard from his waistcoat pocket, Mr. Podgers handed it, with a low bow, to Lord Arthur, who read on it,

Mr. SEPTIMUS R. PODGERS
Professional Cheiromantist
103a West Moon Street

'My hours are from ten to four,' murmured Mr. Podgers mechanically, 'and I make a reduction for families.'

'Be quick,' cried Lord Arthur, looking very pale, and holding his hand out.

Mr. Podgers glanced nervously round, and drew the heavy *portière* across the door.

'It will take a little time, Lord Arthur, you had better sit down.'

'Be quick, sir,' cried Lord Arthur again, stamping his foot angrily on the polished floor.

Mr. Podgers smiled, drew from his breast-pocket a small magnifying glass, and wiped it carefully with his handkerchief.

'I am quite ready,' he said.

CHAPTER II

TEN minutes later, with face blanched by terror, and eyes wild with grief, Lord Arthur Savile rushed from Bentinck House, crushing his way through the crowd of fur-coated footmen that stood round the large striped awning, and seeming not to see or hear anything. The night was bitter cold, and the gas-lamps round the square flared and flickered in the keen wind; but his hands were hot with fever, and his forehead burned like fire. On and on he went, almost with the gait of a drunken man. A policeman looked curiously at him as he passed, and a beggar, who slouched from an archway to ask for alms, grew frightened, seeing misery greater than his own. Once he stopped under a lamp, and looked at his hands. He thought he could detect the stain of blood already upon them, and a faint cry broke from his trembling lips.

Murder! that is what the cheiromantist had seen there. Murder! The very night seemed to know it, and the desolate wind to howl it in his ear. The dark corners of the streets were full of it. It grinned at him from the roofs of the houses.

First he came to the Park, whose sombre woodland seemed to fascinate him. He leaned wearily up against the railings, cooling his brow against the wet metal, and listening to the tremulous silence of the trees. 'Murder! murder!' he kept repeating, as though iteration could dim the horror of the word. The sound of his own voice made him shudder, yet he almost hoped that Echo might hear him, and wake the slumbering city from its dreams. He felt a mad desire to stop the casual passer-by, and tell him everything.

Then he wandered across Oxford Street into narrow, shameful alleys. Two women with painted faces mocked at him as he went by. From a dark courtyard came a sound of oaths and blows, followed by shrill screams, and, huddled upon a damp door-step, he saw the crook-backed forms of poverty and eld. A strange pity came over him. Were these children of sin and misery predestined to their end, as he to his? Were they, like him, merely the puppets of a monstrous show?

And yet it was not the mystery, but the comedy of suffering that struck him; its absolute uselessness, its grotesque want of meaning. How incoherent everything seemed! How lacking in all harmony! He was amazed at the discord between the shallow optimism of the day, and the real facts of existence. He was still very young.

After a time he found himself in front of Marylebone Church. The silent roadway looked like a long riband of polished silver, flecked here and there by the dark arabesques of waving shadows. Far into the distance curved the line of flickering gas-lamps, and outside a little walled-in house stood a solitary hansom, the driver asleep inside. He walked hastily in the direction of Portland Place, now and then looking round, as though he feared that he was being followed. At the corner of Rich Street stood two men, reading a small bill upon a hoarding. An odd feeling of curiosity stirred him, and he crossed over. As he came near, the word 'Murder,' printed in black letters, met his eye. He started, and a deep flush came into his cheek. It was an advertisement offering a reward for any information leading to the arrest of a man of medium height, between thirty and forty years of age, wearing a billy-cock hat, a black coat, and check trousers, and with a scar upon his right cheek. He read it over and over again, and wondered if the wretched man would be caught, and how he had been scarred. Perhaps, some day, his own name might be placarded on the walls of London. Some day, perhaps, a price would be set on his head also.

The thought made him sick with horror. He turned on his heel, and hurried on into the night.

Where he went he hardly knew. He had a dim memory of wandering through a labyrinth of sordid houses, of being lost in a giant web of sombre streets, and it was bright dawn when he found himself at last in Piccadilly Circus. As he strolled home towards Belgrave Square, he met the great waggons on their way to Covent Garden. The white-smocked carters, with their pleasant sunburnt faces and coarse curly hair, strode sturdily on, cracking their whips, and calling out now and then to each other; on the back of a huge grey horse, the leader of a jangling team, sat a chubby boy, with a bunch of primroses in his battered hat, keeping tight hold of the mane with his little hands, and laughing; and the great piles of vegetables looked like masses of jade against the morning sky, like masses of green jade against the pink petals of some marvellous rose. Lord Arthur felt curiously affected, he could not tell why. There was something in the dawn's delicate loveliness that seemed to him inexpressibly pathetic, and he thought of

174

all the days that break in beauty, and that set in storm. These rustics, too, with their rough, good-humoured voices, and their nonchalant ways, what a strange London they saw! A London free from the sin of night and the smoke of day, a pallid, ghost-like city, a desolate town of tombs! He wondered what they thought of it, and whether they knew anything of its splendour and its shame, of its fierce, fiery-coloured joys, and its horrible hunger, of all it makes and mars from morn to eve. Probably it was to them merely a mart where they brought their fruits to sell, and where they tarried for a few hours at most, leaving the streets still silent, the houses still asleep. It gave him pleasure to watch them as they went by. Rude as they were, with their heavy, hob-nailed shoes, and their awkward gait, they brought a little of a ready with them. He felt that they had lived with Nature, and that she had taught them peace. He envied them all that they did not know.

By the time he had reached Belgrave Square the sky was a faint blue, and the birds were beginning to twitter in the gardens.

CHAPTER III

WHEN Lord Arthur woke it was twelve o'clock, and the midday sun was streaming through the ivory-silk curtains of his room. He got up and looked out of the window. A dim haze of heat was hanging over the great city, and the roofs of the houses were like dull silver. In the flickering green of the square below some children were flitting about like white butterflies, and the pavement was crowded with people on their way to the Park. Never had life seemed lovelier to him, never had the things of evil seemed more remote.

Then his valet brought him a cup of chocolate on a tray. After he had drunk it, he drew aside a heavy *portière* of peach-coloured plush, and passed into the bathroom. The light stole softly from above, through thin slabs of transparent onyx, and the water in the marble tank glimmered like a moonstone. He plunged hastily in, till the cool ripples touched throat and hair, and then dipped his head right under, as though he would have wiped away the stain of some shameful memory. When he stepped out he felt almost at peace. The exquisite physical conditions of the moment had dominated him, as indeed often happens in the case of very finely-wrought natures, for the senses, like fire, can purify as well as destroy.

After breakfast, he flung himself down on a divan, and lit a cigarette. On the mantel-shelf, framed in dainty old brocade, stood a large photograph of Sybil Merton, as he had seen her first at Lady Noel's ball. The small, exquisitely-shaped head drooped slightly to one side, as though the thin, reed-like throat could hardly bear the burden of so much beauty; the lips were slightly parted, and seemed made for sweet music; and all the tender purity of girlhood looked out in wonder from the dreaming eyes. With her soft, clinging dress of *crêpe-de-chine*, and her large leaf-shaped fan, she looked like one of those delicate little figures men find in the olive-woods near Tanagra; and there was a touch of Greek grace in her pose and attitude. Yet she was not *petite*. She was simply perfectly proportioned—a rare thing in an age when so many women are either over life-size or insignificant.

Now as Lord Arthur looked at her, he was filled with the terrible pity that is born of love. He felt that to marry her, with the doom of murder hanging over his head, would be a betrayal like that of Judas, a sin worse than any the Borgia had ever dreamed of. What happiness could there be for them, when at any moment he might be called upon to carry out the awful prophecy written in his hand? What manner of life would be theirs while Fate still held this fearful fortune in the scales? The marriage must be postponed, at all costs. Of this he was quite resolved. Ardently though he loved the girl, and the mere touch of her fingers, when they sat together, made each nerve of his body thrill with exquisite joy, he recognised none the less clearly where his duty lay, and was fully conscious of the fact that he had no right to marry until he had committed the murder. This done, he could stand before the altar with Sybil Merton, and give his life into her hands without terror of wrongdoing. This done, he could take her to his arms, knowing that she would never have to blush for him, never have to hang her head in shame. But done it must be first; and the sooner the better for both.

Many men in his position would have preferred the primrose path of dalliance to the steep heights of duty; but Lord Arthur was too conscientious to set pleasure above principle. There was more than mere passion in his love; and Sybil was to him a symbol of all that is good and noble. For a moment he had a natural repugnance against what he was asked to do, but it soon passed away. His heart told him that it was not a sin, but a sacrifice; his reason reminded him that there was no other course open. He had to choose between living for himself and living for others, and terrible though the task laid upon him undoubtedly was, yet he knew that he must not suffer selfishness to triumph over love. Sooner or later we are all called upon to decide on the same issue—of us all, the same question is asked. To Lord Arthur it came early in life—before his nature had been spoiled by the calculating cynicism of middle-age, or his heart corroded by the shallow, fashionable egotism of our day, and he felt no hesitation about doing his duty. Fortunately also, for him, he was no mere dreamer, or idle dilettante. Had he been so, he would have hesitated, like Hamlet, and let irresolution mar his purpose. But he was essentially practical. Life to him meant action, rather than thought. He had that rarest of all things, common sense.

The wild, turbid feelings of the previous night had by this time completely passed away, and it was almost with a sense of shame that he looked back upon his mad wanderings from street to street, his fierce emotional agony. The very sincerity of his sufferings made them seem unreal to him now. He wondered how he could have been so foolish as to rant and rave about the inevitable. The only question that seemed to trouble him was, whom to make away with; for he was not blind to the fact that murder, like the religions of the Pagan world, requires a victim as well as a priest. Not being a genius, he had no enemies, and indeed he felt that this was not the time for the gratification of any personal pique or dislike, the mission in which he was engaged being one of great and grave solemnity. He accordingly made out a list of his friends and relatives on a sheet of notepaper, and after careful consideration, decided in favour of Lady Clementina Beauchamp, a dear old lady who lived in Curzon Street, and was his own second cousin by his mother's side. He had always been very fond of Lady Clem, as every one called her, and as he was very wealthy himself, having come into all Lord Rugby's property when he came of age, there was no possibility of his deriving any vulgar monetary advantage by her death. In fact, the more he thought over the matter, the more she seemed to him to be just the right person, and, feeling that any delay would be unfair to Sybil, he determined to make his arrangements at once.

The first thing to be done was, of course, to settle with the cheiromantist; so he sat down at a small Sheraton writing-table that stood near the window, drew a cheque for £105, payable to the order of Mr. Septimus Podgers, and, enclosing it in an envelope, told his valet to take it to West Moon Street. He then telephoned to the stables for his hansom, and dressed to go out. As he was leaving the room he looked back at Sybil Merton's photograph, and swore that, come what may, he would never let her know what he was doing for her sake, but would keep the secret of his self-sacrifice hidden always in his heart.

On his way to the Buckingham, he stopped at a florist's, and sent Sybil a beautiful basket of narcissus, with lovely white petals and staring pheasants' eyes, and on arriving at the club, went straight to the library, rang the bell, and ordered the waiter to bring him a lemon-and-soda, and a book on Toxicology. He had fully decided that poison was the best means to adopt in this troublesome business. Anything like personal violence was extremely distasteful to him, and besides, he was very anxious not to murder Lady Clementina in any way that might attract public attention, as he hated the idea of being lionised at Lady Windermere's, or seeing his name figuring in the paragraphs of vulgar society—newspapers. He had also to think of Sybil's father and mother, who were rather old-fashioned people, and might possibly object to the marriage if there was anything like a scandal, though he felt certain that if he told them the whole facts of the case they would be the very first to appreciate the motives that had actuated him. He had every reason, then, to decide in favour of poison. It was safe, sure, and quiet, and did away with any necessity for painful scenes, to which, like most Englishmen, he had a rooted objection.

Of the science of poisons, however, he knew absolutely nothing, and as the waiter seemed quite unable to find anything in the library but *Ruff's Guide* and *Bailey's Magazine*, he examined the book-shelves himself, and finally came across a handsomely-bound edition of the *Pharmacopoeia*, and a copy of Erskine's *Toxicology*, edited by Sir Mathew Reid, the President of the Royal College of Physicians, and one of the oldest members of the Buckingham, having been elected in mistake for somebody else; a *contretemps* that so enraged the Committee, that when the real man came up they black-balled him unanimously. Lord Arthur was a good deal puzzled at the technical terms used in both books, and had begun to regret that he had not paid more attention to his classics at Oxford, when in the second volume of Erskine, he found a very interesting and complete account of the properties of aconitine, written in fairly clear English. It seemed to him to be exactly the poison he wanted. It was swift—indeed, almost immediate, in its effect—perfectly painless, and when taken in the form of a gelatine capsule, the mode recommended by Sir Mathew, not by any means unpalatable. He accordingly made a note, upon his shirt-cuff, of the amount necessary for a fatal dose, put the books back in their places, and strolled up St. James's Street, to Pestle and Humbey's, the great chemists. Mr. Pestle, who always attended personally on the aristocracy, was a good deal surprised at the order, and in a very deferential manner murmured something about a medical certificate being necessary. However, as soon as Lord Arthur explained to him that it was for a large Norwegian mastiff that he was obliged to get rid of, as it showed signs of incipient rabies, and had already bitten the coachman twice in the calf of the leg, he expressed himself as being perfectly satisfied, complimented Lord Arthur on his wonderful knowledge of Toxicology, and had the prescription made up immediately.

Lord Arthur put the capsule into a pretty little silver *bonbonnière* that he saw in a shop window in Bond Street, threw away Pestle and Hambey's ugly pill-box, and drove off at once to Lady Clementina's.

'Well, *monsieur le mauvais sujet*,' cried the old lady, as he entered the room, 'why haven't you been to see me all this time?'

'My dear Lady Clem, I never have a moment to myself,' said Lord Arthur, smiling.

'I suppose you mean that you go about all day long with Miss Sybil Merton, buying *chiffons* and talking nonsense? I cannot understand why people make such a fuss about being married. In my day we never dreamed of billing and cooing in public, or in private for that matter.'

'I assure you I have not seen Sybil for twenty-four hours, Lady Clem. As far as I can make out, she belongs entirely to her milliners.'

'Of course; that is the only reason you come to see an ugly old woman like myself. I wonder you men don't take warning. *On a fait des folies pour moi*, and here I am, a poor rheumatic creature, with a false front and a bad temper. Why, if it were not for dear Lady Jansen, who sends me all the worst French novels she can find, I don't think I could get through the day. Doctors are no use at all, except to get fees out of one. They can't even cure my heartburn.'

'I have brought you a cure for that, Lady Clem,' said Lord Arthur gravely. 'It is a wonderful thing, invented by an American.'

'I don't think I like American inventions, Arthur. I am quite sure I don't. I read some American novels lately, and they were quite nonsensical.'

'Oh, but there is no nonsense at all about this, Lady Clem! I assure you it is a perfect cure. You must promise to try it'; and Lord Arthur brought the little box out of his pocket, and handed it to her.

'Well, the box is charming, Arthur. Is it really a present? That is very sweet of you. And is this the wonderful medicine? It looks like a *bonbon*. I'll take it at once.'

'Good heavens! Lady Clem,' cried Lord Arthur, catching hold of her hand, 'you mustn't do anything of the kind. It is a homoeopathic medicine, and if you take it without having heartburn, it might do you no end of harm. Wait till you have an attack, and take it then. You will be astonished at the result.'

'I should like to take it now,' said Lady Clementina, holding up to the light the little transparent capsule, with its floating bubble of liquid aconitine. I am sure it is delicious. The fact is that, though I hate doctors, I love medicines. However, I'll keep it till my next attack.'

'And when will that be?' asked Lord Arthur eagerly. 'Will it be soon?'

'I hope not for a week. I had a very bad time yesterday morning with it. But one never knows.'

'You are sure to have one before the end of the month then, Lady Clem?'

'I am afraid so. But how sympathetic you are to-day, Arthur! Really, Sybil has done you a great deal of good. And now you must run away, for I am dining with some very dull people, who won't talk scandal, and I know that if I don't get my sleep now I shall never be able to keep awake during dinner. Good-bye, Arthur, give my love to Sybil, and thank you so much for the American medicine.'

'You won't forget to take it, Lady Clem, will you?' said Lord Arthur, rising from his seat.

'Of course I won't, you silly boy. I think it is most kind of you to think of me, and I shall write and tell you if I want any more.'

Lord Arthur left the house in high spirits, and with a feeling of immense relief.

That night he had an interview with Sybil Merton. He told her how he had been suddenly placed in a position of terrible difficulty, from which neither honour nor duty would allow him to recede. He told her that the marriage must be put off for the present, as until he had got rid of his fearful entanglements, he was not a free man. He implored her to trust him, and not to have any doubts about the future. Everything would come right, but patience was necessary.

The scene took place in the conservatory of Mr. Merton's house, in Park Lane, where Lord Arthur had dined as usual. Sybil had never seemed more happy, and for a moment Lord Arthur had been tempted to play the coward's part, to write to Lady Clementina for the pill, and to let the marriage go on as if there was no such person as Mr. Podgers in the world. His better nature, however, soon asserted itself, and even when Sybil flung herself weeping into his arms, he did not falter. The beauty that stirred his senses had touched his conscience also. He felt that to wreck so fair a life for the sake of a few months' pleasure would be a wrong thing to do.

He stayed with Sybil till nearly midnight, comforting her and being comforted in turn, and early the next morning he left for Venice, after writing a manly, firm letter to Mr. Merton about the necessary postponement of the marriage.

CHAPTER IV

IN Venice he met his brother, Lord Surbiton, who happened to have come over from Corfu in his yacht. The two young men spent a delightful fortnight together. In the morning they rode on the Lido, or glided up and down the green canals in their long black gondola; in the afternoon they usually entertained visitors on the yacht; and in the evening they dined at Florian's, and smoked innumerable cigarettes on the Piazza. Yet somehow Lord Arthur was not happy. Every day he studied the obituary column in the *Times*, expecting to see a notice of Lady Clementina's death, but every day he was disappointed. He began to be afraid that some accident had happened to her, and often regretted that he had prevented her taking the aconitine when she had been so anxious to try its effect. Sybil's letters, too, though full of love, and trust, and tenderness, were often very sad in their tone, and sometimes he used to think that he was parted from her for ever.

After a fortnight Lord Surbiton got bored with Venice, and determined to run down the coast to Ravenna, as he heard that there was some capital cock-shooting in the Pinetum. Lord Arthur at first refused absolutely to come, but Surbiton, of whom he was extremely fond, finally persuaded him that if he stayed at Danieli's by himself he would be moped to death, and on the morning of the 15th they started, with a strong nor'-east wind blowing, and a rather choppy sea. The sport was excellent, and the free, open-air life brought the colour back to Lord Arthur's cheek, but about the 22nd he became anxious about Lady Clementina, and, in spite of Surbiton's remonstrances, came back to Venice by train.

As he stepped out of his gondola on to the hotel steps, the proprietor came forward to meet him with a sheaf of telegrams. Lord Arthur snatched them out of his hand, and tore them open. Everything had been successful. Lady Clementina had died quite suddenly on the night of the 17th!

His first thought was for Sybil, and he sent her off a telegram announcing his immediate return to London. He then ordered his valet to pack his things for the night mail, sent his gondoliers about five times their proper fare, and ran up to his sitting-room with a light step and a buoyant heart. There he found three letters waiting for him. One was from Sybil herself, full of sympathy and condolence. The others were from his mother, and from Lady Clementina's solicitor. It seemed that the old lady had dined with the Duchess that very night, had delighted every one by her wit and *esprit*, but had gone home somewhat early, complaining of heartburn. In the morning she was found dead in her bed, having apparently suffered no pain. Sir Mathew Reid had been sent for at once, but, of course, there was nothing to be done, and she was to be buried on the 22nd at Beauchamp Chalcote. A few days before she died she had made her will, and left Lord Arthur her little house in

Curzon Street, and all her furniture, personal effects, and pictures, with the exception of her collection of miniatures, which was to go to her sister, Lady Margaret Rufford, and her amethyst necklace, which Sybil Merton was to have. The property was not of much value; but Mr. Mansfield, the solicitor, was extremely anxious for Lord Arthur to return at once, if possible, as there were a great many bills to be paid, and Lady Clementina had never kept any regular accounts.

Lord Arthur was very much touched by Lady Clementina's kind remembrance of him, and felt that Mr. Podgers had a great deal to answer for. His love of Sybil, however, dominated every other emotion, and the consciousness that he had done his duty gave him peace and comfort. When he arrived at Charing Cross, he felt perfectly happy.

The Mertons received him very kindly. Sybil made him promise that he would never again allow anything to come between them, and the marriage was fixed for the 7th June. Life seemed to him once more bright and beautiful, and all his old gladness came back to him again.

One day, however, as he was going over the house in Curzon Street, in company with Lady Clementina's solicitor and Sybil herself, burning packages of faded letters, and turning out drawers of odd rubbish, the young girl suddenly gave a little cry of delight.

'What have you found, Sybil?' said Lord Arthur, looking up from his work, and smiling.

'This lovely little silver *bonbonnière*, Arthur. Isn't it quaint and Dutch? Do give it to me! I know amethysts won't become me till I am over eighty.'

It was the box that had held the aconitine.

Lord Arthur started, and a faint blush came into his cheek. He had almost entirely forgotten what he had done, and it seemed to him a curious coincidence that Sybil, for whose sake he had gone through all that terrible anxiety, should have been the first to remind him of it.

'Of course you can have it, Sybil. I gave it to poor Lady Clem myself.'

'Oh! thank you, Arthur; and may I have the *bonbon* too? I had no notion that Lady Clementina liked sweets. I thought she was far too intellectual.'

Lord Arthur grew deadly pale, and a horrible idea crossed his mind.

'*Bonbon*, Sybil? What do you mean?' he said in a slow, hoarse voice.

'There is one in it, that is all. It looks quite old and dusty, and I have not the slightest intention of eating it. What is the matter, Arthur? How white you look!'

Lord Arthur rushed across the room, and seized the box. Inside it was the amber-coloured capsule, with its poison-bubble. Lady Clementina had died a natural death after all!

The shock of the discovery was almost too much for him. He flung the capsule into the fire, and sank on the sofa with a cry of despair.

CHAPTER V

MR. Merton was a good deal distressed at the second postponement of the marriage, and Lady Julia, who had already ordered her dress for the wedding, did all in her power to make Sybil break off the match. Dearly, however, as Sybil loved her mother, she had given her whole life into Lord Arthur's hands, and nothing that Lady Julia could say could make her waver in her faith. As for Lord Arthur himself, it took him days to get over his terrible disappointment, and for a time his nerves were completely unstrung. His excellent common sense, however, soon asserted itself, and his sound, practical mind did not leave him long in doubt about what to do. Poison having proved a complete failure, dynamite, or some other form of explosive, was obviously the proper thing to try.

He accordingly looked again over the list of his friends and relatives, and, after careful consideration, determined to blow up his uncle, the Dean of Chichester. The Dean, who was a man of great culture and learning, was extremely fond of clocks, and had a wonderful collection of timepieces, ranging from the fifteenth century to the present day, and it seemed to Lord Arthur that this hobby of the good Dean's offered him an excellent opportunity for carrying out his scheme. Where to procure an explosive machine was, of course, quite another matter. The London Directory gave him no information on the point, and he felt that there was very little use in going to Scotland Yard about it, as they never seemed to know anything about the movements of the dynamite faction till after an explosion had taken place, and not much even then.

Suddenly he thought of his friend Rouvaloff, a young Russian of very revolutionary tendencies, whom he had met at Lady Windermere's in the winter. Count Rouvaloff was supposed to be writing a life of Peter the Great, and to have come over to England for the purpose of studying the documents relating to that Tsar's residence in this country as a ship carpenter; but it was generally suspected that he was a Nihilist agent, and there was no doubt that the Russian Embassy did not look with any favour upon his presence in London. Lord Arthur felt that he was just the man for his purpose, and drove down one morning to his lodgings in Bloomsbury, to ask his advice and assistance.

'So you are taking up politics seriously?' said Count Rouvaloff, when Lord Arthur had told him the object of his mission; but Lord Arthur, who hated swagger of any kind, felt bound to admit to him that he had not the slightest interest in social questions, and simply wanted the explosive machine for a purely family matter, in which no one was concerned but himself.

Count Rouvaloff looked at him for some moments in amazement, and then seeing that he was quite serious, wrote an address on a piece of paper, initialled it, and handed it to him across the table.

'Scotland Yard would give a good deal to know this address, my dear fellow.'

'They shan't have it,' cried Lord Arthur, laughing; and after shaking the young Russian warmly by the hand he ran downstairs, examined the paper, and told the coachman to drive to Soho Square.

There he dismissed him, and strolled down Greek Street, till he came to a place called Bayle's Court. He passed under the archway, and found himself in a curious *cul-de-sac*, that was apparently occupied by a French Laundry, as a perfect network of clothes-lines was stretched across from house to house, and there was a flutter of white linen in the morning air. He walked right to the end, and knocked at a little green house. After some delay, during which every window in the court became a blurred mass of peering faces, the door was opened by a rather rough-looking foreigner, who asked him in very bad English what his business was. Lord Arthur handed him the paper Count Rouvaloff had given him. When the man saw it he bowed, and invited Lord Arthur into a very shabby front parlour on the ground floor, and in a few moments Herr Winckelkopf, as he was called in England, bustled into the room, with a very wine-stained napkin round his neck, and a fork in his left hand.

'Count Rouvaloff has given me an introduction to you,' said Lord Arthur, bowing, 'and I am anxious to have a short interview with you on a matter of business. My name is Smith, Mr. Robert Smith, and I want you to supply me with an explosive clock.'

'Charmed to meet you, Lord Arthur,' said the genial little German, laughing. 'Don't look so alarmed, it is my duty to know everybody, and I remember seeing you one evening at Lady Windermere's. I hope her ladyship is quite well. Do you mind sitting with me while I finish my breakfast? There is an excellent *pâté*, and my friends are kind enough to say that my Rhine wine is better than any they get at the German Embassy,' and before Lord Arthur had got over his surprise at being

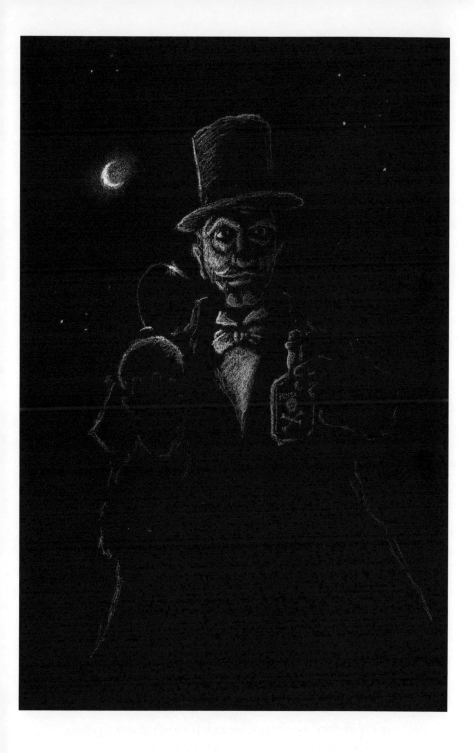

recognised, he found himself seated in the back-room, sipping the most delicious Marcobrünner out of a pale yellow hock-glass marked with the Imperial monogram, and chatting in the friendliest manner possible to the famous conspirator.

'Explosive clocks,' said Herr Winckelkopf, 'are not very good things for foreign exportation, as, even if they succeed in passing the Custom House, the train service is so irregular, that they usually go off before they have reached their proper destination. If, however, you want one for home use, I can supply you with an excellent article, and guarantee that you will he satisfied with the result. May I ask for whom it is intended? If it is for the police, or for any one connected with Scotland Yard, I am afraid I cannot do anything for you. The English detectives are really our best friends, and I have always found that by relying on their stupidity, we can do exactly what we like. I could not spare one of them.'

'I assure you,' said Lord Arthur, 'that it has nothing to do with the police at all. In fact, the clock is intended for the Dean of Chichester.'

'Dear me! I had no idea that you felt so strongly about religion, Lord Arthur. Few young men do nowadays.'

'I am afraid you overrate me, Herr Winckelkopf,' said Lord Arthur, blushing. 'The fact is, I really know nothing about theology.'

'It is a purely private matter then?'

'Purely private.'

Herr Winckelkopf shrugged his shoulders, and left the room, returning in a few minutes with a round cake of dynamite about the size of a penny, and a pretty little French clock, surmounted by an ormolu figure of Liberty trampling on the hydra of Despotism.

Lord Arthur's face brightened up when he saw it. 'That is just what I want,' he cried, 'and now tell me how it goes off.'

'Ah! there is my secret,' answered Herr Winckelkopf, contemplating his invention with a justifiable look of pride; 'let me know when you wish it to explode, and I will set the machine to the moment.'

'Well, to-day is Tuesday, and if you could send it off at once—'

'That is impossible; I have a great deal of important work on hand for some friends of mine in Moscow. Still, I might send it off to-morrow.'

'Oh, it will be quite time enough!' said Lord Arthur politely, 'if it is delivered to-morrow night or Thursday morning. For the moment of the explosion, say Friday at noon exactly. The Dean is always at home at that hour.'

'Friday, at noon,' repeated Herr Winckelkopf, and he made a note to that effect in a large ledger that was lying on a bureau near the fireplace.

'And now,' said Lord Arthur, rising from his seat, 'pray let me know how much I am in your debt.'

'It is such a small matter, Lord Arthur, that I do not care to make any charge. The dynamite comes to seven and sixpence, the clock will be three pounds ten, and the carriage about five shillings. I am only too pleased to oblige any friend of Count Rouvaloff's.'

'But your trouble, Herr Winckelkopf?'

'Oh, that is nothing! It is a pleasure to me. I do not work for money; I live entirely for my art.'

Lord Arthur laid down £4, 2s. 6d. on the table, thanked the little German for his kindness, and, having succeeded in declining an invitation to meet some Anarchists at a meat-tea on the following Saturday, left the house and went off to the Park.

For the next two days he was in a state of the greatest excitement, and on Friday at twelve o'clock he drove down to the Buckingham to wait for news. All the afternoon the stolid hall-porter kept posting up telegrams from various parts of the country giving the results of horse-races, the verdicts in divorce suits, the state of the weather, and the like, while the tape ticked out wearisome details about an all-night sitting in the House of Commons, and a small panic on the Stock Exchange. At four o'clock the evening papers came in, and Lord Arthur disappeared into the library with the *Pall Mall*, the *St. James's*, the *Globe*, and the *Echo*, to the immense indignation of Colonel Goodchild, who wanted to read the reports of a speech he had delivered that morning at the Mansion House, on the subject of South African Missions, and the advisability of having black Bishops in every province, and for some reason or other had a strong prejudice against the *Evening News*. None of the papers, however, contained even the slightest allusion to Chichester, and Lord Arthur felt that the attempt must have failed. It was a terrible blow to him, and for a time he was quite unnerved. Herr Winckelkopf, whom he went to see the next day was full of elaborate apologies, and offered to supply him with another clock free of charge, or with a case of nitro-glycerine bombs at cost price. But he had lost all faith in explosives, and Herr Winckelkopf himself acknowledged that everything is so adulterated nowadays, that even dynamite can hardly be got in a pure condition. The little German, however, while admitting that something must have gone wrong with the machinery, was not without hope that the clock might still go off, and instanced the case of a barometer that he had once sent to the military Governor at Odessa, which, though timed to explode in ten days, had not done so for something like three months. It was quite true that when it did go off, it merely succeeded in blowing a housemaid to atoms, the Governor having gone out of town six weeks before, but at least it showed that dynamite, as a destructive force, was, when under the control of machinery, a powerful, though a somewhat unpunctual agent. Lord Arthur was a little consoled by this reflection, but even here he was destined to disappointment, for two days afterwards, as he was going upstairs, the Duchess called him into her boudoir, and showed him a letter she had just received from the Deanery.

'Jane writes charming letters,' said the Duchess; 'you must really read her last. It is quite as good as the novels Mudie sends us.'

Lord Arthur seized the letter from her hand. It ran as follows:—

THE DEANERY, CHICHESTER,

27th May.

My Dearest Aunt,

Thank you so much for the flannel for the Dorcas Society, and also for the gingham. I quite agree with you that it is nonsense their wanting to wear pretty things, but everybody is so Radical and irreligious nowadays, that it is difficult to make them see that they should not try and dress like the upper classes. I am sure I don't know what we are coming to. As papa has often said in his sermons, we live in an age of unbelief.

We have had great fun over a clock that an unknown admirer sent papa last Thursday. It arrived in a wooden box from London, carriage paid, and papa feels it must have been sent by some one who had read his remarkable sermon, 'Is Licence Liberty?' for on the top of the clock was a figure of a woman, with what papa said was the cap of Liberty on her head. I didn't think it very becoming myself, but papa said it was historical, so I suppose it is all right. Parker unpacked it, and papa put it on the mantelpiece in the library, and we were all sitting there on Friday morning, when just as the clock struck twelve, we heard a whirring noise, a little puff of smoke came from the pedestal of the figure, and the goddess of Liberty fell off, and broke her nose on the fender! Maria was quite alarmed, but it looked so ridiculous, that James and I went off into fits of laughter, and even papa was amused. When we examined it, we found it was a sort of alarum clock, and that, if you set it to a particular hour, and put some gunpowder and a cap under a little hammer, it went off whenever you wanted. Papa said it must not remain in the library, as it made a noise, so Reggie carried it away to the schoolroom, and does nothing but have small explosions all day long. Do you think Arthur would like one for a wedding present? I suppose they are quite fashionable in London. Papa says they should do a great deal of good, as they show that Liberty can't last, but must fall down. Papa says Liberty was invented at the time of the French Revolution. How awful it seems!

I have now to go to the Dorcas, where I will read them your most instructive letter. How true, dear aunt, your idea is, that in their rank of life they should wear what is unbecoming. I must say it is absurd, their anxiety about dress, when there are so many more important things in this world, and in the next. I am so glad your flowered poplin turned out so well, and that your lace was not torn. I am wearing my yellow satin, that you so kindly gave me, at the Bishop's on Wednesday, and think it will look all right. Would you have bows or not? Jennings says that every one wears bows now, and that the underskirt should be frilled. Reggie has just had another explosion, and papa has ordered the clock to be sent to the stables. I don't think papa likes it so much as he did at first, though he is very flattered at being sent such a pretty and ingenious toy. It shows that people read his sermons, and profit by them.

Papa sends his love, in which James, and Reggie, and Maria all unite, and, hoping that Uncle Cecil's gout is better, believe me, dear aunt, ever your affectionate niece,

JANE PERCY.

PS.—Do tell me about the bows. Jennings insists they are the fashion.

Lord Arthur looked so serious and unhappy over the letter, that the Duchess went into fits of laughter.

'My dear Arthur,' she cried, 'I shall never show you a young lady's letter again! But what shall I say about the clock? I think it is a capital invention, and I should like to have one myself.'

'I don't think much of them,' said Lord Arthur, with a sad smile, and, after kissing his mother, he left the room.

When he got upstairs, he flung himself on a sofa, and his eyes filled with tears. He had done his best to commit this murder, but on both occasions he had failed, and through no fault of his own. He had tried to do his duty, but it seemed as if Destiny herself had turned traitor. He was oppressed with the sense of the barrenness of good intentions, of the futility of trying to be fine. Perhaps, it would be better to break off the marriage altogether. Sybil would suffer, it is true, but suffering could not really mar a nature so noble as hers. As for himself, what did it matter? There is always some war in which a man can die, some cause to which a man can give his life, and as life had no pleasure for him, so death had no terror. Let Destiny work out his doom. He would not stir to help her.

At half-past seven he dressed, and went down to the club. Surbiton was there with a party of young men, and he was obliged to dine with them. Their trivial conversation and idle jests did not interest him, and as soon as coffee was brought he left them, inventing some engagement in order to get away. As he was going out of the club, the hall-porter handed him a letter. It was from Herr Winckelkopf, asking him to call down the next evening, and look at an explosive umbrella, that went off as soon as it was opened. It was the very latest invention, and had just arrived from Geneva. He tore the letter up into fragments. He had made up his mind not to try any more experiments. Then he wandered down to the Thames Embankment, and sat for hours by the river. The moon peered through a mane of tawny clouds, as if it were a lion's eye, and innumerable stars spangled the hollow vault, like gold dust powdered on a purple dome. Now and then a barge swung out into the turbid stream, and floated away with the tide, and the railway signals changed from green to scarlet as the trains ran shrieking across the bridge. After some time, twelve o'clock boomed from the tall tower at Westminster, and at each stroke of the sonorous bell the night seemed to tremble. Then the railway lights went out, one solitary lamp left gleaming like a large ruby on a giant mast, and the roar of the city became fainter.

At two o'clock he got up, and strolled towards Blackfriars. How unreal everything looked! How like a strange dream! The houses on the other side of the river seemed built out of darkness. One would have said that silver and shadow had fashioned the world anew. The huge dome of St. Paul's loomed like a bubble through the dusky air.

As he approached Cleopatra's Needle he saw a man leaning over the parapet, and as he came nearer the man looked up, the gas-light falling full upon his face.

It was Mr. Podgers, the cheiromantist! No one could mistake the fat, flabby face, the gold-rimmed spectacles, the sickly feeble smile, the sensual mouth.

Lord Arthur stopped. A brilliant idea flashed across him, and he stole softly up behind. In a moment he had seized Mr. Podgers by the legs, and flung him into the Thames. There was a coarse oath, a heavy splash, and all was still. Lord Arthur looked anxiously over, but could see nothing of the cheiromantist but a tall hat, pirouetting in an eddy of moonlit water. After a time it also sank, and no trace of Mr. Podgers was visible. Once he thought that he caught sight of the bulky misshapen figure striking out for the staircase by the bridge, and a horrible feeling of failure came over him, but it turned out to be merely a reflection, and when the moon shone out from behind a cloud it passed away. At last he seemed to have realised the decree of destiny. He heaved a deep sigh of relief, and Sybil's name came to his lips.

'Have you dropped anything, sir?' said a voice behind him suddenly.

He turned round, and saw a policeman with a bull's-eye lantern.

'Nothing of importance, sergeant,' he answered, smiling, and hailing a passing hansom, he jumped in, and told the man to drive to Belgrave Square.

For the next few days he alternated between hope and fear. There were moments when he almost expected Mr. Podgers to walk into the room, and yet at other times he felt that Fate could not be so unjust to him. Twice he went to the cheiromantist's address in West Moon Street, but he could not bring himself to ring the bell. He longed for certainty, and was afraid of it.

Finally it came. He was sitting in the smoking-room of the club having tea, and listening rather wearily to Surbiton's account of the last comic song at the Gaiety, when the waiter came in with the evening papers. He took up the *St. James's*, and was listlessly turning over its pages, when this strange heading caught his eye:

SUICIDE OF A CHEIROMANTIST.

He turned pale with excitement, and began to read. The paragraph ran as follows:

Yesterday morning, at seven o'clock, the body of Mr. Septimus R. Podgers, the eminent cheiromantist, was washed on shore at Greenwich, just in front of the Ship Hotel. The unfortunate gentleman had been missing for some days, and considerable anxiety for his safety had been felt in cheiromantic circles. It is supposed that he committed suicide under the influence of a temporary mental derangement, caused by overwork, and a verdict to that effect was returned this afternoon by the coroner's jury. Mr. Podgers had just completed an elaborate treatise on the subject of the Human Hand, that will shortly be published, when it will no doubt attract much attention. The deceased was sixty-five years of age, and does not seem to have left any relations.

Lord Arthur rushed out of the club with the paper still in his hand, to the immense amazement of the hall-porter, who tried in vain to stop him, and drove at once to Park Lane. Sybil saw him from the window, and something told her that he was the bearer of good news. She ran down to meet him, and, when she saw his face, she knew that all was well.

'My dear Sybil,' cried Lord Arthur, 'let us be married to-morrow!'

'You foolish boy! Why, the cake is not even ordered!' said Sybil, laughing through her tears.

CHAPTER VI

WHEN the wedding took place, some three weeks later, St. Peter's was crowded with a perfect mob of smart people. The service was read in the most impressive manner by the Dean of Chichester, and everybody agreed that they had never seen a handsomer couple than the bride and bridegroom. They were more than handsome, however—they were happy. Never for a single moment did Lord Arthur regret all that he had suffered for Sybil's sake, while she, on her side, gave him the best things a woman can give to any man—worship, tenderness, and love. For them romance was not killed by reality. They always felt young.

Some years afterwards, when two beautiful children had been born to them, Lady Windermere came down on a visit to Alton Priory, a lovely old place, that had been the Duke's wedding present to his son; and one afternoon as she was sitting with Lady Arthur under a lime-tree in the garden, watching the little boy and girl as they played up and down the rose-walk, like fitful sunbeams, she suddenly took her hostess's hand in hers, and said, 'Are you happy, Sybil?'

'Dear Lady Windermere, of course I am happy. Aren't you?'

'I have no time to be happy, Sybil. I always like the last person who is introduced to me; but, as a rule, as soon as I know people I get tired of them.'

'Don't your lions satisfy you, Lady Windermere?'

'Oh dear, no! lions are only good for one season. As soon as their manes are cut, they are the dullest creatures going. Besides, they behave very badly, if you are really nice to them. Do you remember that horrid Mr. Podgers? He was a dreadful impostor. Of course, I didn't mind that at all, and even when he wanted to borrow money I forgave him, but I could not stand his making love to me. He has really made me hate cheiromancy. I go in for telepathy now. It is much more amusing.'

'You mustn't say anything against cheiromancy here, Lady Windermere; it is the only subject that Arthur does not like people to chaff about. I assure you he is quite serious over it.'

'You don't mean to say that he believes in it, Sybil?'

'Ask him, Lady Windermere, here he is'; and Lord Arthur came up the garden with a large bunch of yellow roses in his hand, and his two children dancing round him.

'Lord Arthur?'

'Yes, Lady Windermere.'

'You don't mean to say that you believe in cheiromancy?'

'Of course I do,' said the young man, smiling.

'But why?'

'Because I owe to it all the happiness of my life,' he murmured, throwing himself into a wicker chair.

'My dear Lord Arthur, what do you owe to it?'

'Sybil,' he answered, handing his wife the roses, and looking into her violet eyes.

'What nonsense!' cried Lady Windermere. 'I never heard such nonsense in all my life.'

ALTHOUGH the story ends badly for Podgers, it has a sunny conclusion for its homicidal protagonist: released from his duty to murder, he is now free to marry and progenerate. A classic Oscar Wilde parable, the message of this story consists of a very serious premise being delivered by a very ludicrous means. At its heart it critiques the British devotion to social obligation, wondering how far such a feeling could drive a man. While very few sane persons would feel compelled to murder based merely on a palm-reader's prophecy, there are countless thousands of people, Wilde implies, who have entered into the indentured slavery of public expectations. Men who marry women they don't love, take on professions they loathe, accept promotions they detest, or live lives they abhor – all to avoid public censure or the disappointment of a few meddling relatives – are no less insane than Lord Arthur whose desire to be a murderer is driven by nothing more than an obligation to fulfill a side-show prediction. While Dorian is corrupt and evil because he is a slave to public attention (be it good, bad, or scandalous), Lord Arthur's corruption stems from the ostensibly better motive of avoiding public condemnation, but in many ways he is a far more dangerous monster than Dorian Gray, since his motivation comes from what he believes to be a noble and worthy impulse to "do one's duty." Through this black comedy Wilde crafts a powerful critique of British social mores and ends up presenting us with Dorian's polar opposite (no less of a danger to the public), for while Dorian's evil came from selfishness, vanity, and reckless indulgence, Lord Arthur's comes from a misguided devotion to selflessness, deferment, and reckless responsibility. Nothing is more dangerous, in other words, than a obedient man who has decided that nothing can dissuade him from accomplishing his duty.

AT their core, most Victorian ghost stories are oblique commentaries on the discombobulating transition from agrarian pre-modernity to industrial capitalism. There is, of course, far more to them than this, but ghost stories found a peculiar vogue during the Industrial Revolution as Britons (who were increasingly middle-class, urban, and intellectual) struggled to reconcile these drastic developments with many, many centuries as superstitious, rural, peasants. Folklore had the glue of English society prior to the 18th century, where the same families had nestled in the same rainy villages for centuries, using the same technologies and hearing the same ghost stories for many generations. With capitalism and industrialism came new technologies, better medicine, longer lives, and more mobility, and this lead many people to wonder if humanity was evolving beyond the morals of past centuries. In ghost stories by Charles Dickens, Rhoda Broughton, Mrs. Oliphant, Elizabeth Gaskell, J. S. Le Fanu, Charlotte Riddell, Amelia B. Edwards, and Wilkie Collins, English readers were encouraged to question how far we truly had evolved. These tales generally decided that steam-engines, Darwinian biology, and mass-market publishing may have prettied mankind up a bit, but we were still subject to the same crimes, temptations, and terrors of our agrarian forefathers. The clash between the not-so-distant past and the steam-powered future lead to a tremendous fashion of ghosts, providing a convenient and navigable space for modern Britons to ponder the rapidly developing times that they lived in. Was there still justice? Did morals still matter? Had we outgrown social accountability? Ghost stories answered these questions and soothed the aching growing pains of Victorian society as the next hundred years saw humanity graduate from candles, lancets, and buggies to electricity, penicillin, and automobiles. "The Canterville Ghost" is one of the most unusual entries in this genre, because it ponders the same problems with humor rather than horror. This is, of course, not the first example of this (in many ways this story is done in the tradition of Charles Dickens, whose comical ghost stories "The Lawyer and the Ghost," "The Bagman's Uncle," and "Baron Koeldwethout's Apparition" also used the supernatural as a comedic arbiter of the changing times), but it is without a doubt the most famous comic ghost story in British literature. Wilde goes a step further and introduces yet another frightening development of the Victorian Age to act as a threat to England's national traditions – the looming, farcical enemy of so many stodgy, English characters in his plays and stories: the American nouveau riche.

The Canterville Ghost:
A Hylo-Idealistic Romance
{1887}

CHAPTER I

WHEN Mr. Hiram B. Otis, the American Minister, bought Canterville Chase, every one told him he was doing a very foolish thing, as there was no doubt at all that the place was haunted. Indeed, Lord Canterville himself, who was a man of the most punctilious honour, had felt it his duty to mention the fact to Mr. Otis when they came to discuss terms.

'We have not cared to live in the place ourselves,' said Lord Canterville, 'since my grandaunt, the Dowager Duchess of Bolton, was frightened into a fit, from which she never really recovered, by two skeleton hands being placed on her shoulders as she was dressing for dinner, and I feel bound to tell you, Mr. Otis, that the ghost has been seen by several living members of my family, as well as by the rector of the parish, the Rev. Augustus Dampier, who is a Fellow of King's College, Cambridge. After the unfortunate accident to the Duchess, none of our younger servants would stay with us, and Lady Canterville often got very little sleep at night, in consequence of the mysterious noises that came from the corridor and the library.'

'My Lord,' answered the Minister, 'I will take the furniture and the ghost at a valuation. I come from a modern country, where we have everything that money can buy; and with all our spry young fellows painting the Old World red, and carrying off your best actresses and prima-donnas, I reckon that if there were such a thing as a ghost in Europe, we'd have it at home in a very short time in one of our public museums, or on the road as a show.'

'I fear that the ghost exists,' said Lord Canterville, smiling, 'though it may have resisted the overtures of your enterprising impresarios. It has been well known for three centuries, since 1584 in fact, and always makes its appearance before the death of any member of our family.'

'Well, so does the family doctor for that matter, Lord Canterville. But there is no such thing, sir, as a ghost, and I guess the laws of Nature are not going to be suspended for the British aristocracy.'

'You are certainly very natural in America,' answered Lord Canterville, who did not quite understand Mr. Otis's last observation, 'and if you don't mind a ghost in the house, it is all right. Only you must remember I warned you.'

A few weeks after this, the purchase was completed, and at the close of the season the Minister and his family went down to Canterville Chase. Mrs. Otis, who, as Miss Lucretia R. Tappan, of West 53rd Street, had been a celebrated New York belle, was now a very handsome, middle-aged woman, with fine eyes, and a superb profile. Many American ladies on leaving their native land adopt an appearance of chronic ill-health, under the impression that it is a form of European refinement, but Mrs. Otis had never fallen into this error. She had a magnificent constitution, and a really wonderful amount of animal spirits. Indeed, in many respects, she was quite English, and was an excellent example of the fact that we have really everything in common with America nowadays, except, of course, language. Her eldest son, christened Washington by his parents in a moment of patriotism, which he never ceased to regret, was a fair-haired, rather good-looking young man, who had qualified himself for American diplomacy by leading the German at the Newport Casino for three successive seasons, and even in London was well known as an excellent dancer. Gardenias and the peerage were his only weaknesses. Otherwise he was extremely sensible. Miss Virginia E. Otis was a little girl of fifteen, lithe and lovely as a fawn, and with a fine freedom in her large blue eyes. She was a wonderful amazon, and had once raced old Lord Bilton on her pony twice round the park, winning by a length and a half, just in front of the Achilles statue, to the huge delight of the young Duke of Cheshire, who proposed for her on the spot, and was sent back to Eton that very night by his guardians, in floods of tears. After Virginia came the twins, who were usually called 'The Stars and Stripes,' as they were always getting swished. They were delightful boys, and with the exception of the worthy Minister the only true republicans of the family.

As Canterville Chase is seven miles from Ascot, the nearest railway station, Mr. Otis had telegraphed for a waggonette to meet them, and they started on their drive in high spirits. It was a lovely July evening, and the air was delicate with the scent of the pine-woods. Now and then they heard a wood pigeon brooding over its own sweet voice, or saw, deep in the rustling fern, the burnished breast of the pheasant. Little squirrels peered at them from the beech-trees as they went by, and the rabbits scudded away through the brushwood and over the mossy knolls, with their white tails in the air. As they entered the avenue of Canterville Chase, however, the sky became suddenly overcast with clouds, a curious stillness seemed to hold the atmosphere, a great flight of rooks passed silently over their heads, and, before they reached the house, some big drops of rain had fallen.

Standing on the steps to receive them was an old woman, neatly dressed in black silk, with a white cap and apron. This was Mrs. Umney, the housekeeper, whom Mrs. Otis, at Lady Canterville's earnest request, had consented to keep on in her former position. She made them each a low curtsey as they alighted, and said in a quaint, old-fashioned manner, 'I bid you welcome to Canterville Chase.' Following her, they passed through the fine Tudor hall into the library, a long, low room, panelled in black oak, at the end of which was a large stained-glass window. Here they found tea laid out for them, and, after taking off their wraps, they sat down and began to look round, while Mrs. Umney waited on them.

Suddenly Mrs. Otis caught sight of a dull red stain on the floor just by the fireplace and, quite unconscious of what it really signified, said to Mrs. Umney, 'I am afraid something has been spilt there.'

'Yes, madam,' replied the old housekeeper in a low voice, 'blood has been spilt on that spot.'

'How horrid,' cried Mrs. Otis; 'I don't at all care for blood-stains in a sitting-room. It must be removed at once.'

The old woman smiled, and answered in the same low, mysterious voice, 'It is the blood of Lady Eleanore de Canterville, who was murdered on that very spot by her own husband, Sir Simon de Canterville, in 1575. Sir Simon survived her nine years, and disappeared suddenly under very mysterious circumstances. His body has never been discovered, but his guilty spirit still haunts the Chase. The blood-stain has been much admired by tourists and others, and cannot be removed.'

'That is all nonsense,' cried Washington Otis; 'Pinkerton's Champion Stain Remover and Paragon Detergent will clean it up in no time,' and before the terrified housekeeper could interfere he had fallen upon his knees, and was rapidly scouring the floor with a small stick of what looked like a black cosmetic. In a few moments no trace of the blood-stain could be seen.

'I knew Pinkerton would do it,' he exclaimed triumphantly, as he looked round at his admiring family; but no sooner had he said these words than a terrible flash of lightning lit up the sombre room, a fearful peal of thunder made them all start to their feet, and Mrs. Umney fainted.

'What a monstrous climate!' said the American Minister calmly, as he lit a long cheroot. 'I guess the old country is so overpopulated that they have not enough decent weather for everybody. I have always been of opinion that emigration is the only thing for England.'

'My dear Hiram,' cried Mrs. Otis, 'what can we do with a woman who faints?'

'Charge it to her like breakages,' answered the Minister; 'she won't faint after that'; and in a few moments Mrs. Umney certainly came to. There was no doubt, however, that she was extremely upset, and she sternly warned Mr. Otis to beware of some trouble coming to the house.

'I have seen things with my own eyes, sir,' she said, 'that would make any Christian's hair stand on end, and many and many a night I have not closed my eyes in sleep for the awful things that are done here.' Mr. Otis, however, and his wife warmly assured the honest soul that they were not afraid of ghosts, and, after invoking the blessings of Providence on her new master and mistress, and making arrangements for an increase of salary, the old housekeeper tottered off to her own room.

CHAPTER II

THE storm raged fiercely all that night, but nothing of particular note occurred. The next morning, however, when they came down to breakfast, they found the terrible stain of blood once again on the floor. 'I don't think it can be the fault of the Paragon Detergent,' said Washington, 'for I have tried it with everything. It must be the ghost.' He accordingly rubbed out the stain a second time, but the second morning it appeared again. The third morning also it was there, though the library had been locked up at night by Mr. Otis himself, and the key carried upstairs. The whole family were now quite interested; Mr. Otis began to suspect that he had been too dogmatic in his denial of the existence of ghosts, Mrs. Otis expressed her intention of joining the Psychical Society, and Washington prepared a long letter to Messrs. Myers and Podmore on the subject of the Permanence of Sanguineous Stains when connected with Crime. That night all doubts about the objective existence of phantasmata were removed for ever.

The day had been warm and sunny; and, in the cool of the evening, the whole family went out for a drive. They did not return home till nine o'clock, when they had a light supper. The conversation in no way turned upon ghosts, so there were not even those primary conditions of receptive expectation which so often precede the presentation of psychical phenomena. The subjects discussed, as I have since learned from Mr. Otis, were merely such as form the ordinary conversation of cultured Americans of the better class, such as the immense superiority of Miss Fanny Davenport over Sarah Bernhardt as an actress; the difficulty of obtaining green corn, buckwheat cakes, and hominy, even in the best English houses; the importance of Boston in the development of the world-soul; the advantages of the baggage check system in railway travelling; and the sweetness of the New York accent as compared to the London drawl. No mention at all was made of the supernatural, nor was Sir Simon de Canterville alluded to in any way. At eleven o'clock the family retired, and by half-past all the lights were out. Some time after, Mr. Otis was awakened by a curious noise in the corridor, outside his room. It sounded like the clank of metal, and seemed to be coming nearer every moment. He got up at once, struck a match, and looked at the time. It was exactly one o'clock. He was quite calm, and felt his pulse, which was not at all feverish. The strange noise still continued, and with it he heard distinctly the sound of footsteps. He put on his slippers, took a small oblong phial out of his dressing-case, and opened the door. Right in front of him he saw, in the wan moonlight, an old man of terrible aspect. His eyes were as red burning coals; long grey hair fell over his shoulders in matted coils; his garments, which were of antique cut, were soiled and ragged, and from his wrists and ankles hung heavy manacles and rusty gyves.

'My dear sir,' said Mr. Otis, 'I really must insist on your oiling those chains, and have brought you for that purpose a small bottle of the Tammany Rising Sun Lubricator. It is said to be completely efficacious upon one application, and there are several testimonials to that effect on the wrapper from some of our most eminent native divines. I shall leave it here for you by the bedroom candles, and will be happy to supply you with more should you require it.' With these words the United States Minister laid the bottle down on a marble table, and, closing his door, retired to rest.

For a moment the Canterville ghost stood quite motionless in natural indignation; then, dashing the bottle violently upon the polished floor, he fled down the corridor, uttering hollow groans, and emitting a ghastly green light. Just, however, as he reached the top of the great oak staircase, a door was flung open, two little white-robed figures appeared, and a large pillow whizzed past his head! There was evidently no time to be lost, so, hastily adopting the Fourth Dimension of Space as a means of escape, he vanished through the wainscoting, and the house became quite quiet.

On reaching a small secret chamber in the left wing, he leaned up against a moonbeam to recover his breath, and began to try and realise his position. Never, in a brilliant and uninterrupted career of three hundred years, had he been so grossly insulted. He thought of the Dowager Duchess, whom he had frightened into a fit as she stood before the glass in her lace and diamonds; of the four housemaids, who had

gone off into hysterics when he merely grinned at them through the
curtains of one of the spare bedrooms; of the rector of the parish, whose

candle he had blown out as he was coming late one night from the library, and who had been under the care of Sir William Gull ever since, a perfect martyr to nervous disorders; and of old Madame de Tremouillac, who, having wakened up one morning early and seen a skeleton seated in an arm-chair by the fire reading her diary, had been confined to her bed for six weeks with an attack of brain fever, and, on her recovery, had become reconciled to the Church, and broken off her connection with that notorious sceptic Monsieur de Voltaire. He remembered the terrible night when the wicked Lord Canterville was found choking in his dressing-room, with the knave of diamonds half-way down his throat, and confessed, just before he died, that he had cheated Charles James Fox out of £50,000 at Crockford's by means of that very card, and swore that the ghost had made him swallow it. All his great achievements came back to him again, from the butler who had shot himself in the pantry because he had seen a green hand tapping at the window pane, to the beautiful Lady Stutfield, who was always obliged to wear a black velvet band round her throat to hide the mark of five fingers burnt upon her white skin, and who drowned herself at last in the carp-pond at the end of the King's Walk. With the enthusiastic egotism of the true artist he went over his most celebrated performances, and smiled bitterly to himself as he recalled to mind his last appearance as 'Red Ruben, or the Strangled Babe,' his *début* as 'Gaunt Gibeon, the Blood-sucker of Bexley Moor,' and the *furore* he had excited one lovely June evening by merely playing ninepins with his own bones upon the lawn-tennis ground. And after all this, some wretched modern Americans were to come and offer him the Rising Sun Lubricator, and throw pillows at his head! It was quite unbearable. Besides, no ghosts in history had ever been treated in this manner. Accordingly, he determined to have vengeance, and remained till daylight in an attitude of deep thought.

CHAPTER III

THE next morning when the Otis family met at breakfast, they discussed the ghost at some length. The United States Minister was naturally a little annoyed to find that his present had not been accepted. 'I have no wish,' he said, 'to do the ghost any personal injury, and I must say that, considering the length of time he has been in the house, I don't think it is at all polite to throw pillows at him'—a very just remark, at which, I am sorry to say, the twins burst into shouts of laughter. 'Upon the other hand,' he continued, 'if he really declines to use the Rising Sun Lubricator, we shall have to take his chains from him. It would be quite impossible to sleep, with such a noise going on outside the bedrooms.'

For the rest of the week, however, they were undisturbed, the only thing that excited any attention being the continual renewal of the blood-stain on the library floor. This certainly was very strange, as the door was always locked at night by Mr. Otis, and the windows kept closely barred. The chameleon-like colour, also, of the stain excited a good deal of comment. Some mornings it was a dull (almost Indian) red, then it would be vermilion, then a rich purple, and once when they came down for family prayers, according to the simple rites of the Free American Reformed Episcopalian Church, they found it a bright emerald-green. These kaleidoscopic changes naturally amused the party very much, and bets on the subject were freely made every evening. The only person who did not enter into the joke was little Virginia, who, for some unexplained reason, was always a good deal distressed at the sight of the blood-stain, and very nearly cried the morning it was emerald-green.

The second appearance of the ghost was on Sunday night. Shortly after they had gone to bed they were suddenly alarmed by a fearful crash in the hall. Rushing downstairs, they found that a large suit of old armour had become detached from its stand, and had fallen on the stone floor, while, seated in a high-backed chair, was the Canterville ghost, rubbing his knees with an expression of acute agony on his face. The twins, having brought their pea-shooters with them, at once discharged two pellets on him, with that accuracy of aim which can only be attained by long and careful practice on a writing-master, while the United States Minister covered him with his revolver, and called upon him, in accordance with Californian etiquette, to hold up his hands! The ghost started up with a wild shriek of rage, and swept through them like a mist, extinguishing Washington Otis's candle as he passed, and so leaving them all in total darkness. On reaching the top of the staircase he recovered himself, and determined to give his celebrated peal of demoniac laughter. This he had on more than one occasion found extremely useful. It was said to have turned Lord Raker's wig grey in a single night, and had certainly made three of Lady Canterville's French governesses give warning before their month was up. He accordingly laughed his most horrible laugh, till the old vaulted roof rang and rang again, but hardly had the fearful echo died away when a door opened, and Mrs. Otis came out in a light blue dressing-gown. 'I am afraid you are far from well,' she said, 'and have brought you a bottle of Dr. Dobell's tincture. If it is indigestion, you will find it a most excellent remedy.' The ghost glared at her in fury, and began at once to make preparations for turning himself into a large black dog, an accomplishment for which he was justly renowned, and to which the family doctor always attributed the permanent idiocy of Lord Canterville's uncle, the Hon. Thomas Horton. The sound of approaching footsteps, however, made him hesitate in his fell purpose, so he contented himself with becoming faintly phosphorescent, and vanished with a deep churchyard groan, just as the twins had come up to him.

On reaching his room he entirely broke down, and became a prey to the most violent agitation. The vulgarity of the twins, and the gross materialism of Mrs. Otis, were naturally extremely annoying, but what really distressed him most was, that he had been unable to wear the suit of mail. He had hoped that even modern Americans would be thrilled by the sight of a Spectre In Armour, if for no more sensible reason, at least out of respect for their national poet Longfellow, over whose graceful and attractive poetry he himself had whiled away many a weary hour when the Cantervilles were up in town. Besides, it was his own suit. He had worn it with great success at the Kenilworth tournament, and had been highly complimented on it by no less a person than the Virgin Queen herself. Yet when he had put it on, he had been completely overpowered by the weight of the huge breastplate and steel casque, and had fallen heavily on the stone pavement, barking both his knees severely, and bruising the knuckles of his right hand.

For some days after this he was extremely ill, and hardly stirred out of his room at all, except to keep the blood-stain in proper repair. However, by taking great care of himself, he recovered, and resolved to make a third attempt to frighten the United States Minister and his family. He selected Friday, the 17th of August, for his appearance, and spent most of that day in looking over his wardrobe, ultimately deciding in favour of a large slouched hat with a red feather, a winding-sheet frilled at the wrists and neck, and a rusty dagger. Towards evening a violent storm of rain came on, and the wind was so high that all the windows and doors in the old house shook and rattled. In fact, it was just such weather as he loved. His plan of action was this. He was to make his way quietly to Washington Otis's room, gibber at him from the foot of the bed, and stab himself three times in the throat to the sound of slow music. He bore Washington a special grudge, being quite aware that it was he who was in the habit of removing the famous Canterville blood-stain, by means of Pinkerton's Paragon Detergent. Having reduced the reckless and foolhardy youth to a condition of abject terror, he was then to proceed to the room occupied by the United States Minister and his wife, and there to place a clammy hand on Mrs. Otis's forehead, while he hissed into her trembling husband's ear the awful secrets of the charnel-house. With regard to little Virginia, he had not quite made up his mind. She had never insulted him in any way, and was pretty and gentle. A few hollow groans from the wardrobe, he thought, would be more than sufficient, or, if that failed to wake her, he might grabble at the counterpane with palsy-twitching fingers. As for the twins, he was quite determined to teach them a lesson. The first thing to be done was, of course, to sit upon their chests, so as to produce the stifling sensation of nightmare. Then, as their beds were quite close to each other, to stand between them in the form of a green, icy-cold corpse, till they became paralysed with fear, and finally, to throw off the winding-sheet, and crawl round the room, with white bleached bones and one rolling eye-ball, in the character of 'Dumb Daniel, or the Suicide's Skeleton,' a *rôle* in which he had on more than one occasion produced a great effect, and which he considered quite equal to his famous part of 'Martin the Maniac, or the Masked Mystery.'

At half-past ten he heard the family going to bed. For some time he was disturbed by wild shrieks of laughter from the twins, who, with the light-hearted gaiety of schoolboys, were evidently amusing themselves before they retired to rest, but at a quarter past eleven all was still, and, as midnight sounded, he sallied forth. The owl beat against the window panes, the raven croaked from the old yew-tree, and the wind wandered moaning round the house like a lost soul; but the Otis family slept unconscious of their doom, and high above the rain and storm he could hear the steady snoring of the Minister for the United States. He stepped stealthily out of the wainscoting, with an evil smile on his cruel, wrinkled mouth, and the moon hid her face in a cloud as he stole past the great oriel window, where his own arms and those of his murdered wife were blazoned in azure and gold. On and on he glided, like an evil shadow, the very darkness seeming to loathe him as he passed. Once he thought he heard something call, and stopped; but it was only the baying of a dog from the Red Farm, and he went on, muttering strange sixteenth-century curses, and ever and anon brandishing the rusty dagger in the midnight air. Finally he reached the corner of the passage that led to luckless Washington's room. For a moment he paused there, the wind blowing his long grey locks about his head, and twisting into grotesque and fantastic folds the nameless horror of the dead man's shroud. Then the clock struck the quarter, and he felt the time was come. He chuckled to himself, and turned the corner; but no sooner had he done so, than, with a piteous wail of terror, he fell back, and hid his blanched face in his long, bony hands. Right in front of him was standing a horrible spectre, motionless as a carven image, and monstrous as a madman's dream! Its head was bald and burnished; its face round, and fat, and white; and hideous laughter seemed to have writhed its features into an eternal grin. From the eyes streamed rays of scarlet light, the mouth was a wide well of fire, and a hideous garment, like to his own, swathed with its silent snows the Titan form. On its breast was a placard with strange writing in antique characters, some scroll of shame it seemed, some record of wild sins, some awful calendar of crime, and, with its right hand, it bore aloft a falchion of gleaming steel.

Never having seen a ghost before, he naturally was terribly frightened, and, after a second hasty glance at the awful phantom, he fled back to his room, tripping up in his long winding-sheet as he sped down the corridor, and finally dropping the rusty dagger into the Minister's jack-boots, where it was found in the morning by the butler. Once in the privacy of his own apartment, he flung himself down on a small pallet-bed, and hid his face under the clothes. After a time, however, the brave old Canterville spirit asserted itself, and he determined to go and speak to the other ghost as soon as it was daylight. Accordingly, just as the dawn was touching the hills with silver, he returned towards the spot where he had first laid eyes on the grisly phantom, feeling that, after all, two ghosts were better than one, and that, by the aid of his new friend, he might safely grapple with the twins. On reaching the spot, however, a terrible sight met his gaze. Something had evidently happened to the spectre, for the light had entirely faded from its hollow eyes, the gleaming falchion had fallen from its hand, and it was leaning up against the wall in a strained and uncomfortable attitude. He rushed forward and seized it in his arms, when, to his horror, the head slipped off and rolled on the floor, the body assumed a recumbent posture, and he found himself clasping a white dimity bed-curtain, with a sweeping-brush, a kitchen cleaver, and a hollow turnip lying at his feet! Unable to understand this curious transformation, he clutched the placard with feverish haste, and there, in the grey morning light, he read these fearful words:—

YE OLDE GHOSTE
Ye Onlie True and Originale Spook.
Beware of Ye Imitationes.
All others are Counterfeite.

The whole thing flashed across him. He had been tricked, foiled, and outwitted! The old Canterville look came into his eyes; he ground his toothless gums together; and, raising his withered hands high above his head, swore, according to the picturesque phraseology of the antique school, that when Chanticleer had sounded twice his merry horn, deeds of blood would be wrought, and Murder walk abroad with silent feet.

Hardly had he finished this awful oath when, from the red-tiled roof of a distant homestead, a cock crew. He laughed a long, low, bitter laugh, and waited. Hour after hour he waited, but the cock, for some strange reason, did not crow again. Finally, at half-past seven, the arrival of the housemaids made him give up his fearful vigil, and he stalked back to his room, thinking of his vain hope and baffled purpose. There he consulted several books of ancient chivalry, of which he was exceedingly fond, and found that, on every occasion on which his oath had been used, Chanticleer had always crowed a second time. 'Perdition seize the naughty fowl,' he muttered, 'I have seen the day when, with my stout spear, I would have run him through the gorge, and made him crow for me an 'twere in death!' He then retired to a comfortable lead coffin, and stayed there till evening.

CHAPTER IV

THE next day the ghost was very weak and tired. The terrible excitement of the last four weeks was beginning to have its effect. His nerves were completely shattered, and he started at the slightest noise. For five days he kept his room, and at last made up his mind to give up the point of the blood-stain on the library floor. If the Otis family did not want it, they clearly did not deserve it. They were evidently people on a low, material plane of existence, and quite incapable of appreciating the symbolic value of sensuous phenomena. The question of phantasmic apparitions, and the development of astral bodies, was of course quite a different matter, and really not under his control. It was his solemn duty to appear in the corridor once a week, and to gibber from the large oriel window on the first and third Wednesday in every month, and he did not see how he could honourably escape from his obligations. It is quite true that his life had been very evil, but, upon the other hand, he was most conscientious in all things connected with the supernatural. For the next three Saturdays, accordingly, he traversed the corridor as usual between midnight and three o'clock, taking every possible precaution against being either heard or seen. He removed his boots, trod as lightly as possible on the old worm-eaten boards, wore a large black velvet cloak, and was careful to use the Rising Sun Lubricator for oiling his chains. I am bound to acknowledge that it was with a good deal of difficulty that he brought himself to adopt this last mode of protection. However, one night, while the family were at dinner, he slipped into Mr. Otis's bedroom and carried off the bottle. He felt a little humiliated at first, but afterwards was sensible enough to see that there was a great deal to be said for the invention, and, to a certain degree, it served his purpose. Still, in spite of everything, he was not left unmolested. Strings were continually being stretched across the corridor, over which he tripped in the dark, and on one occasion, while dressed for the part of 'Black Isaac, or the Huntsman of Hogley Woods,' he met with a severe fall, through treading on a butter-slide, which the twins had constructed from the entrance of the Tapestry Chamber to the top of the oak staircase. This last insult so enraged him, that he resolved to make one final effort to assert his dignity and social position, and determined to visit the insolent young Etonians the next night in his celebrated character of 'Reckless Rupert, or the Headless Earl.'

He had not appeared in this disguise for more than seventy years; in fact, not since he had so frightened pretty Lady Barbara Modish by means of it, that she suddenly broke off her engagement with the present Lord Canterville's grandfather, and ran away to Gretna Green with handsome Jack Castleton, declaring that nothing in the world would induce her to marry into a family that allowed such a horrible phantom to walk up and down the terrace at twilight. Poor Jack was afterwards shot in a duel by Lord Canterville on Wandsworth Common, and Lady Barbara died of a broken heart at Tunbridge Wells before the year was out, so, in every way, it had been a great success. It was, however, an extremely difficult 'make-up,' if I may use such a theatrical expression in connection with one of the greatest mysteries of the supernatural, or, to employ a more scientific term, the higher-natural world, and it took him fully three hours to make his preparations. At last everything was ready, and he was very pleased with his appearance. The big leather riding-boots that went with the dress were just a little too large for him, and he could only find one of the two horse-pistols, but, on the whole, he was quite satisfied, and at a quarter past one he glided out of the wainscoting and crept down the corridor. On reaching the room occupied by the twins, which I should mention was called the Blue Bed Chamber, on account of the colour of its hangings, he found the door just ajar. Wishing to make an effective entrance, he flung it wide open, when a heavy jug of water fell right down on him, wetting him to the skin, and just missing his left shoulder by a couple of inches. At the same moment he heard stifled shrieks of laughter proceeding from the four-post bed. The shock to his nervous system was so great that he fled back to his room as hard as he could go, and the next day he was laid up with a severe cold. The only thing that at all consoled him in the whole affair was the fact that he had not brought his head with him, for, had he done so, the consequences might have been very serious.

He now gave up all hope of ever frightening this rude American family, and contented himself, as a rule, with creeping about the passages in list slippers, with a thick red muffler round his throat for fear of draughts, and a small arquebuse, in case he should be attacked by the twins. The final blow he received occurred on the 19th of September. He had gone downstairs to the great entrance-hall, feeling sure that there, at any rate, he would be quite unmolested, and was amusing himself by making satirical remarks on the large Saroni photographs of the United States Minister and his wife, which had now taken the place of the Canterville family pictures. He was simply but neatly clad in a long shroud, spotted with churchyard mould, had tied up his jaw with a strip of yellow linen, and carried a small lantern and a sexton's spade. In fact, he was dressed for the character of 'Jonas the Graveless, or the Corpse-Snatcher of Chertsey Barn,' one of his most remarkable impersonations, and one which the Cantervilles had every reason to remember, as it was the real origin of their quarrel with their neighbour, Lord Rufford. It was about a quarter past two o'clock in the morning, and, as far as he could ascertain, no one was stirring. As he was strolling towards the library, however, to see if there were any traces left of the blood-stain, suddenly there leaped out on him from a dark corner two figures, who waved their arms wildly above their heads, and shrieked out 'BOO!' in his ear.

Seized with a panic, which, under the circumstances, was only natural, he rushed for the staircase, but found Washington Otis waiting for him there with the big garden-syringe; and being thus hemmed in by his enemies on every side, and driven almost to bay, he vanished into the great iron stove, which, fortunately for him, was not lit, and had to make his way home through the flues and chimneys, arriving at his own room in a terrible state of dirt, disorder, and despair.

After this he was not seen again on any nocturnal expedition. The twins lay in wait for him on several occasions, and strewed the passages with nutshells every night to the great annoyance of their parents and the servants, but it was of no avail. It was quite evident that his feelings were so wounded that he would not appear. Mr. Otis consequently resumed his great work on the history of the Democratic Party, on which he had been engaged for some years; Mrs. Otis organised a wonderful clam-bake, which amazed the whole county; the boys took to lacrosse, euchre, poker, and other American national games; and Virginia rode about the lanes on her pony, accompanied by the young Duke of Cheshire, who had come to spend the last week of his holidays at Canterville Chase. It was generally assumed that the ghost had gone away, and, in fact, Mr. Otis wrote a letter to that effect to Lord Canterville, who, in reply, expressed his great pleasure at the news, and sent his best congratulations to the Minister's worthy wife.

The Otises, however, were deceived, for the ghost was still in the house, and though now almost an invalid, was by no means ready to let matters rest, particularly as he heard that among the guests was the young Duke of Cheshire, whose grand-uncle, Lord Francis Stilton, had once bet a hundred guineas with Colonel Carbury that he would play dice with the Canterville ghost, and was found the next morning lying on the floor of the card-room in such a helpless paralytic state, that though he lived on to a great age, he was never able to say anything again but 'Double Sixes.' The story was well known at the time, though, of course, out of respect to the feelings of the two noble families, every attempt was made to hush it up; and a full account of all the circumstances connected with it will be found in the third volume of Lord Tattle's *Recollections of the Prince Regent and his Friends*. The ghost, then, was naturally very anxious to show that he had not lost his influence over the Stiltons, with whom, indeed, he was distantly connected, his own first cousin having been married *en secondes noces* to the Sieur de Bulkeley, from whom, as every one knows, the Dukes of Cheshire are lineally descended. Accordingly, he made arrangements for appearing to Virginia's little lover in his celebrated impersonation of 'The Vampire Monk, or, the Bloodless Benedictine,' a performance so horrible that when old Lady Startup saw it, which she did on one fatal New Year's Eve, in the year 1764, she went off into the most piercing shrieks, which culminated in violent apoplexy, and died in three days, after disinheriting the Cantervilles, who were her nearest relations, and leaving all her money to her London apothecary. At the last moment, however, his terror of the twins prevented his leaving his room, and the little Duke slept in peace under the great feathered canopy in the Royal Bedchamber, and dreamed of Virginia.

CHAPTER V

A FEW days after this, Virginia and her curly-haired cavalier went out riding on Brockley meadows, where she tore her habit so badly in getting through a hedge, that, on her return home, she made up her mind to go up by the back staircase so as not to be seen. As she was running past the Tapestry Chamber, the door of which happened to be open, she fancied she saw some one inside, and thinking it was her mother's maid, who sometimes used to bring her work there, looked in to ask her to mend her habit. To her immense surprise, however, it was the Canterville Ghost himself! He was sitting by the window, watching the ruined gold of the yellowing trees fly through the air, and the red leaves dancing madly down the long avenue. His head was leaning on his hand, and his whole attitude was one of extreme depression. Indeed, so forlorn, and so much out of repair did he look, that little Virginia, whose first idea had been to run away and lock herself in her room, was filled with pity, and determined to try and comfort him. So light was her footfall, and so deep his melancholy, that he was not aware of her presence till she spoke to him.

'I am so sorry for you,' she said, 'but my brothers are going back to Eton to-morrow, and then, if you behave yourself, no one will annoy you.'

'It is absurd asking me to behave myself,' he answered, looking round in astonishment at the pretty little girl who had ventured to address him, 'quite absurd. I must rattle my chains, and groan through keyholes, and walk about at night, if that is what you mean. It is my only reason for existing.'

'It is no reason at all for existing, and you know you have been very wicked. Mrs. Umney told us, the first day we arrived here, that you had killed your wife.'

'Well, I quite admit it,' said the Ghost petulantly, 'but it was a purely family matter, and concerned no one else.'

'It is very wrong to kill any one,' said Virginia, who at times had a sweet Puritan gravity, caught from some old New England ancestor.

'Oh, I hate the cheap severity of abstract ethics! My wife was very plain, never had my ruffs properly starched, and knew nothing about cookery. Why, there was a buck I had shot in Hogley Woods, a magnificent pricket, and do you know how she had it sent up to table? However, it is no matter now, for it is all over, and I don't think it was very nice of her brothers to starve me to death, though I did kill her.'

'Starve you to death? Oh, Mr. Ghost, I mean Sir Simon, are you hungry? I have a sandwich in my case. Would you like it?'

'No, thank you, I never eat anything now; but it is very kind of you, all the same, and you are much nicer than the rest of your horrid, rude, vulgar, dishonest family.'

'Stop!' cried Virginia, stamping her foot, 'it is you who are rude, and horrid, and vulgar, and as for dishonesty, you know you stole the paints out of my box to try and furbish up that ridiculous blood-stain in the library. First you took all my reds, including the vermilion, and I couldn't do any more sunsets, then you took the emerald-green and the chrome-yellow, and finally I had nothing left but indigo and Chinese white, and could only do moonlight scenes, which are always depressing to look at, and not at all easy to paint. I never told on you, though I was very much annoyed, and it was most ridiculous, the whole thing; for who ever heard of emerald-green blood?'

'Well, really,' said the Ghost, rather meekly, 'what was I to do? It is a very difficult thing to get real blood nowadays, and, as your brother began it all with his Paragon Detergent, I certainly saw no reason why I should not have your paints. As for colour, that is always a matter of taste: the Cantervilles have blue blood, for instance, the very bluest in England; but I know you Americans don't care for things of this kind.'

'You know nothing about it, and the best thing you can do is to emigrate and improve your mind. My father will be only too happy to give you a free passage, and though there is a heavy duty on spirits of every kind, there will be no difficulty about the Custom House, as the officers are all Democrats. Once in New York, you are sure to be a great success. I know lots of people there who would give a hundred thousand dollars to have a grandfather, and much more than that to have a family Ghost.'

'I don't think I should like America.'

'I suppose because we have no ruins and no curiosities,' said Virginia satirically.

'No ruins! no curiosities!' answered the Ghost; 'you have your navy and your manners.'

'Good evening; I will go and ask papa to get the twins an extra week's holiday.'

'Please don't go, Miss Virginia,' he cried; 'I am so lonely and so unhappy, and I really don't know what to do. I want to go to sleep and I cannot.'

'That's quite absurd! You have merely to go to bed and blow out the candle. It is very difficult sometimes to keep awake, especially at church, but there is no difficulty at all about sleeping. Why, even babies know how to do that, and they are not very clever.'

'I have not slept for three hundred years,' he said sadly, and Virginia's beautiful blue eyes opened in wonder; 'for three hundred years I have not slept, and I am so tired.'

Virginia grew quite grave, and her little lips trembled like rose-leaves. She came towards him, and kneeling down at his side, looked up into his old withered face.

'Poor, poor Ghost,' she murmured; 'have you no place where you can sleep?'

'Far away beyond the pine-woods,' he answered, in a low dreamy voice, 'there is a little garden. There the grass grows long and deep, there are the great white stars of the hemlock flower, there the nightingale sings all night long. All night long he sings, and the cold, crystal moon looks down, and the yew-tree spreads out its giant arms over the sleepers.'

Virginia's eyes grew dim with tears, and she hid her face in her hands.

'You mean the Garden of Death,' she whispered.

'Yes, Death. Death must be so beautiful. To lie in the soft brown earth, with the grasses waving above one's head, and listen to silence. To have no yesterday, and no to-morrow. To forget time, to forgive life, to be at peace. You can help me. You can open for me the portals of Death's house, for Love is always with you, and Love is stronger than Death is.'

Virginia trembled, a cold shudder ran through her, and for a few moments there was silence. She felt as if she was in a terrible dream.

Then the Ghost spoke again, and his voice sounded like the sighing of the wind.

'Have you ever read the old prophecy on the library window?'

'Oh, often,' cried the little girl, looking up; 'I know it quite well. It is painted in curious black letters, and it is difficult to read. There are only six lines:

When a golden girl can win
Prayer from out the lips of sin,
When the barren almond bears,
And a little child gives away its tears,
Then shall all the house be still
And peace come to Canterville.

But I don't know what they mean.'

'They mean,' he said sadly, 'that you must weep for me for my sins, because I have no tears, and pray with me for my soul, because I have no faith, and then, if you have always been sweet, and good, and gentle, the Angel of Death will have mercy on me. You will see fearful shapes in darkness, and wicked voices will whisper in your ear, but they will not harm you, for against the purity of a little child the powers of Hell cannot prevail.'

Virginia made no answer, and the Ghost wrung his hands in wild despair as he looked down at her bowed golden head. Suddenly she stood up, very pale, and with a strange light in her eyes. 'I am not afraid,' she said firmly, 'and I will ask the Angel to have mercy on you.'

He rose from his seat with a faint cry of joy, and taking her hand bent over it with old-fashioned grace and kissed it. His fingers were as cold as ice, and his lips burned like fire, but Virginia did not falter, as he led her across the dusky room. On the faded green tapestry were broidered little huntsmen. They blew their tasselled horns and with their tiny hands waved to her to go back. 'Go back! little Virginia,' they cried, 'go back!' but the Ghost clutched her hand more tightly, and she shut her eyes against them. Horrible animals with lizard tails, and goggle eyes, blinked at her from the carven chimney-piece, and murmured 'Beware! little Virginia, beware! we may never see you again,' but the Ghost glided on more swiftly, and Virginia did not listen. When they reached the end of the room he stopped, and muttered some words she could not understand. She opened her eyes, and saw the wall slowly fading away like a mist, and a great black cavern in front of her. A bitter cold wind swept round them, and she felt something pulling at her dress. 'Quick, quick,' cried the Ghost, 'or it will be too late,' and, in a moment, the wainscoting had closed behind them, and the Tapestry Chamber was empty.

CHAPTER VI

ABOUT ten minutes later, the bell rang for tea, and, as Virginia did not come down, Mrs. Otis sent up one of the footmen to tell her. After a little time he returned and said that he could not find Miss Virginia anywhere. As she was in the habit of going out to the garden every evening to get flowers for the dinner-table, Mrs. Otis was not at all alarmed at first, but when six o'clock struck, and Virginia did not appear, she became really agitated, and sent the boys out to look for her, while she herself and Mr. Otis searched every room in the house. At half-past six the boys came back and said that they could find no trace of their sister anywhere. They were all now in the greatest state of excitement, and did not know what to do, when Mr. Otis suddenly remembered that, some few days before, he had given a band of gypsies permission to camp in the park. He accordingly at once set off for Blackfell Hollow, where he knew they were, accompanied by his eldest son and two of the farm-servants. The little Duke of Cheshire, who was perfectly frantic with anxiety, begged hard to be allowed to go too, but Mr. Otis would not allow him, as he was afraid there might be a scuffle. On arriving at the spot, however, he found that the gypsies had gone, and it was evident that their departure had been rather sudden, as the fire was still burning, and some plates were lying on the grass. Having sent off Washington and the two men to scour the district, he ran home, and despatched telegrams to all the police inspectors in the county, telling them to look out for a little girl who had been kidnapped by tramps or gypsies. He then ordered his horse to be brought round, and, after insisting on his wife and the three boys sitting down to dinner, rode off down the Ascot Road with a groom. He had hardly, however, gone a couple of miles when he heard somebody galloping after him, and, looking round, saw the little Duke coming up on his pony, with his face very flushed and no hat. 'I'm awfully sorry, Mr. Otis,' gasped out the boy, 'but I can't eat any dinner as long as Virginia is lost. Please, don't be angry with me; if you had let us be engaged last year, there would never have been all this trouble. You won't send me back, will you? I can't go! I won't go!'

The Minister could not help smiling at the handsome young scapegrace, and was a good deal touched at his devotion to Virginia, so leaning down from his horse, he patted him kindly on the shoulders, and said, 'Well, Cecil, if you won't go back I suppose you must come with me, but I must get you a hat at Ascot.'

'Oh, bother my hat! I want Virginia!' cried the little Duke, laughing, and they galloped on to the railway station. There Mr. Otis inquired of the station-master if any one answering the description of Virginia had been seen on the platform, but could get no news of her. The station-master, however, wired up and down the line, and assured him that a strict watch would be kept for her, and, after having bought a hat for the little Duke from a linen-draper, who was just putting up his shutters, Mr. Otis rode off to Bexley, a village about four miles away, which he was told was a well-known haunt of the gypsies, as there was a large common next to it. Here they roused up the rural policeman, but could get no information from him, and, after riding all over the common, they turned their horses' heads homewards, and reached the Chase about eleven o'clock, dead-tired and almost heart-broken. They found Washington and the twins waiting for them at the gate-house with lanterns, as the avenue was very dark. Not the slightest trace of Virginia had been discovered. The gypsies had been caught on Brockley meadows, but she was not with them, and they had explained their sudden departure by saying that they had mistaken the date of Chorton Fair, and had gone off in a hurry for fear they might be late. Indeed, they had been quite distressed at hearing of Virginia's disappearance, as they were very grateful to Mr. Otis for having allowed them to camp in his park, and four of their number had stayed behind to help in the search. The carp-pond had been dragged, and the whole Chase thoroughly gone over, but without any result. It was evident that, for that night at any rate, Virginia was lost to them; and it was in a state of the deepest depression that Mr. Otis and the boys walked up to the house, the groom following behind with the two horses and the pony. In the hall they found a group of frightened servants, and lying on a sofa in the library was poor Mrs. Otis, almost out of her mind with terror and anxiety, and having her forehead bathed with eau-de-cologne by the old housekeeper. Mr. Otis at once insisted on her having something to eat, and ordered up supper for the whole party. It was a melancholy meal, as hardly any one spoke, and even the twins were awestruck and subdued, as they were very fond of their sister. When they had finished, Mr. Otis, in spite of the entreaties of the little Duke, ordered them all to bed, saying that nothing more could be done that night, and that he would telegraph in the morning to Scotland Yard for some detectives to be sent down immediately. Just as they were passing out of the dining-room, midnight began to boom from the clock tower, and when the last stroke sounded they heard a crash and a sudden shrill cry; a dreadful peal of thunder shook the house, a strain of unearthly music floated through the air, a panel at the top of the staircase flew back with a loud noise, and out on the landing, looking very pale and white, with a little casket in her hand, stepped Virginia. In a moment they had all rushed up to her. Mrs. Otis clasped her passionately in her arms, the Duke smothered her with violent kisses, and the twins executed a wild war-dance round the group.

'Good heavens! child, where have you been?' said Mr. Otis, rather angrily, thinking that she had been playing some foolish trick on them. 'Cecil and I have been riding all over the country looking for you, and your mother has been frightened to death. You must never play these practical jokes any more.'

'Except on the Ghost! except on the Ghost!' shrieked the twins, as they capered about.

'My own darling, thank God you are found; you must never leave my side again,' murmured Mrs. Otis, as she kissed the trembling child, and smoothed the tangled gold of her hair.

'Papa,' said Virginia quietly, 'I have been with the Ghost. He is dead, and you must come and see him. He had been very wicked, but he was really sorry for all that he had done, and he gave me this box of beautiful jewels before he died.'

The whole family gazed at her in mute amazement, but she was quite grave and serious; and, turning round, she led them through the opening in the wainscoting down a narrow secret corridor, Washington following with a lighted candle, which he had caught up from the table. Finally, they came to a great oak door, studded with rusty nails. When Virginia touched it, it swung back on its heavy hinges, and

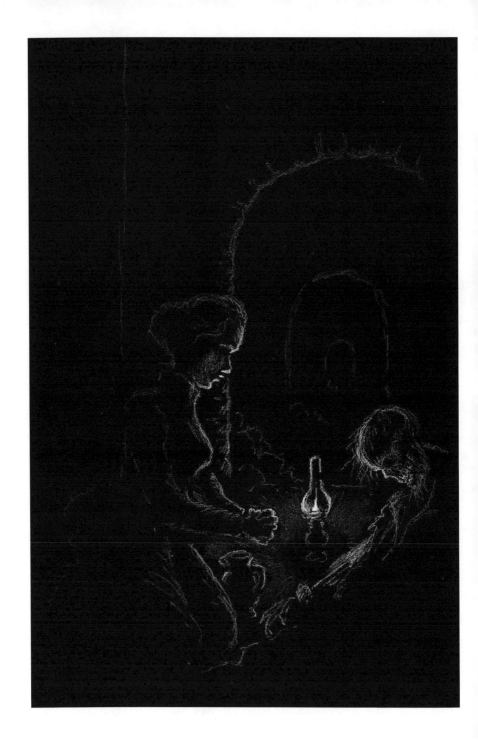

they found themselves in a little low room, with a vaulted ceiling, and one tiny grated window. Imbedded in the wall was a huge iron ring, and chained to it was a gaunt skeleton, that was stretched out at full length on the stone floor, and seemed to be trying to grasp with its long fleshless fingers an old-fashioned trencher and ewer, that were placed just out of its reach. The jug had evidently been once filled with water, as it was covered inside with green mould. There was nothing on the trencher but a pile of dust. Virginia knelt down beside the skeleton, and, folding her little hands together, began to pray silently, while the rest of the party looked on in wonder at the terrible tragedy whose secret was now disclosed to them.

'Hallo!' suddenly exclaimed one of the twins, who had been looking out of the window to try and discover in what wing of the house the room was situated. 'Hallo! the old withered almond-tree has blossomed. I can see the flowers quite plainly in the moonlight.'

'God has forgiven him,' said Virginia gravely, as she rose to her feet, and a beautiful light seemed to illumine her face.

'What an angel you are!' cried the young Duke, and he put his arm round her neck and kissed her.

CHAPTER VII

FOUR days after these curious incidents a funeral started from Canterville Chase at about eleven o'clock at night. The hearse was drawn by eight black horses, each of which carried on its head a great tuft of nodding ostrich-plumes, and the leaden coffin was covered by a rich purple pall, on which was embroidered in gold the Canterville coat-of-arms. By the side of the hearse and the coaches walked the servants with lighted torches, and the whole procession was wonderfully impressive. Lord Canterville was the chief mourner, having come up specially from Wales to attend the funeral, and sat in the first carriage along with little Virginia. Then came the United States Minister and his wife, then Washington and the three boys, and in the last carriage was Mrs. Umney. It was generally felt that, as she had been frightened by the ghost for more than fifty years of her life, she had a right to see the last of him. A deep grave had been dug in the corner of the churchyard, just under the old yew-tree, and the service was read in the most impressive manner by the Rev. Augustus Dampier. When the ceremony was over, the servants, according to an old custom observed in the Canterville family, extinguished their torches, and, as the coffin was being lowered into the grave, Virginia stepped forward and laid on it a large cross made of white and pink almond-blossoms. As she did so, the moon came out from behind a cloud, and flooded with its silent silver the little churchyard, and from a distant copse a nightingale began to sing. She thought of the ghost's description of the Garden of Death, her eyes became dim with tears, and she hardly spoke a word during the drive home.

The next morning, before Lord Canterville went up to town, Mr. Otis had an interview with him on the subject of the jewels the ghost had given to Virginia. They were perfectly magnificent, especially a certain ruby necklace with old Venetian setting, which was really a superb specimen of sixteenth-century work, and their value was so great that Mr. Otis felt considerable scruples about allowing his daughter to accept them.

'My lord,' he said, 'I know that in this country mortmain is held to apply to trinkets as well as to land, and it is quite clear to me that these jewels are, or should be, heirlooms in your family. I must beg you, accordingly, to take them to London with you, and to regard them simply as a portion of your property which has been restored to you under certain strange conditions. As for my daughter, she is merely a child, and has as yet, I am glad to say, but little interest in such appurtenances of idle luxury. I am also informed by Mrs. Otis, who, I may say, is no mean authority upon Art—having had the privilege of spending several winters in Boston when she was a girl—that these gems are of great monetary worth, and if offered for sale would fetch a tall price. Under these circumstances, Lord Canterville, I feel sure that you will recognise how impossible it would be for me to allow them to remain in the possession of any member of my family; and, indeed, all such vain gauds and toys, however suitable or necessary to the dignity of the British aristocracy, would be completely out of place among those who have been brought up on the severe, and I believe immortal, principles of republican simplicity. Perhaps I should mention that Virginia is very anxious that you should allow her to retain the box as a memento of your unfortunate but misguided ancestor. As it is extremely old, and consequently a good deal out of repair, you may perhaps think fit to comply with her request. For my own part, I confess I am a good deal surprised to find a child of mine expressing sympathy with mediævalism in any form, and can only account for it by the fact that Virginia was born in one of your London suburbs shortly after Mrs. Otis had returned from a trip to Athens.'

Lord Canterville listened very gravely to the worthy Minister's speech, pulling his grey moustache now and then to hide an involuntary smile, and when Mr. Otis had ended, he shook him cordially by the hand, and said, 'My dear sir, your charming little daughter rendered my unlucky ancestor, Sir Simon, a very important service, and I and my family are much indebted to her for her marvellous courage and pluck. The jewels are clearly hers, and, egad, I believe that if I were heartless enough to take them from her, the wicked old fellow would be out of his grave in a fortnight, leading me the devil of a life. As for their being heirlooms, nothing is an heirloom that is not so mentioned in a will or legal document, and the existence of these jewels has been quite unknown. I assure you I have no more claim on them than your butler, and when Miss Virginia grows up I daresay she will be pleased to have pretty things to wear. Besides, you forget, Mr. Otis, that you took the furniture and the ghost at a valuation, and anything that belonged to the ghost passed at once into your possession, as, whatever activity Sir Simon may have shown in the corridor at night, in point of law he was really dead, and you acquired his property by purchase.'

Mr. Otis was a good deal distressed at Lord Canterville's refusal, and begged him to reconsider his decision, but the good-natured peer was quite firm, and finally induced the Minister to allow his daughter to retain the present the ghost had given her, and when, in the spring of 1890, the young Duchess of Cheshire was presented at the Queen's first drawing-room on the occasion of her marriage, her jewels were the universal theme of admiration. For Virginia received the coronet, which is the reward of all good little American girls, and was married to her boy-lover as soon as he came of age. They were both so charming, and they loved each other so much, that every one was delighted at the match, except the old Marchioness of Dumbleton, who had tried to catch the Duke for one of her seven unmarried daughters, and had given no less than three expensive dinner-parties for that purpose, and, strange to say, Mr. Otis himself. Mr. Otis was extremely fond of the young Duke personally, but, theoretically, he objected to titles, and, to use his own words, 'was not without apprehension lest, amid the enervating influences of a pleasure-loving aristocracy, the true principles of republican simplicity should be forgotten.' His objections, however, were completely overruled, and I believe that when he walked up the aisle of St. George's, Hanover Square, with his daughter leaning on his arm, there was not a prouder man in the whole length and breadth of England.

The Duke and Duchess, after the honeymoon was over, went down to Canterville Chase, and on the day after their arrival they walked over in the afternoon to the lonely churchyard by the pine-woods. There had been a great deal of difficulty at first about the inscription on Sir Simon's tombstone, but finally it had been decided to engrave on it simply the initials of the old gentleman's name, and the verse from the library window. The Duchess had brought with her some lovely roses, which she strewed upon the grave, and after they had stood by it for some time they strolled into the ruined chancel of the old abbey. There the Duchess sat down on a fallen pillar, while her husband lay at her feet smoking a cigarette and looking up at her beautiful eyes. Suddenly he threw his cigarette away, took hold of her hand, and said to her, 'Virginia, a wife should have no secrets from her husband.'

'Dear Cecil! I have no secrets from you.'

'Yes, you have,' he answered, smiling, 'you have never told me what happened to you when you were locked up with the ghost.'

'I have never told any one, Cecil,' said Virginia gravely.

'I know that, but you might tell me.'

'Please don't ask me, Cecil, I cannot tell you. Poor Sir Simon! I owe him a great deal. Yes, don't laugh, Cecil, I really do. He made me see what Life is, and what Death signifies, and why Love is stronger than both.'

The Duke rose and kissed his wife lovingly.

'You can have your secret as long as I have your heart,' he murmured.

'You have always had that, Cecil.'

'And you will tell our children some day, won't you?'

Virginia blushed.

By the 1880s the United States had unexpectedly been able to survive the Revolutionary War, the constitutional crisis, the War of 1812, several economic depressions, the assassination of two presidents, several complete transformations of its core political parties, the national sin of chattel slavery, and the great Civil War. Up to this point Britain had been the uncontested super power of the Western world, and although this supremacy would go unchallenged until World War One, everyone could see America's star rising in world affairs. Transatlantic relations between the two countries began to become more balanced: before the Civil War, Americans were hopelessly out of their depth, and though charmingly provincial, were still desperate for acceptance by their English cousins. But by the Grover Cleveland administration, the United States had become a formidable economic power on the global stage, and cocksure Yankees were flooding British society – shocking Britain's elite with their unapologetic optimism and charming the middle class with their sunny egalitarianism. In "The Canterville Ghost" the meeting between the Otis's (the name of a well-respected New England family, by the way) and Sir

Simon is more than transatlantic culture shock – in many ways it is a deeply spiritual reconciliation between both countries' deepest insecurities. Americans were decidedly vulgar, petty, shallow, materialistic, and overly optimistic. Britons, on the other hand, were decidedly classist, grave, melodramatic, obsessed with the past, and overly pessimistic. Wilde, who adored Americans, has the two parties address one another's insufficiencies: the Americans learn to appreciate history, gravity, and metaphysics, while the British learn to be proactive, confrontational, and to let go of the past. Virginia – Wilde's typical unsullied, American belle – serves as the hinge between the two parties. She lacks her parents' (and her brothers') servile faith in capitalism (manifested in their hilarious belief in the ability of mass-market consumer products to solve all metaphysical problems), but has the youthful innocence needed to break the curse (a rare find in morbid, sardonic Britain). The story is absolutely hysterical, but notably ends on a somber, spiritual note whereby the Americans lose their bumbling silliness and the Britons learn to move beyond the past by addressing historical sins head-on. Virginia's wedding to the duke is the culmination of this transatlantic reunion, promising to help the two countries heal their vices and move on from their insecurities. Sir Simon is brought to peace by Virginia's belief in grace (while so many other women were driven mad, brought to fits, and made suicidal by their encounters with him) and her faith in forgiveness (a notably rare trait in Wilde's British women – e.g. the name-conscious Gwendolyn and Cecily in "Being Ernest"). Like Sibyl Vane in "Dorian Gray," Virginia is not interested in public spectacles or falsified emotions: both women stand out from Wilde's menagerie of characters for being open-hearted, accepting, and sincere. But unlike Sibyl, whom Dorian rejects, Virginia is able to break the curse of sin by facing it unflinchingly, and providing Sir Simon with unwavering moral support. Guided by her kindness and acceptance, he is able to pass into the afterlife, and the story ends with a hopeful prospect for Britain and America's transatlantic relationship.

THE theme of public attention and appearance is dominant throughout Wilde's plays and stories. In "The Importance of Being Earnest," it is far more important to be "Ernest" than "earnest" because of the apparent appeal of the name. Reality and illusion – truth and perception – are perennially at odds with one another, and while his characters care little for reality or truth, illusion and perception are absolutely everything. Basil repeatedly doubts that Lord Henry is as cynical as he claims, and Lord Henry does very little to deny this claim: perhaps it is true, after all, but his public image is that of a disparaging mocker, so he plays the role expected of him (much like Lord Arthur Saville, I might add). In his own marriage Lord Henry delights that he and his wife tell each other "stories" about their time spent apart, but we must wonder what kind of stories they are? The implication is that they are both having affairs and lying about it over the breakfast table, but what if the truth was that they were having no affairs but telling each other about their fictional lovers? This would certainly be worthy of Wilde. In "The Sphinx Without a Secret," the mysterious protagonist is equally shrouded in intrigue – an intrigue of her own fabrication.

The Sphinx Without a Secret:
An Etching
{1887}

ONE afternoon I was sitting outside the Café de la Paix, watching the splendour and shabbiness of Parisian life, and wondering over my vermouth at the strange panorama of pride and poverty that was passing before me, when I heard some one call my name. I turned round, and saw Lord Murchison. We had not met since we had been at college together, nearly ten years before, so I was delighted to come across him again, and we shook hands warmly. At Oxford we had been great friends. I had liked him immensely, he was so handsome, so high-spirited, and so honourable. We used to say of him that he would be the best of fellows, if he did not always speak the truth, but I think we really admired him all the more for his frankness. I found him a good deal changed. He looked anxious and puzzled, and seemed to be in doubt about something. I felt it could not be modern scepticism, for Murchison was the stoutest of Tories, and believed in the Pentateuch as firmly as he believed in the House of Peers; so I concluded that it was a woman, and asked him if he was married yet.

'I don't understand women well enough,' he answered.

'My dear Gerald,' I said, 'women are meant to be loved, not to be understood.'

'I cannot love where I cannot trust,' he replied.

'I believe you have a mystery in your life, Gerald,' I exclaimed; 'tell me about it.'

'Let us go for a drive,' he answered, 'it is too crowded here. No, not a yellow carriage, any other colour—there, that dark green one will do'; and in a few moments we were trotting down the boulevard in the direction of the Madeleine.

'Where shall we go to?' I said.

'Oh, anywhere you like!' he answered—'to the restaurant in the Bois; we will dine there, and you shall tell me all about yourself.'

'I want to hear about you first,' I said. 'Tell me your mystery.'

He took from his pocket a little silver-clasped morocco case, and handed it to me. I opened it. Inside there was the photograph of a woman. She was tall and slight, and strangely picturesque with her large vague eyes and loosened hair. She looked like a *clairvoyante*, and was wrapped in rich furs.

'What do you think of that face?' he said; 'is it truthful?'

I examined it carefully. It seemed to me the face of some one who had a secret, but whether that secret was good or evil I could not say. Its beauty was a beauty moulded out of many mysteries—the beauty, in fact, which is psychological, not plastic—and the faint smile that just played across the lips was far too subtle to be really sweet.

'Well,' he cried impatiently, 'what do you say?'

'She is the Gioconda in sables,' I answered. 'Let me know all about her.'

'Not now,' he said; 'after dinner,' and began to talk of other things.

When the waiter brought us our coffee and cigarettes I reminded Gerald of his promise. He rose from his seat, walked two or three times up and down the room, and, sinking into an armchair, told me the following story:—

'One evening,' he said, 'I was walking down Bond Street about five o'clock. There was a terrific crush of carriages, and the traffic was almost stopped. Close to the pavement was standing a little yellow brougham, which, for some reason or other, attracted my attention. As I passed by there looked out from it the face I showed you this afternoon. It fascinated me immediately. All that night I kept thinking of it, and all the next day. I wandered up and down that wretched Row, peering into every carriage, and waiting for the yellow brougham; but I could not find *ma belle inconnue,* and at last I began to think she was merely a dream. About a week afterwards I was dining with Madame de Rastail. Dinner was for eight o'clock; but at half-past eight we were still waiting in the drawing-room. Finally the servant threw open the door, and announced Lady Alroy. It was the woman I had been looking for. She came in very slowly, looking like a moonbeam in grey lace, and, to my intense delight, I was asked to take her in to dinner. After we had sat down, I remarked quite innocently, "I think I caught sight of you in Bond Street some time ago, Lady Alroy." She grew very pale, and said to me in a low voice, "Pray do not talk so loud; you may be overheard." I felt miserable at having made such a bad beginning, and plunged recklessly into the subject of the French plays. She spoke very little, always in the same low musical voice, and seemed as if she was afraid of some one listening. I fell passionately, stupidly in love, and the indefinable atmosphere of mystery that surrounded her excited my most ardent curiosity. When she was going away, which she did very soon after dinner, I asked her if I might call and see her. She hesitated for a moment, glanced round to see if any one was near us, and then said, "Yes; to-morrow at a quarter to five." I begged Madame de Rastail to tell me about her; but all that I could learn was that she was a widow with a beautiful house in Park Lane, and as some scientific bore began a dissertation on widows, as exemplifying the survival of the matrimonially fittest, I left and went home.

'The next day I arrived at Park Lane punctual to the moment, but was told by the butler that Lady Alroy had just gone out. I went down to the club quite unhappy and very much puzzled, and after long consideration wrote her a letter, asking if I might be allowed to try my chance some other afternoon. I had no answer for several days, but at last I got a little note saying she would be at home on Sunday at four and with this extraordinary postscript: "Please do not write to me here again; I will explain when I see you." On Sunday she received me, and was perfectly charming; but when I was going away she begged of me, if I ever had occasion to write to her again, to address my letter to "Mrs. Knox, care of Whittaker's Library, Green Street." "There are reasons," she said, "why I cannot receive letters in my own house."

'All through the season I saw a great deal of her, and the atmosphere of mystery never left her. Sometimes I thought that she was in the power of some man, but she looked so unapproachable, that I could not believe it. It was really very difficult for me to come to any conclusion, for she was like one of those strange crystals that one sees in museums, which are at one moment clear, and at another clouded. At last I determined to ask her to be my wife: I was sick and tired of the incessant secrecy that she imposed on all my visits, and on the few letters I sent her. I wrote to her at the library to ask her if she could see me the following Monday at six. She answered yes, and I was in the seventh heaven of delight. I was infatuated with her: in spite of the mystery, I thought then—in consequence of it, I see now. No; it was the woman herself I loved. The mystery troubled me, maddened me. Why did chance put me in its track?'

'You discovered it, then?' I cried.

'I fear so,' he answered. 'You can judge for yourself.'

'When Monday came round I went to lunch with my uncle, and about four o'clock found myself in the Marylebone Road. My uncle, you know, lives in Regent's Park. I wanted to get to Piccadilly, and took a short cut through a lot of shabby little streets. Suddenly I saw in front of me Lady Alroy, deeply veiled and walking very fast. On coming to the last house in the street, she went up the steps, took out a latch-key, and let herself in. "Here is the mystery," I said to myself; and I hurried on and examined the house. It seemed a sort of place for letting lodgings. On the doorstep lay her handkerchief, which she had dropped. I picked it up and put it in my pocket. Then I began to consider what I should do. I came to the conclusion that I had no right to spy on her, and I drove down to the club. At six I called to see her. She was lying on a sofa, in a tea-gown of silver tissue looped up by some strange moonstones that she always wore. She was looking quite lovely. "I am so glad to see you," she said; "I have not been out all day." I stared at her in amazement, and pulling the handkerchief out of my pocket, handed it to her. "You dropped this in Cumnor Street this afternoon, Lady Alroy," I said very calmly. She looked at me in terror but made no attempt to take the handkerchief. "What were you doing there?" I asked. "What right have you to question me?" she answered. "The right of a man who loves you," I replied; "I came here to ask you to be my wife." She hid her face in her hands, and burst into floods of tears. "You must tell me," I continued. She stood up, and, looking me straight in the face, said, "Lord Murchison, there is nothing to tell you."—"You went to meet some one," I cried; "this is your mystery." She grew dreadfully white, and said, "I went to meet no one."—"Can't you tell the truth?" I exclaimed. "I have told it," she replied. I was mad, frantic; I don't know what I said, but I said terrible things to her. Finally I rushed out of the house. She wrote me a letter the next day; I sent it back unopened, and started for Norway with Alan Colville. After a month I came back, and the first thing I saw in the *Morning Post* was the death of Lady Alroy. She had caught a chill at the Opera, and had died in five days of congestion of the lungs. I shut myself up and saw no one. I had loved her so much, I had loved her so madly. Good God! how I had loved that woman!'

'You went to the street, to the house in it?' I said.

'Yes,' he answered.

'One day I went to Cumnor Street. I could not help it; I was tortured with doubt. I knocked at the door, and a respectable-looking woman opened it to me. I asked her if she had any rooms to let. "Well, sir," she replied, "the drawing-rooms are supposed to be let; but I have not seen the lady for three months, and as rent is owing on them, you can have them."—"Is this the lady?" I said, showing the photograph. "That's her, sure enough," she exclaimed; "and when is she coming back, sir?"—"The lady is dead," I replied. "Oh sir, I hope not!" said the woman; "she was my best lodger. She paid me three guineas a week merely to sit in my drawing-rooms now and then." "She met some one here?" I said; but the woman assured me that it was not so, that she always came alone, and saw no one. "What on earth did she do here?" I cried. "She simply sat in the drawing-room, sir, reading books, and sometimes had tea," the woman answered. I did not know what to say, so I gave her a sovereign and went away. Now, what do you think it all meant? You don't believe the woman was telling the truth?'

'I do.'

'Then why did Lady Alroy go there?'

'My dear Gerald,' I answered, 'Lady Alroy was simply a woman with a mania for mystery. She took these rooms for the pleasure of going there with her veil down, and imagining she was a heroine. She had a passion for secrecy, but she herself was merely a Sphinx without a secret.'

'Do you really think so?'

'I am sure of it,' I replied.

He took out the morocco case, opened it, and looked at the photograph. 'I wonder?' he said at last.

"WOMEN are meant to be loved, not understood," is one of this story's most compelling lines. It could also read "women are made to be talked about, not known." Lady Alroy trades a life of personal relationships and authenticity for a fabricated charade of mystique, and in some ways is one of Wilde's most tragic characters (at least from his comic works). One wonders how many hundreds of hours of her life were spent sitting in silence, just for the chance to stir up a little drama. Wilde's implication is that there are many such people in the world whose lives are far more dull and commonplace, yet who succeed in crafting an aura of scandal and intrigue. But what is the cost? As with Lord Arthur Saville and Sir Simon – and Dorian, Basil, and Lord Henry, for that matter – we are forced to wonder at the staggering costs of crafting a false persona. What is lost when we invest so much of our lives into a pretense? Surely in our own social media era this parable is even more applicable than it was in 1887, when sites like Instagram, Facebook, Snapchat, Twitter, and Pinterest allow us to cultivate an illusion of grandeur that looks very different from the sad, empty soul on the other side of the screen. Lady Alroy has a "mania for mystery," and while in some ways she got what she wanted, in others her life is darkly tragic. Hopefully it is a story that can resonate with us in the 21st century and remind us that when we invest most of our life in crafting an illusion, the ones we're really playing the trick on are ourselves.

—FURTHER READING—
Critical, Literary, and Biographical Works

Beckson, Karl. *The Oscar Wilde Encyclopedia.* AMS Press, 1998.

Ellmann, Richard. *Oscar Wilde.* Aldred A. Knopf, 1988.

Frankel, Nicholas. *The Picture of Dorian Gray: An Annotated, Uncensored Edition.* Belknap Press of Harvard University Press, 2011.

Frankel, Nicholas. *The Uncensored Picture of Dorian Gray.* Harvard University Press, 2012.

Gal, Michalle. *Aestheticism: Deep Formalism and the Emergence of Modernist Aesthetics.* Peter Lang, 2015.

Wilde, Oscar, and Ian Small. *Complete Short Fiction.* Penguin Classics, 2003.

ABOUT THE EDITOR AND ILLUSTRATOR

Michael Grant Kellermeyer -- OTP's founder and chief editor -- is an English professor, bibliographer, illustrator, editor, critic, and author based in Fort Wayne, Indiana. He earned his Bachelor of Arts in English from Anderson University and his Master of Arts in Literature from Ball State University. He teaches college writing in Indiana where he enjoys playing violin, painting, hiking, and cooking.

Ever since watching Bing Crosby's *The Legend of Sleepy Hollow* as a three year old, Michael has been enraptured by the ghastly, ghoulish, and the unknown. Reading Great Illustrated Classics' abridged versions of classic horrors as a first grader, he quickly became enthralled with the horrific, and began accumulating a collection of unabridged classics; *Edgar Allan Poe's Forgotten Tales* and a copy of *The Legend of Sleepy Hollow* with an introduction by Charles L. Grant are among his most cherished possessions. Frequenting the occult section of the Berne Public Library, he scoured through anthologies and compendiums on ghostly lore.

It was here that he found two books which would be more influential to his tastes than any other: Henry Mazzeo's *Hauntings* (illustrated by the unparalleled Edward Gorey), and Barry Moser's *Great Ghost Stories*. It was while reading through these two collections during the Hallowe'en season of 2012 that Michael was inspired to honor the writers, tales, and mythologies he revered the most.

Oldstyle Tales Press was the result of that impulse. Its first title, *The Best Victorian Ghost Stories*, was published in September 2013, followed shortly by editions of *Frankenstein* and *The Annotated and Illustrated Edgar Allan Poe*.

In his free time, Michael enjoys straight razors, briarwood pipes, Classical music, jazz standards from the '20s to '60s, sea shanties, lemon wedges in his water, the films of Vincent Price, Alfred Hitchcock, and Stanley Kubrick, sandalwood shaving cream, freshly-laundered sheets, gin tonics, and mint tea.

Made in the USA
Monee, IL
21 June 2020